It's
Conspiracy
By
Any
Name

Other Books by D. A. Williams:
    Bishops Revenge
    It's Conspiracy By Any Name
    Just An Average Dilemma

Published by Raccoon Press
5638 West Lisa Court, Spokane, Washington 99208
Visit our website at http://raccoonpress.com/

ISBN: 978-1-4507-1435-8

Printed in the United States of America

"Here with a Loaf of Bread beneath the bough, A Flask of Wine, a Book of Verse—and Thou Beside Me Singing in the Wilderness—and Wilderness is Paradise Now…"
—from the Rubiayat of Omar Khayam

In loving memory of Socks—he was my buddy…
I miss you, Budrick!

Prelude

It began one morning three months ago when James Mortensen visited my office. A passing acquaintance from the real estate firm three doors down had given me his name, suggesting I contact Mortensen to secure a new mortgage for my property, upon which there had been a foreclosure filed earlier that week. I was encouraged when Mortensen convinced me that he was quite capable of saving my real estate. What I didn't know was that he made a telephone call that afternoon.

✳✳✳✳

On the third ring, Antonio Tafino's gruff voice boomed through the receiver, "Yeah! Hello!"

"Tony? Mortensen here. I have something you might be interested in."

"Okay. Give it to me!"

"I just left a meeting with a fellow who has a small shopping center, that's recently been placed in foreclosure. The property has a short-term note of about two hundred thousand dollars, with a market value of at least four hundred fifty thousand. I thought you might want to go by and take a look at it."

"How old is this place?"

"That's good news, too, Tony. It's brand new. Never been occupied."

"How in the hell did a brand new building get thrown into foreclosure?"

"Obviously, this guy's pretty naive and he didn't check the city's plans for street expansion. No sooner did he get the building completed when the city started a street widening project. The street's all torn up and he hasn't been able to lease any spaces. His mortgage commitment expired and the bank has called his short-term note. I think Frontier National would have extended it, except they've just been sold to that conglomerate in New York and the higher-ups called the loan. This guy has about ninety days to get a mortgage or the bank takes the property."

"How long before Phoenix has the streets fixed?"

"Probably another three, maybe four months. But, Tony, even vacant, you could sit on this for a year and still come out two hundred thousand to the good."

"Humph. Think you can stall this pigeon for ninety days?"

"Hey, Tony, don't worry. I've done this before— remember?"

"Okay, give me the address and I'll go look at it."

The next morning, Mortensen's telephone rang.

"Tafino here. I looked at that property yesterday. I'm interested. Let's do it." Click.

PART ONE

Chapter 1

"Sold!" The trustee barked, as he pounded his gavel with authority. He glanced around at the sparse gathering with a look of finality then turned his eyes to the two short men standing to his right. Speaking softly, he explained to the heavier of the two, "Mr. Tafino, the law states that the proceeds are due in cash or certified funds at the time of sale, but tradition allows you to bring the funds to our office within twenty-four hours."

"Yeah, I know," Tafino answered in a surly voice. "I've bought twenty-some other properties this way before."

As I stood there watching, a strong feeling of defeat swept over me. Tafino's manner, like that of his silent brother, standing alongside and rolling an unlit cigar around in his mouth, reeked of a cockiness that comes with the power of wealth.

For a fleeting moment, I had thoughts of challenging the foreclosure sale, since the law did state that the funds were due immediately. But realistically, I knew I couldn't actually stop it. I merely wanted to harass those jackasses a little. At the same time, I thought—*what's the use?* I walked out.

The chill of the February day slapped me in the face as I stepped from the building. I pulled my coat collar tightly around my neck and headed west into the biting wind. *Damn! I've been in Arizona for fifteen years, but it's never been this cold in Phoenix, not even in February.* At that very moment, it dawned on me. *Whoa! Today is Valentine's Day.* This has been like the Valentine's Day massacre all over again. But unlike the other one, the only blood spilled here in 1978 was mine, Owen J. Hunter, and it was just emotional blood.

With each step clicking against the concrete, I forged ahead against the frigid air with my hands tucked into my coat pockets. I considered each of my feelings at that moment. Sadness and disgust were there, and, ironically, a touch of relief, knowing I no longer had to worry about

1

losing my property. But mostly, I felt the defeat. I tried to separate these feelings and read an analysis into each one. The defeat was the hardest to handle right now. I had truly believed that my property would somehow be saved from the foreclosure. Surely the Gods would not allow me to lose it. *Perhaps I could have done something more. Or something differently.*

Or else someone would certainly recognize the energy I'd put into it and help me out. That's what that damn mortgage broker was supposed to do—the mealy-mouthed hypocrite! I envisioned the look of James Mortensen just a few minutes ago when the sale was over. An expression of relief showed on his face when he brushed quick regrets to me before he anxiously turned to congratulate the purchasers with a handshake and a big grin. What a horse's ass! Kissing up to those goons and all their money! Oops, hatred is suddenly interfering with my feeling of defeat. I guess I can't separate them.

The sadness, of course, is because of the failure and the huge loss, but the relief is there all by itself. It tells me that the anxiety of the past several months is over. I can now continue my life without the worry and the ongoing struggle of all this. I'm free from that, now. As I reached my van in the parking lot, I decided, at present, to stick with the relief.

****

Once I'd climbed inside, I inserted the key into the ignition and started the motor, leaving the key chain and other keys to swing aimlessly back and forth when I removed my hand. They quickly came to a halt. I was in no hurry to leave, so while I waited for the engine to warm up, I lit a cigarette and leaned back into the plaid captain's chair. I puffed long and hard on the Marlboro, watching the expelled smoke drift up to the top of the slightly opened window, where it escaped outside and disappeared.

With a brief half-smile, I witnessed two coatless, young Mexican women, shivering and chattering, clamber into the car next to me and leave in a rush. The only word I understood was "Hurry!"

While sitting there, I rehashed the foreclosure sale I'd just left then my mind began to drift backward in time. I thought of all the hard work I'd put in, going all the way back to when I'd finished school.

"Owen J. Hunter," the president of Southwest Missouri State University called, as I proudly climbed the platform stairs to receive my diploma. With unlimited enthusiasm and this piece of parchment, I was going to set the world on fire. After graduation, I took a job with a large construction company as an on-site accountant, transferring around to several areas of the country for a few years before settling in Phoenix.

Through ROTC and enlistment in the Army Reserves, coupled with pure, dumb luck, I managed to escape the Vietnam mess. I would have gone, had I been ordered to, but I wasn't about to volunteer for such a thing. I'd lost my high school sweetheart to someone else while I was away at college, so I half-heartedly drifted between romances almost as often as I changed job locations. In my mind, none of them quite matched up to my memory of her.

Then, wholly by chance, I became involved in public accounting. While working in the western regional office of my employer, I was approached by two of our sub-contractors to perform accounting services for them as a sideline to my regular job. Word spread, I secured other clients, and within ten months, with my supervisor's blessing, I'd quit the job and opened my own office. After a whirlwind romance with my secretary, Joyce, we ended up married. *My god! Was that really twelve years ago?*

As time went by, the practice grew and we both toiled long, hard hours, slowly accumulating a degree of wealth. But one day, Joycie decided—it seemed overnight—to become a housewife rather than a business partner and left the firm in my hands. She was tired of the stress and long hours dictated by the nature of the work. But the business suffered an irreplaceable loss with her absence. Employee after employee couldn't take her place, simply because they just didn't have that ownership interest that drove her so

3

hard. Consequently, I worked more and longer hours as our marriage eventually drifted into emptiness.

Then along came the torrid fling with Annette. An interior decorator. One of our clients. A sultry beauty, whose overtures impulsively waltzed me into ardent sex, illicit lies, and wrongful deceit. That short, regrettable affair led to the divorce, which led to the crashing downfall of my little empire. Plus, by that time, I was a real black sheep in everyone's eyes—my clients, Joyce's family, hell, even my own family—like I said—everyone.

With all this going on, I decided it was best to sell the practice, which led to my investing in properties, which led to the construction of my strip shopping center, which led to the foreclosure sale I'd just left. In the span of one year, I'd lost my marriage, my business, and my property.

Feeling a chill, I turned on the heater, backed out of the parking lot and headed for home.

Chapter 2

Three days later, while I ate a tasteless supper of half-cold, fast food hamburgers, I began to rattle this foreclosure crap around in my head once more. Several perplexing questions, with no apparent answers, were haunting me and I started to wonder. Had this been a conspiracy against me? Had that damned Mortensen strung me along until the foreclosure sale, just so those wops could steal my building right out from underneath me?

Rising from the recliner, I turned off the television and began pacing back and forth. My mind churned over the events of the past few months. With the land paid for from the sale of my accounting business, I'd hired an architect to draw the plans based on my own design. Frontier National Bank had granted an interim construction loan, using as collateral the mortgage commitment from Purity Life Insurance Company. Shortly after construction of the building had been completed, my Certificate of Occupancy had been issued by the City of Phoenix. The following week, the city began a revision to the sewer system fronting the property, together with a widening of the street from two lanes to four. The architect had told me of the long-range plan for this, but it was not to have taken place for another five years. *Damn! I should have checked it myself.*

Naturally, with the street completely torn up and with very limited access for the next ten months, it was impossible for me to lease any of the spaces in my commercial building. The commitment from Purity Life contained a vacancy factor and since the building was unoccupied when the commitment expired, they used this as a basis for not funding the loan, thereby essentially leaving me with a short-term note at the bank on a newly constructed building. Purity Life also retained the twenty-eight thousand dollars in fees that I had advanced to them for the commitment, all non-refundable, of course.

Meanwhile, in a quiet, unceremonious transaction I had not learned of, the bank was sold to a syndicate from

New York and when my short-term financing came due, they decided to call the loan rather than issue an extension. Considering I read it every day—why didn't I read about that transaction in the business section? Obviously, I answered myself, there had to have been a squash put to the story by a behind-the-scenes investor with connections to the newspaper. I was given thirty days to pay the balance prior to the filing of foreclosure. Having used most of my remaining funds to pay the monthly interest installments on the short-term note, I didn't have the money with which to pay off the loan. So, the foreclosure was filed and I needed a mortgage within ninety days. With no visible means of income—hell, I didn't even have a job—I couldn't qualify for a new mortgage with normal lending institutions. Assuming that real estate agents have contacts with mortgage companies, it was then I asked the broker down the hall for a reference. Enter James Mortensen.

I recalled the first time he came to the small office I was renting, and from which I was conducting my business affairs. He was about three inches taller than my six-foot frame, yet he was quite thin, perhaps fifty years old. His coarse, dark brown hair showed a touch of gray at the temples and was combed straight back. Horned-rim, brown-framed glasses rested on his hawk-like nose and his brown eyes peered through them in a manner that made them appear too small for his narrow, Roman face. Even the new suit he was wearing was brown. My first thought was Jewish—but with the name of Mortensen? *Perhaps from his mother's side.*

After introductions, he smoothly explained that his company represented private investors, pension funds, and similar sources that offer mortgage loans with only the property as collateral, assuming that the property in question warrants a value sufficient to secure the financing. He opened his briefcase—brown of course—and presented to me a packet of forms to be completed to initiate the mortgage application.

As this recall came to me, I stopped pacing for a

moment and voiced aloud to my pet cat, Socko. "Ya know, Bud, I'm positive I told that jerk-wad about that foreclosure situation! Right there at that first meeting!"

Alarmed by my outburst, Socko's eyes popped open and he stared up at me with apprehension, but after receiving a scratch on his black head, he yawned and stretched in his favorite chair. Resting his chin on his front paws, he then gave me a look of appreciation and closed his eyes again. Taking this as his agreement with my statement, I rubbed his head again and continued my pacing, returning my thoughts to Mortensen.

During the ninety days that followed that first meeting, I telephoned Mortensen countless times, inquiring about the progress of the mortgage. He had a raft of excuses as to why the mortgage had not been approved. *'I submitted it to three companies who aren't interested due to the amount.'* Either, *'Their floor is higher than the amount we're requesting.'* Or, *'Their ceiling is lower.'* However, *'I am submitting it to two others today.'* Toward the end I even heard, *'the girl who normally types these forms for me is out for a few days. She has a terrible case of the flu.'*

With time becoming short, I offered to come to his office to type the forms myself, if that's what was needed. Taken a bit by surprise, he stammered and stuttered and finally appeased me by stating that he would stay late and type the forms himself, assuring me that a mortgage commitment was imminent with these last submissions.

Then a mere five days before the scheduled foreclosure sale, he appeared at my office with his brown guise and presented to me another packet of forms to be completed for update purposes. By then, my nerves were frayed and I erupted. "What in the hell do you need more forms and information for? You know that damned foreclosure sale is only five days away! I want you to get a mortgage approved by somebody and I want you to get it now!"

"What foreclosure sale?"

"The foreclosure sale on my building!" I shrieked.

"I'm sorry—I don't know what you're talking about. What foreclosure sale? What do you mean?" He was totally calm.

I was stunned. "What do I mean? I mean the sale on my building. I told you my property is in foreclosure! I told you that the very first day you were in my office!"

"Oh, no, no, no, Mr. Hunter. I was totally unaware of that. Goodness. That changes the picture entirely."

"I know I told you that! Why do you think I've been pushing you to get this thing done? Wake up, man!"

"Mr. Hunter, I swear I had no idea there was a foreclosure involved." He rose part way from his chair with a palms down motion, persuading me to remain calm. Then he said, "Well, that does change things dramatically, I must say… but I know I can get this done for you so you won't lose your building. I truly wish I'd been aware…and this sale takes place in only five days you say? Whew, that is soon. But don't worry—I have an investor or two who will most probably be interested. We'll have to hurry, but these gentlemen do have a real history of getting things accomplished in these rescue type situations. They specialize in financially stressed properties."

God, he was smooth. Too, so believable. And I had really trusted him right up to the day of the sale.

I answered him sarcastically. "Well, I'm sure that I told you about the foreclosure and if you hadn't dragged your feet, I wouldn't be in a 'rescue type situation'!"

"Honestly," Mortensen obviously lied, "I was totally unaware of the foreclosure, but now that I am, I'm telling you—I know what it is I have to do. Please let me submit your package to the investors I mentioned and I'm sure I can convince them that this is a worthwhile investment, considering your building is new construction."

"Looks like I don't have much of a choice!" I exhaled loudly and tossed the pencil I'd been twirling, onto the desk in disgust. "So, how do we go about this?"

"I'll present it to my people and see what they come up with. I will tell you this—they'll probably want more in interest than your present loan is, considering the time element involved in getting it pushed through."

"How much more?"

Staying in complete control, Mortensen was ignoring my anguish. "Mm..." he pondered, looking toward the ceiling before returning his gaze to me, "I'd say, probably two percent more than you had with your construction loan with Frontier National."

My mind came back to the present for a moment. At the time this took place, I recalled thinking that he did seem sincere about not knowing of the foreclosure. Doubting myself, even now, I wondered. *Maybe I didn't tell him.* I returned my thoughts to that meeting.

Looking at Mortensen, I heaved a sigh of disgust. "So, all right, I'll ask you again—what the hell do we have to do to get this thing rolling?"

"Okay, here's what's needed. If you can get this new packet finished this evening, I'll pick it up tomorrow and present it to my investors. I should have a favorable response from one or more of them by the next day then we can schedule a closing for the day after. I dare say I feel somewhat apologetic that I didn't have all the facts from the beginning. I assumed we had all the time in the world to get your mortgage processed, but don't worry, Mr. Hunter, we'll pull this off."

Before I could reiterate my opinion that he did have all the facts, he stood up, closed his briefcase, and extended his hand. He pointed to the package of papers he'd earlier placed on my desk and asked, "Do you think you can get these forms completed this evening?"

I heaved a disgusted sigh. "Uh, yeah. Sure..."

"Good! Then I'll see you in the morning." Snatching his briefcase, he whirled around and whisked away before I could say anything else. He called out a cheerful "Good-bye, Mr. Hunter!" as the door closed behind him.

The next day, he picked up the papers in a rush and told me he would call me in the afternoon to inform me of the status, which he did. He stated that he had presented the package to two investors who had shown considerable interest and we should have a confirmation of their approval the following day. I had four days left until the sale on Tuesday.

With the next day being Saturday, it meant that the closing would have to take place on Monday. On Saturday morning, stewing until the anxiety became too much, I attempted to contact Mortensen at his office without success. Not having his unlisted home telephone number or home address, I was unable to reach him the entire weekend, despite leaving numerous messages. I remembered the feeling of frenzy I'd had on Monday morning, as, still, no one was answering his phone. Distraught, I felt completely helpless.

At mid-morning, my office door opened and Mortensen entered the room, accompanied by two other men. They were both short and heavy, one being considerably larger than the other. Dressed in their swarthy, pinstriped suits, dark blue shirts, white ties and fedoras, they looked like they had just walked from the screen of *The Godfather*. Their sullied complexions, large diamond rings and stickpins complemented the thought. The first word that entered my mind was *Mafia*. In my recall, I was finding it hard to believe that this had all taken place only a few days ago.

I remembered that conversation too. Mortensen offered a handshake as he spoke to me. "Mr. Hunter, this is Antonio Tafino and his brother, Louis. They're the investors I spoke to you about on Friday."

"How do ya do, Hunter?" bellowed the fat one, who had been introduced to me as Antonio. He thrust his chubby fingers in my direction, grasped my hand, and roughly pumped it up and down. The other brother offered no acknowledgement of my existence. He merely pulled a chair up to the desk and sat down with a smirk across his thin lips. Protruding from his face was an unlit cigar, which he constantly kept twirling in the fingers of his left hand. His right hand remained thrust into his suit coat pocket.

Mortensen said, "We'll get right to it, Mr. Hunter.

Here's what Antonio would like to propose with regard to your mortgage problem on your building. They don't have a real interest in a long-term mortgage situation, ah—"

"Nah, we're too old for that," interrupted Antonio, laughing with a snort.

Mortensen threw an overly patient smile in Antonio's direction then continued, "Yes, uh, but they would like to help you buy some time here in order to save your property. You see—"

"Here's what we're proposin' to do, Hunter," the powerful voice of Antonio took over the conversation. "We would like to assume the position the bank now holds." He not only expected me to be in complete comprehension of what he was saying, his attitude conveyed a foregone conclusion that I would jump at the offer.

My blank look triggered Mortensen to speak again. "What Antonio is saying is this—for your payment of some points, they will pay off the bank and continue to hold a short-term loan for a period of time until—"

Antonio interrupted again, jerking his thumb in the direction of Mortensen as he spoke. "That way, you'll be able to take some time until Mortensen here can get a good mortgage lined up for you. You'll be able to keep your building that way." The other one was still there twisting his cigar, stiff-lipped and silent, looking at the ceiling, the walls, the floor, the painting on the wall.

My eyes glanced between Mortensen and Antonio as each of them took turns speaking. This time it was Mortensen. "What Antonio means is, and I'll repeat this, for the few points you will pay to them, they will pay the bank and continue to hold a short-term loan until we can obtain a mortgage for you, the proceeds of which will be used to pay them back. During that time, until the permanent mortgage is in place, you can continue to make the interest only payments to them."

"Yeah, that's what we mean." The Italian was now convinced that I not only understood the proposal, but that I would automatically accept it. Leaning back in his chair, he exhaled triumphantly through his thick nose. Louis was still fingering the cigar and staring at the light fixture above his head.

I felt uneasy about the whole scene. Hesitating, I asked, "Exactly how much money are we talking about here?—for the points, I mean?"

After a short pause to allow Tafino to re-settle himself in his chair, Mortensen answered, "Well, Mr. Hunter, according to my calculations, it would be somewhere in the neighborhood of roughly twenty thousand dollars."

"What?" I asked in disbelief. "They want me to give them twenty thousand dollars, and in exchange for that they are going to pay off the bank and I'll still owe them what I owe the bank right now? Plus, I'll be paying them interest at a higher rate than I'm currently paying the bank?"

"Well, uh, mm, basically, yes." Mortensen squirmed on his chair as he replied. Louis glanced in my direction for a moment before continuing his fascination, now with the clock on the wall, having tired of the light fixture. His fingers didn't miss a beat with the cigar. Antonio gazed directly into my face, showing no emotion, waiting for my answer.

Incensed, I spat the words in the direction of the mortgage broker. "This is certainly not what I anticipated when I talked with you on Thursday and Friday! And, again, it's not what you led me to believe! If you'd explained it fully to me then, you'd know there's no way I can come up with twenty thousand dollars!"

Antonio broke in before Mortensen could react. "Okay, Hunter, how much can you come up with?"

I glared at Mortensen, who was shifting uncomfortably on his chair. Without moving my eyes from him, I answered Antonio through gritted teeth. "Right now, I have seventeen thousand dollars and that's every cent I have. And I'm in no position to borrow any more, anywhere!"

"Ah, hell, Hunter, we'll do it for seventeen grand. We'd just like to help you keep your building." With that, I saw Louis's gaze become fixed on me, with his never changing, cigar twirling smirk firmly in place.

Leaning back in my chair, I pondered all this before answering. Indicating Mortensen with a nod of my head, I said, "Mr. Tafino, he's had ninety days to get a mortgage for me and, so far, he's accomplished absolutely nothing. How do I know you won't go down in thirty days and file a foreclosure the same as the bank has done? Then if he still doesn't get a mortgage in time, you'll have all of my money, *plus* my building."

Obviously, Tafino was used to getting his own way and he visibly subdued his temper before answering in a strained tone, trying miserably to disguise it as pleasantness. "Hunter, we are not the least bit interested in your building, but we are interested in making a few dollars on our investment. Naturally, we want Mortensen to get your mortgage as fast as he can, but in the meantime, we'll be making money in interest. More in fact than we'd make at that damn bank or any other bank for that matter."

"That's probably true, Mr. Tafino, but—"

"Please! Call me Antonio."

Right—I thought—*and what do I call your idiot brother sitting there? Harpo?* My smile was to myself for my private left field humor. I really didn't like these guys. My eyes met Antonio's. "As I was saying, all this is probably true, but it's a lot for me to consider and I would like to have a little time to think about it before I do anything." Taking a turn at each, I exchanged glances with the three of them.

Raising his crusty voice, Tafino barked, "Well, Hunter, we can give you a little time, but we have to know before two o'clock this afternoon whether you're going to accept our offer or not. We gotta finish the paperwork and get it recorded in the morning before the sale takes place at ten o'clock."

With that said, Antonio rose, followed by the others, and they all turned to leave. This time, nobody offered to shake hands.

****

Returning my mind to the present for a moment, I

said to Socko the cat, "Hey, Budrick, if they weren't interested in my building, how did they know the sale was to take place at ten in the morning?" That crazy cat actually has four names I throw at him and believe it or not, he actually responds to all of them, but he only meows to Budrick. He did this time before leaving the room for the kitchen and the food bowl.

****

Recalling once again, it was ten minutes before two when Mortensen telephoned me. Feeling the need for even more time to think, I allowed the answering machine to take the call. "Mr. Hunter, have you made a decision on the offer from the Tafinos? I need to know as quickly as possible, so it's imperative that you please return my call as fast as you can. Thank you."

I had one more quick idea. Reaching for the phone, I dialed Ed Blake at Frontier National Bank. With our dealings having reached a first-name basis, Ed had always worked with me in the past and the periodical construction draws had never been questioned. But my interest payments to them had always been timely made, as well. I explained to him the offer from the Tafinos. "Let me do a little checking, Owen, and I'll call you right back."

His return call came less than fifteen minutes later. Through the answering machine, I recognized his voice and picked up the receiver. "Yeah, hello, Ed."

"Didn't take much checking, Owen. These guys came to town about five years ago with a lot of money. They're not customers of ours, but I've learned they own a lot of commercial and residential real estate. And, Owen, most of it was acquired through foreclosures and tax lien sales. I'd be careful."

"Huh. Well, knowing that, I may as well ask you one more time if there's any possibility I might get an extension of this foreclosure date. Since Mortensen hasn't done anything with the mortgage, I'd like to try somewhere else, but, of course, I'll need some time to do that."

"Man alive, Owen, if it were up to me personally, I'd

do it in a minute, you know that. It's the guy upstairs. He feels we have to close this transaction out."

"But Ed, you know I've made all my interest payments on time and I'll continue to do so. The bank is making good money off of me. Doesn't that count for anything?"

"I know that, Owen, but the higher-ups feel they want to move the money we have invested here to different markets. My hands are tied."

"But you won't have the money, Ed. You'll have my building!" I pleaded.

"Well, technically that's true, unless an investor buys it at the sale. But even if nobody does, with the value of the property, we'll convert the note balance to cash in a short time, Owen, you know that."

"Yes, I suppose you will." I answered icily. "Well, Ed, if you don't have the power to extend it, then let me talk to this 'guy upstairs'. I'll explain it to him and maybe I can change his mind."

Hesitating a bit awkwardly, he said, "Uh, I can't do that, Owen. The people upstairs don't deal with the customers directly. That's what I'm here for. But I do want you to know I have talked to them on your behalf, several times, and I couldn't change their minds. I doubt that you could, either."

There was silence on the line for several uncomfortable seconds. Finally, breathing a disgusted sigh, I broke it. "Okay, Ed, with what you've told me about the Tafino brothers, I think I'll pass on their offer and just let the damn building go. I guess I should say thanks for the help you've been in the past, but you know that without the bank's extension, I'm losing practically everything I have. So, don't take this personally, but I can't let go without saying that I think you have a thankless job and I wouldn't want the damn thing for one single day."

"I understand how you feel, Owen, and I can't say I blame you. And, believe me when I say it isn't easy for me to have to say no. I really wish it wasn't that way."

"I believe you, Ed, I'm just blowing steam."

"That's allowed. Good luck, Owen."

I cradled the receiver without saying goodbye.

Calling Mortensen, I told him of my decision not to accept Antonio Tafino's offer.

"Well, it seems to me that his offer is more than fair, and I think you should reconsider. It guarantees you some time until I can secure a mortgage for you."

"Sorry, I've made my decision."

I hung up before he could say anything else. Click.

For curiosity's sake, I attended the sale that following morning and wasn't the least bit surprised when Antonio Tafino bid one cent more than what I owed the bank. They now owned the building that they weren't the least bit interested in.

****

Returning my thoughts to the present, I grabbed a beer from the refrigerator and sat on the sofa in my silent living room. Ever loyal Socko jumped up to lie beside me and my hand automatically moved to rub the fur on the side of his face. With his eyes closed, he started to purr.

After reviewing over and over in my mind the scenes and conversations from the past several months, I'd now convinced myself that this had been a conspiracy against me from the very first time I talked with Mortensen. Being a trusting person as well as a greenhorn in the real estate investment world, I would never have suspected such a thing while it was taking place. But now, it would be interesting to find out how many ill-gotten mortgages had been obtained by Mortensen for the Tafino brothers, and to discover just how many foreclosed properties have been purchased by them from information they've received from him. How many other people had trusted him to obtain mortgage funding, only to find at the last minute that their only option was a completely unacceptable offer from those thugs!

Considering the facts, I even started to wonder if there was any possibility I could recover something from this or perhaps have the conspirators prosecuted. *Heck, might*

there even be a chance I could get my building back?
I decided to find out.

Chapter 3

It was unusually warm for February and since the temperature outside was fifty-five degrees higher than it had been merely a week ago, I was dressed in casual slacks and a short-sleeved shirt when I entered the office of Richard L. Warner, Attorney. A few years ago, Richard had been a tenant in the same office building where my accounting practice had been located until he migrated downtown to be closer to the courthouses. Except for that common-tenant relationship we'd shared, I'd had no business dealings with him, but we had become friends during that time and I believed his answers would be accurate, direct, and honest.

I declined an offer of coffee from the young brunette stationed behind the reception desk and took a seat on a brown leather chair, ignoring the magazines on the table in front of me. I looked around the reception area. The decor was a reflection of the man. The beige color of the plush carpet extended to the wall covering, which was adorned with several motley sand paintings and the framed documents of his profession. Alongside these were displayed all of the plaques and awards that had been bestowed upon Richard L. Warner. There were many. Healthy, live plants were evenly spaced throughout the office in colorful, southwestern pots. No plastic plants here.

"Hi, Owen." Richard greeted me as he appeared from somewhere down the hall. "It's been a while since I've seen you. How've you been?"

Standing, I extended my hand to accept his, while candidly taking in his appearance. His sandy hair had receded a little and he'd gained a few pounds, but his soft hazel eyes still portrayed his likable warmth. Quite average in size, clean-shaven, and dressed in dark blue trousers, white shirt and colorful tie, Richard was still a rather handsome man. Despite his mannerly comments on my looking good, he had to be surprised at the thirty or so—okay, make it forty or so—pounds that I'd gained. But I still had all of my curly hair and there was no gray appearing in the dark brown curls yet, even though I'd earned some.

After Richard ushered me into his office, he walked around his maple desk and pointed toward a chair across from him. After I sat down, he said, "I noticed your name in the appointment book, Owen. So, how can I help you?"

"Well, Richard, I have a story to tell, and some questions to ask."

As he took notes, he listened intently while I related to him the facts of my construction venture, beginning with the sale of my accounting practice and ending with the foreclosure of my building. I told him about everything that had transpired in between, including my conspiracy theory involving Mortensen and the Tafino brothers. I ended with an obvious question. "In a nutshell, Richard, do you think there's a possibility of convicting these guys? Or recovering anything from them?"

"Perhaps. However, Owen, my practice is primarily limited to corporate law, for a couple of reasons. One, I simply don't have any desire to handle divorces, child custody, accident claims, etcetera. Just don't have the personality to deal with those things." Then he mused, "And, two, with criminal and civil law, eh, I know just enough to get by, mostly to keep my corporate clients out of jail. Now then, if you can deal with that admission, I'll be glad to help you with your situation, assuming we have a case."

"Fair enough, Richard," I smiled. "So, based on what I've told you, I'll ask again—do you think I have a case?"

"Oh, I definitely believe this was an out and out conspiracy for the Tafinos to get your building. Unfortunately, you just happened to pick the wrong guy to get your mortgage. However, conspiracy is the hardest crime on the books to prove. Did you happen to record any of your telephone conversations with this Mortensen character?"

"I thought wire-tapping was against the law?"

"Ah. A very common misunderstanding. You see, Owen, recording a telephone conversation is not wire-tapping. Besides, only a law enforcement agency can 'tap' a phone line. Everyone else merely records telephone conversations and under Arizona law, as long as one of the parties has knowledge of it, a recording is admissible in court as evidence."

"You mean the other guy doesn't even have to know about it?"

"Nope."

"Well, I'll be damned. I didn't know that."

"Most people don't. See there? I've just revealed one of the best kept secrets in the state." He grinned at me.

My response was preceded by a sheepish grin of my own. "Well, Richard, to answer your question—no, I didn't record any of the conversations."

"Did you happen to have any witnesses to the phone conversations? Anyone listening in? Or any witnesses to those meetings that took place in your office—especially the very first one or two?"

"No."

"Do you have any copies of any written correspondence, where either you or Mortensen reveal any knowledge of the pending foreclosure?"

"No. Everything was verbal, either in person at my office, or on the telephone."

"Ouch! Owen, I believe that what we have here is that age-old problem of lack of proof. I do think you have validity for what you believe about these jerks, but I also think we're going to be hard pressed to do anything with it, because of that lack of proof. It comes down to your word against theirs, and there are three of them. These people have evidently had practice at this sort of thing and they've covered their butts exceptionally well."

At the risk of sounding redundant, I repeated, "So, in your opinion, it's not even worth pursuing, huh?"

"Owen, you'd be throwing your money away. I'm sure that any lawsuit would be immediately thrown out of court for lack of evidence, and, I'll go so far as to say, that the judge would probably reprimand me for filing such a frivolous action. Frivolous being the court's terminology, not mine. God, I'm sorry…" He sympathetically shrugged his shoulders.

I couldn't hide my disappointment. "Well, Richard, that wasn't the answer I was hoping for, but at least I know where I stand. And I'm sure that if there were any way you could help me, you would. But what the hell, despite the outcome, it was good seeing you again."

Reaching for the checkbook in my shirt pocket, I opened it and began to write. With a wave of his hand, Richard refused. "No, no, Owen. Put that away. You don't owe me a dime. After all, I couldn't do anything for you. Honest to God, I wish I could. I mean, you certainly didn't deserve to lose what you did, and those scumbags shouldn't be allowed to get away with what they're doing. But, unfortunately, the world is filled with unscrupulous people that get by with this sort of thing every day. I sincerely wish this had a better ending for you. I really do."

I appreciated the note of disappointment in his voice. It was genuine. "I know, Richard. Thanks."

Pushing his chair away, he stood up and began edging his way around the desk. "However, I do agree with one thing. It *was* good that we got to see each other again. We should do it more often, but definitely with more favorable circumstances next time."

"Absolutely."

As I started to leave, my friend fell into step beside me. Walking with me to the reception area, he placed his hand on my shoulder, gave a gentle squeeze, and wished me luck. After a handshake and a final voicing of my thanks, I dejectedly walked outside to my waiting van.

****

For the next three months, I became reclusive by burying myself into remodeling the small house I'd bought following the divorce. I would go days without shaving or changing clothes, not really caring, content to take my frustrations out on the lumber, drywall, ceramic tile, wallpaper, and other projects. I moved my furniture from the office I'd been renting and arranged everything in one of the empty bedrooms. I reasoned that this would save me the money I was paying in rent, and it filled the room. Plus, with no office to go to, it made it easier to remain in seclusion.

Then, one day as I was nearing completion of the remodeling, I needed a few final pieces of wood trim. After shaving, I showered, dressed in clean clothes and left to buy the material. On the way back from the lumber company, an intersection wreck made me detour to McDowell Road, the street where the commercial building I'd once owned was located.

The avenue was now wide and freshly paved with asphalt, which hadn't yet had a chance to fade. It was still very black. The bright yellow and white striping had not had time to dim from the constant beating of traffic rolling over it day after day and the newly poured sidewalks were clean and barren of scuffling foot traffic and graffiti. As I approached the strip center I'd built, I saw that it was now fully occupied.

All at once, angered by the memory of those people and what they'd done to me, I felt heat beneath my shirt collar from a fast-rising burn that was boiling clear down to my chest. Nearly losing control of the van, I whipped into the parking lot and screeched to a stop. Staring at the building, my rage continued to well when I saw all the newness and busy activity. I gazed at the arched entries, which I'd designed and drawn on scratch paper for the architect with my own hands. I studied the desert-colored slump block of the exterior, which I'd selected from a color chart with my own eyes. This entire dream I'd molded into a reality with my own mind and heart seemed to stare back at me. *Damn it! This place should still be mine!*

As I sat there, a gritty determination began to envelop me and, nearly as quickly as it had arisen, the incense within me subsided. A quiet resolve was filling the spot where the anger had been. I silently made a declaration. *There has to be a way for me to get even with those jerks!*

I thought of them all, one by one. Mortensen—that, full-of-bullshit, ass-kisser! Then, good old loud-mouthed Antonio. He'd look more at home in prison stripes, rather than pin stripes. And finally, 'Harpo'. I'd like to personally shove that putrid cigar right down his throat until he choked on the damn thing!

Thus, I vowed, right then and there. *Owen, you're going to get this building back and you're going to put those people where they belong. What you need is a plan. So, today you finish the last room in that house and tomorrow, you start on that plan!*

I smiled for the first time in a long while and left for home.

Chapter 4

The following morning, sitting at my dark cherry-wood desk, I began to take stock. I had fourteen thousand dollars remaining in the bank and no means of income. It had taken me twelve years and a lot of hard work and long hours to accumulate the amount I'd lost on my property. I now needed a lot more money, and in a much shorter period of time. Having finished the remodeling of my house was a plus for two reasons. I could sell it and bank the equity, about twenty thousand, and, just as importantly, I would be able to relocate to an undisclosed location. Unless they checked the public records, nobody would know where I'd be living unless I wanted them to.

Then, I considered my intangible assets. I believe I have sufficient knowledge to operate a construction company and, through my accounting training and experience, I can certainly form and manage trust accounts. Plus, having finally overcome my youthful bashfulness, I can personably deal with most people on nearly all levels. I don't always like it, but I can do it. And with good fortune, I'd been genetically blessed with my late father's intelligence and my mother's youthful appearance.

I mentally listed my intangible liabilities as well. I'm too trusting and prudent, probably again from my mother. Plus, too easily, I have periods of procrastination. And, basically, I'm a bit of a coward.

Physically, I'm pale, overweight by forty pounds and, following twelve years of sitting behind a desk with no exercise, I'm horribly out of shape. Three months of driving nails into drywall and hanging wallpaper has made me a little stronger in the arms, but it's done nothing for my gut. In short, changes would have to be made to both sides of my ledger, inside and out.

Walking to the kitchen, I poured a cup of coffee and returned to my office. Propping my feet on the desk, I leaned back in the chair and casually lit a cigarette. Socko raised his head in annoyed defiance of the barking dog next door, then resumed his restful position of snoozing on the brown carpet beneath my chair. While inhaling and exhaling the smoke, I gazed out the open window at the blue of the morning sky and the fresh greenery of the mulberry trees. An invisible dove cooed from one of the branches. Enjoying this, I knew the balmy May weather would soon be gone and everyone in Phoenix, believing they had died and gone to hell, would once again make the almighty air conditioner their king.

The cigarette was finished sooner than I wanted for it to be, ending my reverie. Sighing, I smashed the butt into an ashtray and stood on my feet. Carrying the receptacle and the still half-full cigarette package to the kitchen, I emptied both into the trash, and with a longing last look at the Marlboros in the wastebasket, I had one thought. *This won't be easy.*

Following a hasty shave and shower, I quickly dressed and went back into the office. *Okay, Owen, before you can radiate an inward confidence, you must first exude an outward one.* I picked up the Yellow Pages and reached for the telephone. Thumbing through the book, I found a small gym with a personal trainer located near-by and I scheduled an appointment for that afternoon.

Lifting the receiver again, I contacted the classified department of the newspaper and placed an ad to sell the house. I gave no consideration to a real estate agent. I wanted to save the expense of a commission, as well as forcing a test of my promotional ability and sales technique. Satisfied, I snatched my keys and billfold from the desk and left the house for a trip to the book store, a sign shop, and the barber.

****

For the next several weeks, I followed the advice of the personal trainer and restricted my food intake according to the dictation of The Fat Book. Meanwhile, enrolling the services of a local tanning salon, I found myself naked and mesmerized under the lamps each afternoon. I really missed the Marlboros.

Finally, after three months of grueling work and

treatment, I was becoming 'tanned and toned'. And, according to the strength guru, "You've done well, Owen. Now, it's just a matter of maintenance."

During this time, I also busied myself with other important things as well. Spending numerous hours at the Recorder's Office, I learned that the Tafino brothers owned many properties, all acquired within the past five years, just as Blake had told me. Mostly commercial, some residential, and, also as Blake had informed me, all obtained through foreclosures and tax liens. Unfortunately, every one of their holdings indicated the seller to be the name of each respective financial institution that had filed the foreclosure. Nowhere could I find out upon whom the foreclosures had been filed, and I had no idea how I could find out. A cross-reference check of the addresses for each property only listed current information, nothing prior.

Every parcel owned by the Italians had been re-financed with new mortgages from various institutions and labor organizations. The proceeds of these new mortgages obviously went right back into their bank accounts. An intelligent method. Allow the rents collected to pay for the properties, increase your cash position by borrowing more than what was paid for them, and keep your own money as well. Even the brothers' personal residences in elite Paradise Valley were foreclosed homes. Surreptitiously making a list of all this information, I couldn't learn from where the Tafinos had migrated.

The limited information I found on Mortensen revealed that he and his wife, Margo, are indebted for a home in Tempe. He is the proprietor of the mortgage brokerage firm and, until recently resigning, she was employed as a loan manager at Valley National Bank. They have excellent credit.

While reading the classified ads every day, I committed to memory the values of real estate for every location inside of Maricopa County. Within six weeks, after I'd put a sales price much higher than what I really wanted for the place, I sold the house for even more than I'd originally anticipated, and added twenty-two thousand dollars to my bank account. I had thirty days to vacate.

Two short weeks later, I acquired a fix-up, four-bedroom home, for nearly thirty thousand dollars below market, with very little down and a quick closing. Luckily, my own credit rating had not been impaired by the foreclosure. I started the repairs even before Socko and I moved in, with the extra fourth bedroom providing a perfect training and workout room.

For the next four months, I toiled at remodeling the house and continued my information gathering and health program. I began making a practice of shopping at various new locations whenever possible, and of traveling different routes to and from the necessary frequented places I'd go. Plus, I always parked the van in the garage, out of sight. I was avoiding pattern setting and I was laying the blocks for the foundation of my own conspiracy.

It was nearing the end of December when my remodeling was completed, but with the holidays looming, I'd wait until the first of the year before placing the house on the market. With that sale, I would then be in a position to make an offer on something within the commercial listings.

When doing that, however, I realized that I must remain behind the scenes, to maintain an element of surprise with my targets. I judged that the Tafinos and Mortensen probably would not consider the possibility of retaliation against them, but there was no way I could merely place myself into a foreclosure situation and simply call Mr. Mortensen again.

Consequently, with the Christmas spirit all around, I began to reminisce one evening and I saw Joyce's face in my mind's eye. Happy with her divorce settlement, she was remarried and, as I was learning to be with mine, content with her new life.

Fleetingly, I wondered about Annette. I could still envision her ravishing beauty, gorgeous body, and those come-hither eyes. *Naw. You'd better stay away from her, Owen.* So, I simply finished my beer and went to bed.

The next morning, while leaving for the bank, I saw the neighbor's teen-aged daughter standing in their front yard. Not having the cold heart to place Socko in a kennel, I approached her about baby-sitting him for a week.

"Oh, do you mean that black and white cat? He's yours? Sure! He comes over here all the time. I just love him to death! He's so cool!" I knew that Socko would be in good hands. Rest assured.

That was the first part of my idea. Two days later, I boarded a plane to Springfield, Missouri to spend Christmas with my mother and my younger sister's family. That was the second part. The third part would have to wait until I got there.

Chapter 5

With all of her other belongings loaded into her packed car, Judy Carmelle had just closed her remaining suitcase, ready to leave the dormitory. She was making a final check for anything she may have overlooked, when her roommate bolted through the door and cheerfully greeted her. "Hi, Jude! You goin' home for the holidays?"

"Hi, Sonya." Judy responded, sounding dejected. "Yeah, headin' for good old Yuma. How about you?"

"Not right away. I'm gonna work a coupla nights first, then," she sang the last words, "It's homeward bound."

Flopping onto her bed and grunting while she removed her shoes, Sonya Waverly whooshed, "Man, I'm glad classes were cut short today. I'm bushed!" After that, with her left hand gripping the edge of the mattress, she reached her right one beneath her sweater and fumbled with her bra strap, finally unhooking it. "Whew! That's a relief!"

Judy simply stood there, silently watching her friend's gyrations, as Sonya was now stretched out on the bunk with her mouth wide open, giving out a huge yawn. Finally, holding her head in her hand, propped by her elbow, Sonya again turned her attention to Judy. "So, babe, are you coming back early, or are you gonna be gone for the full boat?"

With hesitation in her voice, Judy answered, "Uh, I'm not sure." Then she looked into her friend's face. "No, that's not true, Sonya. At first, I thought about not waiting around to tell you this, mainly because I hate tearful goodbyes, but I felt I owed it to you to let you know. Truth is…I, uh, won't be back."

"What?" Sonya exclaimed. She sat straight up at the edge of her twin bed. "What in the hell do you mean—you won't be back?"

"Just that. I won't be back."

"Okay, babe, let's get this straight. Let's see, we've been together in this dormitory for almost three and a half years now, and you're simply going to tell me that you're leaving me here all alone and that you won't be back. Huh-uh, girl, that doesn't fly! What's up?"

"Oh, just something at home..." Judy's voice trailed, as she changed the valise from her tired right hand to her left.

With feigned anger, Sonya Waverly raised her voice. "Judy Carmelle! You are pissing me off! After being friends for as long as we have, do you really think you're just gonna tell me, 'there's somethin' at home', and that's it? You put that suitcase down and come over here. You're gonna tell me the whole story!"

Heaving a sigh, Judy obediently set the satchel on the blue carpet and traipsed across the room. She took a seat on her own bed across from her blonde schoolmate then gave her an appreciative half-smile. "Sonya, I don't want to bother you with this," she said, apologetically.

"Go ahead—bother me."

"Well, it's quite simple, really. I just don't think Mother can continue working as hard as she is just to keep me in college. I think it's time I start taking care of myself and maybe help her a little bit for a change. With Nathan being a junior in high school now, all the expense is simply too much for her."

"So, what are you going to do—give up your plans to be a lawyer and just stay a waitress all your life?"

"Well, no. I figure maybe in a year or two, I can start back to school again. With a good job, I can save some money and when Nathan is on his own, I can always finish then."

"Bullshit!"

Judy had to laugh. "What do you mean, 'bullshit!'?"

"Just that. Bullshit!"

"Well, what do you mean by that? It's not bullshit. It's a cold, hard fact. Look, even with my waitress job here, Mother has had to help me out a lot. And, Sonya, let's face it, I'm going to be twenty-seven years old next month and, like I said, it's about time I stopped being a burden to her and help her out for a change. That's not bullshit."

"I say it's bullshit. You've got what—less than two

years to go before you graduate? Judy, come on—listen, here's what you need to do! You get your degree, pass the bar, and after a few simple accident cases—you're rich! Then you help your mother out!"

"But, Sonya, you don't understand. With Mother working two jobs, it gives my little brother too much time to himself. She thinks Nathan might be hanging with the wrong crowd and it's going to lead him astray! So, if I give her a hand, maybe she can be more of a mother to him. And if he can stay out of trouble and keep playing football—he's pretty good—then he can go to college. So, you see, I've got to stay home when I go. I guess he needs me as much as she does."

But the disappointment in Judy's voice didn't escape her friend. Sonya felt the same disappointment. *Oh, hell, no! I don't want her to leave! I've got to think of something!* She instantly knew of one answer, but she didn't want to pursue that. *Huh-uh, Sonya. There's got to be another way. But, Jeez! You need time to think!*

Just then, the door burst open and a girl with short, brown hair peeked in. The rushing noises from students moving up and down the hallway came in with her. She yelled above the din. "Hey, Sonya! You want to go down to Marco's and eat with us?"

"Not right now, Sandy. Maybe I'll catch you guys there a little later."

"Oookay. Bye. Hi, Judy—have a good trip home."

"Thanks, Sandy. Bye." The door slammed shut as quickly as it had been opened.

Turning to her roommate, Judy offered, "Sonya, if you want to go ahead and go with them, it's okay. I have to leave anyway. It's a pretty long drive home."

"Ha! You're not getting rid of me that easily. We haven't finished talking about this, yet."

"There's nothing more to talk about," Judy exclaimed.

But Sonya wouldn't buy that. *Yeah, there is! I just haven't figured out exactly what, yet! I need time to think, damn it!* With her index finger pressed against her pursed

31

lips and her eyebrows curled into a frown, the thought flashed through Sonya's mind to simply blurt out the only solution she could immediately think of. *No! I can't do that! What would she think? Crap, I just wish the hell she wasn't leaving so soon!* All of a sudden, her crystal blue eyes shot wide open and her lips spread into a wide grin. *Wait a minute, that's it!*

She grabbed Judy by the forearm. "Hey, babe, I just got a brilliant idea! Why don't you go down to Marco's with us? Then you can stay here tonight and head out in the morning. That way, we can talk later and you can drive home tomorrow in daylight. I mean, it's gonna be dark soon and that's a cold, lonely trip at night. Besides, you'll be more alert and a lot fresher in the morning."

"I don't know, Sonya. I promised Mother I'd be home tonight."

"You can call her. One more day won't make a difference." Casting guilt, Sonya quickly added, "Besides, if you're not coming back to school, you can't just leave, not without spending at least one more evening with your friends!"

Judy knew that she would miss them. And their camaraderie. "Oohh, Sonya," she groaned, before relenting. "Well, all right, I suppose."

"Great! Now then, don't you dare mention anything to any of the others about not coming back! Wait until you leave tomorrow. Tonight, let's just have a good time—okay?"

"Sure, Sonya. Okay."

****

Several hours later, lying across her bed in her powder blue, baby-doll pajamas, Judy admitted, "That was fun, Sonya. I'm glad I stayed."

"Yeah, babe, I had a good time, too. That Sandy is so damned funny." She chuckled.

Stretched out on her bunk, Sonya Waverly wrapped her white terrycloth robe around her long legs then rested her head against her folded hands on her pillow. The soft light from the lamp on their nightstand was casting a small shadow on the ceiling. The young blonde stared at it and mentally scolded herself. *Dammit, Sonya! You've thought about this all evening and you haven't come up with any other answer! I guess there just isn't one. And, girl, you owe it to Judy to let her in on the one possible thing that could keep her here. She may be totally disgusted with you when she knows, but if you don't tell her and she somehow finds out later that you didn't, she might be really hurt.* Out of the corner of her eye, Sonya peeked at Judy, now sitting on her bed with her feet curled Indian style, putting on fingernail polish. *Yeah, I suppose you're right—better disgusted than hurt. So, okay, here goes!* She cleared her throat. "Judy, you don't have to drop out of school, you know. Not if it's a matter of money."

"Here we go again, Sonya. That's easy for you to say! You've got money comin' out the ying-yang. I mean, I'm not jealous or anything. You know me well enough to know that's not the case, but once again, it's just another cold, hard fact. Sure, I don't want to leave school—and I don't know how else to say this—but I simply cannot come back. I don't have any other choice!"

"Well, uh, maybe you do. Maybe I know of a way you can stay in school and help your mother at the same time."

"What? Rob a bank?" Judy pshawed.

"No, silly, I'm serious. But I, uh, I'm not sure how you might take this."

It was only with a slight touch of curiosity that Judy shot a glance in Sonya's direction, but, when she saw her nibbling on a fingernail, she stopped brushing her nail in mid-stroke and curled her eyebrows into a small frown. *Oh-oh, that means she's really nervous about something! What in the world does that girl have going on inside that head of hers?* "Take what?"

Sonya sighed heavily. "Oh boy, where do I start? Okay, first of all, babe, I think you already know that you're the best friend I've ever had. And having you stay in school really means a lot to me. I mean—a whole lot! Otherwise, believe me I wouldn't ever bring up this particular subject to you."

"Particular subject? What particular subject?" With skepticism, Judy raised one eyebrow toward her friend and set the nail polish on the nightstand.

Sonya then fixed her stare back onto the shadow on the ceiling and nervously exhaled another long sigh with a loud whoosh. "All right—here goes. You know that I've been working my way through school—right?"

"Yeah. So?"

"Well, I've never really told you what I work at."

A bit puzzled, Judy exclaimed, "Sure you have. You're a hostess out at the country club."

"Uh, no, not exactly. I know that's what I've told you for three years, but that's not really what I do."

"Oh?"

Sonya rolled onto her side and studied the other girl's eyes for several moments before stating, "Judy, like I just said, your friendship means a great deal to me and it's only because of that, that I'm going to tell you what I'm going to tell you. I mean, babe, you've got to finish college! But, if I reveal something that'll probably really shock you, will you promise that nothing will change? Will you promise me you won't hate me? And please! Will you promise not to tell anyone else?"

Exasperated, Judy shrilled, "Tell anyone what, for heaven's sake? Spit it out, woman!"

"Do you promise?"

"Yes, of course, I promise! Now, would you please tell me whatever the hell it is you have to say? And, tell me how this earth-shaking news is going to keep me in school!"

"Damn, Judy! Cut me a little slack! This isn't easy!" Sonya took another deep breath. "Oh, hell! I guess the best thing to do is just blurt it right out. So, all right, what the hell! I don't work as a hostess for some country club! I work for an escort service."

Judy sprang straight to the edge of her bed with a wide-eyed stare. Without thinking, she blurted, "What? What did you say? Are you trying to tell me that you're a prostitute?"

However, Judy was shocked nearly as much by her own bluntness as she was with Sonya's statement. She at once attempted to atone by waving her hand in the air, as if to erase the words. "No, wait, Sonya—wait. I'm sorry! I didn't mean that! You just surprised me, that's all, and that was the first thing that came to my mind."

An awkward hush filled the room, with neither of them wanting to look at the other. Eventually, almost whispering, Judy ventured, "So, okay, explain it to me. What exactly is an escort service? What do you do there? What, uh...?" She questioningly shrugged.

Sonya squirmed and shot a glance Judy's way before settling back and re-fixing her blue eyes on the familiar shadow. "Uh, okay. I'll try."

Looking down, Judy began nervously picking at a stubborn little hangnail with her fingers. For a short time, it was the only sound in the room, save the ticking of their clock on the nightstand. At length, Sonya took a deep breath, then she turned onto her side again and propped her head with the palm of her hand. Once settled, she gazed at her classmate and gamely recited, "Okay, here's how it works. You see, there are a lot of rich businessmen who come to Phoenix, uh, well, obviously for business and sometimes they—well, they want a young lady to be on their arm at various types of functions and they call the escort service. The service gives the assignment to one of us girls and we go out with them for the evening. To dinners, banquets, meetings, conventions, those types of things. That's all." Awkwardly pursing her lips and shrugging her shoulders, Sonya brushed a few loose strands of hair back onto her head then she continued to stare at Judy, waiting for a reaction.

"Oh, hell, Sonya, that's not so bad! My God, I thought you were really going to tell me something horrible! So. That's it? That's all you do?"

Sonya didn't say a word. And when she didn't, Judy instantly had an alarming afterthought. "Wait a minute! You don't hafta have sex with these old geezers, do you?"

Sonya involuntarily giggled. "Hey, a lot of them aren't old geezers! In fact, more often than not, they're really young, good-looking guys."

Judy cocked her head. "Sonya, you didn't answer my question! Do you?"

"Uh, let me see. How shall I put this? Naturally, we get approached sometimes—actually, most of the time, really. And, uh, well, babe, that's where the really big money can be made. The service doesn't require that we do that, but they discreetly take their cut if we do. And, crap, Judy, some of these guys are willing to pay up to a thousand dollars!"

"Damn, Sonya! That's sick! You actually go to bed with a different guy every night and let him have sex with you?"

"Oh, hell, no! Crime-a-netlee, Judy! You make it sound gross! It's not like that, not one bit! I mean, a lot of them aren't interested in that at all and don't even mention it. They merely want some company. Or they want a pretty girl on their arm to impress somebody. Besides, it's not different ones all the time. Both the service and each of us girls have customers who are regulars, so it's usually the same men over and over. And if we're with someone we don't feel comfortable with, we just tell them it's not permitted by the service because they could lose their license and we'd lose our job."

Still sitting at the edge of her bed, Judy's mouth was wide open and her eyes were bugged in disbelief. Aghast, she screeched, "Holy crap, Sonya! That's still sick! I am really shocked. How long have you been doing this? And why did you keep this from me? *How* did you keep this from me?"

Sonya nervously laughed and when Judy saw what she guessed to be guilt on Sonya's face, together with her simpering, she quickly suspected that something about all this was amiss. "Ah, hell, Sonya, wait a minute! You're kidding me, right? Good heavens! You had me believing you! Shame on you. That's a helluva joke to play on somebody!"

Between involuntary giggles, Sonya fidgeted with a loose strand of fiber on her yellow blanket. She looked up and said, "No, I'm not kidding. Uh, let's see—how did I keep it from you? Believe me, it wasn't easy, busybody that you are. Why did I keep it from you? Well, that should be perfectly obvious. Aaaand, I've been doing this for about three years."

Judy shook her head in disbelief. "I don't believe this. You really are serious, aren't you? Sonya, how in the hell did you get started into something like this? And why?"

"Well, do you remember that girl who roomed across the hall from us the first year we were here? Belinda Shepherd?"

Thinking momentarily, Judy recalled Belinda's pretty face. "Yeah, sort of. What about her?"

"Well, she was working there and she told me about it. It sounded exciting, so I had her get me placed at the service. And, be sure, darlin', the money is excellent!"

"My God, Sonya, you're making light of all this and it really isn't funny. I still can't believe it." Judy's shrill voice squeaked with the word believe and all at once, a rush of warmth came into her face and her cheeks felt hot. "Oh-oh, hold on a minute."

"You okay?"

Without answering, Judy jumped to her feet and marched into the bathroom. Hurriedly turning on the faucet, she splashed cool water against her face, once, twice, three times, before systematically massaging it onto her skin. Standing there, she held her eyes closed until the cool water did its magic of taking the fire away. When she finally opened them, she looked at her reflection in the mirror. Then she couldn't keep from grinning. *Can you believe this? That girl actually managed to keep this from me for over three years!*

Of course, despite this totally unexpected revelation, Judy's feelings toward Sonya were no different. She liked her for who she was and how she was treated by her and she knew that wouldn't change. *But, damn! This is a shock!*

She grabbed a thick, soft towel from the rack and held it to her face, allowing it to soak up the water for a moment. Then, after expelling one last huge sigh, Judy slowly trudged back to her seat on the edge of the bed, keeping the towel with her. In time, she peeked through the terrycloth and suddenly burst into laughter. "Good heavens, Sonya! This whole thing is effing bizarre!" When she realized her own unpremeditated choice of words, Judy laughed again.

Sonya's wide grin was not so much for the unintentional humor as it was one of relief. *Thank you, babe. You're still Judy.* She blushed because of both reasons. "Ha, Judy. That's real funny."

"Honest to God, Sonya! I really can't believe you kept this from me for three whole years!" Judy screeched, sandwiching her words between bursts of laughter. "So, tell me, Blondie. By letting me in on this, how is it supposed to keep me in school? Are you so rich from all that extracurricular activity that you're going to support me?" She laughed out loud.

With a Cheshire grin on her face, Sonya raised one seductive eyebrow and dragged out the words. "Oh, no."

Like a thunderbolt, Sonya's meaning hit her. "Wait a minute, girl! You aren't suggesting I do the same thing?"

"Sure. Why not?"

Judy was stupefied. "Why not? Why not? Are you crazy? Oh no, Sonya, you can't be serious?"

"Of course, I'm serious. Why, honey, with that dark, auburn hair of yours and those deep, brown, mysterious eyes, you can make a fortune. Not to mention you have a personality like nobody I've ever met and a body that won't quit! Those wealthy s-o-b's would be absolutely fighting over you."

"Holy crap, Sonya! I couldn't do that!" Judy exclaimed. "I don't even know how you can do it!"

"Sure you could. You like money and sex, don'tcha?"

"Not like that! Not when they're both used in the same sentence! I mean, ut—going to bed with complete strangers? Hell's bells, Sonya! It gives me the creeps just thinking about it!"

"Hey, I was pretty nervous about it at first, too. I'll admit that. But you'll get over it. Honestly. Especially when the bank account builds up."

"Now it's my turn to say bullshit!"

"And it's my turn to tell you that it's not bullshit." Sonya vowed. "Seriously, Judy, you do get used to it. After you get several regulars, you learn a lot about them and really get pretty comfortable in their company. And believe me, all of them are perfect gentlemen. In fact, some of them will be in total awe of you. So you see? Besides the great bucks, you also get treated like an absolute queen. What do you say?"

"I say you're nuts! I mean, Sonya, I appreciate your concern about my schooling and all, and that you'd go so far as to tell me about this, but I just couldn't do it, I really couldn't." Judy blushed.

"Okay, I won't push you. But, I will tell you this; Judy—you're getting really close to graduation and babe, time goes by so rapidly. Only three more short semesters and you're there! Jeez, it's hard for me to believe I'm only six months away! And I've already got more than a one hundred thousand dollar kicker to start the rest of my life with! So, why don't you do something for me—for yourself, really? Go on home for the holidays. Take that couple of weeks to think it over. Then if you decide you want to give it a try, come on back. I know I could get you into the service. No problem there! They'd jump at you, babe!"

"Literally!" Judy scoffed.

"Ha, again!"

Allowing the whole idea to digest for a moment, the young blonde reached over and placed her manicured hand on Judy's forearm, giving her a gentle squeeze. "Seriously, Judy, at least promise me you'll think about it. Okay? I'll really miss you if you don't come back."

Judy raised her gaze to meet Sonya's and, looking into her chum's searching, brilliant blue eyes, she coupled hands with her. "All right, Sonya, I'll consider it. I really will."

Her response was intended to merely appease her friend for that moment, but after they'd said goodnight and she'd slipped under the covers, Judy lay restlessly awake in the darkness for a long time, thinking and arguing with herself. She'd managed to struggle through college for more than six long years and, as Sonya had reminded her, with merely three semesters to go, she desperately didn't want to stop now. *Maybe Sonya's right, since it's only for a year and a half, maybe it wouldn't be so bad.*

Wouldn't be so bad? Are you crazy? It would be horrible!

Yes. It would. But so would leaving school.

But, I don't want to do that!

Yeah, but you don't want to leave school, either! And it's only eighteen months.

Hell! Eighteen months is a long time!

Well, so is the six years you've already spent! Do you want that to be wasted?

No, of course not. But I can finish school later!

Wait a minute, Judy. Think about that! Think seriously about that! Do you honestly believe that you'll finish later? After you're well past thirty?

Thirty? Egad! No, I can't honestly say that I do. But, I also don't think I can do what Sonya's doing, either!

I believe maybe you can. And if you want to finish school, I believe you have to!

But?

No buts. There just can't be any buts.

So, just before she drifted off to sleep, although petrified with the idea, Judy Carmelle knew. *Sonya's right! I've got to come back!*

Chapter 6

Because the amount of money I needed was not going to be earned with buying and selling fix-up residences, it was time for me to begin laying the groundwork to purchase a commercial property. Before leaving Phoenix for Missouri, I'd opened a checking account in the name of Southwest Desert Life Insurance Company. As part of my plan, I used a different bank from the one where I maintained my real accounts. I'd also rented a post office box so that my newly formed insurance company would have a mailing address to which the bank could mail my new checks.

I had also determined that one of the first things I needed was a new identity, which would be the best way for nothing to be traced back to me when I was ready to tackle the Tafino brothers and Mortensen. I had the obituary section of the St. Louis Post-Dispatch in my briefcase. It was where I would start.

I felt the wheels of the commuter plane touch down as it landed in St. Louis. I'd explained to my mother that I had some insurance business to take care of, and I'd be gone for two or three days. Being aware of her fear of airplanes, I knew she would decline when I offered to take her along, but the touch of guilt I experienced at deceiving her was easily discarded by my concern for her welfare. I reasoned that I wasn't quite sure what I might be entangling myself into with my conspiracy thing, but I certainly didn't want to involve my own innocent mother. Besides, it wasn't a trip to St. Louis that would impress her. It would be my offer to have her accompany me, so she was pleased, and I was in St. Louis by myself. Mission accomplished.

Retrieving my valise and suit-bag from the baggage area, I went outside into the brisk, icy wind to the taxi stand. Of the twenty or more cabs parked there, most were occupied by disheveled drivers, resting behind their steering wheels with their heaters blasting. Hot, smelly exhaust filled the air, helping to melt the remaining patches of slush from a recent snowstorm. The dirty puddles of water splashed airborne with the onrush of noisy traffic, adding new patterns to the muddy designs already sprayed on the doors and fenders of the cars, some of which were much older than from this latest storm. At scattered intervals, a few of the more stalwart cabbies stood outside their hacks in the gray, overcast afternoon, huddling against them for warmth.

There amongst the longhairs, the unshaven, and those with tattered clothes, I noticed a heavy-set black man standing at near attention beside a clean, yellow Chevrolet. The toes of polished, black boots peeked from beneath the cuffs of his crisp, dark green uniform pants, and black leather gloves sheathed his hands. The brown buckskin jacket he had on bore slight creases and worn spots, but still reflected much of its clean, original shine. The smile across his round face was wide and book-ended with a deep dimple in the smooth skin of each cheek. The puffs of foggy breath escaping through his white teeth failed to sway his defiance of the cold weather as being just another hazard of his occupation.

Besides all that, I liked his hat. Atop his close-cropped hair was an olive colored, Greek fisherman's cap, which had plainly been a part of him for a long time. The fading of many launderings had not completely removed the white perspiration stains of summer's telltale heat. Pinned to the right side of it was a button which I couldn't read as I approached him. "Afternoon, sir. Is your cab available?"

"Yessuh!" The smile widened as he reached for the rear door handle.

I halted him before he pulled the door open. "Excuse me. Is it okay if I ride up front with you, uh, Robert?" His name was stitched in red on a white patch sewn over the zippered pocket of his coat.

Pleased that I'd noticed, he stopped and fondly touched the patch. He modestly explained, "My wife sewed that on there for me. Not many folks takes the time to notice it, though. Ever'body's too busy these days," he reflected.

Suddenly alerting himself back to work, he stated a

bit apologetically, "Oh, sorry, suh. Let me put that luggage in the trunk for y'all."

With a return smile, I gave him the bags and let myself into the front seat of the Chevvie.

A moment later, I felt the whole car shake when he slammed the trunk, and then rushed to open the driver's door. Grunting, he squeezed behind the wheel, inserted the key, and started the engine. Rubbing his gloved hands together, he said, "There. That heater's gonna be warmin' up real soon, suh. Now then, where to?"

"Is there a Holiday Inn nearby?"

"Yessuh, right around the corner from the airport here." He pointed toward the direction he meant then turned to peer out the window, checking for a break in traffic.

Wanting to hold his attention, I reached over and touched his big arm, giving no thought to the fact that such a move could be risky. "Say, Robert, before we leave, would you mind answering a few short questions for me?" When he quickly jerked around to face me, I offered him a twenty from my shirt pocket.

Stunned for a second, he stared at it before his perpetual grin came back. He took the bill and stuffed it into his pants pocket, grunting again from the lack of space with which to maneuver his large frame. "Yessuh! I'll sure try. An' thank you, suh!"

But before I could ask him anything, it was his turn to reach across and grip my forearm. He defensively appealed, "Say, I hope you ain't gonna ask me about no prostitoots, or drugs, or anything like that, though, 'cause I don't get involved in that sorta thing. Huh-uh!" I shook my head. "Good. Okay. That's good."

However, when I opened my mouth to speak, he stopped me again. "Oh, and one more thing, suh—uh, sorry to interrupt—but how long will these questions take? I mean, I don't want that dispatcher wonderin' too much about where I might be." He pointed toward the two-way radio.

"Not very long at all, Robert." I then pointed my own finger at the silent speaker, where the invisible dispatcher lurked. "Incidentally, go ahead and turn on the meter. I don't expect the company to give me your conversation for free. And, Robert, I must say that I'm impressed with your show of honesty. It's refreshing." His only reply was another broad smile, accompanied by a slightly bashful nod of appreciation.

"Now then, Robert, in addition to the motel, the next thing I need to find is a good Italian restaurant. I've got a real craving for some spaghetti and meatballs."

"Okay, suh. I can do that. What else?"

"Do you happen to know the location of Greenlawn Chapel?"

His eyes spread wide open in alarm as they glued themselves to me. "You mean the funeral home?"

"Right."

"Yessuh, I know where it's at. Say, y'all don't have somebody there, I hope. I mean, you didn't lose a loved one, or somethin'?"

"No, Robert, nothing like that. But thanks for asking. I just have some business to take care of there tomorrow."

"Oh, good. That's good." He slowly replied.

Keeping his brown eyes riveted on me, he immediately began wondering what kind of business his passenger could possibly have at a funeral home. *Oh, Lordee be! Maybe he's a casket salesman!* He inwardly shuddered, not really wanting to know. Hankering to rapidly change the subject, he blurted, "Suh, you got anything else I can answer for y'all? Or, is you ready to leave?" He quickly checked the traffic again.

Sensing his nervousness, I promptly tried to alleviate any misgivings he might have about me. "Just one more thing, Robert. I'm an insurance representative," I paused to let that sink in, "and in addition to my business at the mortuary, I'll need to visit several other places in town as well. Therefore, I'd like to know your hours so that when I need a cab, I can call and request you. I mean, the company does allow that—right?"

A look of semi-relief showed on his face and the big

grin returned. "Oh, Yessuh. Y'all just call 256-2000, and ask for cab number one, oh, two, two. But only in the evenin's, 'cause I work from four 'til twelve."

There were other things I would need from him later, but I first wanted to ensure that he trusted me because I didn't want him to back away from those things when the time came. So for now, I finished the conversation. "Okay, Robert, I believe that takes care of everything. Guess I'm ready to go to that motel now—I want to freshen up a bit before I tackle that spaghetti. So, when I'm ready to eat, I'll just call and ask for your cab. All right?"

"Oh, Yessuh! Two-five-six-two thousand. Cab ten-twenty-two."

****

Sometime later, I waited outside the motel lobby until I saw Robert wheel the Chevrolet under the canopy. He quickly reached across the seat and opened the passenger door. "Yessuh. Hi there. Hop on in. I'm takin' you to the Wine Gardens. Finest I-talian in St. Louis."

"Sounds perfect, Robert." I climbed into the cab.

While promoting small talk during our drive to the restaurant, I learned that Robert Tanner and his wife, Yvonne, are the parents of a baby girl named Theresa, who is one year old. Robert was born and raised in St. Louis and has been driving a cab for the same company for almost eight years. "And that's about it, suh. Yeah, I been tryin' to save up some money to buy a house, but, man, I tell you, with the prices goin' up all the time, I don't know if I'll ever get there. But, I'm hopin', 'cause that sure would make my wife awful happy."

"You just keep pluggin', Robert, you'll get there," I vowed, as he drove the Chevrolet up to the curb.

"Wellsuh, here we are—The Wine Gardens. Y'all enjoy that spaghetti an' meatballs, you hear? And I'll be back to pick you up in about two hours, just like you asked. No reason to call. I'll be here!"

I handed him a fifty. "Thank you, Robert. Please keep the change. And don't bother coming around for the door—I'll get it."

****

While riding back to the motel after dinner, I felt comfortable enough to filter a few leading questions into our ongoing small talk. These would determine if this big man was the right guy or not. "Say, Robert, there's going to be several times in the next couple of days when I'll be needing transportation in the daytime during your off-duty hours, so I have a suggestion to make. I assume you have a personal car, other than your taxi?"

"Yessuh! I got a brand new Pontiac Grand Prix!" He proudly stated.

"Good. Then what I'd like to suggest is this—I'd like to hire you and your personal car to chauffeur me around when you're not working. It's not that I couldn't take other taxi, it's just that I feel comfortable with you and I thought, with an extra hundred a day, it would be something for you to put away toward that down payment on your house. Now then, Robert, I certainly don't want to cause you any problems with your job, so, if you're concerned they might object, I'll absolutely understand. Of course, when you're on duty, naturally, I'll use your cab. What do you think?"

"Well, suh, I don't rightly know. I sure could use the extra money, but nobody's ever asked me about this before, so I really don't know what the cab company might say—I mean, should they find out." His laugh had a touch of devilment.

"Well, Robert, it's my opinion that if you were to do that sort of thing all the time, they probably wouldn't like it. But since I'm only in town for a few days, it most likely would be just a one time thing for you."

"You is right. Yessuh, you is probably right. An' thinkin' 'bout it, if I don't tell nobody about it, nobody will know." The shady chuckle again before he quickly about-faced. "Course, should they ever ask, I wouldn't lie about it. I'd just explain it to them the way you just explained it to me, an' maybe it wouldn't be no trouble at all. I'd just tell 'em that if they don't want me to do that sorta thing no more, then

46

I won't do it."

"Well, Robert, you can certainly be sure I won't tell them. Like I said, I wouldn't want to cause you any problems and, besides, I also wouldn't want to lose my chauffeur." We both laughed.

"Thank you, suh."

"And one last thing, Robert. Rather than 'sir', why don't you call me O. P.? That's a nickname my grandmother used to call me years ago." That part was true. She'd shortened it from 'Ornery Poop'! Fortunately, when the kind old lady passed away, the nickname went with her.

"O. P? Oh, like that boy on Mayberry? Opie? That'll be easy enough to remember. Yessuh, Opie." He chuckled.

Leaning back into the seat, I'd by now determined that Robert was the guy I wanted and that he would most likely be a good deal of help to me, especially if I approached him exactly the right way. Foremost, he was honest and righteous, but he seemed willing to extend a touch of larceny, if it served a deserving and justifiable purpose. I'd made a friend.

Upon arriving at the motel, I took the paper with his home number scribbled on it, paid the fare with another nice tip and told him good night. I looked forward to the large double bed waiting for me.

****

The following morning, after breakfast, I returned to my room and reached into my briefcase for the obituary notice from the St. Louis Post. I read it again:

> Joseph T. Bowden, 35, of St. Louis, a real estate broker, died December 17, 1978. Born and raised in St. Louis, he is survived by his wife, Jeanette, daughter, Linda, son, Kyle, father, Charles, sisters, Janice Durham and Denise Fletcher, plus several nieces and nephews. Visitation daily, 1 to 8

p.m.   Services will be held at
Greenlawn   Chapel,   1118   West
Mulberry, on Wednesday at 2 p.m.

Reaching for the Yellow Pages, I began to call the real estate offices, beginning with A-Able Realty. Each time, I asked for Joseph T. Bowden. "There's no one here by that name. Could another broker or salesperson help you?"

"No, Mr. Bowden was highly recommended by a mutual acquaintance and, somehow, I misplaced the name of the realty company he works for. However, it's imperative that I speak with somebody soon, so if I can't locate him right away, I'll be sure to call you back." Click.

During my telephone travels, only two people were sharp enough to suggest that I contact the mutual friend and simply ask him for the name, but I compromised that by telling them he couldn't be reached for several days. Finally, nearly an hour later, I found what I was looking for at Mid-America Realty. "Oh dear, haven't you heard? Mr. Bowden was an associate here, but he passed away on Sunday."

"Oh, no. I wasn't aware of that. Had he been with your company a long time?"

"Well, he was only here a little over a year, but we all came to know him quite well. He was, uh, somewhat outgoing. And I must say that it was quite a shock. You don't expect a man his age to have a heart attack."

"No, you certainly don't."

"Anyway, Mr. Taylor is handling Mr. Bowden's accounts now. Shall I transfer your call to him?"

"Uh, no, not right now. My friend and I only discussed Mr. Bowden yesterday, and I'm sure he doesn't know about this. Maybe I should call him first to let him know. I'm sure that, after he hears, he'll want me to talk with your Mr. Taylor. Thank you very much, ma'am and, again, I'm certainly sorry to hear about Mr. Bowden." Click.

I scratched the name and address of Mid-America Realty on the edge of the obituary notice. Now I needed to know the name of a prior firm he'd been associated with.

His real estate license would be a matter of public record. It was the best place to begin looking.

I called Robert, who picked me up and took me to Twenty-Four Hour Printing. I ordered five hundred business cards, five hundred envelopes and one hundred claim forms, all of which I'd designed earlier. Twenty-Four Hour Printing promised to have them ready by noon tomorrow.

Being that I made the mistake of giving him the choice, Robert and I lunched at Steak 'N Shake. Since it was well after noon and there wasn't much else I could accomplish today, I had him chauffeur me past a few sites that I could tell my mother about, even though we'd both seen them numerous times before—the Arch, Busch Gardens, and the St. Louis Zoo. I kept feeling the heavily settled weight of two large hamburgers and french-fries in my stomach. It'd been well over a week since my last workout and it was past time for me to visit a gym. Preferably one with a tanning salon.

Dependable as ever, Robert dropped me at Northwest Fitness Center, a short two blocks from the motel. "Here we are, Opie. Good timin', too. I got to git on home and git ready to go to work."

"Thank you, Robert. I'll just walk back to the motel from here and I'll see you tomorrow morning at nine o'clock."

"Yessuh, Opie." He saluted before driving away.

The next morning was Thursday and Robert drove me to the office of the County Recorder. Searching the records, I discovered that Mr. Bowden's real estate license was first issued fourteen years ago. His sponsoring broker at that time was one James T. Connolly. Finding the trusty Yellow Pages near a pay phone, I turned to the real estate listings and got lucky. Tracing my finger to the C's, I read 'Connolly, James T., Real Estate', in bold print. *Good. I won't have to call them all again to locate Mr. Connolly.*

Dropping a coin into the telephone, I dialed the number and asked to speak to the broker. "May I tell him who's calling?"

Quickly inventing a name, I told her, "Colby Reese,

with Mid-America Realty." She transferred the call.

"Connolly here!" His deep voice boomed through the receiver. "Reese, is it? I don't believe we've ever had any dealings together."

"No, sir, we haven't. I've only had my license for a couple of months. Mr. Connolly, the reason for my call is to let you know, in case you haven't already heard, about the sudden passing of Joseph Bowden. Joe had sort of taken me under his wing to teach me the ins and outs and during the short time we worked together, he told me about having been with your firm. He spoke quite highly of you several times."

"Yes. Jeanette called me the day after he died. Yeah, Joe was with us a long time. Got his start here, as a matter of fact. I was sorry I had to let him go last year. I kept telling him that someday that booze was going to kill him."

"Uh, yes, that seemed to be a problem for him here, too. Anyway, Mr. Connolly, I felt I should call you out of courtesy."

"Certainly. And I appreciate it, Reese." Click.

I had even more than I expected. Good. In addition to revealing Bowden's longevity with his company, Connolly had told me something else. If Joe Bowden was an alcoholic, more than likely, he was also broke.

Returning to the record books, I located two Joseph T. Bowden's, but only one with a wife named Jeanette, so I copied the address from the deed recorded for their residence.

After picking up the printing, Robert and I traveled to the home of Mr. and Mrs. Bowden. As I expected, nobody was there. Our next foray was to Greenlawn Chapel. While a nervous Robert waited patiently in the shiny, green Grand Prix, I went inside.

Signing the name of Phillip Patterson to the visitation register, I walked into Memory Chapel Room, where I was greeted by a curt young man, who escorted me to the casket. Standing there, I viewed one Joseph T. Bowden. The young man posed a question. "Were you a friend of Mr.

Bowden's?"

For a few nervous moments, I wasn't sure I could, or should, go through with this. But I quickly thought about all the months I'd already put into it, plus I reminded myself about the violated feeling I'd had when I realized what had been done to me by Mortensen and the others. Besides, if my prognostication was correct about Mr. Bowden, then I persuaded myself to believe that Mrs. Bowden would be grateful for the compensation she was about to receive for the unaware use of her husband's name.

I again heard the young man standing beside me ask, "Sir?"

"Uh, no. Not exactly. I only met him personally one time." I fibbed. "I, uh, really came to see Mrs. Bowden. As awkward as it may seem, I believe I have a bit of good news for her. Is she at the chapel today?"

He looked at me with critical eyes and I knew exactly what he was thinking. *How in the hell could there be good news at a time like this?* Eventually, he retorted, "Yes, sir. I believe she may be in the lounge downstairs with the family. If you'll please follow me, I'll take you to her."

I was presented in an abrupt manner to a short, very plump lady in a black dress. I waited until the impersonal young man walked away before I spoke to her in a low voice, "Mrs. Bowden, my name is Phillip Patterson. I'm with Southwest Desert Life Insurance Company. I apologize for intruding on you at such a terrible time, but I didn't find anyone at home and, assuming you'd be here, I took the liberty of coming by to personally offer my condolences."

"Were you a friend of Joe's?"

"A long time ago. You see, I sold Joe the small life insurance policy he has with our company, which he acquired while he was with Connolly Real Estate."

"Life insurance? Joe had life insurance?" Surreptitiously glancing around the room to be sure she was out of earshot, she whispered, "Uh, Mr. Patterson is it? Believe me, with the cost of his funeral and everything, this is a Godsend. Can you tell me how much I'll get?"

"The policy is for two thousand dollars. If you'd like—"

"By any chance, do you have the check with you?" She interrupted.

This is going to be much easier than I thought. Reaching into my inside coat pocket, I removed a packet of papers and handed them to her. "No, ma'am. I'll need to have you complete a claim form first. There's no need to do it right away, of course—just fill it out at your convenience and mail it to us in this envelope. After we receive it and get it processed, we should have the check mailed to you within thirty days."

"Oh dear. All right, I'll fill it out this evening and get it in the mail first thing tomorrow." Then she self-consciously looked around the room again and dropped her voice even lower. "But, uh, Mr. Patterson, do you think there's any possibility I might get the check before thirty days?"

It was the opening I'd hoped for. "Well, Mrs. Bowden, if I could have you give me the claim form personally, it would certainly speed things along. Is there any chance I could have it tomorrow?"

"Why, yes, of course. As I said, I'll complete it tonight." Then she timidly hesitated, before asking me, "And, uh, Mr. Patterson, I hate to impose on you, but is there any possibility you could pick it up at our house, first thing in the morning? It's because I have to be here early. His services are tomorrow, you know." With a wistful look, she choked back a sob.

"Yes ma'am. I know. And sure, I'll be glad to do that. As a matter of fact, Mrs. Bowden, I'll tell you what. I have to be in our home office within the next few days, so I'll be more than happy to deliver the claim form in person. And, while I'm there, I'll see to it that it gets processed immediately so that you'll have your money right away. Considering your loss, it's the least I can do."

She touched my arm and gave me a melancholy smile. "Oh, thank you, Mr. Patterson."

Wanting to finalize this and get the hell out of there, I fabricated a reminiscent recollection and answered the one possible question she might have, before she could ask it. "You know, Mrs. Bowden, it's strange, but Joe's policy was one of the very first ones I sold, when I first started out. And I seem to recall that he was just beginning his real estate career at the same time. Anyway, I soon learned that the best way to be successful in the insurance business is to give good service, considering that's mostly what we sell, so I've always cross referenced my files of the policies I've sold with the obituaries every day, and, when I have a match, I don't wait until the beneficiary contacts us. I contact them on my own as soon as I can. And, believe it or not, once in a while, such as in your case, they don't even know the policy exists. Most people have been appreciative of that."

"Well, I certainly am, Mr. Patterson. It'll help a lot."

When I saw tears welling in her eyes, I genuinely felt a lot of sorrow for her. Now, I really wanted to get out of there. I quickly stood up, took her right hand into both of mine and told her. "Mrs. Bowden, I won't keep you from your family any longer and, again, please accept my deepest sympathy."

"Thank you, Mr. Patterson. I'll see you in the morning."

By now, I was probably more nervous than Robert, so without another word, I hurried out of Greenlawn Chapel.

****

The next day, the weather had turned balmy and Robert and I decided to take advantage of it. While seated on a park bench eating my Caesar salad, my cabbie buddy enjoyed three roast beef sandwiches and french-fries. Our conversation started with the usual small talk, but now was the time to approach this gentle giant with what I really needed from him.

Therefore, without a great deal of detail, I discreetly confided to my newly found friend, how someone had stolen my real estate from me, but there was no way to prove it. I also told him how I was in the process of setting the bad guys up to recover what was rightfully mine and to have them prosecuted for it. "But, Robert, I need some help."

"What kinda help, Opie?"

I tactfully explained that I wanted to locate someone who could make fake drivers' licenses and several other forms of identity, and why.

Not even a bit skeptical, Robert had seen that I was honest with him from the beginning, therefore, he not only vowed to help me, but also wished me the best of luck in my pursuit. "Yessuh, Opie, a man tries his best to be honest with everybody and make a decent living, but sometimes they ain't always honest in return. That ain't right. Anyway, I knows a coupla fellas at the cab company who can give me names of places where we can get those licenses. You say you need a Missouri and an Arizona? They can do that. So, when I pick you up to take you to dinner, I'll take you to the moonlight printer's, too." The devilish chuckle again.

"Thank you, Robert."

With the claim form from Jeanette Bowden in my possession, I had all the information I needed. With that, and my new Missouri driver's license, I would be able to obtain a credit report for Joseph T. Bowden, along with his birth certificate, copies of his tax returns, marriage license, real estate license, or anything else I wanted. The Arizona driver's license would establish the identity in Phoenix.

After Robert graciously accepted my five hundred dollars for his help, he drove me to the airport and I left St. Louis to spend Christmas with my family in Springfield.

When I returned to Phoenix, I retrieved a check from the middle of the Southwest Desert Life Insurance Company checkbook and had 'Phillip Patterson' issue it for two thousand dollars to Jeanette Bowden: Proceeds of policy number so-and-so. Then, seeking more help from Robert, I sent it to him so that he could mail it for me. That way, it would have a St. Louis postmark. After her check cleared the bank, I closed the account.

Next, I prepared papers to establish the Joseph T. Bowden Trust. After receiving an identification number from the Internal Revenue Service, I opened a bank account in that name. I was now Joseph T. Bowden.

Chapter 7

After selling the house quickly, Socko and I moved again. I bought another fixer-upper with little money down and a fast closing, and in a better neighborhood. Plus, I now had over seventy thousand dollars in the trust account. By acquiring our next home in the name of Joseph T. Bowden, Owen J. Hunter had virtually disappeared.

Of course, with the vacancy rate for office space at less than four percent, I determined that office buildings were what I needed to concentrate on. Naturally, foreclosure properties were out of the question for two reasons—my limited cash resources for one and just as importantly, my attitude that, unlike Mortensen and friends, I couldn't bring myself to profit from someone else's misfortune.

I scanned the newspapers daily until one day I located a nearly vacant fourteen-unit office building for sale. Somewhat older, it had been grossly neglected and needed substantial work to make it available for rent at today's rising rates. On the plus side, it was in a desirable location, so in addition to the potential for cash flow, it represented an excellent re-sale possibility as well. I also took note of the fact that, with the proper alterations, it could easily be converted to nineteen units, thereby increasing the rent rolls. After checking, double-checking, and re-checking everything with the city and county, I made an offer on behalf of the Joseph T. Bowden Trust. The anxious owners readily accepted it.

By law, having to assume the leases of the few tenants still there, I verified that the longest would be in effect for no more than six months. I offered them a choice of an instant, penalty free escape clause, or, they could stay during remodeling, with the understanding that rents would increase substantially once the reconstruction was completed and their leases expired.

Wanting a fast completion and knowing it would take much too long to do the work myself, I accepted bids from plumbing, roofing, electrical, mechanical, carpentry, and drywall contractors.   It would take most of my trust money to complete the project, but once finished and occupied, I would be able to apply directly for an assumable mortgage without the 'benefit' of a mortgage broker such as Mortensen.   The proceeds of that loan would more than replenish my cash and, with a sale, my profits could also be banked.

Since I was still cultivating my newly found assertiveness, I practiced it by ram-rodding the sub-contractors to completion and inside of three months, the renovations were finished.   I then formed a dummy management company to secure the tenants and within another thirty days, seventeen of the nineteen spaces were leased, after which I obtained the mortgage. With it showing a positive cash flow, the building sold easily and I now had over two hundred thousand dollars in the bank.

In the meantime, I continued to constantly watch the ads, but with the current inflation and interest rates approaching twenty percent, buying had become more difficult than selling. However, with diligence, I managed to secure two more depressed properties in the next sixty days and with constant supervision and a lot of hard work, as the weeks quickly passed, I was able to increase the Bowden Trust to a bankroll in excess of one-half million dollars.

Working evenings and weekends, I also completed the house renovations at the same time and soon, Socko and I were moving one more time. This time, it was to Arcadia, an older, yet very popular area of large homes with values exceeding well over two hundred thousand dollars.   With most of it financed, I paid one hundred thirty-five thousand for ours, but I had a lot of work to do again.

It had now been twenty months since my original building went to foreclosure and I felt good about my accomplishments since that time. Within the next six to nine months, with two more gainful transactions, I fully expected to have more than one million dollars. This time, maybe Socko and I could stay put for a while.

Also, by then, I would be ready to shift to phase two

of my plot, but first I had to find out who the people were that had been foreclosed upon and subsequently had their properties acquired by the Tafino brothers, through Mortensen. I theorized that any potential witnesses I could find would add weight to the case I intended to build against them. *But how can I gain access to Mortensen's office records?* Breaking into his place was certainly out of the question.

One evening, out of the blue, it hit me. *Owen, that just might work.* Reaching for the Yellow Pages, I flipped through them until I came to the classification I was looking for and began to scroll down the list of names. *Whoa. Which one?* I decided to pick one from where the idea came from— out of the blue. I closed my eyes and jabbed my finger onto the page. It settled on a name halfway down the column.

Nervously dialing the number, I heard it ring twice before a sultry voice answered. "Parisian Escort Service. This is Amanda."

"Ah, hello. Yes, I would like to engage one of your escorts for dinner on Friday evening, please."

"All right. Have you employed our service before?"

"Uh, no, I haven't. In fact, I've never employed any service before."

"I see. Well, first of all, may I have your name? And will you be in town for very long?"

"Yes, it's Joseph Bowden. And, I'm a Phoenix resident."

"Okay, Mr. Bowden. How did you hear about us? By referral?"

"Ah, no. Actually, I picked you out of the Yellow Pages. The name intrigued me."

An amiable laugh. "I see. All right, then, please let me tell you a little about the services we provide and our fee structure. First of all, we'll take an application from you and we do require that you place a security deposit with us in the amount of two thousand dollars, which is refundable at anytime you choose to discontinue your association with us."

Amanda wisely paused, silently permitting me an opportunity to drop it right there in the event the deposit would be a problem. I reasoned that it was by design, purely to weed out most of the undesirables and deadbeats right off the bat. I made no comment.

With my silence, Amanda continued. "Okay, Mr. Bowden, once you've been approved, we can schedule a young lady to accompany you for dinner, a convention, a business meeting, or so forth. Our normal fee for a four-hour accompaniment is five hundred dollars, with limousine service being an additional sixty-five dollars per hour. Also, we can arrange for a private, in-your-own-home candlelight dinner for an additional five hundred dollars, which includes a bar, all catering, and a male server. Additional time beyond the four hours will be at the young lady's discretion and fee structure. So, are there any questions I can answer for you?"

She had explained it well. "No. Thank you...well wait, perhaps one—how do I go about completing the application?"

"Simple. I'll take the information right now, if you like."

I told her I liked. Thus, following a series of inquiries to establish that I am who I say I am, and that I'm a legitimate risk and no apparent threat to their young ladies, Amanda came to her last two questions. "Finally, Mr. Bowden, which type of dinner engagement appeals to you? And, will you be paying the deposit and service fee by credit card?"

"I prefer the in-my-own-home arrangement. And, may I use a cashier's check?"

"Yes, of course. You can drop it by our office once your application has been approved. You probably noted that—for security reasons—our address is not listed in the telephone book, so we'll disclose our location to you when we notify you of your approval. Okay?"

"Certainly. And, thank you, Amanda."

"Thank you, Mr. Bowden. And, good night." Click.

****

My approval call came on Wednesday. "Good evening, Mr. Bowden. This is Amanda with Parisian Escort

Service. How are you this evening?"

"Fine, thank you. And you?"

"Oh, I'm great, just great. I'm calling to let you know that your application has been approved and we look forward to providing you with an escort for dinner on Friday evening. Are your plans still for then?"

"Yes, they are."

"Great. Now then, do you have any particular type of young lady in mind? Blonde? Or brunette, perhaps?"

"Uh, no. Actually, the only criteria I'm interested in, is someone relatively mature, somewhat outgoing, and I'd prefer that she be college educated. I'll be interested in conversation."

"No other preferences?"

"No others. That's it." I made the assumption that she'd be attractive.

"Great. Now then..." I could hear the shuffling of papers before, exaggerating the trailing of her words for effect, Amanda sensuously announced, "All right, I think I know just the young lady that fits that bill. Her name is Sonya...she's a tall, gorgeous, blue-eyed, blonde. Quite beautiful, she's, ah, nearing graduation from college. And...she's very outgoing."

She gave me her usual hesitation, expecting me to comment. Once again, I didn't. While ostensibly surprised, she professionally proceeded, awkwardly at first, but recovering nicely. "Well, then, let's see. Okay. The caterers will be there at around six o'clock to set up and Sonya shall be escorted by your server, arriving at around seven. Do these hours meet with your approval?"

"Yes, that sounds fine, Amanda. Thank you. I'll, ah, bring the deposit and fees to you tomorrow afternoon."

Then, after giving me their mysterious address in Scottsdale, she switched back to the sultry voice. "And, Mr. Bowden, thank you for choosing Parisian. I know you'll enjoy Sonya's company."

"I'm sure I will. Thank you, Amanda. Goodnight, now." Click.

Chapter 8

The two people from the catering service were busying themselves in the kitchen, while I nervously paced the living room floor. I heard the doorbell ring and nearly jumped out of my shoes. When I opened the door, I was greeted by a curly-haired body-builder in a tuxedo. "Mr. Bowden? Hi, my name is Mark from Parisian Escort Service, and I'll be your server this evening. May we please come in?" A young lady was standing behind him.

"Yes, of course." I held the door open wide as Mark took her hand and lead her into the house. She literally floated into the room. She was wearing a short, tight, low-cut midnight blue dress and matching high-heeled shoes. Her wavy, Farrah Fawcett hairdo cascaded to well below her shoulders, with several large curls nestling against the dark fabric of a bolero jacket. A petite gold chain with a dainty locket adorned her neck and crystal earrings peeked from within the long locks of her hair. The creamy coffee color of her skin was like a natural suntan and the ruby lipstick on her full lips contrasted with the white teeth of her smile. Her soft ecru make-up, with a mere touch of dusky eye shadow and liner, brought brilliance to her mysterious eyes and created an aura of secrecy about her. Her high forehead, curved cheekbones, and the concave bridge of her petite, slightly tipped nose added to her loveliness. She was absolutely stunning.

While drinking in her beauty, I simply stood there, mesmerized. I felt something stirring inside me—something I'd never experienced before. Finally, it was Mark who spoke first, "Mr. Bowden, I'd like to introduce you to your dinner companion. May I please present—Judy."

Still spellbound, I didn't know what to say. But I also didn't know what she was thinking. *My God, he's handsome! So tanned! And look at those green eyes! What a sparkle! Damn, Judy, say something to the man!* "Hi, Mr. Bowden, I'm Judy." Her voice sang.

"Ah. Hello, Judy. I'm Joe." I clumsily extended my

hand to meet hers. I felt like I was sixteen, again. Worse yet, I was acting like it!

After holding on for a moment, she released her grip from mine and took a step backward. She winsomely tilted her head to one side and her smile widened. "I can see by the surprised look on your face that Amanda didn't call you. Sonya was called out of town on a family emergency today and I agreed to take her place this evening. I hope that's all right?"

"Yes, yes. That's perfectly okay. I'm, uh, merely looking forward to a nice, quiet dinner and some pleasant conversation." I felt myself flush. *Man alive, Owen—you're never going to be able to pull this off!*

Still tilting her head to one side with her weight shifted onto one foot, she stood there, gazing into my eyes. *Well crap, Judy! Quit staring at the guy! He's going to think you're some kind of loony!* Her eyes glanced away, but almost instantly came back as she answered, "That sounds fine, Joe."

"Ah, good." Then I simply stood there again, nervously shifting my weight from one foot to the other. Hell, I was practically dancing! *Lord Almighty, Owen! Why are you being so awkward?* I forced my eyes away from her and glanced around the room, desperately searching for something to say. Just then, my gaze landed on a big smudge on the wall. *Ye gads, she must think this place is a wreck!* I rushed to explain, "I must apologize, Judy, and ask that you please overlook the condition of the house. I've only recently moved in and, although I've managed to get the furniture arranged and the draperies hung, I haven't had time to start on the remodeling I intend to do. Believe me, you won't recognize this place three or four months from now."

She quickly looked around the room. "No need to apologize, Joe. I'm here to enjoy some good food and conversation with you, not to look at your house, although I'm impressed just as it is—you've arranged it quite nicely." *Way to go, Judy! Hell's bells, you don't have to lie to the man! Look at this place. It's a mess! The walls are dirty and need painting, and the carpet's utterly filthy! But you've gotta admit, girl, the place is orderly and his furniture is very nice! So, he's probably being truthful. And now, since he's not saying anything else and since you're the professional here, you should say something! But, since you can't think of anything earth-shaking to say—talk about the house again!* "You know, Joe, I'd like to see the rest of your home. I'd be interested in hearing about your remodeling plans."

"Oh, sure. But, uh, may I offer you a drink first?"

Thank God he said that! Maybe after a couple of mai tais, I won't be so nervous. Incidentally, why am I so nervous? "Yes, a drink sounds nice. I believe I'd like a mai tai."

All the while our bungling introductory conversation was taking place, Mark had been patiently standing nearby and saw this opening. "Mr. Bowden, if you will please direct me to the kitchen, sir, I'll be glad to serve your drinks."

"Thank you, Mark. Right this way."

Within a few moments, with our mai tais in hand, Judy and I began casually strolling from room to room. While explaining my mental blueprint for future designs and decorations, together with the methods I'd use, I started to feel somewhat at ease. Ultimately, we finished our tour in the dining room, where Judy commented with a warm smile, "Joe, I really like your ideas for the changes. Honestly. You're apparently very knowledgeable about what you do." She seemed more relaxed, as well.

At the same time, being Johnny-on-the-spot, Mark entered the room. "Excuse me, I'll be glad to serve dinner any time you'd like."

"Thank you, Mark." Judy and I responded in unison then, catching each other's eye, we both laughed because of it and made our way to the table.

While we leisurely enjoyed a filet mignon with all the trimmings, combined with a couple more drinks, we easily began talking and laughing together. Meanwhile, Mark's service was excellent. Gliding inconspicuously between the kitchen and dining room, he handled everything with scarcely a word, giving us only an occasional smile or nod.

Following dessert, the two of us lazily entered the living room and Judy was answering my latest small talk question. "According to my mother, one-half Italian, one third Hispanic, and the rest Irish, with a drop of French and German thrown in. What about you?"

"Mostly British. My ancestors came from Wales."

While Judy took a seat at one end of the sofa, I set my drink down and pointed toward the stereo. "Would you like some music?"

She did that little tilting thing with her head again and caroled, "Sure. Jazz and blues are my favorite—unless you'd prefer something else."

"Ah, no. They're my favorites, too."

I walked across the room and as I stood there shuffling through the tapes, all at once, I heard Judy squeal. "Eeeee! Oh my God!"

When I quickly turned around to look at her, my eyes captured the silhouette of Mark, who'd sprung to the doorway to investigate her scream. Upon learning the reason for it, I cast a wide grin and nodded toward Mark before I said to Judy, "Ah, I see you've met Socko." He was on her lap.

"Socko, you nearly scared me to death!" Judy exclaimed. Mark slowly retreated to the kitchen.

"It seems he likes you." I chuckled.

"Goodness, he's cute. And look at the size of that big head! Have you had him long?"

"Not really. He showed up on my doorstep about two years ago. He was around eight months old and skinny as a rail, so I fed him. After that, I couldn't chase him away and he's been with me ever since."

Staring at the cat and stroking his chin, Judy said to me, "Joe, don't you know that people don't pick cats? Cats pick people. That's why he stayed. He likes you." Looking up at me, she narrowed her eyes ever so slightly as she studied mine and huskily added, "Probably very much."

Suddenly hearing a rattling noise in the kitchen,

Socko vaulted down as quickly as he'd jumped up and ran away to somewhere down the hall. Standing up, Judy brushed the front of her dress and, as he darted from the room, laughed affectionately after him. "Bye, Socko. Thanks for the short visit."

When he was out of sight, she said to me, "If you'll please excuse me, Joe, I think I'll make a trip to the powder room." Without waiting for an answer, she whirled around and walked away, rolling her eyes. *Damn, Judy, why did you say 'powder room'? You hate that term!*

But before she made her way to the bathroom, she made a quick detour to the kitchen. I heard a short, muffled conversation, after which, Mark appeared, carrying a huge serving tray loaded with an ice bucket, two fresh glasses and a tall pitcher of mai tais. Surveying the room, he nodded to me, then placed the tray on the unit holding the stereo and returned to the kitchen. I strolled to the couch and sat down. Leaning back, I closed my eyes and listened to the music.

****

Quietly shutting the bathroom door behind her, Judy Carmelle looked into the mirror. Leaning closer and devilishly grinning, she pointed her finger at the reflection and silently told herself, *Girl, this has to be the best assignment you've ever had! God, he's so nice! Mm, and so good looking, too. No question about what to do later!* She giggled to herself. *Whoops! You naughty girl!*

After touching her lipstick to her full lips, she examined the result and resumed her silent one-way conversation. *But, what is it about this guy that fascinates me so much? Maybe it's merely because he talks to my face instead of my chest, unlike all the other jerks! Although, he did glance a few times.* She impishly giggled again.

I mean, usually, the locals are always rich, fat guys with sleazy minds and a wide-open wallet, which they think will buy them anything. I figured this to be a short dinner and a quick turn-down. Normally, by this time, I'm fighting off busy hands and snide remarks! But, you know, I really like this man. Maybe it's just chemistry. Who knows?

She then reached into her bag and retrieved a small brush. Carefully touching it against her auburn curls, she gently patted them with her hand while she studied herself in the mirror and pictured Joe's face again. *Funny, though, it's really hard to figure him out. I mean, it seems to me he'd have no trouble getting a date, that's for sure. So why would a good-looking local guy call an escort service? Maybe it's simply because he's super busy or something and just wants some company. Maybe he's not interested in anything else—he certainly hasn't made any advances!*

Suddenly, with admiration, she gave a petite laugh of amusement. *It's kinda cute, though, I mean the fact that he's a little bit bashful—Amanda did say this is his first engagement! In any event, thank goodness Sonya went to Omaha, today. She simply won't believe this when I tell her!* However, as Judy pictured her blonde friend, a twinge of guilt immediately swept through her. *But I sure hope her mother will be okay.*

Re-touching her hair with her hand a final time, Judy took a last glance into the mirror. Satisfied, she left the room with one more thought. *All right, Girl. Let's go see if we can find out about this guy.*

****

In the meantime, as I sat there sipping my drink, I debated. *Okay, Owen—ut—Joe! With her bubbly charm, this girl can definitely do what you want! But, how are you going to approach her about it? I mean, she seems so, I don't know, innocent, maybe?* I envisioned her pretty face. *Whoa there, Owen—damn, I mean Joe—wait a minute! Is it possible that you're confusing yourself here? Perhaps you're letting an infatuation with her beauty influence you. Maybe she's not as virtuous as you seem to want her to be. Could be, it's an act.* I pictured her again and remembered a few minutes ago, when she was sitting across the table from me and laughing. Then, I recalled her refreshing reaction to Socko. *Naw, that's no act. You're likely very right about her, Owen—ut—Joe! Damn it! It's Joe! But, innocence can be several things, so, perhaps it isn't the only word to describe her. Maybe it's honesty, as*

66

well. Yeah, that's it. Honesty! So, your best approach is to simply do it with honesty right back to her, and fella, I believe it's now or never! Here she comes!

****

Judy placed her jacket on a Queen Anne chair as she glided past it then strolled across the room and took a seat right next to me on the sofa. Curling her legs beneath her as she sat facing me, she sipped the last of her drink and chimed, "So, Joseph, what else can we talk about?"

I looked into her root-beer eyes. "Well, now that you've asked, I, uh, do have something I'd like to discuss with you."

Okay, Judy, maybe you were wrong about him— maybe he is interested. Anyway, here comes the pitch. Let's see how he approaches it. "Oh?"

"However, this may be a little difficult, so please bear with me." I glanced at her.

"Okay." She mused.

"You see, I'm looking for a particular person to help me with a project I have going."

"A project?"

"Uh, yes. I'll try to explain this to you the best I can. But it's a bit of a story."

She touched her hand to my forearm. "Well, before you get too deeply into it, would you be an angel and freshen our drinks?" *This is a different approach! A project?*

After serving our mai tais, I sat back down beside her. Still trying to work up courage, I studied her large, brown eyes again then took a deep breath. "All right, Judy, here it is. You see, some time ago, I lost a piece of property to some people who conspired illegally to get this property from me. However, there was no way for me to prove the illegality of their actions, so they ended up with my real estate and I lost practically everything I had. Since then, I've managed to rally from that and make some money rather quickly and I'm in the process of taking steps to recover from them. But to do so, I need certain information from one of them, and since I'd be easily recognized, it's impossible for

67

me to get it by myself. I'll need some help." I stopped for a moment to sip my drink.

And before I could continue, Judy interjected. "I'm not sure I understand, Joe, but I am intrigued. So. You want somebody to get this information for you—is that it?" Studying me, her mahogany eyes instantly bugged open. "Whoa! Wait a minute! You want *me* to get it for you! Am I right? Is that why you brought me here?"

Without answering, I lifted my drink to my lips and looked away. With the mixed sounds of fear and reluctance in her voice, all of a sudden, I was having second thoughts about involving her, for her own sake. But then I reasoned that, being with an escort service, it was fairly likely that she'd been approached with some pretty strange propositions and I readily determined that she was probably very capable of brushing away any that she wasn't comfortable with. *Besides, Joe—hey, I got the name right—this is why you brought her here. Hell, the worst she can do is flat say no and walk out!*

And while I was contemplating all of this, Judy was thinking to herself. *What in the hell is this all about? Whatever it is, it sounds risky! Yet, at the same time, this man seems so sincere and Judy, you know you like him. And, unless he's the biggest con artist of all time, he doesn't seem the type to lure you into something dangerous, so why don't you play along with him? At least, hear what he has to say!*

Wait! Did she just ask me a question? "I'm sorry, Judy, did you just say something?"

"Yes. Where in the world were you?" She giggled. "I was just asking how I would go about doing that. Getting this information, I mean? It sounds fascinating, but wouldn't it be dangerous?"

I felt my face flush. "Well, with what I had in mind, I don't believe there'd be any real risk involved."

"Well, I guess I still don't understand. Don't you have any friends who'd be willing to do this for you? I mean, if there's no danger…"

"No. There's nobody."

With her cheek resting on her fisted hand, Judy leaned her elbow against the back of the flowered sofa and sipped from her glass. She studied my face. "You're really serious about this, aren't you, Joe." It was more of a statement than a question. "But, why someone from an escort service? Wouldn't a private detective be better?"

"Uh, no. An investigator couldn't get it done. You see, I need a lot of information and it's going to take quite some time to gather all of it together. And, of course, it all has to be obtained without the guy suspecting anything, so a detective wouldn't be able to gain access, not without raising suspicions." I looked at her for a reaction.

"Okay, I'm captivated. Tell me more. Do you have a plan in mind to do this?"

I unintentionally laughed. "Uh, yes, I do."

And for some reason, she laughed with me. "This should be good." Then, she laughed again. "Please continue."

"Let's see, how shall I explain this? Okay. I'll tell you the hypothetical I had in mind when I called Parisian. Now then, I'm doing this with the risk that I might offend you, but please, don't be."

She flirtatiously lifted one eyebrow and gave me a mischievous grin then she shook her head.

"Good. You see, I had this idea that most escort services are merely cover-ups for other types of services. At least, ahhh, common rumors have led me to believe that some of them are."

"I see." She moved a little closer to me.

"Again, bear with me here. I'm just talking a hypothetical."

"And, I'm just listening." She teased.

"All right, here goes. I was imagining—no, honestly, I really have to say hoping—that I would find one of those types of escort services when I called Parisian. My far-fetched idea was to hire the services of one of their young ladies to seduce the man who has the information I need and, by doing so, she could get it for me."

Judy giggled. "Joe-Joe, it doesn't work like that! You make it sound too simple." Beginning to feel the mai tais, she cupped her hands to her mouth and pretended to shout, "Hey, Mister, if I go to bed with you, will you give me the information that Joe Bowden needs?" With another laugh, she showed me her empty glass. "I'm sorry, Joe-Joe, I don't mean to make light. I'll tell you what—if you'll re-fill this again, I promise that I'll listen very, very seriously. Okay?"

Grinning back at her, I took the glass from her hand and walked to the makeshift bar. *At least, she seems to be enjoying the conversation.*

When I returned, Judy accepted the drink and cuddled against me. She reached out and began to run her fingers through my hair. "Now, then, Mr. Joe-Joe, where were we? Oh, yeah, you were telling me how this clandestine mystery girl is going to help you get your contraband from the bad guy and I promised to listen seriously. Right? So, tell me, sir, how are we going to accomplish this?"

"Hey, you'll like this part. You see, I was hoping to find that certain young lady who is really wanting to get out of this escort business and by hiring her full time until she completes what I need for her to do, she could possibly make enough to, uh, "escape the lifestyle" she no longer wants. Hell, I even thought that she could entice our target guy into hiring her in his office. That way, she'd be in a position to get the information I need from his files, plus, she'd be earning two salaries for the same job!" I laughed out loud. "Guess I've been reading too many novels, huh?"

She stopped rubbing my hair and placed her hand on my forearm, squeezing ever so slightly. Leaving it there, she moved her face in front of mine and raised one eyebrow. "Galahad, your idea may not be as farfetched as you think it is."

Permitting me a few seconds to digest that thought, Judy kept her brown eyes on mine with a deep, searching look before dropping her gaze to my lapel, just as she moved her hand to my shirt. Caressing the material, she nervously recited, "You see, Joe, as you've perceived, there are many times when each and every one of us girls are propositioned by the men we're escorting. I mean, the service doesn't promote it, of course. They leave such things to our discretion. We have the option to pick and choose as we please. And it's true, most of us have a few regular guys that we're comfortable with, out-of-towners mainly, and they pay well, so..." She shrugged her shoulders and momentarily raised her eyes to mine, before modestly taking them away.

Unsure of what to say, I reached to my left and lifted my drink from the end table. *Why am I feeling this bit of jealousy?*

And with some sort of sixth sense, Judy quickly detected my angst. In response, she said in a lighter vein, "Anyway, Galahad, I think I know just the girl you're looking for. Ever since she started, I really don't believe she's been comfortable doing this, but she's busting her butt to get through law school and only has about a year to go. I've known her for a long time, so if you'd like for me to, I'll be happy to mention this to her. Incidentally, she's also very discreet, so it certainly wouldn't go beyond her. Interested?"

Her hidden meaning didn't escape me. She wanted time to think about it. I furtively decided to play along. "Hey, of course. Please ask her."

"Okay," she chimed. "I'll have a talk with her tomorrow and let you know what she says. How about that?"

"Sounds good to me. Thank you."

"You're welcome, Galahad. Glad I could help." She patted my chest then rested her head against me.

The clean smell of her hair intoxicated me, probably more so than the rum, and I subconsciously began toying with her curls. With a sense of relief for getting this out in the open, I admitted, "Judy, you cannot possibly know how absolutely nervous I was about bringing this whole thing up to you."

"Joseph, you handled that quite well," she laughed. Raising her head, she handed me her once again empty glass. "May I have another?"

Climbing to my feet, I went to the stereo and inserted a Junior Wells cassette before refreshing our mai tais. As soon as I returned, Judy took my arm and placed it around her, then cradled herself against me and cooed, "Oooo. Now that's nice music!"

We listened in silence for a time, before Judy abruptly sat up and looked into my face. "Joe-Joe, let's get back to that help you need for a moment. I really do think I have someone for you, but I have to be certain about something. Are you sure there's no danger involved?"

"Quite sure. I mean, the guy I need the information from is only a pawn for the other people and I get the feeling that danger is certainly not in his vernacular. He's a weenie, trust me. I honestly believe that the worse thing that would happen, should he find out what she's doing, is that she would probably get fired. However, I also believe that if she's careful, she should be able to pull it off without a hitch."

"A covert operation. Oooo, Joe-Joe! It sounds exciting." With that, she immediately placed her head back on my chest, and changed gears again. "Oh, listen! It's playing, "I Could Cry." Didn't Junior write that song?"

"Uh, I don't know."

With her eyes closed, Judy hummed a little of the melody and while lost in some form of dreaminess, she said with a throaty murmur, mostly to herself. "Ohhh, yes! Blues are sooooo sultry!" Then, she brusquely climbed to her knees and sat back on her lower legs, facing me. "Now then, Joe-Joe, I have one more question for you! Do you really want to thank me?"

What is this, now? Looking at her, I traced a lazy smile. "Thank you?"

"Yeah," she said. "For talking to my friend tomorrow."

"Certainly. I thought I did, but I'll say it again. Thank you."

"Naw, Joe-Joe. Merely saying thank you isn't good enough."

"Oh? Well, what else did you have in mind?"

She gave me that tilting of her head again and her dark chestnut eyes bared a look of devilment. "Uh, let me see. Hm. Okay, I'll tell you what. You can let me stay here with you tonight."

"What?"

"You heard me." She giggled.

When I felt myself becoming aroused, I hurriedly scrambled for words. "Uh, Judy, you don't have to do that. I mean, that wasn't the reason I asked you to come here. Besides, how could you consider that to be me thanking you?"

She wriggled her backside, all the while twirling her hair with her fingers as she chimed, "It's what I get paid for, silly man. And I could use the business." She nervously laughed out loud. "My God! I can't believe I'm doing this! I want you to know, sir, that I've never propositioned any man before! Ever! I mean, I've certainly had many of them proposition me, but never the other way around! And, no—before you even think about it—there are far, far more that I've refused than accepted!"

Feeling flushed again, I said, "It must be the rum."

"It ain't the rum, Galahad. It's you!"

All at once, I had this warm feeling. I cleared my throat and said, "Well, I'm, ah, certainly flattered. But, I don't understand. Uhhh—why me?"

"Because, Joe-Joe. One, I think you're super nice and I really like you. Two, you're a gentleman—a real gentleman. Aaaand, three, you've been very straight-forward and honest with me." She giggled and placed both of her hands on my cheeks. "Plus, you serve excellent mai tais and you play the blues. So. What do you say?"

Owen, I think you're falling in love with this woman!
"I say that I'm very tempted. It has been a long time."

Moving her face very close to mine, she cooed, "Then by all means, Galahad, you should give in to temptation. You'll enjoy it." Wistfully gazing into my eyes, while stroking her fingers through my hair again, she wantonly moved her face closer to mine and whispered, "We both will." Then, she pressed her lips to mine, kissing me, long and hard.

Reluctantly pulling away, I questioned her, "Whoa, wait a minute. Uh, what do we do about our friend Mark, out there in the kitchen?"

She threw her head back in playful laughter. "Oh, don't you know? Mark and the caterers have gone. They left through the garage about forty-five minutes ago. It's just you and me, Joe-Joe."

When my face colored, she cackled out loud. I reached for my mai tai. "I think I need another sip of this."

Giggling, Judy lifted herself from my lap then nestled against me and rested her hand on my leg. As she sensitively began to massage my thigh, my arm draped around her shoulder, while my fingers caressed the bare skin of her arm and, for a time, we simply snuggled there, listening to the music. Then, just as the cassette finished playing and the room filled with silence, before I could make a move to replace it, Judy sat straight up and poignantly looked at me. The smile had left her lips, replaced by a pout, and with a hint of reluctance in her voice, she whispered, "Joe-Joe, I, uh, don't want to break the mood, but there is something else I think we should discuss." She looked away.

"Oh?"

"Price?"

When I stared at her with a look of complete surprise on my face, I was instantly thankful that she didn't see it, for, despite my feeling of disappointment, I knew this was part of it. Recovering right away, I simply offered, "Well, first of all, you haven't broken my mood, and secondly, that's something that's not an object for me. Please, Girl, you just name it."

"I like that—you calling me Girl." The impish grin was there again. "Okay, Galahad—here's the deal. You have to fix my breakfast in the morning and take me home."

"What?"

"You heard me. That's the deal!"

74

"Well, what kind of a deal is that?"

Rising up to her knees, she straddled herself across me again and placed her arms around my neck. She moved her face against my cheek and nibbled my ear before whispering, "It's a great deal, Galahad! And not only do I think it's a great deal, I also think it's a done deal!"

Crushing her full lips against mine, she thrust her tongue into my mouth and began to slowly wriggle her body against me. She was absolutely right. It was a done deal.

****

The next afternoon, my telephone rang. "Hello."

"Hi, Joe-Joe. This is Judy. Remember me?"

Game time, again. "Ah, yes. The breakfast girl."

"Right. Hey, I want you to know that I've talked with my friend and she's definitely interested in what you told me. At least, she's interested in talking to you about it. How about that?"

"That's good. That's really good. Can you have her get in contact with me?"

"Well, I could do that, but don't you think it's a better idea to have her come over there this evening and discuss the details with you? Unless you're busy."

"I'm not busy. This evening is fine."

"Great. Then, I'll send her over."

"Will you be with her?"

"Oh, no. I have big plans for tonight. Oh, and one more thing—she wants to know if you cook?" She chuckled. "I mean, besides breakfast?"

I raised my voice in mock alarm. "You told her about that?"

"Sure. She and I have no secrets."

"I see. All right. Does she like seafood?"

"Very much."

"Well then, how would this sound to her? Baked halibut with Mournay sauce, creamed potatoes, broccoli with creamed cheese, and perhaps a tossed salad with choice of dressing? I do that as well as I do breakfast."

"Oooo. I think she'll like that."

"Oh, and I almost forgot. Of course, there'll be dessert."

"Ha! Hey, don't get any ideas about her. I've already told her that I consider you my private reserve. Remember, she's only an employee—hired to seduce Joe Blow—not Joe Bowden." More laughter.

"And that's all I want from her, believe me. Hell, I don't even know what she looks like, so how could I have any ideas?"

"She's gorgeous! I'm tellin' you!"

"Good. That'll make the job easier for her."

"Ha, again!"

"All right. How will seven o'clock sound to her?"

"That works. I'll tell her to be there. Bye, Joe-Joe." Click.

At precisely seven o'clock, the doorbell rang. When I answered it, of course I was not the least bit surprised when Judy's 'mysterious' auburn-haired young lady presented herself with her arms extended and her palms up. "Hi there, Joe-Joe! I'd like to introduce you to the girl I told you about—me! Judy Carmelle."

Chapter 9

Much later that evening, with neither of us wanting any mai tais, Judy and I relaxed on the patio, drinking coffee and listening to the mellow strains of the blues wafting through the open patio door. The dim obscure rays of Malibu lights reflected rainbow shades of blue, green, yellow, and red on Judy's beautiful enigmatic face. Totally enjoying this quiet meditation, I studied the artistry of her as if I were relishing a portrait that has been painted to perfection.

She was sitting curled in a lounge chair, with her hands wrapped around her cup. The cool October wind gently moved her hair around her face, amplifying her mysterious appearance. She made no attempt to brush the strands away. The slight almond shape of her eyes seemed to give them an occult personality all their own as she stared straight ahead. Her perfect generous lips kissed the brim of her mug as she savored the coffee. Lowering my eyes, I could see her breasts straining against the lace front of her white blouse, over which she was wearing an unbuttoned plaid shirt of mine. Tight denims trailed from her slim waist around the graceful curves of her contoured hips to hug against her long legs, stretching to the top of boot-like, black Reeboks.

At length, unknowingly breaking my spell, Judy sat up and positioned herself to face me. "Joe-Joe, I've been thinking. I'm wondering how I can I do what you need for me to do and still continue with school? I mean, I can't be in two places at the same time. If it were summer break, it would be easy."

Watching me, she drank again while she waited for my answer. I thought about it before giving one. "Let's see. All right, this is October, and you graduate in June. Right?"

"Right."

"Okay. June is only eight months from now and it'll be that long before I have enough money to make my next move anyway, so I can wait until then. I just don't want those damn wops to die before I get even with 'em! They're pretty old!" I started to laugh before I immediately recalled her heritage. I sat straight up and blurted, "Oh, crap no, Judy! I shouldn't have used that term. I apologize. I'm sorry—really."

She gave me a silly giggle. "That's all right, Joe-Joe. Believe me, there are Italians, and there are wops." Then, she winked at me. "Just as there are Brits, and there are limeys." She giggled again.

I simply shook my head. "More coffee?"

"Sure, Galahad."

After I returned with the brews and sat back down, Judy picked up the conversation again. "Okay, Joe-Joe, I have another question. In order for us to carry out your plan, you'll need to have the information I'll be getting because you'll have a lot of checking up to do on those people—true? So, wouldn't it be better if I get this sooner, rather than later?"

"Probably. But like I said, I can wait until you graduate."

"Yeah, but that means we have to wait for eight months." Then she wisecracked, "What are you planning to do, pay me, while I do nothing but go to school and study during that time? Huh-uh, I don't think so."

"Of course. Why not?"

"Why not?" She threw me an exaggerated scowl. "I'm not going to let you do that! I mean, despite the fact that I desperately want to get out of that so-called escort business, I can't just quit there and depend on you, especially without doing what you need for me to do in return."

"Sure you can. You're much too close to finishing school, to leave."

"Joe-Joe, please be serious. That wouldn't be fair to you." She pouted.

I put on a harsh look. "Girl! I am being serious and furthermore, I'll determine what's fair for me. All right? Damn! You're making me frigging redundant!"

She gave me that Cheshire grin. Then, after placing

her cup on the umbrella table, she stood up and meandered toward me, all the while keeping the silly smile. Easing herself onto my lap, she straddled her legs across mine and began combing my hair with her fingers. "Okay, Galahad, let's really concentrate on this. Maybe we can work something out. There's got to be another way. Huh?"

I shook my head. "Nope. We'll do this like I just said."

Closing my eyes, I relaxed against the back of the chair and slipped my hand under her borrowed shirt. I began rubbing her back through the fabric of her blouse. A moment later, I bucked alert with a grunt when she thumped her palms against my chest. "Unnnh."

"Joe-Joe, I've got it! Listen to this! If I stay in school full time, I'll finish in June. Okay? However, if I transfer to evening classes, it will only take two more semesters, which would be the following June." I opened my mouth to interrupt, but she placed her finger on my lips, silencing me. "No, no! Last night, you asked me to bear with you while you told me your little story, so tonight, I'm asking you to bear with me. Just hear me out—okay?"

"Okay." I chuckled.

"Good." She squeezed my thighs with her legs and wiggled her backside against me, then placed both of her hands on my chest. "Now then, here's my deal. If I transfer to night school for now, I can get the information you need during the day. Then, after you have it, I can return to school full time and finish the following January, rather than June. You can help me with it, then. Fair enough?"

"You'd actually be willing to do that?"

"Of course. Why wouldn't I be?"

"But—"

"No buts, Joe-Joe. If you agree it's a good idea, then it's a done deal!"

I placed my hands on her shoulders and held her away from me. My turn to do the kidding. "Girl! What is this thing about your "done deals"? Who's in charge of this operation, anyway?"

"Well, I guess you are—when you're right. But when I'm right, then I should be. And, hey, just like last night, this particular time, I'm right!"

"Okay, I'll admit it is worth considering, nevertheless—"

"Good! Than that's it. However, I do have one problem with this arrangement. If I transfer to night school, I won't be allowed to live in the dorm anymore. It's for full-time students only. Oh, now that I think about it, I guess there are two problems, actually. I'll need a place to stay for one, and if I suddenly move out, I'll have to explain why to Sonya. How much can I tell her?"

"As little as possible. The more people who know about this, the less chance we have of succeeding. Not that I think she'd—"

"I understand," she broke in. "Don't worry, I'll make up something to tell her, but, Joe-Joe, I'm sure that she and I will want to stay close, so I guess I'll just have to be really careful. Now then, what about the other problem? Can I stay with you?" With a big grin, she shimmied her derriere against me again.

With only having known this young woman for a little more than twenty-four hours, I was already sensing a bonding like I'd never felt before. Even now, the scent and taste of our lovemaking from last night was still with me, and I hoped it would never go away. I hoped she would never go away.

Wrapping my arms around her, I guided her face down to mine and tenderly moved my mouth against her full lips. I felt that same stirring again. After a long time, I slowly pulled away and stared into those big, brown eyes. "Girl, like you say, that's not only another great deal—I believe that's one more done deal, too."

She touched the end of my nose with her forefinger. "Joe-Joe, I think we're getting pretty good at these done deals. Now then, since we have all this business bullshit out of the way, can I take you to bed?"

And before I could say a word, she throatily laughed

80

and thumped my chest again, then squealed, "Damn! I'm propositioning you again! How do you make me do that?"

"Darned if I know, Girl! It's a complete mystery to me. Believe me."

"Well, don't get the big-head, Galahad. It's simply because it's getting way too cold to stay out here and I need you to come inside and warm me up. That's all!"

"Ah. That explains it."

Shivering, she hurriedly stood up and started pulling on me until I was clumsily out of the chair. "Hurry, Joe-Joe, I'm about to freeze!"

Chapter 10

Late Sunday evening, a very tired Sonya Waverly shuffled through the door of the dormitory room. After dropping her two suitcases onto the floor, she slumped across the bed and closed her eyes. She immediately drifted to sleep.

Sometime later, when Judy walked in and flipped on the light, the young blonde bolted awake. Upon seeing her roommate, she rubbed her eyes, then propped herself onto one elbow and yawned. "Hi, Judy. Jeez, I'm glad you came in! What time is it, anyway? I've got a ton of things to do tonight."

"It's 11:30. How's your mom doing?" Judy asked.

"Holding up good, real good. Hell, everybody's more concerned about her than she is for herself. The, uh, biopsy was malignant and she'll have to start radiation and chemo this week. I'm really worried about her, babe."

"Yeah, it shows. You look pretty beat." Judy walked to her own bed and sat down. "God, Sonya, I'm really sorry to hear this. I really am. But, you know, they've made a lot of progress in treating this stuff and, knowing your mother, she'll do all right."

Sonya sniffled and brushed away a lone tear. "Thanks, babe, that's what we're hoping."

After rubbing the last cobwebs of sleep from her eyes, Sonya stretched her arms above her head and yawned again. She gave Judy a thin smile. "So. What's new with you? Anything exciting?"

"Uh, yeah. But, you won't believe it."

"Well, it must be something good. You seem awfully bubbly. Say, this wouldn't have anything to do with your dinner date on Friday, would it? Which, incidentally, was supposed to be my dinner date."

"Could be." Judy grinned.

Upon seeing Judy's wide smile, Sonya rolled her eyes and exaggerated a show of disbelief. "Oh, my God, no! You've got that look! Don't tell me you're in love?"

Goodness! Does it show that much? Remembering the need for secrecy, Judy waved her hand to discount the notion. "What? Don't be ridiculous! Shoot—the guy didn't even proposition me." She intimately smiled to herself. That part was true.

Sonya's eyes slanted as she skeptically asked, "Are you lyin' to me? You're awfully damned skittish."

"No, Sonya, hell, no! Actually, the truth is, he offered me a really good job." That part was also true.

Sonya laughed erotically. "Oh? What kind of job, huh?"

"Well, it's certainly not what you're thinking. The guy owns a large contracting company and he wants to hire me to be his gopher. Actually, I'll be his assistant. He's super busy, and he needs somebody who is really dependable—and intelligent enough to handle all of his critical errands. Plus, I'll even get to do most of his legal research."

"Gee, that sounds kind of exciting."

"Well, uh, there is one drawback."

"Not enough money?"

"No, that's no problem. I'll be making almost as much as with Amanda. No, my dilemma is this—I'll have to transfer to night school, which will make graduation a year further away. And, uh, Sonya, when I do that, it means that I'll have to leave the dorm."

"I see. Well, uh, won't the additional expense of an apartment make it a lot less lucrative?"

"Huh-uh. He's paying for that, too. As well as for the rest of my schooling."

Sonya's eyes slanted. "And for all of this, you're gonna be running errands? Sounds fishy to me, Judy. I'd watch out for this guy."

"Oh, hell, Sonya, there's a lot more to it than running errands! Truth is, it's a pretty good deal for him, too. Like I said, I'll also be doing most of his legal work, which will cost him a lot less than having a full time lawyer on his staff."

"I guess that makes sense." Sonya confessed. "But

there's something I don't understand. How did this conversation even come up?" Sonya laughed. "Did he purposely contact an escort service to find a girl for that kind of work?"

"Matter of fact, that's exactly what he did." Judy chuckled.

"You're joshin' me, right?"

"Nope. It's the God-awful truth."

"Seriously? But why? That seems a little strange."

"Not at all, Sonya—he's being extremely intelligent. Think about it. He gets to enjoy a lavish dinner, which he can write off. Plus, he gives his criteria to Amanda, who busts her ass to give him exactly the girl he's looking for, so it costs him less time and money overall. Plus, there's no employment agency fee and he doesn't have a pot-load of interviews to wade through. Remember, he insisted on somebody college educated and outgoing, and Amanda recommended you, which fit almost perfectly. But the fact that I took your place, ironically, it worked out even better for him. With my law studies, I was exactly what he was looking for. And, Sonya, I've never been comfortable with this lifestyle—you know that—and this gives me the chance to leave it."

Both of them sat awkwardly hushed for several seconds before Sonya broke the silence. "I'm sorry, Judy, but to me, this whole thing sounds a little bit too good to be true. And, I suppose you're going to tell me that there's no arcane activity involved in this little venture. Right? No hanky-panky?"

"Sonya, I told you, the guy is impressed with my intelligence and he didn't even proposition me. Really. I've spent the whole weekend talking with him and he's a perfect gentleman. Besides, I think he has a girl-friend." She certainly hoped that part was true. "Anyway, I'm going to do this. Those days of sex for money are over with for me. That's another *huge* plus! So, tomorrow, I'm going to administration to transfer to nights."

"And I suppose that means you'll be moving out

really soon. Right?"

"Uh, yeah. And, Sonya, that's the only thing I don't like about it. It's going to be real strange, not being here with you."

"Yeah. I'll sure as hell miss having you around, too." There was a twinge of bitterness in Sonya's voice.

"Listen, Sonya, in a few more months, with graduation, we'd both be leaving here at the same time, anyway. All I'm doing is moving that up a little bit. I mean, it's not like I'm giving up our friendship—just my bunk. Besides, I'm sure you'll get somebody really nice to move in here, and hey, with my night schedule, we'll get to see each other real often. Heck, you can meet me after class and we can study together on the nights you're not working. Don't you think so?"

Sonya looked away and shot her a hollow answer. "Yeah, sure, absolutely."

"Really. We will. I promise."

Sonya glanced back at her friend and saw the unmistakable excitement in Judy's eyes. Yet, she also knew that her friend's concern over having to leave was very genuine. "You're right, Judy. You deserve this. And, thinking about it, I might be able to talk Paulette into moving in here. She's not real happy with Sandy. Too much noise for studying."

"Hey, that's a good idea."

Another uncomfortable silence developed until Judy stretched across the space between them and touched her friend's cheek. "Sonya, I know this is sudden and that I'm taking a big step here, but I have to do it. So, wish me luck, huh, buddy?"

"Oh, Judy, that goes without saying you know that. But how will I get in touch with you, if I need to?"

"As soon as I get settled and have my phone in, I'll let you know," Judy reassured her. "I promise." Then she quickly stood up and chimed, "Now then, I believe we'd both better start getting it together here, or we'll never get to bed tonight."

"Yeah, you're right. Why don't you go first, Jude? I'm gonna rest a few minutes."

"Are you sure?" Judy considered.

"I'm sure, babe." Turning her back, Sonya swiped a tear from her cheek.

Not noticing it, Judy walked into the bathroom and closed the door.

Chapter 11

The next morning, I looked into my telephone listings, found the one I wanted and dialed the number. On the third ring, a man answered. "Hello."

"Hello. Robert?"

"Yessuh, this is Robert."

"Robert, you may not remember me, but this is O. P."

"O. P? Opie. Hey—sure I remember. How ya doin', man?"

"I'm fine, Robert. How about yourself? And the family?"

"Good. Real good. Nice of y'all to call. Say—are you back in town? You needin' more transportation?"

"No, sir. I'm in Arizona, and I need to ask a big favor of you."

"Sure thing. Watcha need? And, say, how are you comin' along with that get-even plan?"

"Thanks for asking, Robert. So far, I'm right on schedule, but it's still going to take a long time. Matter of fact, this call has to do with that. What I need, is another Arizona driver's license. Can you get it for me?"

"I can do that. Same as before?"

"No, sir. This one is for a lady friend of mine."

"Uh-*huh*!"

"She's helping me against the bad guys."

"Aha! So this is part of the get-even plan?"

"That's right. Anyway, Robert, tell you what I'd like to do. I'm going to send you two pictures of her. One you can use on the license and the other you can keep with the extra one of me that you have. I'll also send all the information you'll need to put on it—you know, name, address, and so on. Plus, I'll give you instructions on where to mail it back to me. I'm also sending a money order to cover the cost of the license, the postage, and something for you for doing this. Sound okay?"

"Yessuh. Sounds okay to me, Opie."

"Great. Oh, yes, Robert, and one more thing. I'm

mailing this Special Delivery and I'll include enough money for you to send it back the same way. All right?"

"Yessuh. I can do that."

"Good deal. Say, have you bought that house yet?"

"No, Opie, not yet. I'm gonna need a lot more money for that. But I'm still savin' for it. I'll get there."

"I know you will Robert. You're a good fellow, and you deserve it."

"Thank you, suh."

"You're quite welcome, Robert. And thank you a bunch for doing this."

"No problem, Opie. Anytime." Click.

I had the license four days later and we leased a car for Judy in her new name.

****

The following Monday, she drove her new white Thunderbird to the Carson Office Complex, where Mortensen Mortgage Brokers was located. I drove my own Thunderbird in front of her. After parking, I walked back and slipped into her car on the passenger side. Judy squealed with laughter when she saw me in the white-haired wig I was wearing.

"Well, c'mon, Girl! I don't want our Mr. Mortensen to recognize me!"

Looking out the window, I carefully watched the other side of the street. "He'll be wearing a brown suit. I guarantee it. Now then, what's your name, again?"

"Jane Romero," she sang. Still tickled, she again burst into laughter.

Shaking my head, I tried to feign disgust, but I was unable to keep the smile from my own face. "Are you sure you can do this?"

"I'm sorry, Joe-Joe, I think it's just because I'm a little nervous. But, don't worry, I'll handle it okay."

I glanced across the street again, thinking everything through. Having installed a second telephone line in the house, I'd attached it to a tape recorder and an answering machine, with an outgoing message in 'Jane's' voice. "Now then, do you remember the telephone number?"

"Joe-Joe, please give me a little credit. Of course, I remember. I swear—I believe you're more nervous about this than I am."

At that moment, I saw a man in a brown suit leave the building. "There he is—that's him. Last chance to back out."

Judy leaned toward me and gave me a kiss on the cheek. "Get out of the car, Joe-Joe, he's mine. I'll see you at home later."

****

Judy watched as Mortensen walked into the parking lot at the rear of the building. When she saw him leave in a blue Datsun, she maneuvered a u-turn and pulled into traffic behind him. After traveling a long way west on Bethany Home Road, she eventually saw him swerve into the parking lot of the Rusty Nail Steakhouse. As he pulled into a space, she motored past and drove for a few blocks before turning around to go back. Ten minutes later, she also walked into the Rusty Nail.

Easily picking him out, Judy selected a table close by and sat where she was in his full vision, yet making sure that the lady seated with Mortensen had her back to her. Stalling for time, Judy engaged the hostess in conversation, discussing the rustic wooden decor, the nice mesquite aroma filling the place, the old west design of the menu, the cute western outfits all the waitresses were wearing, and ultimately, she ordered.

Throughout her meal, Judy stared seductively at Mortensen and every time he looked in her direction, she'd smile and hold the gaze until he timidly looked away. Even while talking to his companion, he'd glance at her, failing miserably in his attempts to avoid being caught by either of them. A couple of times, the blue-suited lady half-turned to see what he was finding so fascinating, however, not wanting to appear conspicuous, she tactfully turned only part way, catching but slight glimpses of the beautiful young woman in the low-cut dress. Each time, Judy was looking the other way in total disinterest.

In due time, Mortensen and the lady stood up and as he was shaking her hand, Judy heard him say, "And thank you, Mrs. Roberts. I'm quite sure we'll have an answer for you tomorrow afternoon. I'll call you as soon as I know."

The woman mumbled something in return and left, throwing an icy glare toward the much younger, indifferent lady in the revealing dress. Judy didn't see it, but she felt it.

Smiling once again at Mortensen, Judy saw him fumble with his billfold, place some bills on the table and turn to leave. Passing by her table, he paused momentarily, then hurried to the cashier and paid the check. Looking longingly back at her one more time, he walked out the door.

Slamming her napkin onto the table, Judy grumbled, "Crap!" She toyed with the rest of her meal, waited a full five minutes, then left.

****

The next day, she tailed Mortensen to The Spaghetti Company on Central Avenue and repeated the same routine. Dressed in a very feminine light blue blouse and tight black skirt, she was approached by two other men willing to share their company with her. Drawing from her experience with the escort service, declining them was easy.

Today, Mortensen was dining with a man about forty years old. After they were finished with lunch they started to leave and the mortgage broker, like yesterday, hesitated when he passed by Judy's table. Judy was not about to let him get away today. She gave him a flirtatious smile. "Pardon me, sir, but didn't I see you at the Rusty Nail, yesterday?"

Mortensen pointed at himself to be sure she was talking to him. Judy nodded, keeping the smile in place. Mortensen waved goodbye to the other man and, gathering courage, he walked up to her table. "Why, uh, yes you did."

"I thought I remembered. You were dining with a lady in a blue suit. Right?"

"Why, yes, that's right." He cleared his throat.

"Would you care to sit down?" Judy cooed.

90

He nervously looked around before seating himself across from her. Unsure, he halfway stood back up and offered a handshake. "Oh, sorry. Uh, my name is James Mortensen."

She took his hand, holding on longer than she normally would. "Hi, Mr. Mortensen, I'm Jane Romero."

Sweet Holy Mary, I can't believe this beautiful young girl is coming on to me! He suddenly became braver. "Oh, please, call me James."

"All right, James."

"Okay—Jane is it? All right, Jane, I, uh, see you've finished your lunch, so may I buy you dessert?"

"No, thank you. I'm watching my figure." She alluringly smiled at him. *And apparently, so are you, Mr. Mortensen. Good.*

James studied her pretty face. *Egad! Now what do I say? Okay, I know.* "Well then, uh, how about a drink?"

"Sorry, James. I usually don't drink in the daytime."

"Oh, uh, sure. I understand."

Lifting her cola glass, Judy took a sip and noticed the disappointment showing in his eyes. She lowered the drink back to the table. "But I'll take a rain check."

"What's that? Oh? Well, sure. Okay." He squirmed on his chair and dropped his left hand onto his lap to hide his ring. "You know, I do work late at the office, sometimes. Perhaps some evening?"

She seductively raised one eyebrow. "Absolutely. I'm free every night."

"Well, I certainly don't believe that. A gorgeous young lady such as yourself—free every night? C'mon, you're joking."

Her eyes opened wide. "No, really, it's true. I don't have time to get involved with anyone right now."

"Oh? And what do you do that keeps you so busy?"

"Well, I was going to college full-time, but I've had to drop out to find a job. School is so expensive these days. So now, I intend to work for about six months, then I can go back to finish. Either that, or just continue working and go nights."

"I see. What are you studying to be?"

"I've already minored in business administration, but after taking a few very uninteresting law courses, I switched to psychology about three years ago."

"Those are all good fields."

"Yes, but I really like psychology," Judy sang. She toyed with a long strand of her auburn hair. "As a matter of fact, I have this little game I play in my mind, where I look at someone and try to determine what kind of business they're in." She reached across the table and touched his hand. "Take you for example. You have a look of success about you, which, incidentally, I really admire in a man, so I'd say, uh, stock market. Right?"

"Not so far off. I'm a mortgage broker," he boasted. "It seems you'll be a good psychologist."

"Thank you." There was a melody in her voice. Then, she glanced at her watch. "Well, Mr. Mortensen, it's certainly been nice chatting with you, but I have an interview downtown at two-thirty, so I should probably be leaving."

She stood up and opened her purse. While she fumbled inside, Mortensen jumped from his chair and reached for her guest check. "Here, Jane. At least let me buy your lunch."

In one smooth motion, Judy snapped the pocketbook closed, slung the strap over her shoulder, tilted her head and smiled at him. "Oh, why thank you, James. Oh, and if you have something to write on, I'll give you my number for that rain check."

Thrusting his hand into his jacket pocket, Mortensen swiftly wrapped his fingers around a silver ballpoint. "Yes! I have something. I'll just write it on the back of a business card." He hurriedly visited the pocket again and retrieved two small pasteboards, one of which he presented to her. "Here. I'll give one to you, too. That's how you can reach me."

Taking it, she opened the handbag and gently placed it inside. "Thank you, James. All right. Ready? It's five-

five-five, nine-one-one-three. Jane Romero."

Quickly scribbling it down, Mortensen admired the card before carefully putting it back into his pocket. Then he smiled at her. "Well, uh, when should I call?"

"Anytime, James, anytime," she sang. She gave him a wink and turned to leave. As she sashayed away, she exaggerated the sway of her hips. Near the door, she looked back over her shoulder and gave him a parting smile. Then she went outside and disappeared.

****

Shortly after four o'clock, Judy and I heard the telephone ring and listened to the incoming message. "Hi, Jane, this is James Mortensen. I met you at The Spaghetti Company, today. Remember? Well, it seems that I have to work late at the office tonight and I was just wondering if I could pay off that rain check for the drink this evening. You can call me back at the number on the card I gave you. I'll talk with you later." Click.

Acting serious, I coldly stated, "Okay. Guess it's time to get Jane her own apartment."

"What did you say? What do you mean by "her own apartment"? Joe-Joe, that wasn't part of our deal!"

"Well, you sure as hell can't bring him here."

"I don't want to bring the stupid jerk anyplace!" She screamed at me. "I can't believe you're telling me this! Do you honestly intend to rent an apartment for me?"

"Certainly." Then, unable to keep from laughing, I looked at her wide-open, fiery brown eyes and relinquished the game. "But, don't worry, Girl. You won't have to stay there, or bring our friend, Mr. Mortensen there. It's merely for cover."

She slapped my chest. "Damn it, Joe-Joe! That wasn't funny!" Then she slapped it again and promised with a throaty laugh, "I owe you one, Joseph. Brace yourself."

****

Sometime well after midnight, I was aroused from my sleep by a soft kiss. "Hi, Joe-Joe. How ya doin'?" Judy chuckled.

93

Still drowsy, I mumbled, "Mm, I love your lips."

"They're too big."

I shook my head and settled back onto the pillow, closing my eyes. "Not big, just appetizing."

"Guess what? I got a job. How about that?"

Rising up, I squinted at her. "What? How in the hell did you do that so quick?"

"Oh, I just fed Mr. Mortensen a few margaritas, touched his hand a lot, secretly unbuttoned the top two buttons of my blouse, then I gave him a sob story about the poor little girl who can't find a job and doesn't know what she's going to do, and I start on Thursday morning. Now then, what do you need for me to find out?"

Shaking my head in disbelief, I placed my hand against her neck and began massaging the smooth skin of her cheek with my thumb. With a smile, I muttered, "I'll tell you that, tomorrow. In the meantime, how's about bringing those luscious, big lips back down here again?"

"So!" She pulled away. "You do think they're too big!"

Laughing, I gently drew her face down to mine. "Girl, they're not too big, trust me. They're just delicious, that's all."

Chapter 12

During her first few days at work, Judy spent a lot of time learning the procedures of the office from Mortensen's secretary, Maryann Tolbert, who couldn't understand why Jane was even there.   After all, Maryann had handled everything by herself for more than eight years now. *Does James really believe that the real estate market is going to double in the next six months? Enough for him to open a second office? Oh well, what can I say? He's the boss.*

She glared at Jane, who was standing near the filing cabinet with her back to Maryann. With all of Jane's weight resting on one foot, her curved hip protruded within the tight confine of her short skirt. *Huh! I think I know the real reason she's here! I've seen the way James hangs around her. He drools after her like a puppy dog! It's disgusting!*

Still studying the younger girl, Maryann watched her swivel across the room to her desk and lift the intercom. *Good gracious! James is on that thing with her all the time. Except when he's out here with her! But, surely she couldn't be interested in somebody like him? I mean, after all, she's no bimbo! She's sharp! I've never seen anyone catch on so fast. Except when it comes to the files, though. She can't seem to find anything in there! Sakes alive, she's always looking for something without ever finding it!*

Maryann continued to gaze at Jane, but this time, wistfully. *And, you know, I don't think it's fair that she's that smart. Not with all those looks to go with it. Intelligent and beautiful! Why not me?*

****

In the early afternoon of Judy's fifth day, a short, fat man in a blue, pinstriped suit barged into the office. He rattled the door closed behind him. "Is Mortensen here?" he bellowed to Maryann.

At that moment, Jane was walking from Mortensen's office carrying a handful of correspondence. Her short, navy skirt and frilly, white lace blouse was complimented by her perfectly applied make-up and cascading auburn hair, making her the absolute picture of femininity. Antonio Tafino abruptly stopped in his tracks. He hypnotically stared at her every step while she glided to her desk.

Undressing her with his bloodshot eyes, he leaned across the counter that separated the reception area from the workspace. His voiced boomed. "Well, hello there! Hey, you must be the new girl Mortensen told me about. I'll be an S.O.B, he wasn't lyin', babe! You're gorgeous. By the way, I'm Antonio Tafino. Maybe you and I should have a drink sometime." It was a command, not a question.

Not answering, her cold, calculated stare didn't dissuade him.

"Say, beautiful, you look Italian. Are you?"

He reminded her of the escort service locals. No longer looking at him, she icily answered. "Just a very small part."

He gave her a squalid laugh. "Well, it shows, gorgeous. And quite nicely, I might add!"

"I'm mostly Mexican." She proudly stated. "That's the part that shows."

"Humph! You still look Italian to me."

Judy's eyes finally met his and shot daggers. She then scooped up her purse, stomped around Maryann's desk and marched through the gated opening. Brushing past the intruder without looking at him, Judy reached the door, then turned and said to the other woman, "Maryann, I'm beginning to feel ill. I'll be in the restroom." Promenading into the entry hall, she banged the door shut behind her.

Glaring after her at the closed door, Antonio gave Jane a surly grumble, together with a wave of dismissal. Ignoring Maryann, he then forged his way into Mortensen's office. Jerking his thumb toward the outer office, he bellowed, "What's with that bitch?"

Surprised, Mortensen rose from his chair. "Who? What? What are you talking about, Tony?"

"That stupid Mexican broad you hired. What a stuck-up bitch!"

"Mexican? You mean Jane?"

Calming as fast as he'd angered, Tafino blared, "Oh, to hell with her!" He dismissed her from his mind.

Turning his thoughts to the reason for his visit, Antonio barked at Mortensen. "What about that Cooke building? How much longer till the sale?"

"Just a week or so away. Why?"

"Because, Carpitto down at First Federal Savings called me today, that's why! This guy—Cooke? Carpitto told me this jerk has applied for a mortgage down there and Carpitto was wantin' to know if I'd be interested in puttin' up the dough!"

"Hell, that's nothing to worry about, Tony. Carpitto won't be able to approve him. That's why he called you. He obviously knows that Cooke is looking for a rescue."

"Yeah, but what if Carpitto calls a few of his other outside investors and somebody else gets interested in the place. And suppose they loan the money to this asshole? Where does that leave us?"

"I see what you mean. All right. I'll call Carpitto and tell him I've been working on a deal for this character named Cooke for months and that I can't find anybody willing to do it. I'll ask him if he can find somebody for me. Hell, we all use the same people for funding and Carpitto will assume that if I can't find anybody, he won't be able to either. He'll pretend he doesn't know Cooke and secretly think I'm doing him a favor by saving a lot of his time, knowing he doesn't need to go searching for a dead mule."

"Good. I figured you'd take care of it."

"Consider it done, Tony."

"Yeah. We want that one."

Reaching for a folder on the corner of his desk, Mortensen opened it and leafed through the papers inside. "Well, since you're here, Tony—that foreclosure sale is scheduled for next Tuesday, so should I introduce you and Lou to Cooke on Friday? Or, should I make it Monday?"

"Make it Friday. Maybe we can squeeze some points out of this pigeon."

"Naw, Tony, forget it. He's flat broke."

"You sure?"

"I'm positive. He's near bankruptcy."

"Okay, then make it Monday. And you'll make yourself scarce this weekend. Right?"

Mortensen smiled and nodded. With a parting wave of his hand, Antonio turned and walked to the door. Holding it open, he looked back at Mortensen with a lustful grin on his oily face. Signaling with his head toward Jane's vacated desk, he animalized, "So? Are you beddin' down that Mexican bitch, yet?"

Turning crimson, Mortensen stared at him with a sheepish grin.

"You ain't!" Tafino roared. Then he slammed the door. Mortensen could hear the Italian's laughter all the way into the hall.

Chapter 13

After telephoning me from school, Judy and I met later for pizza and beer to celebrate her discovery of the first six names from Mortensen's files. Sitting together in a corner booth at Pizza Hut, she leaned across the table and told me, "Oh, by the way, Joe-Joe, I met one of the wops today. Talk about gross!"

Knowing that Harpo couldn't, or wouldn't, talk, I knew it had to be Antonio. Picturing him in my mind, I remembered the first thought I'd had about him. *Mafia.* I secretly glanced at Judy. It hadn't dawned on me that she could possibly have contact with them. I scolded myself. *Why in the hell didn't I think of that?* Taking a sip of my beer, I told her, "Girl, I'm beginning to be sorry I got you into this."

"Why's that?" she asked, surprised. "He's just a dirty old fart that makes my skin crawl, that's all. Nothing to worry about." She shrugged. Then, changing the subject completely, Judy re-filled our glasses from the pitcher of beer and commented, "Joe-Joe, this is good. Pizza's the best late-night snack in the world."

"Yeah, I agree. But I won't be able to eat anything else for the next three days."

"Ha! You? I'm the one with the big ass!"

"Girl, it's not big. Just nice and round. Mm-Mm." I laughed.

Smiling, she shook her head and rolled her eyes at me, then reached for another slice of pizza and showed it to me. "Well, Galahad, I'm gonna make it bigger and rounder."

After taking a huge bite, Judy suddenly held her forefinger up, vying for patience. Chomping on the food and washing it down with a big swig of beer and a gasp, she exclaimed, "Oh, Joe-Joe, you'll be happy to hear this, too! Seriously! I discovered something interesting in one of the files today."

She covertly looked around to be sure we were out of earshot. Leaning closer, she lowered her voice. "There's this guy named Edwin Cooke who owns a building on Cave Creek Road and his mortgage application is almost three months old. The file is supposed to be active, but as far as I can tell, Mortensen hasn't submitted it to anyone yet for a mortgage. Anyway, this fella, Cooke? He's called the office every day since I've been there. When I answered the phone and talked with him today, he sounded really anxious, especially when I told him Mortensen wasn't in. He insisted that I have Mortensen call him back immediately to advise him about the two applications Mortensen told him he'd submitted last week. That's what prompted me to look in the file. Voila! No applications. Of course, I merely gave Mortensen the message that he'd called, not the reason why. Oh yeah, and one more thing. Cooke has a large balloon payment that was due about a month before he applied to Mortensen and as far as I can tell, it hasn't been paid yet. It's with First National Bank's mortgage department."

"Hey—good girl—that's all very interesting. But what can I do with it?"

"Well, I also got Cooke's phone number from the file. If he's in foreclosure, maybe you should call him to warn him about Mortensen and the wops."

"Too risky. If I call Cooke, chances are, he'll call Mortensen and raise hell. And even though Mortensen wouldn't recognize my name, I don't want to take the gamble of having it traced back to me and blowing my cover. On the other hand, if I do it anonymously, Mortensen might suspect that the information about him could only have come from you. So, that's no good."

"Your cover?" She questioned between bites. "What do you mean your cover?"

Stunned by my own slip, I blankly stared at her, not answering.

Leaning back against the seat, Judy placed her pizza back onto her plate. Silently sitting there, she just looked at me, with the latest un-chewed bite of crust bulging inside her cheek.

I had to tell her something. "Well, what I mean is

this—Mortensen might remember me and get suspicious."

With her voice muffled by the mouth full of pizza, she said, "Huh-uh, you didn't say that he might remember you. You said he couldn't recognize your name, yet he might trace it back to you and blow your cover. What cover?"

As I sat there looking at her, I found myself wishing for that proverbial hole to crawl into. Finally moving her mouth into motion, she chomped vigorously on the pizza and quickly washed it down with two large gulps of beer, all the while glaring at me until she'd swallowed the last of it. "You know what? I'm just thinking about something. Let's see, what's the expression? Bear with me? Well, looking back on it, I thought it was sort of ridiculous at the time, changing my name to Jane Romero. But, what was it you said? Oh yeah, 'Well, Judy, when you leave Mortensen's for good, he might not take no for an answer. This way, he can't pursue you, he can't stalk you. He won't be able to find Jane Romero'." She let that sink in before adding, "Now then, I want to ask you something else. Who is Owen?"

Oh, no. Damn! Why didn't I tell her everything? Incredulously overwhelmed by her perception, without thinking, I dug my own hole a little deeper. "What? Owen? Owen who?"

"That's what the hell I want to know—Owen who!"

At that moment, it felt like those large, brown eyes were burning a hole right through me. Trying to gather my senses, I sighed. "Okay. How did you come up with Owen?"

"I discovered that inadvertently." She smirked, folding her arms in front of her. "Remember that day not very long ago when I helped you clean the house? Well, I was dusting in the bedroom, when I accidentally knocked over that picture on the dresser and it fell out of the frame. You know, the picture of your sister, her husband, and their kids—if that's really who they are. Well, the writing on the back of it says, "To My Dear Brother, Owen." I wondered about it at first, but I figured it might be your middle name until I remembered that your middle initial is T. So? Maybe it's a nickname, I thought. Anyway, I just passed it off.

However putting two and two together here, it now seems to me that there might be something with regard to Owen that I should know about. So, Mystery Man! You want to explain it?"

Fidgeting with my beer mug, I exhaled loudly and leaned back against the booth. I forced a thin smile. "Owen is my real name. Owen Hunter."

"So, were you eventually going to tell me this? Or, were you making it so that after all this is finished, I won't be able to stalk you?" She slammed her napkin onto the table.

"Of course, I was going to tell you."

A tear escaped from her eye and ran down her cheek. She brushed it away, not moving her eyes from mine. Sniffling, she blurted, "Do you know what? In two weeks it's going to be Thanksgiving. I wanted to go home and visit my mother. I even told her that I intended to bring Joe—the man I've fallen in love with—with me! Now, what do I tell her? Any suggestions, Houdini?"

"Well, first of all, you can tell her that Joe's also fallen in love with you."

"And what about Owen? Who does he love?" Her sarcasm shot like darts.

"He loves you, too. Look, Judy, I know it was probably wrong for me not to tell you from the get-go. And except for omitting the name thing, I have told you everything else, and everything I've told you is the truth. I simply figured that if you didn't know my real name, you couldn't accidentally let it slip out. Now then, besides me, you're the only person who even knows about this conspiracy thing. Hell, even my own mother doesn't know." I momentarily forgot about Robert. But Judy knew about him, sort of.

"Well, I really liked calling you Joe-Joe. Now, I don't know what to call you."

"Well, forget about calling me Owen. That could eventually become dangerous. Just keep on calling me Joe-Joe. I'm used to it. Besides, I like it."

Shuddering, she searched my eyes again and said,

"My God, Joe, this whole thing is beginning to get a little thick. And I have to admit, that Antonio character scares me a little. I think we've got to start being very careful."

"You want out?"

"No! Absolutely not! Hell, you'd probably call another escort service and end up with some dizzy blonde with big boobs, who'd blow the whole thing for you. Sorry, Charley, you're stuck with me. Guess I'm just a little disappointed, that's all. I'll get over it."

I took her hands into mine. "Well, all I can do, Girl, is tell you I'm sorry, and promise you that from now on, you'll know everything there is to know about all of this. Incidentally, I should also tell you that you're going to be one hell of a lawyer."

A trace of a smile crossed her lips as she looked away from me and stared down at our coupled hands. "You mean that, when you said you love me?"

"Yes I did. Very much." When I squeezed her hands, she glanced up and I stared deeply into her large, root beer eyes, letting my answer register. She returned the squeeze.

Kissing the back of her hands, I grinned. "Now then, Girl, let's go home—okay? You're gonna love it when I tell you how I got to be Joseph T. Bowden."

Chapter 14

As I parked the car at the curb, I mentally thanked Judy for listing the mortgage companies that Mortensen's clients owed money to, prior to hiring Mortensen. Armed with six money orders in my coat pocket, I became Phillip Patterson again and started with the name at the top of her list. The first two people I visited merely took the money and thanked me.

I rang the bell at the third house and waited at length for the door to open. When it did, I cheerfully greeted the thin, silver-haired lady who answered it. "Good morning. Mrs. Blake?"

"Yes."

I held up the paper and told her, "Mrs. Blake, my name is Phillip Patterson. I'm with United Savings & Loan and I have a check for you."

The frail woman suspiciously balked behind the counterfeit security of the screen door. "A check, you say? What in the devil for?"

"Please allow me to explain, ma'am. You see, following an audit by our independent accounting firm, it was discovered that when your loan was paid off three years ago, there was an overpayment of one hundred, twenty dollars and rather than send out a simple form letter, management felt that a personal apology for not discovering this sooner would better represent our company. Therefore, I've come to deliver the check to you and Mr. Blake."

"Mr. Blake is dead."

It was my turn to hesitate. I cleared my throat and stammered, "My goodness, I was not aware of that. I'm sorry."

"And our loan wasn't paid off. Our house was stolen from us."

"Stolen?"

"That's right, stolen. We never really blamed you folks too much, though. You did try to help us as much as you could. After all, it wasn't your fault Ralph couldn't find work and his unemployment ran out."

"Please excuse me, Mrs. Blake, but I don't understand. What do you mean, your house was stolen from you?"

"Well, it's pretty simple, Mr. Patterson. When you people foreclosed on us, we went to some fella named Mortensen to get another mortgage and ended up losing our home."

I played ignorant. "Your house was foreclosed? I wasn't aware of that, either. I assumed it was paid off. I've only been with the company for about a year... I moved here from Chicago. The records didn't indicate a foreclosure—only that your loan was paid off. Not how, or by whom."

"Nope. Foreclosed. Three years ago. Afterward, poor Ralph always thought that Mortensen character stalled us along just so those crooks could buy our house right out from underneath us at the foreclosure sale. Or I guess, steal it from us would be a better word. And, Mr. Patterson, it was a beautiful home."

"Well, ma'am, I'm curious. Tell me more about what happened with this man, Mortensen. Uh, who exactly is he? And what was it you said about crooks? I'm sorry, but I'm a little lost here."

Mrs. Blake proceeded to tell me, in detail, the same story I could have told her. She ended with, "Yeah, poor Ralph wanted to file lawsuits against all of them. He threatened to go to the newspapers, the Corporation Commission, the Banking Commission, the Real Estate Board—everyone. But, the poor devil never got a chance."

"Oh?"

"No. He got killed in his truck, two weeks after we lost the house. He loved that old truck, too. Guess it's only fittin' that he should die in it, if he had to go."

"Oh, dear. How did the accident happen?"

"It's my understanding that the brakes failed. He was on his way back from a fishin' trip up to Lake Roosevelt and he went around a sharp, downhill curve on that rugged dirt road up there, with no brakes. He lost control and the truck went off the road and rolled over several times. It threw him clear out and the truck landed on him. Lucky he didn't kill someone else with him, I suppose."

"Gee, Mrs. Blake, I don't know what to say, except I am truly sorry." My genuine show of concern teamed with Mrs. Blake's reminiscence and her attitude toward me started to soften considerably.

"Thank you, Mr. Patterson. I miss him a lot, even now."

"I'm sure you do, ma'am." I stood there, sympathetically shaking my head, and despite feeling very awkward, I hastily tried to determine if there was anything else she could tell me that might be useful. Then it clicked. "Mrs. Blake, how did you happen to know it was the brakes that failed on Mr. Blake's truck?"

"Why, the police told me. I guess they inspected it at the junkyard where it was taken."

"I see. But you don't mean a junkyard—you mean the police impound yard. Right?"

"No, it was a junkyard. It was called Pull Your Own Parts, Incorporated, or something like that. Anyway, it's located somewhere down on Broadway Road. They called me to come down there and pick it up, if I still wanted it. But after the accident, I had no interest in it. Besides, they wanted an arm and a leg for storing the damn thing! I guess they just kept it, though, because they asked me to send them the title to it since I didn't want to pay their outlandish storage fees."

"I understand."

"But, Mr. Patterson, do you want to know what the strangest part of this whole thing is?"

"Certainly. What's that?"

"With Ralph's life insurance, I would've had enough money to pay off the house, only it was two weeks too late."

That was enough for me. I quickly offered my sympathy one more time, gave her the check, and left.

****

After bidding adieu to Mrs. Blake, my curiosity was

peaked. I stopped at a nearby service station and changed into a pair of Levi's and a work shirt, which I'd gotten used to keeping in the trunk, with all the remodeling I was doing. I headed for Broadway Road.

Mrs. Blake was right about the junkyard's name. Under the pretext of needing a fender, I gained entrance to the vehicles. Searching through the pick-up trucks, I luckily found a beat-up old Dodge with several papers bearing Ralph Blake's name in the glove box. I had one goal. After crawling beneath the dilapidated heap, I brushed the spider webs out of the way and inspected the front wheels.

Although there were no cuts or frays in the rubber brake lines, the brake cylinders both showed signs of leaking. The stains on the drums and hubs had long since dried, but due to the telltale discoloration, the seepage was obvious. Being an early fifties' model, I knew it had a single chamber master cylinder for all four wheels, so if any one of the lines had worked loose and leaked, the brakes would have failed completely. But even with my somewhat limited mechanical ability, it seemed impossible to me that both line nuts could work loose at the same time. I gripped one of them between my thumb and forefinger, but I couldn't loosen it. I tried the second wheel. They were both securely tightened. Dragging myself from beneath the old Dodge, I marched to the sales counter in the out-dated trailer at the front of the yard.

"Excuse me," I said to the man in charge, "would it be possible to borrow a half-inch, open end wrench?"

"There's a five dollar deposit on it 'til you bring it back."

I quickly handed the man a fiver, took the tool and hurried back to the truck. Scrambling beneath it again, I placed the wrench on the nut. With plenty of grunting and shoving, it finally broke loose and a few drops of thin liquid trickled from the cylinder. Sliding across the ground, I tried the other wheel and got the same result. The bit of remaining brake fluid in the system had settled down the lines and only leaked once the nuts were loosened. When I re-tightened both fittings, the flow of liquid immediately stopped.

I shuddered. *Hell's bells! These nuts had to have been loosened before the accident and then re-tightened after it!* With it being an old vehicle, I reasoned that it would be easy for a police officer inspecting it, to attribute it all to age. Yet, if Ralph loved his old truck as much as Mrs. Blake told me he did, everything surely would have been working fine prior to the wreck. I also realized that my suspicion about all of this would not be sufficient to prove that any kind of tampering had taken place.

I slowly climbed out from under Ralph Blake's old truck and brushed the dirt from my clothes. I returned to the office trailer. When I replaced my five-dollar bill to its proper place in my billfold, I retrieved one of the business cards I'd had printed in St. Louis. As I handed the card to the burly man on the other side of the counter, I read his nametag. "Excuse me, Bill, my name is Phillip Patterson. I'm with Southwest Desert Life Insurance Company. We're trying to settle a claim for a Mrs. Blake and I just came by to inspect her late husband's truck—"

"Thought you wanted a fender?" Bill gruffly interrupted.

"I'm sorry, Bill, but I made that up. I was afraid you wouldn't let me in to look at it if I told you what I was really here for. Now then, can you please answer a couple of questions for me?"

"Wait a minute, fella! You're askin' me to help you out after you just lied to me? Huh-uh! Stick it up yer ass!"

I defensively held up my hands. "Bill, I understand your anger, really I do. But truthfully, it's not for me. It's just that we'd like very much to settle the policy and the poor old widow could certainly use the money. So, you'd actually be helping her. Not me."

He took a slow puff from his cigarette, all the while glaring at me. "Well, I shouldn't, but if it's fer an old lady— what is it you want to know, anyway?"

"Do you happen to have in your files, the name of the

policeman who ordered it towed in here? Or, the name of the officer who inspected it?"

Bill suspiciously looked at me with one eye squinted closed. "Why do you need to know that?"

I heaved a sigh, treating the whole affair like I was complaining about my job. "Just a formality, Bill. You know—damned paperwork! I have to get a copy of the police report for our files before I can issue the policy proceeds to her."

"Okay. Which truck is it again?"

I pointed through a dirty window toward the lot. "It's that light blue '52 Dodge. Belonged to a fellow named Ralph Blake."

Grumbling under his breath, the junkyard man thumbed through a dusty, gray file cabinet and pulled out a grease-spotted folder. "Yeah, here it is." He gave it a quick study. "Hey, wait a minute! I remember that old truck! Hell, yes! It was brought in here by some fly-by-night tow truck operator. I'd never heard of him before. Ain't ever seen him since, either. Some great big guy with a crew-cut. Ugly as hell. I can't imagine how he was able to talk the police into lettin' him haul it in here but my guess is he slipped a pay-off to one of the deputies at the scene. Probably got a big fat paycheck from some insurance company for towin' it, too."

"You don't happen to have this towing guy's name by any chance? Or his license number?"

"Naw. And besides his bein' so friggin' ugly, the only other thing I can remember about him is, he was drivin' an old Chevvie. Hell, he shoulda left the tow truck here too, beat up as the damn thing was!" Bill heehawed before he turned his attention back to the folder.

Chuckling with him, I waited while he sifted through the few items in the file. In due time, he lifted up a yellow paper and grunted. "Aw, here we go. Detective Bearden from the Phoenix Police Department was the guy who inspected it. I'd say it was a couple of days later. He's the one who gave me the okay to either release it to Mrs. Blake, or apply for a salvage title." As I jotted down the name, he told me, "But I hope you don't need anything else. The only other thing in here is the title—the old gal mailed it to me."

"No, Bill, I believe that gives me what I need. Now I can write up my inspection report so that Mrs. Blake can get her money. Thanks."

Bill's stance toward me was softening just as Mrs. Blake's had earlier. Guess I was having that effect on people today. He summed it up, "Glad to help. But say, it seems to me you insurance guys are usually out here right away. How's come you waited three years? Hell, you're lucky that old heap hasn't been crushed. But since parts that old are hard to find, that's the only reason I kept it."

"Kind of a long story about the three years, Bill, and I won't bore you with it, but there was some kind of mix-up in the claims department and I got the job of cleaning it up. Anyway, thanks again for your help. Please take this for your trouble." I placed twenty dollars on the beat-up plywood sales counter and turned to leave.

"Hey, Patterson." He called after me.

"Something else, Bill?"

"Well, thanks for the twenty. And I gotta say—you're pretty damn sharp! You were right. I most likely wouldn't have let you in here if I knew you were an insurance guy."

I grinned at him and walked out the door. Neither of us had any way of knowing that the old Chevvie tow truck had been crushed by another junkyard, just minutes after leaving Ralph Blake's Dodge at Pull-Your-Own-Parts, Incorporated.

Chapter 15

Judy Carmelle bounced into the house, and then locked the front door behind her. "Hey, Joe-Joe, I smell something good. You got supper ready?"

"I picked up Chinese. Come in here, Girl, we've got to talk."

"Why so serious? What's up?"

"Sit down. I'll tell you while we eat."

As we dined on lemon chicken, stir-fried vegetables and egg-fried rice, Judy listened while I told her about Ralph Blake and my theory. I finished my meal and my story at the same time. "Judy, I believe that poor old man was murdered."

"Murdered? Shoo, Joe-Joe. Don't get carried away. It was probably just an unfortunate accident."

"It couldn't have been an accident. Brakes just don't do that. Those line nuts had to have been loosened by somebody then re-tightened later. Probably that tow truck driver, whoever the hell he is."

"C'mon, Joe-Joe, I think you're just being paranoid. After all, it was an old truck. Couldn't they have simply worked themselves loose over time?"

"Okay, let's assume they did. Then, how did they get tightened back up again—by themselves? Even discounting that, if they'd slowly worked loose, the brakes would have shown gradual failure and Mr. Blake would have fixed them, according to what his wife told me about his love affair with the old heap."

"Well, if somebody did loosen them, why wouldn't they just leave them that way? I mean, why go to the trouble of re-tightening them?"

"Simple. If they were left that way, there could always be room for suspicion that they were loosened, especially if both of them were loose. Re-tightening them makes it look like they were old lines that merely developed a leak. Especially to somebody who casually checked them following the wreck. More than likely, they wouldn't have tried to loosen the nuts like I did today."

"Okay, I'll ask you again. How do you know that's not what happened? Maybe they did leak on their own."

Judy, this is becoming a bit frustrating. Patience, Joe. "Because of the way they started leaking again when I loosened the nuts, sweetheart. If they had developed a slow leak all by themselves, all of the fluid would have drained from the lines. There wouldn't have been anything left in there to leak!" I didn't realize I was steadily raising my voice.

Not looking at me while she sifted through the containers for more food, which she shoveled onto her plate, Judy said, "Don't raise your voice to me, Joseph. After all, I'm no mechanic and I can't say that I understand all that stuff. However, I do think it's a bit of a stretch. Why would somebody kill an innocent, old man like Blake? Well, unless the old lady did it for the insurance." She bantered.

I ignored her quip. "Okay. How about this—with all the threats of exposure that Blake was making, maybe the Tafino boys or Mortensen had him killed to silence him?"

She shook her head in disbelief and gave me an amused laugh. "This time, Joe-Joe, I do think you've been reading too many novels, and if you really believe that, maybe you should forget about getting even with them." She continued to busy herself with the food.

"Judy, please stop clowning around. I'm serious. And I'll admit, this has actually got me a little bit scared and I think you should be, too! Now then, according to your rule—since I'm the one who's right this time, I'll tell you what I want you to do. Thanks to your good help, I believe I have enough information to go it alone from here on, so what I'd like for you to do is quit the job at Mortensen's, go back to day school and move quietly into the background."

"Baloney! I've already told you, Joe-Joe, you got me hooked into this thing and if you think you're going to dump me that easily, you're full of it! If you intend to continue with it then believe me, I'm going to continue with it right alongside you." She finally stopped what she was doing with the food and reached out to touch my hand. She looked at me. "But, okay, I'll promise to be careful. How's that?"

"Huh! I wonder if we can be careful enough."

"Joe-Joe, all we have right now is one little suspicion. Let's at least check out some more people. Okay? Incidentally, speaking of that, I've got eight more names for you." She hurriedly reached into her purse and whisked out a sheet of paper. As she handed it to me, she simpered, "But, Joe-Joe, please don't find any more dead ones."

Chapter 16

One of the names on Judy's latest list sounded familiar, but I couldn't place it—Wayne Meeks. So, with most recent addresses and more money orders in my pocket, I began with that one. When Wanda Meeks explained to me about her husband, I remembered seeing it on the news broadcasts a couple of years ago. Wayne Meeks was an ironworker who had fallen nearly two hundred feet to his death.

According to Wanda, it seemed to be a continuation of the bad luck that had besieged them for over a year. His accident happened on his first day of work, following a long absence from a hunting injury, for which he couldn't qualify for compensation. With no income and with several vacancies in the small commercial building that was to someday supplement their retirement, they were unable to make their mortgage payments on the place. When a foreclosure was filed, they'd contacted Mortensen. I listened to the same old story about the mortgage broker and his Italian friends. And just like Ralph Blake, a suspicious Wayne Meeks had also threatened lawsuits and exposure. It was less than two weeks later that he died.

"The way it was explained to me, Mr. Patterson, Wayne had been sent up to install girder bolts in a beam, but as soon as he stepped away from the crane that hoisted him up, he slipped on some form oil, lost his footing and just fell off."

"Did you say form oil?"

"Yes. I understand it leaked from a barrel placed up there for the carpenters. They were about to set their forms."

"You mean the forms weren't even set yet?"

"No, that's why Wayne was up there to replace the missing bolts—so the carpenters could get started. Mr. Patterson, I probably wouldn't even know enough to tell you this much about it, except that Wayne loved his work a whole lot, so he talked about it all the time."

As she was telling me this, my memory flashed back

to my earlier days as a field accountant and some of the construction things I learned. *Why in the world was that form oil up there in the first place? Hell, they don't even coat the forms until the day they pour the concrete, long after the forms are already set! Especially on a high-rise building. Those carpenters need all the space they can get up there and those barrels would just be in their way.* I saw no reason to mention this to Wanda Meeks. "Just one more question, ma'am. Why was your husband placed up on the twentieth floor just after he'd returned from a long absence?"

"I understand they were running behind schedule and since Wayne was the closest ironworker there, somebody asked him to volunteer. Knowing Wayne, he did. Incidentally, Mr. Patterson, I'm curious—why are you asking me all these questions?"

"Well, Mrs. Meeks, knowing that you lost your building and our company, although not me personally, had a hand in that by filing the foreclosure, I feel terrible that you lost your husband as well. I was simply trying to determine if you had a basis for a lawsuit. I certainly think you should recover something."

She gave me a soft chuckle. "I appreciate your concern, Mr. Patterson, I really do, but I guarantee you, I've already received a very handsome settlement from the contractor's insurance company."

Just like before, I hurriedly repeated my sympathy, gave her the check and left with several questions burning in my head. Old newspapers would give me the account of the ironworker's death, so I headed for the library.

With the kind help of a knowledgeable librarian and after only thirty minutes of browsing, I found the story in a back copy of *The Arizona Republic* and discovered when I read it that luck was with me. After thanking the librarian, I left and pointed the Thunderbird north toward Camelback Road. My old supervisor, Stan Murdock, would be surprised to see me.

****

Feeling the plush carpet literally crush beneath my

feet, I was quickly escorted into Stan's richly furnished burl-paneled office by a perfume wearing, heavy-set secretary. I declined her offer of coffee.

I shook Stan's hand and we both exchanged pleasantries. As we sat down across from each other, Stan asked, "You're doing what? Private investigating? I'd heard you were out of public accounting, but I was told that you were into real estate— or something like that. So, now what? You're spying on people to see who's sleepin' with who?" Stan laughed out loud.

"That's a pretty good one, Stan, but I haven't quite elevated myself to that level yet. I'm actually into insurance investigation—real low-life stuff—trying to track people down."

"So, how can I help you with that?"

"It happens that I'm looking for a couple of men we want to serve with a summons to appear in a civil suit. And you may not believe this, but I don't even know either of these characters' names."

"Do I?"

"Probably not. But I believe you can find out for me."

"I'm a little lost here, Owen. How do I do this?"

It seemed strange to hear somebody address me as Owen. "First of all, Stan, let me jog your memory. When you guys built the United Bank Building downtown, there was a man killed on that job. An ironworker named Wayne Meeks. He fell off the twentieth floor."

"Oh, yeah, now that you mention it, I remember. But say, wasn't the litigation on that all settled?"

"All except for one thing. You might also recollect that Nevada-Utah Iron & Steel was the sub-contractor on that job for all the ironwork. Now then, your insurance company and Nevada-Utah's carrier both settled out of court with the widow, very quickly. However, and this goes against my grain, she's attempting to file a wrongful death claim against the ironworker foreman and the crane operator. I've been hired by her ambulance chaser lawyer to locate these guys, so, what I need is their names and addresses. I could easily have gone to Nevada-Utah to find this out, but this gives me a good excuse to visit you." That part was only partly true because without Stan's help, I probably wouldn't have gotten a thing from Nevada-Utah. They would have wanted credentials I didn't have.

"Owen, old buddy, as if you ever needed an excuse. Let's see what I can do." Lifting his telephone, Stan pushed a button and waited. Holding his hand over the mouthpiece, he commented to me, "By the way, Owen, I gotta say—you're sure lookin' good. You been vacationing in Hawaii? Whoops. Hang on a minute, Owen. Stella, will you get Brownie from Nevada-Utah on the phone for me, please?"

While he waited, Stan offered me a cigarette. I hadn't given it a thought in months and declining was easy. Momentarily, Stan spoke into the phone again. "Brownie? This is Murdock. I need a favor."

It took three telephone conversations. After hanging up from the last one, Stan told me what he'd learned. The crane operator that day had been a fill-in from the union and since Nevada-Utah's payroll records only went back two years, they had no information regarding his name. Next call, the union told Stan that this guy had apparently been a member for less than six months, therefore he didn't qualify for Health & Welfare benefits, and consequently, his name didn't appear on any of Nevada-Utah's report forms for that time period. Finally, the only thing the job superintendent could remember about the guy was that he was a "big, mean-acting, ugly guy with a crew-cut." Didn't say much. In the police investigation, the crane operator had satisfactorily answered their few questions. He'd merely lifted the ironworker to the top aboard the crane and the man's death had been caused by the spilled form oil. Nobody ever figured out how that leaky barrel got up there. And no, the superintendent couldn't remember what kind of car the guy drove and the foreman on that job died last year from liver cancer.

Stan summed it up. "Sorry, Owen, guess I wasn't much help."

"Thanks anyway, Stan. At least I got a description of the guy. Looks like my next step, is to contact all of the crane contractors and rental companies."

"Yeah, and I'd assume that your widow's lawsuit against the foreman is a lost cause—unless she can collect from a corpse!" Stan laughed.

As I stood to leave, I winked at him and grinned. "You know, Stan, that's not beyond the realm of possibility. The man may have left a large estate."

After momentarily gazing at me with a surprised look on his face, Stan's chuckle returned when he said goodbye.

Heading home, I mentally compared notes between Blake and Meeks and, besides the identical association they shared with Mortensen and his crowd, I could only make one other connection.   The tow-truck driver and the crane operator had to be the same guy.

Chapter 17

During supper, Judy gave me a troubled look when I told her about Wayne Meeks. "I'm beginning to believe you're right, Joe-Joe. This is probably too much to be just a coincidence. So, now what do we do?"

"I'm not sure. I thought I had this whole thing planned out. I mean, at first, I was merely going to nail those scumbags for fraud and get my building back. But, Girl, it appears to be a whole lot more than that now. These guys could be killers. And if that's true, we can't let them get away with it."

"I agree. And not only that, we need to prevent it from happening to somebody else. So, I'll ask you again—what do we do next?"

"First thing we're going to do is what I wanted to do yesterday and this time, I'm insisting! I want you to get away from Mortensen and stay out of the picture."

"There you go with that crap again! Damn, Joseph! You're more than redundant—you're a freaking broken record!"

"Judy, please! Listen to me! Look, when I first contacted that escort service, I had one little thing in mind for some girl to do. All right? I had no idea that I would end up falling in love with her and I certainly didn't know there'd be any danger involved. Remember that? Remember me telling you there'd be no danger? Well, by having you out of this from now on, I'm merely keeping my word."

"All right, Owen, if I'm out, then so are you! I don't want you having any accidents when you come up against those people again!"

I heaved a sigh. "Judy, why won't you please listen to me? Look here, I have to admit I've been pretty naive about all this. I should have realized that other people would have figured out these guys' methods before I did. But who would've guessed they'd be killed for it? Hell, I just wonder if there's any more, other than those two. And now, I'm beginning to realize one other thing. Since this undercover conspiracy type thing is all new to me, I'm having to learn a lot of things as I go, therefore, it becomes doubly dangerous and that's why you're out of it. This is my deal from now on."

"Just like that. I'm out. So okay, Owen, go call the escort service again and get the blonde with the big boobs. Maybe you'll get one without big lips and without big hips! Who knows, maybe she'll be kind enough to go to bed with both, you and Mortensen! And since you aren't in love with her, it's no matter if she screws it up and you both get blown away. Who'll care?" Folding her arms across her chest, Judy slumped against the sofa, scowling at me. "*Now*, who's feeling redundant?"

I couldn't keep from grinning. "Damn! Am I glad you don't ever get really mad at me!"

Keeping her eyes glued to mine, she clenched her teeth and snapped, "I am really mad at you!"

Crossing her legs, she briskly bounced her foot up and down, not budging from her stare. "Well? Don't just sit there, Owen! Go call Amanda! Have her send the bimbo over here tonight! And believe me—she's got plenty of them. Then, while I'm at school, you can fill her in. With the details, I mean."

At first not realizing what she'd just said, Judy suddenly caught the double connotation and burst into nervous laughter. Holding her stomach, she fell back against the sofa and a stream of hot tears started running down her face. For a time, she simply sat there, laughing and crying at the same time. I waited until it was over.

Eventually, she leaned forward and brushed the tears from her cheeks. When she looked at me, there was concern showing in those root-beer eyes. "My God, Joe-Joe, I have to be honest with you. I really am scared by all of this. Can't we just go to the police?"

"I wish we could, gorgeous. But all we have are a few wild suspicions and a bit of circumstantial evidence. And nothing that ties any of this to Mortensen and his bunch. We have to get more. A lot more."

Instantly changing moods again, she bubbled, "Hey! You said we. Does this mean I'm back in?"

Without even looking at her, I deliberately stood to my feet and walked to the bar to mix us some mai tais. Once I had the drinks in my hand, I strolled across the room and handed one to her, then took a seat at the other end of the couch. I took a sip and said, "Okay, I surrender. But it certainly isn't without a lot of reservation."

Judy hurriedly set her drink on the coffee table and scrambled across the sofa. She straddled my lap and gripped my chin in her hand, then teasingly shook it. "Now then, that's better. See? But, hell, Joe-Joe, I should have known you'd give in! I momentarily forgot—you like these big lips and big hips." A quick wiggle and the devilish grin again.

"Damn! How do you do that?"

"Do what?" She innocently asked.

"How can you go from being scared to death one minute to becoming Bozo the Clown, the next?"

"Easy. I'm serious when it calls for it, but the rest of the time, I simply enjoy us. This is what we are together. Can't you see that? Of course you can. You do the very same thing! Just not as good! For example—watch this." She squeezed my thighs with her legs and the grin left her face, replaced by a sultry look. She then placed her arms around my neck and slowly lowered her lips against mine, softly manipulating her mouth, gently tugging, pulling, pressing and eventually releasing, all the while rubbing her breasts against me. Slowly pushing away from me with her hands on my chest, she said, "Okay, that's enough seriousness." The seductive stare was quickly replaced with a broad grin again as she shimmied against my lap once more and impishly declared, "Okay, Galahad, despite what I feel happening to both of us down there, that's all you get for now." With that, she lifted herself from me and returned to the other end of the couch.

"What in hell was that about?"

"You know, a little bit of serious, a little bit of Bozo." She giggled. "But now, Joseph, it's time for us to get serious again, really serious. We have a lot of things to discuss on the subject of what to do about Mortensen and company. So, where do we start? Any ideas?"

"Well, miss teaser, for your information, actually, yes I do have some. The first one being that we both need another mai tai."

"A very good beginning." She handed me her already emptied glass.

When I returned with the fresh drinks, I told her, "As a matter of fact, there's one really good idea that I've already put into play. Remember that gray wig I wore?"

Beaming a wide grin, she said, "Joe-Joe, my dear, that's something I won't *ever* forget."

Rolling my eyes toward the ceiling, I smiled and sipped from my drink. "Seriously, I really have done a lot of thinking about this and the gray wig was the first part of it. Now then, the two buildings I bought a few weeks ago will be renovated in about ten weeks, maybe twelve. The house may take a little longer. And when those are sold, phase two can begin because I'll have enough money to frame our Mr. Mortensen and the Tafino brothers. However, when that time comes, I'm going to have to deal with Mortensen again and I asked myself how I was going to do that without being recognized and remembered by him. After much careful thought and deliberation, I came up with an answer. I enrolled in Salon Arizona."

"And what, pray tell, is Salon Arizona?"

"It's a school for theatrical costuming and make-up, and once I learn it, I'll be able to completely disguise myself. I can be any age. I can be scarred for life. I can be a blonde or a brunette, or gray-haired, or even a hunchback. Whatever I want to be. Just so long as he doesn't recognize me. Anyway, I started it a few weeks ago. That's where the gray wig came from."

"Ingenious. Just don't try to wear the stupid thing to bed." Like a pixie, she winked and took a sip of the mai tai. "Okay. What other ideas you got, Mr. Hollywood?"

"Remember me telling you about the attorney?"

"The one you went to see after your foreclosure? Warner?"

"Yes. Well, in a roundabout way, he gave me all the information I need to develop a strong case. When I'm ready for Mortensen, I intend to rent an office, in which I'm going to bug the phones and install hidden cameras and tape recorders. But that's a good ways down the road and it'll only serve to snare them for their racketeering."

"Okay. But, Joe-Joe, knowing what we suspect about Blake and Meeks, what can we do about that?"

"What I'd like to do is put a bug on Mortensen's telephone. Maybe there's a chance they'll slip up and say something incriminating, then we can lasso them for the killings, as well. But if I do that, I don't want you in there anymore."

"That's kinda smart and dumb at the same time. Seems to me I *have* to stay there. Who's going to monitor the thing and get the tapes for you?"

"Well, I certainly can't let you do that, so don't even think about it. What if he discovers the stuff?"

"Give me some credit, Joe-Joe. If he finds it, I'll just act innocent and make something up. Trust me—I can get the horny so-and-so to believe anything."

"Damn it, Judy! No! It's too dangerous!" I slammed my hand against the sofa cushion for emphasis.

Judy slammed her own hand with equal authority. "Right. And the only danger for you is that you might get caught breaking and entering. So, you'll go to jail for ten years, the wops will die, Mortensen will still be after my ass, I'll be home broken-hearted, and the case is closed."

"Thank God, I'll have you to defend me." I mused.

"Don't count on it. I want smarter clients than that."

Chuckling, I reached for my mai tai and took another drink. "Well, I'll have to break in once to set the damn thing up."

"Wait a minute, Joe-Joe." Lifting her purse from the floor, she reached inside and pulled out a key ring. Waving it in my face, she sang, "You won't have to break in,

Hollywood. I've got a key."

I felt my face flush. "Okay, then here's the short-term plan. After I get the sub-contractors started tomorrow, I'll pick up what we need at the electronics store so we can get it installed at Mortensen's. Better do it late at night. You doin' anything after class tomorrow evening?"

"No plans, Joe-Joe. And speaking of class, look at the time! Jeez, I better get going right now."

I stood up and grabbed her hands, pulling her to her feet. I took her into my arms. "Okay. But prepare yourself, Girl, 'cause when you get home tonight, I'm gonna proposition you for a change. How's that?"

"Well, it's about time, Hollywood. See ya later."

Chapter 18

For the third night in a row, James Mortensen sat in the blue Datsun outside the Arizona State University psychology building. He was experiencing frustration, disappointment, even a touch of anger. Not once had he seen Jane Romero come out of the building after classes had finished.

He glanced at his newly installed car phone and instantly changed his mind about trying to call Jane at home. He was too afraid. He didn't want it buzzing busy if Margo called. Although expensive, he'd put the phone in for just that purpose. With the new service of call forwarding installed in his office, he could re-direct his wife's late night calls to the car phone without her even knowing it. "I'll be right on my way home, dear. I'm just leaving the office," he would lie.

Impatiently sitting there, he kept nervously tapping his fingers against the steering wheel. He was trying to reason everything to himself, but he wasn't finding any answers. At least, none that satisfied him.

Why did Jane tell me that she was in school every night? Sometimes I wonder about her. Like today—finally saying that I could come to her place for a drink, then whispering to me about being on her period. "So, James, don't get any ideas," she'd said with that sexy laugh. Hell, I want her, not a damn drink!

Then James Mortensen alibied. *But she must like me, though. She's always touching my arm, she smiles at me all the time, brings me coffee. She certainly doesn't treat any of the men who come to the office that way. They all think she's conceited. Especially Tony. He hates her.*

You know what? I just thought of something. I'll bet it's because she knows I'm married. Yes, that's got to be the answer! I'll bet if I was single, we'd be doin' it every night! He automatically stiffened when he imagined it.

All at once, he was alerted by the noise of chattering students leaving the building next to the one he'd been watching. He stared out the window at them, studying them all. *Wait a minute! There she is!* Crouching down in the seat, he watched as Jane Romero moved past, busily chatting with somebody. James rose up for a closer look. *Who's that blonde with her? Thank goodness she's with another girl.* James looked at the blonde again. *But why wouldn't she be? She told me she doesn't have a boy friend.* Squirming, James felt his face go hot. *I couldn't stand the thought of some other guy doing her. I'd have Tony get him killed!*

Breathing heavily, James held his hand to his chest, trying to calm himself. It helped. But what helped even more was visualizing what Jane would be like naked, lying there, waiting for him, smiling up at him. He felt himself stiffen again.

Crouching lower behind the wheel, he watched from the corner of his eye as they crossed to the other side of the street. *Wonder what they're laughing about so much? Probably discussing all the different guys who've been doing them!* Becoming angered again, he studied the blonde, blaming her. Recording her face into his memory, he instantly despised her. Still glaring at her, he noticed the choreographic sway of her hips, which caused him to partly overturn his first emotion about her. *Look at that ass! Hell, maybe I'd like to have that one, too! Maybe Jane could introduce us if she's not going to put out pretty soon. No, that won't work. She'd wonder where I saw the blonde and know I was spying on her.*

Breathing a sigh of exasperation, he looked at the other students streaming from the building. *Wait a minute! That's the law building! Why did Jane come out of the law building? She's not studying law! Oh, hell, wait a minute. I know. She went over there from the psychology building to meet that blonde—she's the one who's studying law. Stupid me! There's probably a back way into that building. I should have thought of that before! I'll bet she's been leaving by the back way every night. Tomorrow, I'll wait there. Maybe Jane will be alone. But, crap! What good will it do if she is? She'd probably get mad as hell if I'd show up there unannounced.*

Besides, she's on that damned period! Oh, hell—how I hate this damned waiting. I've got to have her pretty soon.

Straining for one more look, James watched them disappear around the corner, trying to hold the vision of their tight Levi's in his mind's eye. But no longer having them in sight, the vision disappeared and he became depressed. Starting the car, he muttered, "Guess I'll go home to Margo."

Chapter 19

Antonio Tafino's fat finger pushed the numbers on the pay telephone. As soon as he recognized the gravelly voice of the man who answered, he grumbled into the mouthpiece. "Yeah, Alex. It's me, Tafino!"

"What's up, boss?"

"Got a little job for you."

"Good. I've been itchin' for somethin' to do."

"This one won't be easy. Meet me at the club in two hours and I'll give you the details. And for God's sake, Alex, wear a suit." Click.

****

When Edwin Cooke left for work at the new job he'd finally found, he paid no attention to the white Cadillac sitting across the street from his house. It had taken him eight months to find employment and he didn't want to be late, and he didn't mind at all that he had to work on the day after Thanksgiving. After all, Alice had to work, too. Running ten minutes behind his wife, he screeched out of the driveway and raced away.

Alex Bigotti patiently waited fifteen minutes before exiting the white Cadillac. When he approached the front door of the Spanish style house, he read the nametag inside the small gold frame. *Edwin and Alice Cooke.* He rang the bell and waited. No answer. He rang the bell again.

Acting casual, he rubbed his hand across his crew-cut while slowly scanning the nearby houses for activity. Everything was quiet. Since it was a very average neighborhood, there were probably not a lot of people living around here who got today off from work. *Good.*

After three minutes, he secretly tried the doorknob. It was locked. He pushed the button a third time, just to be certain, and heard only the muffled sound of the chimes behind the closed door. Then it became quiet again.

Returning to his car, Alex drove away from the curb and sped around the corner. He parked a short block away on a side street. Lifting his large six-foot frame from the vehicle, he cursed Cooke, wondering why the stupid jerk didn't live on a corner lot. That would be easier. *There's no alley, either! Damn!*

Back-tracking along the side street, he stopped before he reached Cooke's street. Lighting a cigarette for cover, he cupped his gloved hands around it and peered over them through a chain link fence, which surrounded most of the corner home's back yard. The far side was enclosed by a block fence, separating it from the adjacent house. Bigotti frowned at that.

He took a careful look around the yard and the patio and didn't see any toys. Or dogs. He'd already inspected the driveway in front when he drove past, noting the absence of any cars.

Still watching the neighborhood, he snuffed the smoke and stuck the butt into his pocket, not wanting to leave any evidence. Certain he hadn't been seen, he sauntered from the sidewalk to the rear corner of the house and raised the gate latch. The unlocked gate opened and Bigotti stepped inside, quietly closing the gate behind him.

Briskly crossing the lawn, he looked over the top of the block fence, checking the back of the next house. He perked. It was vacant. He remembered seeing the for sale sign in front. Scaling the wall, he marched to the opposite side of the yard and climbed over another wall on the other side. He found himself standing beside Edwin Cooke's swimming pool.

Concealing his big body behind a potted rubber tree plant on the patio, Alex tested the sliding door. It was locked. Removing a screwdriver from his coat, he expertly dislodged the screws from the casing surrounding the entryway and put them into his jacket pocket. Using his strength, he easily lifted the heavy door from its frame and leaned it against the outside wall. Taking one more look around, he peered over the top of the rear wall toward the house behind Cooke's. No movement. Finally, sure that nobody was watching, Bigotti entered the house.

Once inside, he began searching, starting with the

bedroom. Being careful to replace everything exactly as he'd found it, he rifled through drawers one at a time, and with each step he took, he made sure no shoeprints were detectable in the thick carpeting.

Not finding what he came for in the bedroom, he reasoned that the second room of choice was the family room. Despite his hulking frame, he moved catlike back down the hallway.

He knew it was here, someplace. After all, the boss had told him it was here. Deftly checking the most obvious hiding places, Bigotti finally found the item he was searching for tucked toward the back of a curio cabinet drawer. *Now then, just one more thing. Good thing the weather's turned cold at night.*

Not even deliberating, he passed through the kitchen to the living room, aiming his silent feet toward the guest closet near the front door. Ignoring the family photographs mounted on the wall, he walked past them. He didn't care. This was business. Opening the closet door, he peered inside and immediately saw what he wanted. It was time to leave.

Within fifteen minutes, the patio door was carefully re-installed and Alex Bigotti was opening his car door. He plopped onto the seat, quickly inserted the key into the ignition, started the Cadillac and roared away. They would never know he'd been there.

Chapter 20

The return shuttle flight from Yuma was uneventful and while Judy and I walked through the airport concourse, Judy was rambling to me. "Mother just fell in love with you, Joe-Joe, except she thinks you're a little too old for me. At least, she did until she got to know you. And you really made an impression on Nathan. He was amazed at how much you know about football. Huh! They didn't either one give me any credit for picking you to fall in love with."

Holding my hand tightly, she pressed her head against my arm as we walked along. With only carry-on luggage, we made our way directly to the parking garage where I'd left the Thunderbird. As I began to pull out of the parking space, I said, "We'd better visit Mortensen's office before we go home. Got your key?"

"Yes. And I'm sorry, Joe-Joe. I guess in all the excitement of wanting to take you home to meet mother, I simply forgot to remove the tape. Forgive me?"

"Once we have the tape, then I'll forgive you." I teasingly scolded.

****

Having been stuffed with turkey and all the trimmings for four days, I wasn't the least bit hungry when we walked into the house a little while later, only tired. After unpacking and showering, Judy and I sat in the living room with a glass of red wine, listening to *Santana*.

Judy gave me a tranquil look. "You know, Joe-Joe, it's kinda nice being alone with you again. And thanks for building the fire."

Sitting sideways on the sofa with her feet curled Indian style, she fingered the lacy front of her see-through nightie and asked, "Did you know I bought this just for you? Do you like it?" I did and I said so.

Talkative, she straightened her long coffee-colored legs across the sofa and picked up her glass of wine from the table. "Is it too late to go next door and get Socko? I guess you know, Joe-Joe, that besides loving you, I also love your blue-collar cat, too. I've missed him. Haven't you?"

I got up from the couch. "I'll see if their lights are on."

When I opened the front door, Socko waltzed in as if we hadn't even been gone.

"Good!" Judy exclaimed. "C'mon, Socko, now I can take you both to bed. C'mon, Joe-Joe, I'm tired."

"Huh-uh, Girl, no can do just yet. Not until we listen to that tape."

"Oh, gee, you're right. I forgot about it again."

She sat back down on the sofa with the cat while I placed the cassette in the machine. Only one conversation was of interest.

****

"Hello."

"Tony? We may have problems. That guy Cooke just came into the office, mad as hell."

"Yeah? So what's the problem?"

"He's threatening all sorts of things, like lawsuits, going to the newspapers, the Corporation Commission, the Banking Commission, or anybody else who'll listen to him. Swears uphill and down I knew about the foreclosure from day one."

"Don't worry about it. You handled him like all the others. Right?"

"Absolutely. No record of it anywhere."

"Then, Mortensen, don't concern yourself. He's just upset that he lost his building. He'll cool off."

"Tony, you don't understand. The short little fart threatened to kill me! Came in here wavin' a gun around! He only left because I picked up the phone and started to call the cops. Scared the living crap right outta me!"

Laughter. "Mortensen, there's only one thing that's gonna kill you. That's if you're ever lucky enough to get a piece of that Mexican ass that's workin' for you!" More laughter.

"Tony, this isn't funny! He truly scared the hell out of me!"

"Mortensen, it's good you called me. However, don't worry about this Cooke guy—I don't think he'll be giving you any more problems. You just enjoy Thanksgiving with Margo and I'll talk to you next week. Oh, and one more thing, don't call the cops." Click.

****

After listening to it, I retrieved the tape, dated it, marked the content on the label and placed it in the cabinet with the others. Before I could comment, Judy exclaimed, "Joe, I don't remember Cooke being in the office last week. That must have happened while I was at lunch. And Maryann didn't even mention it to me. That's incredible! Of course, she doesn't tell me much of anything. She resents me being there in the first place. But if some idiot came in there waving a gun around, surely you'd think she'd tell me about that!"

"Maybe she had orders not to tell you."

"I can't think of a solitary reason why. No, it's just her. Guess I'm just damn glad I wasn't there."

Taking a seat on the Queen Anne chair, I reached for my glass and swallowed the last bit of my wine. With my brow furrowed, I said, "Well, I'll tell you what, Girl, there's something that really concerns me about that conversation. Thinking about Blake and Meeks, I just hope it doesn't mean anything. Didn't you hear Tafino tell Mortensen that Cooke wouldn't give him any more problems?"

"Joe-Joe, maybe you really should give Cooke an anonymous call from a pay phone tomorrow. I'm serious. I mean, this man could be in real trouble. Joe-Joe, we have to warn him. Please—do it for me?"

I stood up to refill our wine glasses. "Okay, you're probably right. But I'll have to do it in such a way that it doesn't blow us out of the water."

"I know." Shaking her head back, she combed her fingers through her auburn hair, moving it away from her face, watching me with anticipation.

I started to pace the floor and looked at her, sitting curled on the sofa, waiting, her teeth clenched against a painted fingernail of one hand while her other stroked the cat's contented face. After a time, I said, "Okay, I think I've come up with something. I'll put on my best scowl and be, uh, Detective Rogers. How does this sound?"

I formed an imaginary telephone with my hand and began to walk back and forth in front of Judy. I cleared my throat. "Mr. Cooke, this is Detective Rogers with the Phoenix Police Department. The reason I'm calling you is to warn you to back away from this Mortensen guy. We're tapping his phone and we've got his office wired because of other complaints we've had against him. That's how we know you were in there raising hell and threatening him. Now then, one reason I want you to steer clear is because we think his friends could be dangerous. The other is because we don't want you screwing up our sting for us. Now listen to me, Mr. Cooke, when we get enough evidence, there's a good chance you might be able to recover something from your loss, but in the meantime, don't contact this Mortensen anymore. Lay low and keep quiet. And don't breathe a word about Mortensen or this phone call to anybody. No newspapers, no banking commission, no lawyers, nobody. Our department will contact you as soon as we have something solid. Besides, we may ask you to be a witness. Incidentally, Mr. Cooke, do you have a permit for that gun?" I hung up the imaginary phone.

Bowing slightly, I grinned at Judy. "I'm pretty sure he'll buy it because he'll wonder how anybody but those in the office could know he was in there. He'll think the place has to be bugged by the police. What do you think?"

"Joe-Joe, sometimes you scare me. How do I know that you're not just acting with me?"

"You don't." I mused with a clandestine laugh.

"Aha! There! You see? You just did it!"

"Did what?"

"Hop-scotched!"

"Hop-scotched?"

"Yes, hop-scotched! You went from serious to Bozo the Clown—just like that!" She snapped her fingers.

134

I sensed her relief with knowing I'd call Cooke.

Standing, she leaned down to place Socko on the floor. He headed for the kitchen. Turning her back, she placed her weight on one foot, thrust her left hip toward me and patted her derriere. "Getting back to that tape for a moment, Hollywood—don't worry—as big as it is, Mortensen ain't gettin' a piece of it! After all, I wouldn't want to be responsible for killing the horny jackass!" A ping of sarcasm.

I laughed. "I believe you. But, how about me?"

Putting her arms around my neck and pressing her body against mine, she pretended to scoff. "Huh! If you're just acting with me, you don't deserve it."

She took my hand and placed it squarely against her buttock, then murmured, "But, Hollywood, I don't think you're acting, I think you're very real, so I guess so. You'd better hurry, though, I'm supposed to start the curse tomorrow."

Slightly parting her lips, she moved her mouth to mine. The instant I felt her darting tongue, I answered her kiss, becoming instantly aroused. Picking her up in my arms, I carried her to the bedroom.

Kissing, touching and caressing, we raced to remove each other's pajamas, until at last, our bodies were freed. My hands moved to massage her swelled, firm breasts as my fingers gently squeezed her hardened nipples. Moaning, she took my tongue into her mouth, pulling with her full lips in frantic desire.

I allowed my hand to drift from her chest to the curvature of her stomach, her hips, her thighs. I traced a path over her smooth flesh with feathery strokes, brushing, touching and gently squeezing the softness of her delicate skin, relishing the delicious touch of her writhing body beneath my hands.

In rambling bliss, I kissed her hair, her forehead, her eyes, her cheeks, her neck, finally returning my lips to her mouth as my hands urgently explored her. All the while, her own magical hands were moving to caress me, squeezing, teasing, fondling.

Her impatience impelled her to begin tugging and pulling on me, urging my body above hers, then gently placing me inside of her. Rising and falling in unison with my movements, she shuddered, quivering and shaking. The deep murmur in her throat rose in pitch as her ecstasy quickly reached a crest, together with my own.

Trembling, she fell panting against the pillow while her delicate hands stroked my face and her soft breasts pressed up against me. Slipping her hand to the back of my neck, she nudged my face down to her own and caressed a kiss to my cheek, once, twice, three times. The clean, musky scent of her rich, auburn hair filled my senses with every breath I inhaled as my face rested against hers.

Whispering into my ear, she lowered her hands and placed them firmly on the small of my back, holding me inside of her. Slowly, we began to pirouette our bodies in entwined togetherness until we turned to our sides facing each other. Feeling the satiny skin of her firm, round backside beneath my hands as they rested there, I temperately squeezed her, keeping myself against her.

Closing our eyes to quiet the quake of our love making, we quickly drifted to sleep in each other's embrace.

Chapter 21

The white Cadillac sat empty between two other vehicles in a parking lot next to Calloway Park. Its owner was three blocks away, not the least bit interested in the park or the people playing tennis there beneath the lights. The chill of the late November air didn't affect him as he strode up a driveway toward the parked car sitting there.

Looking skyward, Alex Bigotti thinly smiled to himself. *Good, there's no moon.* Cleverly unlocking the door with a slim-jim, he climbed into the back seat of the Buick and waited. He'd only stay until midnight, then he'd leave and try again tomorrow night, just as he'd done the previous two nights.

At eleven o'clock, the front door of the house opened and a short, stocky man came outside. Bigotti heard a woman's voice call after the man. "Honey, pick up a loaf of bread while you're there."

Acknowledging her request as he unlocked the car door, the man climbed in behind the steering wheel. Starting the engine, the driver turned to look behind him to check for traffic before backing into the street.

Without warning, he found himself looking directly into the ugly face of Alex Bigotti, not more than a foot from his own. Filled with alarm, his body bolted toward the front of the seat, hurling him against the steering wheel while his foot automatically slammed on the brake pedal, jarring his glasses loose to the tip of his nose. Feeling his heart pounding, he tried to scream, but couldn't.

Pushing the eyeglasses back into place, he finally squeaked, "Who the hell are you? What are you doing in my car?"

Deciding to not wait for an answer, the man grasped for the handle and tried to open the door, but immediately felt the strong grip of the intruder holding his arm away from the latch. The man heard Alex say, "Wait. I'm not here to rob you. I merely wanna talk to you."

Still shaky, the stocky man's fear alloyed with anger.

137

"What the hell do you want to talk to me about? Especially at this time of night? If you want to talk to me, then do it properly and at a decent hour. Now, get out of my car and get the hell out of here."

"Hey, I said I wanna talk to you and I intend to do it right now. Believe me, after I tell you what I have to say, I'll go away and leave you alone. Okay?" Bigotti's hold on the man's arm tightened and his cold, malefic stare told the stocky fellow to listen.

"All-all right, but make it quick."

"That's better." Bigotti snarled. "Are you Edwin Cooke?"

"Yes. How do you know my name? And I'll ask you again, who in the hell are you?"

"That doesn't matter. Now then, please turn off the engine and put the gearshift in park. And turn off those damn headlights! Then we'll talk."

Too frightened not to, Cooke did what Bigotti demanded.

Releasing his hold on Cooke's arm, Bigotti leaned back, appearing to relax his mood a bit. "Good. That's better. Now then, what I wanna tell you is—you shouldn't have threatened my friends."

"What? What the hell are you talking about?"

"My friends who bought your building. You lost the damn thing and you should have left it at that."

"Well, I don't think that's any of your business!"

"This makes it my business." Waving it in front of Cooke's face, Bigotti showed him a pistol.

Cooke took a closer look. "Wait a minute—is that what I think it is in your hand?"

Bigotti laughed in a mongrel tone. "Yes, Mr. Cooke—it's a gun. Matter of fact, it's your gun. And these are your bullets, too."

"Oh my God!" Cooke screeched, petrified. "What the hell are you doing with my gun and how did you get it?"

Reaching into his coat pocket, Bigotti ignored Cooke's question and snorted, "Oh, yeah, I almost forgot—

these are your gloves, too."

Raising them to show Cooke, he cackled grotesquely then tossed them onto the front seat. "Please put 'em on."

"No wonder I couldn't find them! How the hell did you get my gun and my gloves? And, for the last time—who in the hell are you?" He clawed at the door handle again.

Bigotti again clamped a strong hand on Cooke's arm and told him, "Tut-tut, Mr. Cooke, that's a mistake—reaching for the door handle. Don't make me use this thing." He waved the gun again.

Cooke's short fuse lit up. "Listen, you big ugly pig, don't you threaten me. You'd better get the hell out of my car before I go in and call the cops!"

"Mr. Cooke, shame on you for calling me such names. And I think you've forgotten that I'm the one holding the gun. And it's loaded." Abruptly twisting his gargoyle face into a wretched look of hatred, Bigotti fairly screamed, aiming the pistol between Cooke's eyes. "I'm tired of being patient with you, Cooke! Now do as I say and put on these gloves or I'll blow your damn brains out! Do it, asshole!"

With a sudden panic stampeding through his chest, Cooke did as he was told, picking up the gloves and nervously shoving his shaking hands into them. He had no way of knowing that the right one was covered with powder residue from shots fired earlier in the day.

Grinning repulsively, Bigotti stated, "All right. That's better."

"There. I've put on the damn gloves. Now then, please get the hell out of here and go tell your friends I won't say any more about the building. Tell them I got their message—you've scared the crap outta me and I know better than to say any more. Okay?"

"Naw! I really don't think I can trust you to keep your mouth shut, Mr. Cooke. You seem to have this hot temper—" Bigotti aimed the pistol at him again.

"Oh, my God! Yes you can! I swear!"

"Cooke, we both know better than that. The minute I walk away from here, you'll buzz right in there and call the cops. I can't allow you to do that."

"I won't, I swear! I got the message—I'm tellin' you that I got the frigging message! Now, for Chrissakes, please leave!" Cooke whimpered.

"All right, Cooke. I believe you did get the message." Bigotti chuckled, reaching for the door latch. Edwin Cooke breathed a momentary sigh of relief. But before he could enjoy it, Bigotti swiftly raised the Smith & Wesson to Cooke's head and jerked the trigger. The sharp crack of the small twenty-two was largely muffled by the confine of the closed car.

Swiftly placing the pistol in Cooke's limp right hand, the killer then slipped from the back seat of the Buick and scampered to a cluster of oleanders for cover. Biding several precarious seconds, he watched and listened. It stayed quiet. Seeing no movement or porch-lights flashing on, he crept away, using trees, parked cars and bushes for cover.

An hour later, Alex Bigotti was drinking a beer in front of the late show when Alice Cooke went out to see if Ed had returned from the store. He didn't hear her screams.

Chapter 22

The next morning, I poured two cups of fresh coffee and handed one to Judy as she shuffled into the kitchen. With her eyes closed, she stretched toward me with a good morning kiss. Before sitting down, she trudged across the floor and turned on the television in the family room just as the morning news was coming on. Pulling her robe tightly around her, she sat on the sofa and curled her dainty feet beneath her. She motioned for me to sit beside her.

****

"Good Monday morning. This is Channel Three News, at six. I'm Bill Carpenter. Our lead story this morning is the gruesome discovery of a Phoenix man found dead in his own driveway, just after midnight last night. Phoenix police received a nine-one-one call from the victim's wife and found a man identified as Edwin Cooke shot to death in his car. He suffered a single gunshot wound to the head. According to his wife, Alice, Mr. Cooke was extremely despondent over recent financial troubles and apparently took his own life."

"We have this report from police lieutenant, Curtis Mattix, who is still at the scene in north Phoenix. Lieutenant Mattix? We understand this is being treated as a suicide. Can you add anything further?"

"Well, Bill, a gun registered to Mr. Cooke was found in the car and what appears to be powder burns were found on his glove. All indications are that he was shot in the temple at very close range, all consistent with a self-inflicted gunshot wound. However, further investigation is still under way."

"Have you found a suicide note?"

"We haven't discovered one at this time, Bill, but as I mentioned, the scene is still being investigated."

"Lieutenant, do you suspect there could have been foul play involved here?"

"We haven't completely ruled that out, Bill, but all indications are—it was a self-inflicted wound."

"Thank you for that report, Lieutenant Curtis Mattix of the Phoenix Police Department."

Turning to face another camera, the announcer caricatured a grim look on his face and continued, "As further developments take place in this case, you'll hear them here first, on Channel Three news. Turning to other news, the Phoenix City Council will be in session today to discuss—"

Judy flicked off the television then looked at me with fear in her eyes. "My God, Joe! That has to be our Edwin Cooke! Do you think this and that tape could be just coincidence? Please say yes."

"Knowing what we know, Girl? I don't really think so. According to that," I point at the television, "he killed himself, but I can't believe it. Yet, if he didn't, how in the world did they do it? I mean, the police found Cooke's gun in the car, and powder burns on his glove."

"Oh, no! I'm getting sick." Judy ran to the bathroom.

Several minutes later, with her slippers scuffing slowly across the floor, she returned. She stopped to pour a fresh cup of coffee on her way back. Her scrubbed face appeared swollen and red around her eyes. Walking over to her, I held my arms around her and she laid her head on my chest as I held her close to me.

Looking totally spent, she mumbled, "I, uh, think I'm all right now. My God, Joe! That was quite a shock. Whew!"

"Sure you're okay?"

"Yeah."

Caressing her hair, I kissed her on the forehead. "Now then, Judy, while you were back there, I did some serious thinking. If we hadn't heard that tape, maybe I could accept the suicide thing with Cooke. But this all ties together too closely. I mean, hearing Tafino tell Mortensen that he'd have no more problems with Cooke convinces me the poor guy was murdered somehow. This whole mess just keeps getting deeper by the day, so I've decided something. There's no way you're going back to that idiot's office again."

Judy heaved a patient sigh. "Joe, I understand your concern, I really do. And I love you for it, believe me. But all this thinking you've just been doing hasn't been done very clearly. Suppose I don't go in and Mortensen rifles my desk and finds that recorder?"

"I really don't care if the dumbass does find it!"

Jerking away from me, she screeched, "Damn, Joseph! Do you realize what you're saying? If he finds that thing and tells those frigging wops, chances are, you'll be finding my body in a car someplace pretty soon!"

That hit me squarely between the eyes. I knew she was right. "So what do we do? Judy, I'm afraid for you."

"Look, it's already six-thirty and we don't have time to re-hash this whole damned get-little-Judy-out-of-this-thing conversation again! Now then, I'm going into that bathroom and I'm going to put on my strongest face and get my ass down to that office before that perverted Mortensen shows up! Let me get through today and after school tonight, we'll go get the damn thing!" With that, she turned and pounded her feet toward the bathroom.

"Hey!" I yelled after her.

Stopping, she turned her face toward me and asked in a soft voice, "What?"

"I love you."

"Thank you, Joe-Joe. I love you, too."

Chapter 23

Maryann burst through the office door and slammed it shut behind her. She rushed through the entry gate to her desk and blurted, "Holy moley, Jane! Did you hear what happened last night? That poor Mr. Cooke shot himself!"

"What? Was that our Edwin Cooke?" Judy feigned surprise.

"Yes!" Maryann exclaimed. "You remember—sort of a short, stocky man, receding hairline, glasses—"

"Oh, I know who he is. I just didn't make the connection to the report on the news this morning." She allowed her words to drift. "Maybe if they'd shown his picture..."

Maryann nervously exclaimed, "I, uh, don't think you heard about what happened in here last week. Huh?"

"I'm not sure. What are you talking about?"

"Well, I, uh, guess I forgot to tell you. Last Wednesday, Mr. Cooke came storming into the office waving a gun around! He actually threatened to kill Jim! My goodness, he was mad!"

Pretending disbelief, Judy screeched, "In this office? When did this happen? Where was I?"

"You, uh, were at lunch. Man alive, it was scary."

"And you forgot to tell me this? How could you forget such a thing?" Maryann looked down at the floor, not knowing what to say.

Allowing herself to enjoy Maryann's embarrassment for only a moment, Judy continued, "Well, I'm sure as hell glad I missed that! What in the world could he have been so mad about? Did I hear them say he went bankrupt or had some kind of financial problems, or something? I only half-listened to the news broadcast."

"Yeah, that's what he came in here all upset about. You know that building on Bell Road? The one we were trying to get mortgaged for him? I guess he blamed Jim for losing it...said that Jim knew it was in foreclosure from the moment he hired us to get the loan and that Jim was in cahoots with Mr. Tafino to buy the place all along. Isn't that ridiculous? But anybody can look in the files for themselves. There's no mention of a foreclosure in there. Jim didn't know anything about it, but he had a hard time convincing Mr. Cooke of that. I swear, he seemed half-crazy and only left when Jim picked up the phone to call the cops."

To now, Judy had had very little conversation with Maryann and preferred to leave it that way. *The less you talk, Girl, the less there's a chance you'll slip up. Let's not allow this discussion to go much further.* "Hmm. Well, from what you're telling me, Maryann, it seems to me that he was most likely distraught over going broke. My psychology professor says that when really bad things happen to people—you know—a sudden death, a divorce, or in Mr. Cooke's case, a bankruptcy, things like that, they always look for a reason why and usually try to find someone to blame it on. In any event, let's hope there's no more of that kind of excitement in here again. Whew!"

Before Maryann could say anything else, Judy sat down and cast a quick glance toward Mortensen's office door. With a sideways look at the other woman, she pointed at the files on her desk and lowered her voice. "I guess I'd better get to work."

But Maryann wasn't finished talking. "Uh, Jane, there's one more thing I'd like to say to you first. This is a little embarrassing, but I have to admit that when you first started to work here, I couldn't understand why Jim had hired you. I suppose it was because I've been here by myself for so long, I didn't believe I needed any help. But, I've got to say, since you've been here, things have gone so much smoother. I believe I owe you an apology. You're really a very nice person."

"Why, thank you, Maryann." *Finish it, Girl!*

Judy shot her a smile, then signaled for secrecy with a finger to her lips and whispered, "Listen, just between you and me, in about two months, I'll have my degree and I'll be going into psychology full time. Believe me, Maryann, when that happens, this place is all yours again."

Maryann's grin was one of relief.

****

Sometime later, Judy found herself alone in the office, sitting at her desk and holding her head in her hands. She had to force herself to be calm. *Good heavens! My nerves are shot! Perhaps Joe-Joe's right. Maybe it is time for me to get out of here.* All at once the office door sprang open, causing her to bolt upright. It was Maryann, returning from a trip to the ladies' room. She looked at Judy. "Jane, are you okay?"

"Yeah, I'm fine. Just have a headache, that's all."

"I've got some pills."

"No, that's okay. I'll be all right."

"Well, when I first came in today, I noticed you look pretty tired. Are you sick?"

At that moment, Judy saw Mortensen from the corner of her eye as he started into the reception area, then hesitated and pulled back out of sight behind the door. It was for his benefit that she explained to Maryann, "No, not really. For one thing, it was a long trip home for Thanksgiving and I got in kind of late last night. That's part of it. But I really think it's because I'm having complications with my period. It's been going on for about fifteen days now. I mean, I normally only go four or five days, but this time, I've had severe cramps, headaches and the damned thing doesn't seem to want to stop. If it continues, I'm going to see my gynecologist."

"Oooo, maybe you should. I have trouble sometimes, too. After a while, it becomes depressing." Placing her purse in the desk, Maryann added, "And say, hon, if you don't feel like working the rest of the day, I can cover for you. I know Jim won't mind if you go. Not if you're sick."

"Thanks, Maryann, but I'll tough it out. However, I think it's my turn to go to that ladies' room." Judy picked up her purse, cupped her hand to her mouth and whispered, "Gotta go change!"

That part was true. On top of everything else, she had started this morning. *Grrr!*

****

From behind the door casing, James Mortensen secretly watched Jane leave. He waited until she was out of sight before he came out and placed some papers on Maryann's typewriter stand. With a scowl, he told her to hold his calls. Then he trudged back to his office, shut the door behind him and took a seat behind his desk. His burdened mind began to wander.

I wonder where she really went for Thanksgiving. Said she was going to visit family. Humph. Probably met some jerk someplace. Wouldn't surprise me if he's right here in town! And, I don't believe that crap about period complications. He immediately empathized. *But, she does look tired... Huh! Most likely from having some young stud wearing her out! I swear—if I find out who it is, I'll have Tony kill him!* Disgustedly shaking his head, Mortensen slammed the pencil he'd been twirling onto the desk.

Changing gears, he couldn't really concern himself too much about Jane this morning. Picking up the newspaper, James Mortensen reviewed the front-page story about Edwin Cooke. He was having extreme difficulty dealing with the guilt caused by the man's death. He slapped the newspaper against the arm of his chair before tossing it back onto his desk. He began to think again.

That stupid, pigheaded Antonio! Ignorant dago! Doesn't he know these losers we set up don't have any proof when they raise so much hell? Crap! I always see to that with the way I handle everything. If he'd just leave them alone, they'd eventually go away! The stupid dumbass doesn't have to have them killed! Sometimes I wish I'd never gotten involved with him in the first place. Addlebrained boneheads, him and his brother, both. What was it he told me when he first came to my office?

Oh, yeah, him and Lou had decided to retire with all their money from their business in New York. They moved to Arizona to invest in real estate. Buy it cheap and sell it high. That's what he'd said. Best way to buy it cheap is with foreclosures and tax liens. That's when he made the proposition. Steer them onto some good foreclosure properties and it will be worth my while. But I swear, except for the money, I wish I'd never met them. And, now, they've gone and killed three people over this! Stupid, ignorant wops!

I will have to admit, though, I can't feel quite as badly about this Cooke character. My God, I thought I was gonna wet my pants when he pointed that damn pistol at me!

With sweat popping out on his forehead, Mortensen wiped it away with a handkerchief. Standing up, he felt a bead of moisture trickling down his body inside his stained shirt. His armpits were soaked. Pacing back and forth, he wanted desperately to find some kind of reason with everything, but all the solutions to these problems evaded him as they usually did. Still pacing, he walked to the window and looked outside at nothing, holding his clammy hands behind his back.

But, God help me! How can I escape this madness? It was so easy in the beginning. Until that old fart, Blake came along—and now, there's two more since him! Hell, maybe it's my fault they're all dead. If I hadn't told Antonio about them in the first place, it probably would have blown over, each and every time. But, I was afraid not to. If it had caused problems for him and Lou, then my ass would have been in a sling!

Still forlornly looking out the window, he meditated to an even earlier time, sighing heavily. *Before they came along, I had an excellent reputation...and I am good at what I do. I know this business inside and out. I follow the market closely—and take a look at all the first-rate mortgages I've placed over the years. If only these foreclosure properties would all go as smoothly as a normal deal. I mean, handling the people and lying to them is easy. And I don't really feel badly about these idiots losing their properties. Hell, if they're not smart enough to be able to hang on to them, then they deserve to lose 'em.*

It's the way Antonio does things that bothers me. And even he's not too bad when everything turns out right. But he should quit. Hell's bells, I've made him a lot of money the past five years! What's he going to do with all of it, anyway?

Sometimes, I don't even think it's the money with him. I swear, I wonder if he's not just playing a game to see how much he can get away with. Oooohhh, Mother of Mary, I wish I could talk to someone about all of this!

Maybe I should tell Margo. He quickly re-thought that. *No, she'd never understand it. Hmm, let me think about this a little more. Hey, wait a minute. I've got it! Jane's studying psychology—maybe I could talk to her. Ha, this is funny! I've heard that patients sometimes have affairs with their psychologists. That's what I'll do! I can boink her and tell her my problems at the same time!*

Silently laughing to himself, Mortensen returned to his chair. Leaning back, he placed his folded hands behind his head and sighed heavily again while he continued his foray into his own mind.

Let's be realistic here, James. You know you couldn't tell Jane. First of all, she hasn't finished school yet and she has no experience. Secondly, you'd have to fire her because you couldn't have your counselor working for you. And you know you're not going to do that.

He bantered with himself. *But, hey, on the other hand, I could call her into my office any time I wanted, under the pretext of needing counseling.*

Momentarily amused, Mortensen's eye caught another glimpse of the newspaper picture of Edwin Cooke resting on his desk. The levity immediately became replaced with the anxiety he'd felt before. Rising once more from his chair, he strolled to the window again and re-clasped his hands behind his back. Looking at the blue sky, he analyzed the entire scenario over and over again.

James, you know you were only kidding and that realistically, there's no way you could possibly ask Jane to be your counselor. Just imagine that seriously for a moment. You certainly couldn't tell her about your involvement with Antonio! First of all, she'd have a total lack of respect for you, and then you'd never be able to have her. And secondly, if Tony found out about it somehow, he'd have her wiped out! Crap! He might have you done in as well for telling her!

All at once, another thought leaped into his mind. Racing to his desk, he frantically studied the appointment calendar. He was instantly relieved when he saw he had no appointments until late afternoon the next day. Wiping the perspiration from his brow again, he pranced back to his chair behind the desk, but changed his mind about sitting down. Instead, he began pacing again, still searching for some genuine answers. *Man alive, I have to talk to somebody about all of this! But who?*

He continued to rack his brain until the obvious nearly jumped up and slapped him. *Hey, wait a minute, that's it! Why didn't I think of that before? Of course! I'll just go out and find a psychiatrist!*

All at once relieved with that decision, James Mortensen looked at his watch. Although looking forward to calling the doctor, for now he merely wanted to be with somebody for a little while. A person he felt comfortable with.

Taking his brown suit jacket from the hall tree, he put it on and adjusted it, making sure he looked calm. Opening his office door, he walked into the reception area and moved past the two women. When he reached the outer door, he turned back to tell Maryann, "I may be a little late this afternoon. I'm going home for lunch."

Holding up some papers to show him, the secretary yelled, "Jim, I have two important messages for you." He was already out the door when she added, "One of them is from a Detective Bearden."

Chapter 24

I raised my voice to Judy. "No, no, no! You're not talking me into it!"

"But, Joe-Joe, I got through today okay and besides, I haven't finished what I have to do in there. I haven't had even the remotest chance to search Mortensen's files in his private office yet."

"Absolutely not. It's far too dangerous."

She ignored me. "Besides, you heard the latest tape. Without the wops around, it should get real quiet in there and we both know the only way we're going to get solid evidence is if we leave the recorder there and I stay to monitor it."

"Judy, we're going to get that damned machine out of there and we're going to get you out of there! That's final!"

"Hey, Mister Grouch! If you keep on trying to have this conversation with me, time after time after time, I *will* quit and you can call Amanda for the bimbo waiting in the wings!"

"I just might do that!"

"You wouldn't dare!"

"You're right, I probably wouldn't. But that doesn't mean—"

"Joe-Joe, please? Just for a little while longer?" Her captivating tilt of the head was there, accompanied by the Cheshire grin. "Incidentally, how are the buildings coming along?"

Sighing, I didn't answer. *Damn! That look makes me melt every time!* Climbing to my feet, I made my way to the bar to mix some mai tais. Taking longer than usual, I eventually meandered back to the sofa and handed a glass to her. "Okay, you win. Let's give it one more week."

"Two."

"All right. But only one week at a time."

"I'll accept that. Now then, I'll ask you again. How is the remodeling coming along on the two buildings? Seriously, Joe-Joe, I'm interested."

"You know where I am with that—we're still at least three months away from putting them on the market. You're just asking me about them to change the subject away from the danger you're in at Mortensen's."

"Ah, yes, my dear... Yore, ah, favorite topic. We must, ah yes, get that poor girl out of, ah, that situation."

"Forget it, Bozo. That's the poorest W. C. Fields I've ever heard."

Laughing out loud, she pinched my nose. "Damn, Joe-Joe, sometimes you are absolutely, frigging hopeless. All this good help you're getting and you don't even appreciate it. Not to mention the good loving you're getting on top of it. Of course, I believe you do appreciate that. But, I'll admit, not any more than me, Big Guy. Seriously, now—"

Bursting into laughter again, her eyes suddenly flooded with tears. Placing her head on my shoulder, she held me tightly and shuddered. "My God, Joe, my nerves are shot. We both need a break from all this. Tell me again—how soon is Christmas?"

Rubbing her back, I said quietly, "Two more weeks, babe."

Standing straight up, she brushed the tears from both cheeks and staunchly proclaimed, "Well, hell, I can last for two more weeks. I'll be okay."

Checking her watch, she said with alarm, "Jeez, I'd better get to school! I'd really like to stay here and be with you, but...Wait up for me?"

"Sure."

Kissing my cheek, she leaped from the sofa and said, "Thanks, Joe-Joe—you're a peach. Later, Hollywood."

****

As soon as she left, I played the most recent tape again.

****

"Hello."

"Tony, it's Mortensen. We got another problem."

"What the hell is it this time?"

"Tony, the police were here today. They were asking

all kinds of questions about that Cooke foreclosure."

"What did you tell 'em?"

"I told them I knew nothing about it until a day or two before the sale. Also told them that Mr. Cooke should have filed his bankruptcy before the sale, not after. Hell, I said, I tried to inform Mr. Cooke that he could have possibly saved his building that way, but I couldn't convince Mr. Cooke of that."

"Good. Did they talk to those two broads working for you?"

"Not really. Just a few standard questions. They pretty much ignored the girls and grilled me."

"Then don't worry about it, you did all right."

"What do you mean, don't worry about it? Tony, I think we better lay low for a while. I mean, I don't think either of us needs any trouble. What do you say?"

"Okay, Mortensen, I agree. Besides, after the holidays, Lou and I are takin' our families overseas for about four months, anyway. During that time, we just don't buy any properties. Now then, if the cops contact you again, just answer their questions like you been doin'. You know what to say—your records show you're clean. I'll call you when we get back." Click.

****

Turning off the machine, I went to the workout room to pump some iron.

Chapter 25

It seemed like *déjà vu*, departing the plane from Yuma again. After deciding to split the Christmas holidays between families, Judy and I were walking to gate twenty in Phoenix for a flight to St. Louis to spend a week with my mother. We'd just spent seven days with Mrs. Carmelle and Nathan, who'd come home from Miami University.

Although Nathan wasn't a starter—he was still only a freshman—he was playing a lot of football with the back-up unit. At first disgruntled with the switch from running back, he was now happy to be a wide receiver, especially with Miami and their vaunted passing attack. His grades were above average and he had a cheerleader girl friend. Enjoying himself at home for the holidays, he devoured everything he could hear about football and weight lifting from Joe, not to mention all the food he could get his hands on. *I'd probably get to talk with Joe even more if Judy would keep her hands off of him and leave the poor guy alone for a few minutes.*

Marie Carmelle was excited during the entire week, rushing around in an effort to make everyone feel comfortable and at home. She was extremely happy. With Nathan in college on a scholarship and Judy having such a good job, Marie's health had improved tremendously since she was now working only one part time job. The money from Judy helped a lot. *And Joe is so nice! I'm so glad Judy found him!*

Judy's voice poofed my recollection daydream away. "Here's number twenty, Joe-Joe. Damn, I just hope I can get used to calling you Owen for a week."

"Hey, Girl, don't worry about it. I've got that cute, round butt of yours covered for that one."

I dropped my hand to emphasize and she instantly shoved it away with fabricated prudence. "Oh?"

"Yep. I told Mother you think I'm such a clown, you've taken the habit of calling me Jo-Jo all the time."

"Clever." She squeezed my arm as we reached the line at the boarding counter.

Waiting for our turn, Judy suddenly exclaimed, "Oh, no, I was afraid of this." Turning toward me, she all of a sudden buried her face in my chest and said, "Uh-oh."

Placing my arm around her waist, I queried, "What? What's the matter?"

Without looking up, she told me. "Mother of pearl, Joe-Joe, I just saw that fat-ass wop walk by and I'm sure he recognized me."

"Tafino?"

"Yeah, who else?"

Our turn in line came up and I handed the tickets to the clerk. Judy stayed hidden. "Has he gone, Joe-Joe?" she mumbled.

Peeking north, I scanned the waiting lounge and the walkway from left to right, then back again. Leaning down, I whispered in her ear, "I think so. I don't see him."

While waiting for the boarding passes to print, the young man at the gate counter regarded Judy's strange behavior. Cupping my hand to my mouth, I quietly told him, "Real fear of flying. I'm trying to calm her down."

Despite his youth, he nodded a worldly expression of complete understanding.

Finally taking her face away from me, Judy stood erect and shook her auburn hair back. Tossing the underside of her locks with her hand, she smiled at the young man and gave a bashful shrug of her shoulders. "Sorry."

Upon seeing her face, the young man froze in place, drinking up her beauty with his young, wide eyes. Eventually aiming the boarding passes in my general direction, he kept his gaze fixed on her, gawking that what-a-lucky-guy-he-is stare. The boy was right on target.

****

While in Springfield, I contemplated calling Robert Tanner in St. Louis, but I didn't dare. I don't really know why. But hell, I even considered it a bad idea to send the guy a card. Why take chances?

To Judy, all the dormant trees, gray skies and drab of mid-winter brown seemed dreary. I tried to explain it away.

"Oh, babe, you should see it in spring and summer when the trees bud, the flowers bloom, the grass turns green, the sky is blue and everything is alive." I promised to bring her back.

Little sister Marsha and Judy were fantastic together. With absolutely nothing in common—Marsha, seven years older, a married housewife with a plumber husband and four children, facing childless, unmarried, career minded Judy, it should have been war. However, personality attractions can be strong. The only two things these women have in common, is the fact they are both female and each has her own distinct sense of humor. But it was enough. They laughed together the whole week, a lot of it at the expense of poor Pete and myself.

Pete Widenour is a good man. A hard-working, loyal husband and devoted father. My appreciation of him for that is only equaled by my appreciation for his relationship with Mother. Totally respectful. "Why, Owen, he's over here all the time, helping me with so many things. You'd have to see it to believe it. And he's so good to Marsha and the children."

But Mother's the same way. If it weren't true about Pete, she wouldn't say it. Following the death of Dad several years ago, her children and grandchildren became her whole world and I'm so thankful for Marsha and Pete being there so close to her. And I don't believe she's ever quite given up on the idea of me returning to Springfield. Thus she mentioned, "Owen, you look so good, so tan and healthy." Of course, it wasn't the tanning salon and workout room, it's, "That pretty young lady you've met. It seems she's as good for you as Marsha is for Pete. Do you have plans to marry and settle down soon?"

Sleeping apart was difficult for both, Judy and myself. On our third day there, Marsha and I traveled to the grocery together. With a knowledgeable wink, she said, "Owen, I'm sure that staying at Mother's is tough. Why don't you and Judy spend a night or two at our place? We aren't quite as prudish as Mother."

On one of those evenings, Judy and I escaped for one of our favorites, pizza and beer. We were sitting across from each other in a corner booth. "Joe, I'm still concerned about that wop seeing me at the airport."

"Don't worry about it."

"You can say that—I don't think he got a good look at you. Besides, you look different now, so I wouldn't expect him to remember you from before. But what if he tells Mortensen he saw me?"

"So what if he saw you with your long-lost older brother, who you haven't seen in over two years, who came to Phoenix to go home with you to Omaha, or Tulsa, or wherever you told him you're from."

"Yeah, but we were boarding a flight to St. Louis. How would I explain that?"

"A connecting flight."

"Which is about a thousand miles east of home—which is Oklahoma City, incidentally."

"Easy enough. My ticket was for there because I had some business to take care of. You just came along for the company before we went on to OK City. Why are we even discussing this?"

"Because I'm concerned about it. I don't want that pervert Mortensen to even remotely think I have a boy friend. He's crazy enough to arrange one of Tafino's "accidents" for you. And another thing, what do I do if he wants to meet this long-lost older brother of mine? I can't introduce you—you'd have to come face to face with him and if he remembers you, our deal is blown sky-high."

"You won't have to. Your brother had to go back to Los Angeles to finalize the advertising contract he sold while in St. Louis. Now then, Girl, you can't even be sure Tafino recognized you, so I don't have the faintest notion that our Mr. Mortensen is going to approach you about all this in the first place. Furthermore, there's no way he could convince Tafino to have this crew-cut crane operating, tow-truck driving fella whack me for absolutely no reason, so can we please dispense with this bullshit discussion?"

Laughing, I reached for the pitcher of beer.

Apparently satisfied with my explanation, Judy

served pan pizza to us both without even a reply. Taking a bite, she suddenly changed the mood and the subject of the conversation. "Oooo, Joe-Joe, I love being here with you. I almost wish we didn't have to go back in three days."

"I agree. And do you know the one thing I've enjoyed the most? Besides being with you of course, is the fact that for a whole week, I've been able to be me."

"Yeah, well, you better make the most of it—only three days left—then you gotta go back to being the other you. And one more thing. You better make the most of tonight, too. The next two nights are back at your mother's."

I gave her Robert Tanner's normal response. "I can do that."

"Oh, do I ever know you can! Oooo! Can I have *shome* more beer?"

I picked up the pitcher and poured. It was our third pitcher, and having drunk much more of it than me and at a much faster pace, Judy was becoming giddy and her words were starting to slur. All at once, the jukebox twanged into a country music drone, smashing the hushed atmosphere and bringing an exaggerated frown to her pretty face. "Oh, crap! Like we needed that!"

Cupping my hands to be heard over the drawl, I shouted, "Hey—that sets the mood. I've got something else to discuss with you before we go home."

"You mean home, or home-home?"

"Both. Since you brought up Mortensen earlier in the conversation, I think it's time we review everything before we go back to Phoenix."

"Oh, crap! The grinch is going to ruin the rest of the—hic—holidaze. Okay, I suppose you're right, Owen. Let's hear it."

"First of all, it's been quiet as hell since that Cooke thing. You were right about that. So, is it really necessary to keep tapping Mortensen's phone?"

She stared past me to an imaginary audience and gave them a wink. "Oh, boy, I shoulda known—this ain't no review, boys and girls. This is the old get-the-girl-out lecture." Then she looked at me and pointed a finger, shaking it up and down. "But, hey, I ain't havin' it this time, Owen. Even if the wops go away for a few months, they'll be back, mark my words. And, neither them nor Mortensen is going to stay quiet with this little scam they've got goin'. They'll kick it up again, so we leave the damn thing in there."

Swigging from her glass once more, she sat it down hard on the table and gave me a silly laugh. "Besides, I love listening to those conversations that Mort-uh—hic—Mortensen has with his psych-all-o-gist." She giggled again. "Turns me on to hear, hic, someone talk about me that way. You don't ever do it."

"Girl, you oughtta choke on that pizza. You're downright nasty!"

"Yep! Nasty is the right word. So what else are we gonna review, Owen?"

"Nothing more, Girl. I think the beer's getting to you too much."

"Oh, come on. I'm more aware than you might think, so tell me the rest. Okay?"

I inwardly smiled. *No sense arguing with her, Joseph. She won't remember it in the morning, anyway.* "Well, with the holidays about over, maybe my sub-contractors will feel like working again and I can get those two buildings completed before the wops get back from overseas. Plus, the house is coming along much better than I expected, so maybe I can finish that at the same time as the buildings."

"I'm beginning to—hic—like the house. But I know you have to sell it. There'll be other houses. So, what's after all that?"

"Then we're ready for phase two."

"Good. But you'd better tell me about phase two tomorrow, because if you don't get me to bed pretty soon, I'm gonna phase out. This beer is makin' me shleepy."

"Hell, maybe we should have brought along a couple of Mortensen's tapes to arouse you." I quipped.

At that moment, as suddenly as it had begun, the music stopped and a hush filled the pizza parlor. Slapping

159

my arm, Judy didn't realize how loud she was talking when she roared, "Pretty damned nasty in your own right, ain'tcha, Galahad! Well, just for that re-remark, I'm gonna make you do it aaaalll night long! Yes sir, we're gonna make love until all of that nashtiness is right out of you! C'mon, boy, I'm—hic—tasskin' you home!"

As she jumped up and began jerking on my arm, I glanced around the dimly lit alcove. One grinning young couple was applauding, but I thought the poor old pair in the next booth was going to have a heart attack. I quickly steered us toward the door.

****

The following morning, we all met at Mother's for a day-long trip to St. Louis. Despite the cold weather and despite having visited all the sights in St. Louis before, she'd never forgotten about the places I'd seen when I was there by myself.

During breakfast, Judy almost choked when Mother stated, "Goodness, dear, you look completely worn out. Didn't you sleep well last night? Well, I guarantee you'll sleep better when you come back over here tonight."

Looking away, I bit my tongue to hold back my laughter until it hurt.

Three days later, we were back in Phoenix.

Chapter 26

Toward the end of the following week, Judy came bouncing through the front door, set the tape on the television and declared, "Hey, Joe-Joe, guess what? No classes tonight. What do you say we go out for a steak?"

Hearing only silence, she said to Socko, "Hey, Bud, where is he? His car is here."

Sitting down on the sofa, Judy picked up the cat and placed him on her lap. She began rubbing his face. Kissing him on top of the head, she tried to hold him to her, but Socko wriggled free. Jumping down, he shook himself, looked defiantly up at her and left. I'd told her many times, "Just rub his face, don't clinch him, and he'll sit on your lap forever."

And she'd always defended, "But, Joe-Joe, he's so cuddly. His face is like a teddy bear."

Standing up to chase after him, Judy saw me enter the house, which ended the pursuit. "Hi, Galahad."

"Hi, Girl. You're here early. Have you been doing what I asked?" I scolded.

"Yessir, Master. Been takin' a different route to work and a different route home every day. Not bein' followed by anyone. Besides, sir, if you'll look at your watch, you'll see that I'm not early—you're late. Furthermore, you're a filthy mess. What have you been doing? Aaaand finally, I don't think Socko likes me."

"Don't cuddle him. Save that for me."

"Not the way you look. So, where were you when I came in?"

"I was in the garage putting away some tools and I look this way because I had to show the carpenters where the walls are supposed to be located and I had to settle a dispute between the drywall crew and electricians. Not only that, the insulators insisted I go up into the attic crawl space and make sure they'd placed the amount of insulation I want. Besides, I clean up nicely. Want to help me do that?"

"Only if you're gonna get naked."

****

It was nearly eleven o'clock when we got back from dinner.

"Thank goodness tomorrow's Friday," Judy said as I unlocked the front door.

Once inside, we checked the Mortensen tape and both answering machines, where one message waited on Judy's line. Sonya's wailing voice pleaded, "Oh my God, Judy, I wish you were home. Please, please, please call me when you get in. I don't care what time it is, please call me!"

Grabbing the phone, Judy frantically pressed the buttons for Sonya's number. Respecting her privacy and anticipating a long conversation, I went to the kitchen to make coffee.

****

"Joe, I've got to go to Omaha."

"Hey, you're crying. What's wrong?"

Cradling herself into my outstretched arms, Judy laid her head on my chest. "This is really bad, Joe. Sonya's mother passed away." Drawing in a deep breath and sniffling, she then told me, "And Sonya's going home tomorrow night. I told her I'd go with her."

"Certainly. By all means."

I held her for several minutes until she eventually pulled away. Reaching into the cabinet for a cup, she filled it with coffee, then shuffled to the table and took a seat across from me. Looking into my eyes, she exhaled a very deep sigh then looked away. With her arms propped by her elbows on the table, she rested her chin in the palms of her hands and for a time, she just sat there, silent, staring at nothing.

Finally, she raised her head and brushed away the last tear before she solemnly rationalized, "Joe, I wish you could come too, but if I really think this through, this is not a good time. If I tell Sonya about us now, she'll really be upset that I didn't tell her before. Well, maybe she would be. But to explain it away, I'd have to let her in on everything. Not a good idea."

Taking her left hand in both of mine, I caressed the

162

back of it with my thumbs. "You're right, of course, and I'd love to be with you, but Sonya really needs you right now. So, just go. And speaking of that, when do you plan to leave?"

"I told Sonya I'd meet her at the airport at six o'clock tomorrow evening. The plane leaves at seven-ten, so I'll have to go straight from the office. And I guess, since the funeral is on Sunday, I should be able to come back Sunday night. But don't worry, I'll take the tape with me tomorrow night."

"Good. Now then, I think you should go over to the dorm and be with Sonya tonight. You can pack what you need for the trip and take it with you. And while you're doing that, I'm going to your apartment to remove the recording tapes there, in case there's something on them we need to hear before you leave. I'll check 'em again sometime Sunday night. It'll most likely be late when you get back, anyway."

"Thanks for understanding, Joe-Joe."

Hugging me, she kissed my cheek, then sighed and told me, "Joe-Joe, isn't it funny how life's irony works good and bad at the same time. The night I first came here, Sonya was in Omaha because they had just discovered her mother's illness. So, if her mother hadn't gotten sick, I wouldn't have met you, but now she's died because of it."

Holding her tightly, I kissed her forehead while I stroked her hair, awkwardly lost for words. Sensing this, Judy provided an avenue for me, away from my discomfort. "Now go, Joe. I won't leave until you get back from the apartment."

Little more than an hour later, I walked Judy to her car. Standing on her toes, she tenderly kissed me, pressing herself against me for a long time. Finally releasing her lips from mine, she put her cheek against my own and spoke softly, "Guess I gotta go now. I'll slip away and call you on Saturday. I love you, Joe-Joe."

Fighting back tears, Judy got into the Thunderbird and reversed into the street. Waving, I watched the car as it disappeared around the corner and she was gone.

****

As usual, James Mortensen worked late on Friday night. Thinking of Jane, he was depressed that she had to go out of town for some stupid funeral. *She could have spent tonight with me instead! Crap! She was just gone for two weeks!*

And try as he might, he couldn't concentrate on the stack of papers laid out on the desk in front of him. *Makes me wonder, too, where she really went for Christmas. Huh! Told me she was going to visit family in Oklahoma City, but I'll bet she probably had some stud waiting for her someplace again. And I'll also bet she really hasn't had complications with her period again for the past three weeks, like she said!*

With his breathing coming in short gasps, James traveled deeper into his preoccupation. *And another thing! Every night at school, she walks into that dorm with that blonde bitch!* He pictured them in his mind's eye. *Always laughing, talking, swinging those asses back and forth with every damn step! Always holding the door open for each other, sharing a cola, passing the bless-ed thing back and forth! If a person didn't know better, he'd think they were a couple of lesbians!* James suddenly bolted upright in his chair. *Oh, no, that couldn't be! Not Jane! Could it be possible she's a lesbian?*

The idea sickened him and not wanting to believe it, he fought against the thought, but for some reason, it refused to leave. Heat flushed in his face and he felt a nauseating lump in his throat. Holding his hand to his chest, James closed his eyes, trying to relax. All at once, his mind invented a portrait of them together and he could see them naked, writhing to each other's touch. Becoming aroused, he groaned, still battling against the possibility, but for him, there was too much evidence for it to be to the contrary.

Therefore, James reluctantly relinquished his struggle against this newly discovered paradox. In doing so, it led him to create a more favorable hypothesis. Scintillated, he impetuously reasoned, *I'll bet that's it! Of course! It's not because I'm married that I can't get with her, it's because she's a lesbian! And, oh my God, if she is one, then that's part of the problem. I'll bet she's a virgin and she's probably never ever been with a guy before!* James Mortensen snickered. *I'll fix that!*

Feeling the strain of his throbbing erection pressing downward in his tight trousers, James reached underneath the desk to adjust himself and upon opening his eyes, they all at once fell upon the picture of Margo on his desk. When he saw her image staring back at him, he experienced a twinge of guilt and disgustedly let go of himself. He quickly placed the picture face down. *Ha! Some marriage. Stupid Margo. Every day, always asking me if I'm going to work late again. Hell, I'm making a damn good living. What else does she want? Like it's my fault we don't have kids! I've heard that for years, too! But, ha! Just wait until I get Jane converted and she gets pregnant! Then when I leave Margo and marry Jane, as young and beautiful as she is, Margo will be as envious as hell and know it's her own fault. Stupid bitch! And will I ever be glad! Always riding my ass about something!*

With the image of Margo's photo removed from his sight, James once more envisioned his beautiful secretary. *Jane won't be like that, I know. In fact, I'll wager she'll be so understanding, she'll let me convert that blonde too, and then convince the little whore to come over so all three of us can go at it together. Holy hannah! Just imagine that! What would you think of that, Margo?* He defiantly reclaimed the picture from the desk and stared at the likeness looking back at him.

James studied her face for a moment. *Margo. Automatic Margo. Jeez, even the sex is automatic! Touch a little here, touch a little there, hop on, hop off, and it's over. Thank heavens it won't be that way with Jane. We'll do it a different way every night! And when Blondie is there, sometimes I'll watch them, sometimes one can watch me when I'm with the other one—then we'll switch! Damn, Margo, just thinking about it makes my balls hurt!* Twisting his mouth into a sordid half-laugh, he gently placed the picture back onto his desk, this time face up.

But now, in addition to his strong erection, James Mortensen was also experiencing a splitting headache. He tried to force himself to think about the work he had to do, but with this new revelation, he had to give up the attempt. *It's no use! I'd like to call that ignorant psychiatrist, but at this time of night, I'd more than likely reach that damn answering machine again! He's never there when I really need to talk to him! And, hell, I wouldn't even have to talk to him if it wasn't for Jane!*

Removing his glasses, James rubbed his eyes and swiped his forehead across the sleeve of his shirt. He placed the spectacles back on his nose then leaned back in his swivel chair. Closing his eyes, he began rubbing his temples with the fingers of both hands. *Ooooh, this is all so unclear! You know, I was pretty happy before she came along! Well, except for those killings. But I didn't need to talk to anybody about that. Those people were all fools and that guilt goes away after awhile! But not this! Yuk! I wish Jane would go away, I mean for good, not merely to some damn funeral! Who was it she said died? A girl friend's mother? Probably that other lesbian whore, the blonde! I'm so sick of all this! I wish I'd never met Jane!*

Tears began to well in his eyes and, holding his face in his hands, James shook his head, and then realized what he'd been thinking. *Wait a minute! Why am I saying that? Of course, I'm glad I met her! She really likes me, I know. And my God, she's so beautiful. That would be such a waste if she really is a—.* He couldn't bring himself to say the word again, so he explained the whole idea away, instead. *No, it's not that! It can't be! It's just that she's confused. She merely needs more time. Time for me to get her away from Blondie, that's all. Then it'll be okay.*

As if in confirmation, James looked longingly through his office door, to the space where Jane's vacated desk desolately rested in the near darkness of the outer office. *I really wish she was sitting there right now.* Suddenly spying the copy machine resting on the table next to her space, he perked slightly. *Hey, if I copy these forms I have to finish, I'll at least be able to stand right next to where she works.* Then he quickly glanced at the clock. *Besides, I'd better get to work anyway. Margo's going to wonder where the hell I am.*

With renewed energy, James walked out of his office with a handful of fresh mortgage applications and flipped on the light switch to the outer office. As he strode toward the Xerox, he lost his grip on the papers and they fell from his hand, scattering to the floor. *Damn!*

Heaving a sigh, he leaned down to slowly retrieve them one by one. He found the last page resting almost out of reach under Jane's desk. Still daydreaming, he paused, envisioning her shapely legs under the knee space. Momentarily closing his eyes, he sniffed the area for a scent of her perfume. Lost in fantasy, James began inspecting the whole underside of her desk and all at once his eyes rested on a small black box hidden in the upper right corner. Curious, he casually inspected it, detecting two wires, one leading from each side. *What in the world is this?*

Tracing them, he discovered one going to the telephone jack and the other to the bottom drawer of the desk. Carefully pulling the drawer open, he cautiously burrowed toward the back. Feeling a strange object, he tugged the drawer open further and saw the other wire connected to a cassette tape recorder. A third led from the recorder to an electrical outlet behind the desk. There was no tape in the machine.

Alarmed and confused, James retraced the wiring to be certain he wasn't mistaken. Instantly feeling hurt, he couldn't conceive of why it was there and it would be Monday before he could ask her. Suddenly going cold, something dawned on him. *Holy cow—wake up James! She's probably recorded all those calls to that doctor!*

All at once frightened and panicky, James ripped the wiring loose and threw the machine across the room. Moisture welled in his eyes. *Oh heaven help me! Now what can I do? If only I knew where I could reach her, so I could ask her about this! There's got to be a reasonable explanation!*

167

Rubbing his forehead, he began to pace back and forth. *But what can it be?*

He thought of a possible solution. *Wait! That's it! She's not taping my calls. She's taping Maryann's to find out if she's a lesbian too.* But his momentary relief instantly disappeared when another thought cropped up to replace that one. He groaned. *Oh, no! It's Maryann. Maybe Maryann put this in here for some reason. Maybe she's trying to blackmail me! But about what?* Except it then occurred to him. *No, wait a minute, it couldn't be her—she's not bright enough to think of something like that.*

James's mind went blank for a time before he decided it could only be one other thing. He chilled again. *Since Jane is a lesbian,* this time he had no problem with the word, *she obviously doesn't have a romantic interest in me and she's been leading me on about that, so it has to be the money.*

He began to cultivate this theory. *Yes, that's it! Jane has taped my conversations with Dr. Stone and she intends to blackmail me because she somehow knows about the money from Tony that's stashed in the safety deposit box. Crap, that's over three hundred eighty thousand dollars! But how could she know about that? Unless she's rifled my desk! Damn me and my stupidity! I shouldn't have kept the damn bankbook in there in the first place!*

He hurried back to his own desk to ensure himself that it was still there. It seemed to be exactly where he'd left it. And untouched. Still, he couldn't help thinking, *Damn! I'll bet she's going to approach me about it soon, too! Then I either give her the money, or she goes to Margo with those tapes of the doctor!*

Narrowing that to be the only possibility, James Mortensen pictured Jane once more in his mind and his eyes stung with fresh tears. *If only she'd said something! Hell, I'd give her the money, merely to have her stay with me! Jane, I love you! Don't you understand that?*

Frenzied, he walked back to the copier, where he absent-mindedly picked up the stack of applications and slammed them hard upon the surface of the table. *I just have to talk to somebody about this! But who? I can't tell Margo, that's for sure! She doesn't know about Jane or the money. I've got to try to reach Doctor Stone.*

Picking up the telephone, James dialed the number from memory and listened. *Just as I expected! His damn answering machine!*

Smashing the receiver back onto the base, James kicked at Jane's desk. Slumping down into her chair, he held his head in his hands and cried. Straining to think, he abruptly felt cold once more. *Oh, no! I just thought of something else! The tapes! Where does Jane keep the tapes?*

Frantic, he began to fruitlessly rifle her desk drawers, already sensing they wouldn't be there. *Where in hell could they be? At her apartment? All I know is I've got to get my hands on those things before she goes to Margo. Margo. Sweet, patient, automatic Margo.*

Scared, James wanted to go home. But he couldn't. Not yet. He had to figure out something. Standing, he gripped his hands together behind his back and began pacing again. All at once, he relaxed, knowing the answer.

I know who I can call. Antonio won't be leaving for Italy for another week. He'll know what to do.

Chapter 27

I learned on Saturday that Judy's plane was scheduled to arrive around midnight Sunday evening, so I planned on changing the cassette tapes in her apartment at eleven-thirty. After pumping iron, I went to the bathroom for a quick shower before leaving the house. Even though talking with her yesterday was good, seeing her tonight will be even better. It's no fun listening to that sultry jazz and blues all by myself. Lost in thought when I backed the car out of the driveway, I didn't hear the telephone ringing in the house.

****

The sound of the phone rudely awakened Socko from his slumber. Startled, he jumped down from the desk and looked back up at the phone in disgust. He obviously couldn't understand why he heard Judy's voice and when she stopped talking, he looked up again. Once satisfied the disturbance was over, he decided to continue his nap back up on the desk, but when he sprang up there, the telephone cord got tangled around his foot. Repugnantly trying to free himself, Socko jerked his paw several times, ultimately pulling the cable from the machine. The cord fell limp to the floor behind the desk as the cat nestled down onto the wooden surface and closed his eyes. He was back to sleep in no time.

****

Wheeling the Thunderbird into her apartment's designated parking space, I shut off the engine, exited the car and sprinted up the flight of stairs to Judy's pretend apartment. When I started to jiggle the key into the lock, I saw that the door was ajar. Frightened, I stepped back and looked around. Cautiously peering through the front room window, I cupped my hands around my eyes and stared into blackness. The only thing I could see was that the drapes had been drawn.

For a moment, I considered getting the manager, but quickly discarded that idea because I didn't want any police

170

involved if something was wrong. Besides, with that being the only entrance, I knew that if someone was in there, they'd have to come out right there, so I went back to the car and waited. I watched the door for a full fifteen minutes.

As the dashboard clock edged closer to midnight, I allowed another full five minutes to go by, even though I knew time was becoming a factor. Judy would be home soon and I wanted to be there when she arrived. Allowing for the time she spent retrieving her luggage, finding her car, and driving time, I calculated she'd be at the house at about twelve-thirty, one o'clock at the latest.

And who knows, I thought to myself as I considered the partly opened door, when I removed the tapes on Thursday evening, maybe in my haste I didn't pull the door tightly closed. But I really didn't believe that, so, despite my reservations, I decided I had no choice but to investigate.

Slipping up the staircase as noiselessly as possible, I was shaking and for the first time in my life, found myself wishing I had a gun. I edged closer to the door and after gathering a bit of nerve, I eased it open a couple of inches. Concealing myself against the outside wall, I reached inside and flipped the switch, turning on the overhead light. Hesitating, I listened. Everything was quiet.

Nervously peeking around the casing, I kept listening, all the while inching my way closer into the entryway. Bravely giving the door a final hard shove, I peered into the room and couldn't believe my eyes. All the furniture was overturned and ripped to shreds, and everything that had been on the walls had been thrown to the floor. Books, lamps, and knick-knacks were strewn everywhere. Quickly stepping inside, I closed the door behind me.

After the initial shock wore off a bit, I stood there staring at the mess and I immediately knew—this was no run-of-the-mill burglary. Somebody was looking for something and there could only be one answer. Obviously, Mortensen found the recorder and more than likely, it was Crew-cut who'd been here, presumably looking for tapes. A brisk walk-through revealed his thoroughness. Both phones had been ripped from the walls, cabinet doors were hanging wide open and dishes were smashed all over the kitchen. Clothes had been thrown from the bedroom closet and even the mattress was cut to ribbons. In addition, the tape recorder was gone. It was the only thing missing.

I also realized there was more to this clutter than merely hunting for missing cassette tapes. It was meant to scare the hell out of whoever found it. *Well, that worked!*

I made one final exploration of the place, searching for I don't know what, when another thought suddenly struck me. *What if that ugly moron is out there right now, waiting for me to come back out?* I felt the hair bristle on the back of my neck as a chill went through me. *Well, I guess I have to find out and I've certainly got to get back home before Judy does, so, here goes!* Slipping back to the front door, I dug into my pocket for the car keys and held them in my hand at the ready. Then I switched the doorknob to the lock position, grabbed the handle, flipped off the light and stepped outside, slamming the door shut behind me, seemingly all in one motion.

Leap-frogging two or three steps at a time, I bounded down the stairs, ran to the car, jumped inside, started the engine, jerked the lever into gear and squalled out of the parking lot, all the while keeping an eye peeled through the windows and the rear-view mirror. Taking an indirect route, I circled several blocks to be sure nobody was behind me. Thankfully, I either lost somebody or I was traveling alone.

Arriving home, I saw that Judy's car was not in the driveway yet, so I hopped out of the Thunderbird, went to the family room and nervously waited for her. While checking through the front window every five minutes or so, nearly an hour crawled by and there was no sign of her. Becoming extremely impatient, I picked up the family room extension to Judy's personal line and pressed the re-dial bar that indicated the number to Sonya's dormitory room. There was no answer. Pacing the floor, I waited for another half-hour, constantly checking my watch every minute or two.

Good heavens! It's after two o'clock in the morning! Where in the hell is she?

Becoming more alarmed by the moment, I went to the office for the third or fourth time to re-check the answering machines for both, her line and mine. There were no flashing lights to indicate that any messages had been left. *Damn!*

I racked my brain, trying to think of something I could do other than simply waiting. There was no way I could reach her at Sonya's home in Omaha to find out when they'd left. I didn't have the number. *How stupid of me!*

Leaving the office, I walked to the living room one more time and peered through the draperies at the dark street. There was not even a hint of traffic. From there, I nervously aimed myself into the kitchen to brew a pot of coffee. As I turned the Mr. Coffee on, an idea finally struck me. I waltzed back to the office and looked up the number for the airport, then reached for the telephone. When I lifted the receiver to my ear, there was dead silence. *What the hell?*

Dismayed, I surveyed the top of the desk, then the phone base and finally, the floor, where I spied the cord laying on the carpet. *How in the hell did that happen?* Grabbing it, I pushed the cable into the answering machine. When the message indicator light started blinking, I hurriedly pushed the playback button and listened.

"Hi, Joe-Joe, it's me. How ya doin', big guy? Incidentally, where are you, anyway? You'd better not be out entertaining one of Amanda's bimbos!" Throaty laughter. "Just kidding! Say, Sonya and I couldn't get a flight tonight, so we're coming home in the morning. I'll barely have time to get to the office from the airport, so I'm going directly there. But don't worry, I'll call you from work and I'll see you tomorrow night. Well, I'd better go…getting away to make this call wasn't easy, believe me! I love you, Galahad!" Click.

For a moment, I just stood there, silently staring at the answering machine. *That's no good, Girl. I've gotta somehow get word to you long before you get to that office!*

Feeling a sense of urgency and not coming up with any immediate ideas, I screamed at myself, "Think, damn it! Think!"

I went to the kitchen for a strong cup of that coffee. The best thing would be to meet her at the airport when her plane arrives. *But holy Hannah, I have no idea what flight, or even what airline she'll be on. Damn, Girl, why didn't you tell me that in your message? Argh! Maybe she didn't think I needed to know.* I defended her.

Dragging myself back to the office with coffee in hand, another idea was finally forming. I reached for the Yellow Pages. Starting with the first one, I checked the airlines one by one, soon discovering that there were no flights arriving from Omaha before one o'clock the next afternoon. She had to be on a connecting flight. But from where? Oklahoma City? Denver? Dallas?

Dialing the airlines again, I inquired about arrivals from those places. There were a total of eight flights, all arriving at various different times in the morning at three different terminals. *Jeez! I can't go to the airport on just the slim chance I'll run into her! What if I miss her? Worse yet, Mortensen knew she was going out of town for the funeral! What if they're waiting for her there?* Then I rationalized that thought. *No. They wouldn't do that. How could they even know she'll be there? Not only that, on the slim chance they do, it would be too risky. Too many people around. Besides, they'd have to have an army there to cover all the terminals. No, if they're after her, they'll wait until she gets to the office.*

I trudged to the kitchen for another mug of coffee, and then it was back to the office again. *Wait a minute! Maybe I could have her paged. But when? Every five minutes? And what if she doesn't hear the page? She could be on her way outta there before I could get word to her. No, I have no other choice. I have to beat her to the office. I'll do that.*

Wait a minute, I can't do that! What if Antonio is there? Even if Mortensen, by some slim chance, doesn't remember me, Tafino might recognize me from seeing me at the airport and not only would that destroy our plan, but Judy and I could then be facing the same danger together! Not that I want her to face this alone, or even at all, but at least, for the time being, they don't know about me.

Okay, let's reserve meeting her at the office as a last resort. In the meantime, I have two more ideas to try.

Picking up the telephone, I dialed for directory assistance in Omaha and requested telephone numbers for everybody named Waverly. There were sixteen of them. *Hells bells, I don't even know Sonya's father's name or address, so I can't even narrow it down! So, okay, do I really want to awaken sixteen people in the middle of the night and scare them to death? And what if Sonya's folks have an unlisted number? Then what?*

My only other alternative was to call Marie Carmelle on the slim chance she knew the number. Or at least have some information to eliminate some of the sixteen names I'd scribbled on my desk pad. But I hesitated because I really didn't want to have to explain to Marie why it was so imperative that I reach Judy at this late hour. That's a last resort idea, too.

Trying to think of any other alternatives, I stood up and marched from the office to the kitchen, on to the family room, then back again with no real direction. Only one thing seemed certain. Sleep was out of the question. There's got to be a way to warn her and to do it without blowing all of our hard work to this point.

All of a sudden, it hit me. I knew what I had to do. Although uneasy about the whole idea, I went to the bathroom to get ready. It was time for me to put to use, what I had learned at Salon Arizona. I had to try and disguise myself so that nobody would recognize me.

Chapter 28

A quick glance at my watch told me that time was running out if I intended to be at Mortensen's office before Judy got there. Looking in the mirror one last time, I told myself that I would have to be satisfied with the make-up job. *For the first time doing it, Joseph—not too bad!*

Scrambling to my office room, I quickly scribbled two notes and shoved them into my suit coat pocket, hoping I wouldn't need them. Next, I rushed to our bedroom and gathered the things I needed into a brown paper bag. Praying I wasn't overlooking anything, I believed I was ready.

My plan was to simply get there before her and warn her so we could both just drive away. Another quick check of the time told me I should have about twenty minutes to spare, assuming she didn't arrive real early.

Slamming the front door behind me, I dashed to the Thunderbird and climbed in. *Whew, I'm glad it's cool today! I sure as hell don't want to be sweating. At least no more than I already am!* I inserted the key and tried to start the car. It ground and ground, but refused to fire. Pumping the accelerator, I tried again. No luck. *C'mon. car! Start, damn it—start!* I turned the key again. Still no luck.

Trying desperately to remain calm, I analyzed the situation. *Let's see, plenty of gas in the tank, the battery is turning over okay and there has to be spark—hell, it's a brand new car! Only a couple of other things are possible—the fuel pump, the fuel filter, or the starter! But, crap, I don't have time to fix anything now and it's too late to call a cab! What the deuce do I do now?* I tried again. Same cold result.

Slamming my hand against the steering wheel, I tried to think. Then, it hit me. *Wait a minute! The van!* It was parked in the garage. I hadn't driven it in weeks. There'd been no reason to. Scurrying to the overhead door, I unlocked it and let myself in before instantly recognizing another problem. The Thunderbird was parked right behind it. Running back to the car, I reached inside and threw it into neutral, then started pushing it backward. When it was near the sidewalk, I hopped in, slammed on the brakes and shoved the gear lever into park.

Quickly exiting the car, I hurried to pick up my paper bag cargo where I'd left it on the driveway and rushed back to the van. With one last look, I scrutinized everything before I climbed inside. *Thank heavens, just enough room to back out.* I jumped into the van.

But when I turned the key, I heard the battery merely grind down. Uhrow, uhrow, uhrow. Then silence. *What in the Sam-hell else can go wrong?* Climbing back out, I raised the hood and grabbed two half-inch wrenches from the pegboard wall. After unhooking the cables, I threw the dead battery onto the workbench.

Hurrying, I galloped to the Thunderbird and lifted the hood. *Thank heavens they're both Fords.* They were the same style battery!

While loosening the battery cable bolts, I heard a vehicle screech to a stop in the street. I looked up and saw a young man in a pick-up truck. He yelled at me, "Hey, old-timer. Need some help?"

In my haste, I had forgotten about my disguise, therefore I hadn't given a thought as to how ridiculous it must appear to see an eighty year old man running back and forth between the two vehicles. But fortunately, this man hadn't seen that, only an old man under the hood. Despite his good intentions, I thought fast and hollered back to him, "No thanks, sonny! I might be old, but I have the body of a healthy thirty-five year old! Been runnin' marathons for years. Watch this!"

Lifting the battery out of the car, I ran back to the van and plopped it into place in the engine compartment. I then surged back to the Thunderbird and shut the hood. I saw the young man still sitting there, staring. Heading back toward the garage, I stopped half-way and turned to yell at him, "Say, sonny, I'm gonna be backin' out of here very shortly and I'm in kind of a hurry. Would you mind pullin' out of the way there a little bit?"

Shaking his head in disbelief, the man continued to gawk at me as he slowly began driving away. Scrambling one last time to the van, I was beginning to believe that marathon running statement.

After getting the battery hooked up in record time, I wiped my hands as best I could on a shop rag and climbed back into the seat. Murmuring a prayer, I turned the key and pumped the gas pedal. When I heard the engine burst into a loud roar, I exhaled a sigh of relief. Then I backed out of the garage. After taking time to close the garage door, I peeled around the Thunderbird, out of the driveway and into the street. Jerking it into drive, I smashed my foot to the accelerator and roared away. I'd lost thirty-five minutes.

While checking my watch every thirty seconds or so, I weaved in and out of traffic, all the while changing lanes and driving at jailbreak speed to make green lights. *Good Heavens please, don't let any cops see me!* I was generally driving like a maniac, but I knew I had to hurry.

****

James Mortensen sat stewing in his office on Monday morning. He feared for Jane's safety and he would just as soon forget the whole incident, even if it meant losing the money he'd concealed. Knowing the truth about Meeks, Blake, and Cooke, he'd pleaded this to Antonio, but the ignorant buffoon insisted that those recordings be found and destroyed. Friday night's phone conversation was still fresh in Mortensen's mind.

****

"Mortensen, there's no reason for you to give up that money you've worked so hard for. And don't worry about anything happening to your little Mexican bitch. I mean, we can't eliminate everybody that gives us a problem. Relax. Just do as I say. Put that damn recorder back where you found it and if that broad shows up on Monday morning, you don't mention it to her. You just send her on an errand, first thing when she arrives. Give her some phony mortgage papers and send her out to the Valley National Bank office in Litchfield. We'll have somebody intercept her there and simply convince her that we know about her little blackmail plans against you and we'll threaten to have her arrested unless she turns the tapes over to us. In the meantime, we'll see what we can find in her apartment. If we recover the stupid things, then all you have to do is merely fire her ass, and whatever the hell else you do, Mortensen, don't even think about getting those tapes back on your own. Got me? Now then, give me her address."

****

Reluctantly, James had given it to him and now, knowing that Antonio's man didn't find the tapes, he walked to the window, wondering how he could avoid sending Jane on the fake mission that Antonio had ordered. Looking outside, James noticed the ugly man sitting in a white Cadillac across the street reading a newspaper, but he gave him no mind. He was too busy concentrating on the problem at hand.

His thoughts remained with Jane as he paced back to his desk. *Oh, sure, she's shown up here all right. Says she came directly from the airport, but as refreshed as she looks, I'll bet she's had a real go-around with that lesbian whore girlfriend of hers! And hells bells, if I send her on the wild goose chase Antonio dictated—I'll never get the chance to get her away from that blonde bitch! But I'd better do it, because crossing Antonio would certainly be worse than that!*

Aversely, James trudged across his office toward the reception area. He had the package of phony papers in his hand.

****

At eight-fifteen, I arrived at the Carson Office Complex, wheeled the van around the corner and headed for the parking lot. I didn't see the white Cadillac parked on the side street, nor the man inside with the crew cut, pretending to be reading a newspaper. I screeched to a stop in a handicapped space, right in front. Not having the proper sticker or plate, I was taking a chance, but I had to.

Remembering my get-up, I eased myself from the van and looked around, trying to appear lost. While scanning my surroundings, I suddenly saw Crew-cut sitting across the street, watching me. With mixed emotions, I stared back, trying to record that hideous face to memory. It wasn't hard to do. I moved my eyes away from him and looked around the parking lot. When I spotted Judy's Thunderbird, I breathed a bit easier and even though anguished, I forced myself not to go look inside her car. Common sense told me that considering the heavy traffic and pedestrian activity, they certainly wouldn't be foolish enough to accost her in the parking lot. *Besides, Crew-cut seems to be waiting for someone.* When I looked at him again, he glanced toward her car, then returned his beady eyes to the newspaper, showing indifference to me.

Attempting to show that same indifference, I reached into the van and dragged the paper bag across the seat. I stuffed it under my arm, all the while telling myself to be careful. *Go slow, Joseph—you're eighty years old. Remember?* Moving in a crouch, I shuffled my feet, wishing I had a cane for emphasis, or even self-defense, if it came to that. Fumbling with my parcel, I finally got to the door and bungled my way into the building. Seeing nobody in the hall, I hastened my steps until I reached the office with Mortensen's name on it.

Saying another silent prayer and heaving a sigh for bravery, I opened it and moved inside. Squinting, I looked around the room and saw Mortensen just entering the reception area from his private office with a package of papers in his hand. He looked up at me and stopped in his tracks. I slowly shuffled toward him and a short, chubby, dark-haired woman seated in front of him. *That must be Maryann.* Trying to appear uncertain, my eyes scanned the room and upon seeing Judy out of the corner of my eye to my left, I thanked God and continued my approach.

Waving a paper in my hand, I advanced toward the mortgage broker, who stared petulantly at the rumpled paper bag tucked under my arm. Looking peeved, he rudely turned away and hurried back into his office, shutting his door behind him and leaving me to the girls. I gave the chubby one a toothy grin. With her shoulders stiffened, she immediately looked away from me and began concentrating heavily on the papers in front of her. That left Judy. Seeing me, she stood up and cheerfully asked, "Hi, there. Can I help you?"

With a shaky hand, I held the paper so that only she could see what was written on it and in my best old-man quivery voice, I said, "Heh, heh, such a pritty one, you are."

"Why, thank you." She smiled.

She didn't know! *Damn! I have her fooled!*

"Yore sure welcome, pritty one. Now, say, can you please direct me to where this place is?" I winked at her and nodded at the paper.

"Sure. Let me see it." Reaching out, she gripped my hand and held it still. She read the first of my two messages:

> Don't say a word—it's me, Joe-Joe. You're in danger. I have a note in my other hand. Take it and read it in the ladies' restroom. Now, point me in the direction of that restroom.

Her mouth dropped open in surprise. I winked at her again. Trying to maintain her composure and keep the strain from her voice, she pointed at the door and nervously said, "Well, uh, all right, sir, go back out that door you just came in and go down the hall." She pointed in the direction she meant. "It's right near the end of the hallway. Okay?" Her voice squeaked on the word "Okay?"

"Thank you, missy. I'll find it." Avoiding her eyes, I stepped away from the counter and shuffled in a crouch to the door. Fumbling with the knob a time or two, I slowly pulled it open. Before leaving, I turned to wink at her again, giving her the thumbs up signal. Once outside, I looked both ways and didn't see anybody in sight. *Great!*

Running to the end of the hallway, I spotted the restroom marked "Women" and opened the door. I made sure it was vacant and shoved the paper bag inside. I then went out the front entrance of the building and shuffled my way back to the van. I climbed inside and nervously waited.

Judy allowed no more than thirty seconds before making her move. Grabbing her purse from her desk, she jumped up and stated, "Maryann, I'm going to the restroom. Be back in a few. Okay?"

"Okay."

Moving sprightly, Judy jogged to the ladies' room and, once inside, locked the door behind her. Rapidly unfolding the note, she read it quickly:

> Don't question this until we've gotten you out of here. Mortensen found the recorder and Crew-cut trashed your apartment. Change into those things in the paper bag. Put the clothes you change out of into the bag and throw them into a trashcan. I'm parked in the back lot. Hurry!

Rushing as fast as she could, Judy ripped open the sack and pulled everything out. Shedding her blouse and skirt, she quickly shoved her legs into the blue jeans and snapped them closed, then slipped the sweatshirt over her head. Cramming her feet into the Reeboks, she didn't bother to tie them. The wastebasket wasn't big enough, so she opened the vanity and loosely threw the bag and her clothes inside. With a struggle, she tugged at the blonde wig, prodding her auburn locks with her fingers until they disappeared under the yellow hair. Quickly arranging the sunglasses on her nose, she studied herself in the mirror for a moment, unlocked the door, and walked out as if she owned the place.

As she exited the restroom, two employees from a neighboring office were approaching from the far end of the hallway. *Oh, oh!*

Afraid they might recognize her, despite the disguise, Judy re-traced Joe's steps out the front door and walked briskly around the corner of the building toward the rear parking lot. Half-way there, she realized that she'd pass within three feet of Mortensen's office window in a matter of seconds. *Damn, Judy! You should've gone around the other side! Oh well, don't slow down now!*

Watching carefully, she caught a glimpse of the man in the white car staring at her. Raising her head conceitedly, she adjusted the sunglasses with her left hand to conceal her face as she skirted past the window and kept going. Peripheral vision told her of movement at the window, but not breaking stride, she looked straight ahead.

****

James Mortensen was standing beside a filing cabinet near the window, reluctantly waiting for Jane to return from the restroom, when he caught a fleeting glimpse of the blonde walking past, breaking his train of thought. Jumping closer to the pane, he watched the girl's back as she moved away. *Good Heavens, that looks like Jane's friend from school. I'd recognize that ass anywhere!* He momentarily forgot about Jane's errand.

Straining against the glass, he examined her up and down as she scurried farther along the sidewalk. *No, wait a minute, that can't be her. That hair is too brassy, too yellow. But that round butt?* He studied her again. *Huh, I guess at that age, all those little round asses look alike. From what I've seen at that college, they're all nice!* James then pushed his face against the window until she hurried out of sight around the corner of the building. He didn't notice the man in the white Cadillac scrutinizing him.

****

Rounding the corner, Judy hastened her step when she saw me sitting at the wheel of the van. Not daring to look back, she walked around the rear of the vehicle, making her way to the other side. Delighted at the sight of the opened door waiting for her, she momentarily hesitated. "What about my car?"

"Leave it. Just get in."

She bounced into the seat and slammed the door. "Okay. Then go!"

Thrusting the van into reverse, I backed out much too

quickly and walloped a light post, which stopped us immediately. Ignoring that, I shoved the lever to drive and sped away, bouncing us both in our seats as I careened into the street. Casting a glance into the rearview mirror, I saw the man in the white Cadillac watching in total disbelief. *That old fart shouldn't even be allowed to drive in the first place.*

For me, I was just thankful that Judy and I were parting company with Mortensen and friends. At least for the time being.

With the tires squealing, I raced to make the green light at the next corner. Flying through the intersection, I was grinning from ear to ear.

With an affectionate smile, Judy looked over at me and said, "Joe-Joe, old men aren't supposed to have tears in their eyes. And they're certainly not supposed to drive this way! Slow down, you old coot!"

It was good having both of them back—Judy and Bozo.

Chapter 29

James Mortensen waited nearly two hours before making the dreaded call to Tafino, but spurred by his fear of the Italian, his reasoning eventually impelled him to reach for the telephone.

"What the hell do you mean, she's gone?" Antonio bellowed.

"Just that, Tony. She told Maryann she was going to the restroom over two hours ago. We've searched the whole building for her, but she's just plain vanished. She didn't leave in her own car, though. It's still here."

Tafino blew a disgusted sigh into the telephone. "Mortensen, here's what probably happened. She came in there this morning and saw that recording crap completely rearranged, most likely because you didn't put it back the right way. Then she got scared and high-tailed it outta there, and if this broad is as intelligent as you say she is, of course she wouldn't leave in her own car. She left it there to throw you off her trail and to make you think she was still close by. She'll probably come back for it later. Now then, trust me, when she gets a look at that apartment, I guarantee those pretty little panties you're so anxious to get into will be frightened right off her sweet, little ass and you won't ever see or hear from her again."

Filled with emptiness over the fact that Jane was more than likely gone for good and more than ever wishing he'd never called Antonio about her in the first place, Mortensen knew he couldn't say anything about it, so he gave the only meek reply that he could. "Yes sir, Tony. I'm sure you're right."

"So, Mortensen, I want you to forget about that blackmail bullshit and for your own sake, if it's still in there, make damn sure you get that recording crap out of that office! Burn it! Understand?"

"Yes sir, Tony, but—"

"Don't interrupt me. Now, get this straight—and I am serious about this—we've had a good thing in the past and we've both made a pile of money. The only thing saving your ass is the fact that you're damn good with the pigeons, otherwise, somebody else would be doin' your job from now on. Got me?"

Sweating profusely, the mortgage broker understood completely. He knew he'd be dead. "Yes sir, Tony. I understand. Believe me, I understand."

Crustily barking into the mouthpiece, the gangster continued his tirade, "And one more thing—on Friday, Lou and I are heading for Sicily. We're gonna be gone for three or four months. During that time, I want you to stay at home and quit chasin' skirts. I want you to get your act together and be ready to do some business when we get back. And finally, if that Mexican bitch does happen to contact you about those tapes, or blackmail, or anything else for that matter, you'll have my number over there and you get a-hold of me right away. Do you understand that?"

Mortensen fidgeted in his seat. Loosening his tie, he unfastened the top button of his shirt and mopped the perspiration away from his neck and forehead. "All right, Tony. I understand. Don't worry, I'll do just as you say."

Upon hearing only raspy breathing through the receiver, he swiped his face again with the already damp handkerchief. Extremely nervous, he was desperate to atone and lighten the hoodlum's mood. "By the way, Tony, you and Lou enjoy yourselves over there and I'll be ready when you get back, I promise. In fact, I'm gonna start looking for other properties right away. If I find something really juicy while you're gone, should I call you over there about it?"

"No." Click.

Mortensen didn't hear the second click of the extension phone.

"Lou, we may have a problem. Who knows what the hell that redhead has on those cassettes? We hafta get a-hold of those tapes and see what she's up to. I should be gettin' a report from Bigotti soon. When I talk to him, I'll sic him on her trail and I'm also gonna have him stick to Mortensen like glue while we're gone. Maybe that'll lead us to the redhead."

Louis knowingly smirked as Antonio finally broke into a grin of his own. "In the meantime, let's you and I have a drink. We gotta celebrate gettin' outta here on Friday."

Twirling the cigar, Louis nodded and slowly rose from his easy chair. With a gimpy walk, he went to the liquor cabinet.

****

Taking our fresh coffee from the kitchen into the living room, Judy and I sat on the sofa. I told her about the stress of last night's events, from the time I went to the apartment, right up until the moment we drove away from Mortensen's parking lot. "So, Girl, that's about it. Am I ever bushed? Whew! And relieved."

Playing with my hands in hers, Judy bubbled, "Joe-Joe that took guts. And do you know what? You are going to be so damned cute when you do get old. How long did it take you to create that get up, anyway?"

"About three hours, more or less."

"Pure genius. Honest to God, I didn't recognize you. And I hope you know— you probably got there just in time. According to Maryann, Mortensen was just getting ready to send me on some kind of errand, clear out past Litchfield Park."

I squeezed her hands. "Not to frighten you, precious, but that might've been your last one. I believe I got a look at Mr. Crew-Cut, waiting outside the building in a white car."

Judy shivered. "Yeah, I saw him, too."

A ghostly silence followed and we merely sat there for what seemed a very long time, simply appreciating each other and staring into each other's eyes. Finally, Judy broke the spell by asking in a soft voice, "So, Hollywood, what do we do now?"

"Well, this is where I usually give the let's-get-the-girl-out speech, but I know better, so I suppose we re-think some things, make a few adjustments to the plan and continue to go after 'em. I've got some ideas we can discuss later, but for right now, we've got two vehicles to get rid of. Pronto."

187

"What can I do to help?"

"Call Avis to pick up your car, then help me get this stuff off my face."

Chapter 30

Antonio Tafino stopped swirling the scotch in his glass when the telephone rang. He reached out and picked it up. "Yeah?"

"It's me, Bigotti."

"What the hell went wrong over there today?"

"Don't know. I watched that redhead's car for over three hours and never did see her come out. Then some tow truck came and towed it away."

"Did you follow it?"

"Of course. They took it to an Avis rental lot. I figure she had it leased and dumped it back on 'em. And I'll bet if we could see the rental agreement, it would show that apartment as her address, but you wanna hear somethin' strange, boss? I don't think that broad really lives there."

"What's that supposed to mean?"

"Just that. There was practically no clothes in the place, dust everywhere, no dirty dishes and there was nothin' in the fridge."

"Humph. Okay, if she doesn't live there, she obviously lives someplace else, but she must have rented that damned apartment for some reason. Might be a good idea to watch the place to see if she goes back there. Anything else?"

"Yeah. I drove back to Mortensen's and went inside his office. I pretended to have the wrong place, but I took a good look around. The only broad in there was a chubby, little frump with a butch haircut, so I figured I'd better check out the ladies room, just in case. It was empty, so I searched around in there and guess what I found? The clothes the auburn broad was wearin' this morning were stuffed in the vanity along with a paper bag. Then I remembered somethin' real peculiar that might explain a lot of things. Ya see, boss, I saw her go in this morning, at least from your description I believe it was her, but I never saw her leave and I was watchin' both, the front and back doors, real careful."

"All right—what's the point—get to it," Tafino impatiently huffed.

"Sure. Lemme finish. About fifteen minutes after the auburn broad got there, some old guy showed up and went into the building carrying a big paper bag. When he came back out, he didn't have it with him. I didn't pay much attention to him at the time, even when he didn't leave right away. Then, after another ten minutes or so, some brassy blonde came chargin' outta there, got in his van, and they left together like a bat outta hell."

"Bigotti, just what in hell does this soap opera have to do with anything?"

"Well, boss, after findin' those clothes and puttin' two and two together, I figure it was the auburn broad in a blonde wig who left with that old man."

"I'll be damned! Yeah, I see what yer sayin'. So, did you get a good look at this old guy?"

"No, I told you I didn't pay much attention to him, but he's drivin' a light blue Ford van with a dented up rear bumper. I'll recognize it if I see it again. So, whaddya want me to do next?"

"We gotta find that broad, Bigotti! Do like I said. Keep watchin' that apartment. And somethin' else you could do is go out to the university and try to dig up some information on her. Mortensen said she's a part-time student out there. But, Alex, don't make yourself obvious when you do that."

"Yeah, yeah, sure, boss. What else?"

"Keep your eyes peeled for that old man. You just might spot him someplace. And, Alex, don't pester the old fart. Just let him lead you to the Mexican broad. Incidentally, while you're travelin' around, keep a look-out for her as well; ya never know—you just might run into her by accident."

"Want me to take care of her after I get those tapes back?"

"That depends on what you can prod out of her. Who knows, it just might be she really was merely tryin' to cash in on Mortensen's bucks and maybe she backed out when she realized he'd found that recorder. And if that's the case,

Alex—the blackmail thing with Mortensen—then just get the tapes from her, threaten to expose her, and leave her be."

"What if it's something else? Something that could cause a problem for you and Lou?"

"Then get rid of her."

"Consider it done. Anything else?"

"Just one more thing. While we're away, I want you to watch that damn Mortensen like a hawk. Who knows, maybe he can lead us to that broad. But, more importantly, I want to know everything that dumbass does while we're overseas because if he continues bein' a pervert, we may have to eliminate him, too."

"You got it, boss. Have a good trip."

"We will, Alex." Click.

****

It was nearly midnight before Judy and I managed to crawl into bed. Lying close to each other, we were both too tired to sleep. After talking everything through, we'd gotten a lot of things decided. Needing several more weeks before my properties would be ready to sell, and with the Tafino brothers thankfully out of the country for a while, there wasn't much that Judy could do for the time being. Plus, there was no way she could continue her schooling at Arizona State, yet being so close to graduating, it was also foolish to consider having her drop out altogether.

Propping my head onto my hand and leaning on one elbow, I looked into her face and mentioned, "Vanderbilt has one of the best law schools in the country."

"Vanderbilt? Where's that?"

"Nashville, Tennessee."

She bolted upright in the bed. "Holy smoke, Joe-Joe, that's clear across the country! I mean thousands of miles away!"

"It's about three and a half hours by plane and you can fly home every week-end. Or, I can go there."

"That's foolish, Joe-Joe! And probably very expensive." Biting her lower lip, she threw me an anticipatory look. "What about something closer?"

191

I stared intently into her face without bothering to answer. She studied my gaze for a moment and with a pout, she touched her hand to my cheek and quickly relented. "Okay, okay. Every weekend? You promise?"

Just like that, it was settled. "I promise."

"Good," she said, "and count on me being here, too. After all, I don't want you calling Amanda for a replacement. Which reminds me. About that wig you had in the bag? Just because I keep on telling you to get a big-busted blonde, it doesn't mean you have to try to turn me into one."

"Hell's bells, Girl—that was easy. You've already got half of that combination. All I had to do was provide the yellow hair."

"Shreeeek. Are you telling me that *they're* too big, too?" Pounding her small fists into my chest, she continued to screech while I laughed until my sides ached. And when the laughter subsided, I pulled her to me and kissed her generous lips, gently at first, then deliberately blending into a passionate urgency, ending with us making love.

Much later, after she'd fallen to sleep, I raised my head to look at her. Lovingly kissing her cheek, I discreetly told her, "God, I'm gonna miss you, Girl."

Two short days later, after a tearful goodbye at the gate, she boarded the plane and was gone.

EPILOGUE
PART ONE

James Mortensen sat in the Datsun, waiting for the light to change green. He watched the pedestrians on both sides of the street and strained his eyes to look at the occupants of the other vehicles on the road.

She has to show up sometime. I don't care what that ignorant Antonio says. He can't stop me from looking for Jane. I've got to know why she did that to me when all I ever wanted was to have the chance to be in love with her. I'd have done anything for her. I still would! And good, old Doctor Stone. He thinks I should forget about her, too. What was it he said? Oh, yeah, I remember!

"After all, James, think about everything. You have a good, solid marriage, a highly successful business and you should be very happy right now. Sometimes when we reach this age, we want to recapture some of our youthful adventures, or we want to pursue them now, if we didn't have them when we were young. Believe me, this urge will pass. I know. I experienced it myself. So, I want you to listen to me; I'm trying my best to guide you through this confusing part of your life. Trust me, I've come to learn your personality and if you should actually involve yourself with this Jane, or any other young lady, you'd be so guilt-ridden afterward, you would most likely have to relieve that guilt by confessing to your wife and you could wind up all alone. Please let me help you overcome these temporary impulses and you'll be far better off in the long run."

None of them seem to understand that I can't forget about her. I just can't! So, I'm going to watch everyone everywhere, day and night until I see her! Hell, even if I'd spot that lesbian blonde, it could help! When she hears how much I care for Jane, she'll have to tell me where she is!

Suddenly disgusted with the melancholy nature of the music the car radio was playing, James reached over and turned it off. Then, he tried to reason everything further. *I could go out to the university and look for her, but Antonio and Louis probably have spies all over the place and I wouldn't want them to think I'm doing anything other than what Antonio told me to do. And speaking of them, they'll be back soon. Then I might have to stop looking for Jane altogether.*

The insistent honking of the car behind him jolted James back to the present. Realizing that the light had turned green, he accelerated forward, heading home.

****

Seated in the white Cadillac, Alex Bigotti watched the blue Datsun, a couple of cars ahead of him. Every night he followed James Mortensen from his office and except for an occasional stop at the market, Mr. Mortensen always went straight home and stayed in all evening. Sitting there, Bigotti again witnessed the mortgage broker straining his gaze back and forth as if he was searching for someone. Hoping there might be a tie between Mortensen's awkward behavior and the auburn haired chick, Bigotti scoured with him, wanting to impress Tafino with a good report.

But so far, the only thing to account for is Mortensen's goofy habits of staring at people everywhere he goes. He certainly hasn't done anything out of line. Hell, maybe the horny pervert just gets his kicks from watching all this young stuff prancing around!

Alex hadn't had any luck in spotting the van either, but he had no way of knowing that it was now white and sported a shiny, new bumper. Feeling bored, he looked forward to the boss's return. In the meantime, when the traffic began to move in front of him, Alex continued his pursuit.

****

"Lou, I figure we'll head back around May 30th. I don't wanna leave all that real estate in the hands of that property manager too damn long! Besides, we've seen everybody here and I'm itchin' to get back to work. I certainly hope that stupid-ass Mortensen has his act together. He ain't been the same since he met up with that Mexican broad. Let's hope Alex has her outta the picture by the time we get back. If not, we'll hafta find her and get rid of those tapes, then get her the hell out. Then, Brother, it's back to business, as usual." Antonio Tafino laughed.

Lou twirled his cigar, and with a thin smile nodded his approval.

****

Judy Carmelle sat alone in her dorm room. Rubbing her eyes, she stretched and yawned. She was tired from the long hours of studying. As she often did, she allowed her mind to drift to a vision of Joe and his soft, green eyes, and the memory of his gentle touch. She anticipated being with him on Friday night. This week, he was coming to her. Smiling to herself, she fleetingly recalled the disappointed look on the young man's face in the library earlier in the day when she'd answered his question, frankly and bluntly. "No, I'm sorry, but I'm very much in love with someone and I'm totally committed to him." *I'll give these Tennessee boys credit, though—they are persistent. But I've got my Joe-Joe.*

Looking back on everything, with so much having changed in her life these past eight months, she often found it difficult to grasp. Yet, she relished every moment, every event, since the first time she'd laid her eyes on the temperate man with the tanned body in the leather jacket. Beaming to herself, his presence in her mind rejuvenated her energies and she returned to her task at hand.

****

Feeling alone and sometimes frustrated, I buried myself into finishing the house, while riding herd on the sub-contractors to complete the buildings. Long days ground into weeks and I missed Judy with all my heart. Weekends were filled with updating and lovemaking and nearly every Sunday night, we shared another sad farewell. Because of her heavy schedule of classes and my anxious pursuit of completion of my work, there were a few times when we were forced to miss our rendezvous, which made the next one even that much better.

But as time crept by, the desert bloomed, the trees came alive and the temperature began to rise in Phoenix.

With spring, the hours of daylight increased and the days became longer until near the end of May, I had over one and one-half million dollars in the bank and soon, no place to live.

Plus, just as important, in two weeks, Judy will be graduating, she will come home, and my world will be right again. I can't wait!

PART TWO

D. A. Williams

Chapter 31

On the same day I signed the papers to close the house sale, I telephoned Judy that evening. "Girl, you'd better hurry up and graduate. We're ready for phase two and I need you. Incidentally, don't come home this week-end, we don't have a place to live."

"Then, mister, I suggest you call Holiday Inn. And you might consider looking for another house as well. After all, I'll be back for good in two weeks."

"Ho there, hang on a minute, Girl. I thought I was the boss of this operation."

"Like I told you before—not when I'm right. Besides, I'm not bossing, Joseph. I'm merely inputting."

I passed up the opportunity for some type of japing remark and simply told her, "Okay, but despite your in-put, I already have a plan."

"And, what is that, sir?"

"We still have thirty days before we have to vacate, possibly more if we need it. And this time, I don't want a house in the name of Joseph Bowden or Owen Hunter. Now then, I'm coming to your graduation in two weeks, then we're going to Indianapolis for a few days and we'll decide about another house when we get back here. We may just rent."

"What's in Indianapolis?"

"The beginning of phase two. So, what do you want for a graduation present?"

"Are you supposed to ask me that? Aren't you supposed to surprise me?"

"Call me strange, but I'd prefer to make you happy with what you want rather than surprise you with something you don't. Besides, I do have a surprise for you, but it doesn't count as a gift."

"Don't tell me. Let me guess. A Corvette?"

"Is that what you want?"

"Yes. But I don't want a new one—they're kind of ugly. I want a 1963 Split Window Coupe. Or, a convertible. And I also don't want you to get it. With this piece of paper

I'm gonna receive in two weeks, within two years, I'll get it myself. You can get me a new blonde wig to replace that tacky thing you gave me before. Now then, what's your surprise?"

"Your mother and Nathan are coming with me to your graduation. What color Corvette do you want?"

"Really? You're bringing them? You are so sweet! That's nice, Joe-Joe. I mean really, super nice. I want a red one."

"Red will clash with your hair."

"Not if I'm wearing that new blonde wig! See you on Friday, Hollywood." Click.

****

On the day of Judy's graduation, Marie, Nathan and I stood up and proudly watched as Judy glided to the podium to receive her diploma. Beneath her cap, her dark auburn hair shone brilliantly in the afternoon sun as she faced the university president to accept both, his handshake and her scroll. Walking away, she held the parchment in her right hand and raised it in an exalted signal of triumph as she searched the audience for us. Eventually, she spotted us waving frantically to her and she held up the diploma again before moving to her seat with the other graduates.

Turning to Marie, I wrapped my arm around her shoulders. Seeing the proud tears in her eyes, I nodded toward Nathan and said to her, "Just think, Marie, in another three years, we get to go through this again."

Holding a tissue to her eyes, she nodded.

With a wide grin, Nathan spoke up, "Yeah, but there'll be one big difference next time, Joe."

"Oh? How's that?"

"I want my Corvette to be black." We all laughed and when the ceremonies concluded, we left to celebrate with our new graduate.

****

Spending the next three days with Judy's family, we rented a van and toured the Ozarks, ending with a must-see visit for Marie to Graceland. After Judy and I said good-by to her and Nathan at the airport in Memphis, we returned to Nashville and exchanged the van for Judy's red Corvette.

Heading north on Highway 31E, we drove through Gallatin, and then wove our way on the two-lane road to Glasgow, where we stopped for a late lunch. Continuing from there, we took several pictures along the way as we leisurely motored through a lot of other small towns and magnificent country scenery until we reached Louisville that evening.

After staying in Louisville overnight, we left mid-morning and continued our northerly trek on US31, arriving at Columbus, Indiana, in early afternoon. Making a spur of the moment side trip on State Road 46, we aimed her shiny sports car toward Brown County State Park for a picnic lunch. That evening, we checked into the Speedway Holiday Inn in Indianapolis, using the old stand-by, Phillip Patterson, this time as Mr. and Mrs.

The next morning, following an early breakfast, we ordered a supply of business cards from a fast service print shop, where I paid a premium for four-hour service. We spent the balance of the morning at the Indianapolis Motor Speedway Museum and by two o'clock that afternoon, I was walking into the office of the NAACP. Judy had taken a cab downtown for a shopping spree.

As I closed the door behind me, the young lady seated at the reception desk greeted me. "May I help you, sir?"

Handing her one of the new cards, I introduced myself. "Yes. My name is Phillip Patterson. I'm a free-lance writer and I've been talking with the Association of General Contractors about an article I want to write. The publisher of their quarterly news magazine and I are working on a project that I'd like to do for their next publication. I'm interested in talking with one of your representatives in an effort to determine who the top three or four black general contractors in Indianapolis might be. I'm intending to do an article featuring them and some of the projects they've completed."

Looking dubious, the young lady accepted my card

and scrutinized it. "I see. You'll want to talk to George White." Picking up the intercom, she deliberately announced me to him, all the while looking me over. She then escorted me to his office.

A balding, middle-aged black man moved from behind his desk and extended his hand. "Good afternoon, Mr. Patterson. I'm White, but as you can see, I'm also black."

Laughing with him, I commented, "That's more than I can say, Mr. White. See there, you have me at a disadvantage already."

Keeping his warm smile in place, he queried, "How can I help you, Mr. Patterson?"

Repeating my earlier tale, I concluded, "Mr. White, it's my opinion that with such an article, not only would exposure for the black community be good, I believe it would benefit the entire construction industry. It would afford more opportunities for the quality black contractors and sub-contractors, as well as expanding the number of reliable firms on the bid lists of the white contractors now in the association. Personally, I fail to see how this continuing segregation benefits anyone and if there are quality performers out there, they should be recognized and rewarded for their efforts. Perhaps with my article, everyone can gain something; not only additional monetary opportunities, but also a valuable lesson as well. What do you think, Mr. White?"

"I cannot agree more wholeheartedly, Mr. Patterson."

When I left, I had in my possession, the names, addresses, and a lot of information about the top four companies.

****

That evening, Judy and I enjoyed a home cooked supper of Salisbury steak, mashed potatoes and gravy, whole kernel corn, and all the trimmings, at Hansel & Gretel Storybook Restaurant. While we were eating, she leaned across the table and asked in a hushed voice, "Tell me something, Joe-Joe. Why are you insisting that the contractor you're going to impersonate be a real person? And why a black man?"

"Quite simple, my dear. Back in Phoenix, we'll need all the financial information of a real person to back up our operation and I'm choosing a black man for the protection of the real contractor. Consider this. Suppose that something in our undertaking goes sour and Tafino discovers there's a quote, "real contractor" located in Indianapolis and he decides to send one of his cronies to wipe him out. When Tafino's henchman sees that the "real contractor" is a black man, he'll know it can't be me. So, chances are very good they'll leave the "real contractor" alone."

"Huh. Pretty clever, Hollywood. Say, this supper is delicious—don't you think so?"

I did and I told her so.

****

The next morning, Judy and I traveled across town to Southeastern Avenue, then east on Prospect Street to the location of Worthington Construction Company. Waiting in the car, Judy opened a book and began reading, while I went inside. I approached the black secretary, making a mental note of her nameplate. "Excuse me, Joyce—is Mr. Worthington in, please?"

"Is he expecting you?" she asked, somewhat suspiciously.

"No. I was given his name by Mr. George White, from the NAACP office. I'd like to interview him for an article—"

Interrupting, she blurted, "Oh yeah! Mr. White called us yesterday afternoon. You're the man who's gonna do the story."

"Yes. That's right."

Moderately anxious now, the young lady picked up the intercom phone. "I'm sure Mr. Worthington will see you, Mr....?" She gave me a blank look.

"Patterson. Phillip Patterson." She then announced me.

A dark complexioned, middle-aged black man greeted me as he came through his office door to the reception area. "Yes sir, Mr. Patterson—come on in."

Closing the door behind us, Reginald Worthington ushered me to a leather chair. "Please, sit down, Mr. Patterson, sit down."

Seating myself, I reached into my briefcase for a pencil and notepad as Worthington marched to his own chair behind the desk and commented, "I understand from George White that you're wanting to put together a story for the AGC quarterly. Quite frankly, Mr. Patterson, I doubt if they'll be interested. That organization has shunned the black community for a long, long time. I know. I've tried to join several times. Lots of excuses those folks have, but we all know the main one."

"Well, that's why I plan for it to be more than a story, Mr. Worthington. In addition to what I believe will be interesting reading, I hope it opens some eyes."

"And what is your real interest in this, Mr. Patterson?"

Oh boy, Joseph, this guy has a hard-on and wants to play hardball. Just remember what Daddy always told you. "Son, if you can't dazzle 'em with your brilliance, then baffle 'em with your bullshit!"

Looking Worthington squarely in the eye, I told him, "Just this, Mr. Worthington—it seems that my article will make winners out of everybody concerned, me included. First of all, as you've just told me, you've tried several times to join the fraternity that controls the construction industry in this town and you've failed. Why? Because you're black. And you believe that's unfair. Well, sir, it just so happens, so do I."

I pictured Robert Tanner's deep dimpled face in my mind's eye and then proceeded to rake Mr. Worthington over the coals. "For your information, some of my best friends are hard-working, law-abiding, truthful people, who just happen to black. Not only that, Mr. Worthington, I've done some research on your company and not only do you do quality work, you are also a hard-working, law-abiding, honest person, so why shouldn't you benefit from that by getting more work? I believe you should, and with my article, you will. Furthermore, this will also benefit the association by bringing to their attention, the additional bidding competition and quality workmanship that firms like yours can provide, so they, too, can also make more money. For myself, I intend to command a high dollar for the article, so I benefit as well. Any other questions?"

"You know, Mr. Patterson, I like your style. Truthfully, do you think this article will work?"

"Yes, sir, I do."

"Then tell me how I can help."

I outlined the layout for my intended editorial, explaining that it would include pictures of completed projects, budget guidelines and Critical Path projections. During my discussion with Mr. Reginald Worthington, I casually delivered a complete fabrication. "Incidentally, I mentioned this article idea to my accountant and he tells me you're a client of his as well."

"Oh?"

"Thomas Payne?"

"Mm, no. We use a big eight firm. Arthur Andersen and Company. I usually deal with Samuel Blumberg over there. Is Mr. Payne an assistant of his?"

"No, he's with another firm altogether. Huh, that seems strange. Oh well, maybe I'm mistaken. I probably misunderstood him."

I hastily changed the subject back to my reason for being there, and not trusting my memory to absorb and retain everything, I busied myself with covertly jotting down the names of Joyce, Samuel Blumberg, and Arthur Andersen And Company. However, when I asked the appropriate construction questions, I did rely on my memory for those.

Following our meeting, I left Reginald Worthington's office loaded with pictures of completed projects, details of his company's beginning and subsequent growth, as well as a list of his major sub-contractors.

The next day, taking the time to visit all the other builders given to me by the NAACP, I discovered that, just as

I'd hoped, each of them had been contacted by an industrious George White.

Following the same format I'd used with Reginald Worthington, I quoted the same story about the fictitious accountant, Thomas Payne, and then scribbled the correct information into my yellow tablet as I learned it. After collecting more photos and history from each contractor, Judy and I went to dinner and then to our motel room to piece all of our information together. With her help, I managed to scratch out an article that seemed worthy of publication.

The next morning, I headed for the Association of General Contractors' office on Meridian Street with every intention of selling my story for their next publication. Upon delivering copies of everything to the assistant publisher, he relished the idea. The article would be out in two months.

The following Monday, Judy nervously telephoned the office of Arthur Andersen and Company. "Hi, this is Joyce, with Reginald Worthington's office. May I speak with Samuel Blumberg, please?"

"I'll connect you with his secretary."

"Mr. Blumberg's office," she nasaled.

"Hi, this is Reginald Worthington's secretary, Joyce. Mr. Worthington asked me to call your office and request copies of our corporate tax returns and financial statements for the past three years, together with the most recent one for this year. Oh, and he needs copies of his individual tax returns as well. We've recently joined the Association of General Contractors and they have an article on our company coming out in their next publication. Since we've joined, we've received invitations to bid on some rather large projects and Mr. Worthington is anticipating a need for additional financing. He needs the reports from you to prepare his loan applications. So, may I speak with Mr. Blumberg, please?"

"I can take care of that for you. No need to bother Mr. Blumberg with it. When would you like to pick them up?"

"Oh. You know, if you could please mail them to our post office box, that would be fine."

"I can't do that. You'll have to pick them up."

Judy turned to me and said, loud enough for the secretary to hear, "Mr. Worthington, she's insisting I pick them up."

I growled back, "Tell her to put Blumberg on the phone and I'll talk to him about it."

Before Judy could repeat my message, the secretary intervened, "No need to bother Mr. Blumberg. I'll mail them. I'm sure he won't mind."

"Good. I'll give you the mailing address so you don't have to look it up." Hurriedly quoting it, "Joyce" voiced her thanks and hung up.

Turning to me, Judy shivered. "I hope this works, Hollywood."

"You did fine, Girl. Now then, only three more to go."

****

Switching motels every night as a slight precautionary measure, we waited until Wednesday before checking the four post office boxes. There was a package from an accounting firm in every one. After studying the contents of each, I determined Reginald Worthington to be our guy.

I telephoned Robert Tanner in St. Louis and managed to catch him just before he left for work. The new drivers' licenses and social security cards would be in our post office box in Phoenix by the time we arrived home, one set each for Reginald and Joyce Worthington, as well as Phillip and Patricia Patterson.

On Thursday morning, we left Indianapolis and aimed the Corvette west on Route 40. Placing her head against my shoulder, Judy kissed me on the neck and looked into my face. "Say, Joe-Joe, isn't Springfield right on our way home?"

"That it is."

"Do we have time to stop at your mother's for a few

208

days?"

"That we do."

Chapter 32

Every day for nearly two weeks, Judy and I went to the Planning & Zoning Office of every city and town in the county until we found what we were looking for. There was a widening and sewer project scheduled to begin on Scottsdale Road within six to nine months.

Touring the area together, Judy spotted a for sale sign posted on a commercial piece of land on Scottsdale Road, just south of Cactus Road. It was exactly the size we needed. I called the realty company and learned the asking price was half a million dollars. In my mind, I reasoned they could be stuck with the property for nearly two years while the government's tear-up routine was taking place, so I told him I'd give them three seventy-five cash for an immediate closing. I made sure to mention the city's widening plans. I counted on the broker surmising that the commission on my offer would far exceed the nothing he'd receive from a frustrated owner, who would more than likely fire him for not selling their property, long before the two years had passed.

The next day, they countered with four hundred fifty thousand. I raised my offer to four hundred thousand, take it or leave it. They took it. Step two of phase two was complete.

Judy and I spent the next few weeks forming the Phoenix branch of Worthington Construction Company. We opened bank accounts, rented post office boxes, more printing, hired an architect and submitted applications to the city for building permits. Everything was right on schedule.

With a mortgage commitment from the Joseph T. Bowden Trust, Phillip and Patricia Patterson signed a contract with Worthington Construction Company for the erection of a multi-unit garden-type office complex on our newly acquired land.

This all took place in the dining room of the three-bedroom home the "Pattersons" had leased in Scottsdale. Representing all the principals for every entity, Judy and I sipped mai tais as we laughed and hailed congratulations to each other with every signature. After everything was signed, our invisible Notary Public, whom we named Miss Pamela Wilson, affixed her name and official seal to each document.

In composing the mortgage commitment, we arranged for a short-term interim loan for six months, to be replaced with a permanent mortgage following completion of the project. We designed all of our contracts from those I'd retained when I was Owen J. Hunter, together with Judy's legal input and research for construction and financing law changes since that time. We spent days culminating the necessary documents to place everything in motion. Our various printing bills from shops all over Maricopa County were becoming astronomical.

Needing to provide the Bowden Trust with an appraisal, as well as for later use with Mortensen, we visited our branch manager at First Interstate Bank and secured the names of the top three appraisers in the county. "And good luck with your project, Mr. and Mrs. Patterson."

With plans, projections and deed in hand, we visited Thomas Markham & Associates. Within three weeks, our very expensive, certified, forty page appraisal eventually stated on page thirty-eight that our finished building would be worth two million, four hundred thousand dollars.

Weighing all of our costs for the land, architectural fees, appraisal, construction, and incidentals, we expected to spend one million, four hundred thousand dollars. We granted our mortgage commitment in the amount of one million, eight hundred thousand. It was my intention to lose the property, convict the bad guys and in the process, get back from them the four hundred thousand dollars I should have received two years earlier for my original building. However, assuming that my projections were accurate, it appeared I could be as much as three hundred thousand dollars short of meeting the commitment.

Retiring to the family room, I waited until Judy went to the bedroom to change before I outlined this to her. While

I was selecting a cassette to put into the stereo, I saw her return to the room and place two fresh drinks on our coasters. With the soft, uneven voice of Aaron Neville in the background, I seated myself across from her so that I had a good view of her new, bright green see-throughs.

After explaining my forecast of a probable deficit to her, I summarized, "Girl, we have two options. One is, I can cut back on the size of the project to meet our resources, but that means the past two months have been wasted. We'll have to start over and the bad news about that is—if the city's widening plans are on schedule, we won't have the building completed before they haul out their bulldozers."

"Okay. And option number two is?"

"To barge straight ahead with the original idea and hope that the well doesn't run dry before we get to the end. However, if we do that, there are a couple of small changes I'll need to make, but this part gets good. If Worthington bills one million eight for the construction and only gets paid one million five from the Bowden Trust, Worthington files a lien on the property. Then Bowden looks to Patterson for the additional money, which Patterson doesn't have. So, seeing an opportunity there, Worthington gives Patterson a four hundred thousand dollar note for the land and takes over ownership of the property. He drops the lien and assumes the mortgage with Bowden. However, to secure the note, Patterson then files his own lien. About that time, enter the City of Scottsdale, tearing up the streets. With no tenants, Worthington doesn't make the interest payments, so to protect his one million five and cover the lien, Bowden forecloses for one million nine. Worthington then contacts our Mr. Mortensen."

"And that will be the start of phase three. Am I right?"

"Absolutely right. Plus, there's one other good thing. When the street project is finished, the value of the property should jump to more than three million dollars. A very inviting investment, huh? Finally, when the Tafino brothers buy the property at the foreclosure sale for one million nine,

Bowden gets his money back and Patterson gets paid, thereby removing the lien. Now then, since Worthington has already profited by a couple hundred thousand with the construction, the additional Patterson money is what I got cheated out of in the first place."

"Clever, Hollywood. Very clever. But can you really be sure those dagos will buy the building?"

"Believe me, Girl, as greedy as they are, this'll be too good for them to pass up. I'm positive they'll buy the place. Let's just hope they all buy this little fiasco we're putting together."

She persisted. "But what if the wops *don't* buy the building? What then?"

"Simple. Bowden gains ownership and sells the property for two million four. So we end up with even more money and do it again."

Judy sipped from her drink and gave me that tilted head, raised eyebrow look. "Why don't we just do that in the first place?"

"Two reasons, beautiful. First of all, we'd probably have to sit on the place until Scottsdale finishes their street improvements before we'd be able to sell it, which will take maybe nine to twelve additional months. And, considering we wouldn't have enough money to live on for a year, we'd most likely end up selling it for a lot less than it's worth. After all that, we'd have to take the time to find another suitable property, go through all of this again, build the place, wait out the foreclosure period, and all of that could be yet another year to eighteen months, minimum. Second thing, if we go through all of the above, who knows how many more people will be foreclosed upon by Mortensen and crew during that time, and how many more "accidents" will take place with any of them."

With her eyes fixed on Socko, Judy didn't look at me as she solemnly answered, "Oh, yeah, right. I see. Then, let's do it just like we planned."

Suddenly becoming quiet and sitting on the sofa with her feet curled under her, Judy twirled a long strand of her hair with one hand while she stroked Socko's face with the other. Relishing the sight of her, dressed in those lacy, revealing, green baby-dolls, I wavered with the decision to fix us another mai tai. Logic finally dictated to me that if I were to leave for the chore of mixing them, I could then delight in the view of her with a full glass instead of an empty one. Taking her glass from the coaster on the coffee table, I went to the kitchen.

Upon returning, I handed her the refilled glass and strategically sat in my recliner, positioning myself to again have her in full view. Smiling warmly as she took the drink from my hand, she waited until I was comfortably in my chair before she spoke. "So, Joe-Joe, what's next?"

Vaulting to the front edge of my chair, I furrowed my brow and impersonated, "Oh, Judy, Judy, Judy, don't you know, my darling?"

Judy's sudden outburst of singing laughter caused an annoyed Socko to jump from her lap to the floor. Glaring back at her, he pranced conceitedly toward the kitchen. Waving him away, she told him, "Oh, go ahead and leave, you stuck-up cat! I'm never going to try to pet you again!" That part was not true.

Turning to me, she winked. "Incidentally, Hopscotch, your Cary Grant is far worse than my W. C. Fields. And you didn't answer my question."

"Here it is then. It's time for Reginald Worthington to rent an office for the construction company and let's get started."

Still giggling, Judy gulped the rest of her drink and set her empty glass on the table. Holding her arms toward me, she wiggled her fingers in invitation. "Okay, Joe-Joe, that's it. I'm tired. Come take me to bed."

Chapter 33

Rising an hour earlier than usual the next morning, Judy and I dabbled with our stage make-up for the first time, with Judy insisting we do this in separate bathrooms. After two grueling hours, I was ready to venture into the outside world. Having finished first, I waited for her in the kitchen, using the time to re-fill Socko's food and water bowls. After pouring two cups of fresh coffee, I nonchalantly leaned against the counter and waited. Carefully sipping the hot brew, I caught a glimpse of Judy peeking around the doorjamb. "I hope this works, Joe-Joe."

With a nervous giggle, she clutched the hem of her dress and, performing a small curtsy, entered the kitchen. Momentarily looking down at herself, she raised her eyes to meet mine and although a bit hollowly, she triumphantly exclaimed, "It should fool somebody, though! I look hideous!" That part was true.

Staring at her, I was amazed. *My word, she's really done a good job!* A burn scar traced from her collar to behind her left ear. Resting on her brand new protruding nose was dark, horned-rim glasses, behind which were dull, hazel eyes, thanks to the non-prescription contact lenses. Her brown wig was amply streaked with strands of gray and curled into a bun. It was attached with a hairpiece comb. She'd capped several of her teeth yellow and with a few scattered moles on her forehead and cheek, she was totally ugly.

Her loose fitting dress fell way below her knees to her lower legs, over which were thick, unsightly pantyhose. Since she really couldn't hide her firm breasts, she'd padded them profusely to give them a much larger, bouncy, appearance. I stood there gawking at her.

"Okay, Hollywood, you can quit grinning! You're not exactly beautiful, you know!" That part was also true.

I was wearing a dark brown wig with limp hair as straight as a poker, which fell down over my ears, almost to my collar. Ugly glasses coupled with blue contacts—too blue really—and a gold earring added to my look. All this, plus the gray in my phony mustache and goatee, although purposely insufficient to hide the freshly applied pockmarks, should be enough to fool anyone who hadn't seen me in three years. Posing, I said to her, "Hey, I'll have you know this look will turn quite a few heads."

"Yeah." She chuckled. "Away."

With a huge wish-us-luck sigh, Judy threw her purse over her shoulder and marched toward the door leading to the garage. Stopping halfway there, she leered at me, blinking her dull eyes. Exaggerating, she lowered her voice and seductively uttered, "Okay, Reginald, baby, bring my coffee and let's go."

****

With me handling the scheduling of sub-contractors and performing the accounting duties, Judy acted as my secretary, legal advisor and errand runner. Within six months, the construction of our twenty-unit office complex was nearing completion and we were getting quite adept at applying the disguises, cutting our time to less than an hour. But, by now, I was nearly broke.

Having the holidays behind us and our visitations completed, Judy and I sat in front of the fireplace on a cold January night. Sipping our usual mai tais, I explained to her, "You know, Girl, even though this is costing me less than I originally anticipated, I'm down to less than twenty thousand dollars in the bank and I still have to pay the landscaper. Not only that, we have to live for the next three to five months while the upcoming foreclosure procedure takes place. And, hell, Scottsdale hasn't even started their widening project yet. Undependable idiots! I suppose I could borrow another forty thousand in the name of Bowden or Patterson, but creating a verifiable income for either of them will be difficult."

"Couldn't you have Worthington borrow it?"

"Too risky. The bank would probably want some kind of collateral, plus we'd need new financial statements and credit reports and I'd just as soon leave Indianapolis out

216

of the picture. I don't want to take a chance of anybody contacting the real Worthington. Maybe I should just sell the project quickly and start again."

"You can't do that, Joe-Joe, for all the reasons you explained to me before. Besides, there's no need to. I can help."

"Help how? By trying to borrow it for me? I can't let you do that."

"No, silly, I've got over eighty thousand dollars in the bank and you're welcome to it."

"What?" I asked incredulously.

"Yeah. Surprised? Hey, all that money you've paid me, I've put in the bank. With you paying for everything, I've had nothing else to do with it. And with Nathan on scholarship, Mother hasn't needed much help, and what I did give to her came from my Mortensen paychecks. Plus, I had some of my own from the time before I met you. You want it?"

"You're incredible!"

"Not really. I suppose if I had a real brain, I'd just take the money and run, but I have this problem. You see, I happen to be madly in love with the benefactor who helped provide this little nest egg, so I can't do that. Stupid me, I have to stay and help. Now then, Hollywood, in exchange for my doing that, do you think you could find it within yourself to please replenish this?" She handed me her empty glass.

Like a minx, she giggled. With her head resting against the cushion on the floor, her gorgeous auburn hair cascaded across the pillow. She threw me a kiss before she dreamily laid there and closed her eyes, quickly losing herself into the music.

Several minutes later, I sat mesmerized in the recliner in front of the fireplace, sipping my fresh mai tai, with my eyes resting on Judy's pretty face. I turned them away from her and gazed at the crackling flames, relaxed in the comfortable solidarity which Judy brought to me and totally appreciative of her being. At times, I appraised our situation and burned with a desire to sweep us away from all of this to a world of our own, letting the madness we've created fend for itself. As she'd said, take the money and run. But, with my youthful naiveté gone, I've found my true being and there would be an emptiness in doing that. One that both of us would most likely experience.

Judy broke my spell, bringing me back to the present. "What are you thinking over there, Galahad?"

I decided to keep that to myself, so I simply said, "I need for you to run an errand for me tomorrow morning. I'd like for you to pick up the landscaping plans from the architect and deliver them to Baker's Nursery. I'd do it myself, but I'm meeting with the city inspector about the paving and you know their drill. He'll show up when he's damn good and ready, after which I'll slip him a fifty and he'll approve the parking lot. So, I've got to be there early and it could take all morning."

"Consider it done, sir. But can I do it without the Joyce disguise? I hate wearing that hideous get-up all over town."

"I don't know, Girl. I don't like wearing mine all that well either, but I think you should put it on. You just never know."

"Oh, please, Joe-Joe? Tell you what. After I deliver the plans, I'll come home and dress down then I'll meet up with you at the office. Fair enough?"

"Okay. Fair enough."

She grinned and blew me a kiss. "Thank you, Hollywood."

We stayed silent for several moments when, chewing on a mouthful of chipped ice from her drink, Judy all at once raised up on one elbow, shot a serious looking glance toward me and solemnly mumbled, "Oh yeah, sir, I also want you to know that I want interest on that eighty thousand if you use it."

Hopscotch time. Bozo's back. "Oh yeah? At what rate?"

"Oh, let me think." She scratched her head in mock

seriousness. "Aha! I know. Do you remember that great deal we put together the first night I met you?"

"Oh yeah, the night you seduced me."

"Oh no, Hollywood. I didn't seduce you—I captured you!" That part was very true.

"Well, Galahad, you do serve a mean breakfast and you do make love very nicely, sooooo, if that's an interest rate you can live with, then I think a repeat of that will be sufficient."

I crawled out of the recliner and joined her on the floor. "Sounds to me like another great deal."

"Not only a great deal—consider it another done deal, Galahad." She smoothly slipped out of the brand new red baby-doll pajamas and when we eventually slept, the fire had burned down to mere embers.

Chapter 34

With her large burlap market bag slung over her shoulder, Judy marched toward the architect's office at the end of the corridor. With her high-heeled shoes clicking against the tile floor, she played the juvenile game of not stepping on a crack.

She also drew the attention of three men in the hallway, all of whom halted their conversation to gaze at her long legs, which were moving gracefully beneath her short, dark blue pleated skirt. Oblivious to their stares, Judy continued to walk past them when she unexpectedly heard a familiar voice and she froze. "Jane? Jane, is that you?"

Without looking, she recognized the voice of James Mortensen. Thinking quickly, she walked up to the first office on her right and went inside. Closing the door behind her, Judy threw the lock and stood with her back against the frosted glass entryway. She looked around and saw a receptionist seated at a desk in front of her and approached her. "Oh, my God! You've got to help me! There's a man out in that hallway who's stalking me!"

Startled, the young brunette blurted, "What? Oh dear, I'll call security." She reached for the phone.

"Wait! Not yet!" Judy commanded. "Don't call them yet."

"But?" The girl put the phone down.

Judy made a quick study of the confused young woman and estimated her to be about the same size as herself. Coolly scanning the room, she asked, "Do you have a ladies' room in here?"

"Uh, yes. Right around the corner there." The girl pointed in the direction of it. Just then, they both heard the entrance door rattle and the receptionist jumped up. "Oh, no! That guy could be dangerous. Please let me call security. They'll take care of him."

They both heard the desperate pleading of James Mortensen from beyond the door. "Jane? Please! I just want to talk to you! Okay?" He shook the door again.

"What should I do?" asked the receptionist. "Is that your name? Jane? Does this guy know you?"

"Uh, sort of." Judy replied. Looking first back at the door, then in the direction of the restroom, Judy moved around the girl's desk and gripped the frightened young lady by the arm.

The girl stepped back. "What are you doing? Why don't you just let me call the guards?"

"No! Look, this jerk-wad has been hounding me for months and can't take no for an answer. If you can help me, I'll teach the imbecile a lesson! Come with me."

"What do you want me to do?" The girl whaled.

"Just trust me." Judy reassured, as she led the girl into the restroom and closed the door.

"But?"

Reaching inside her bag, Judy pulled out a wad of bills and started peeling twenties from the roll. She looked into the brunette's face. "Take off your clothes. I'll give you two hundred dollars for that skirt and blouse."

"What?" The baffled girl shrieked.

"Here." Judy slapped the money into the girl's hand and directed, "Here's two hundred dollars. Trade clothes with me."

Not waiting, Judy stripped off her own skirt and blouse then shoved them in the direction of the young woman, who grappled with them to keep them from falling to the floor. Without hesitation, Judy jerked a blonde wig from the bag and mentally thanked Joe for insisting that she have it with her at all times. She quickly stretched it over her auburn hair, tugging at it and pushing her own locks underneath it. She looked into the mirror, then at the brunette. "Hurry up, get your clothes off!" Judy barked.

"Wait a minute! I get it! You're disguising yourself so that guy won't recognize you!"

"Right. Now you've got it." Judy gave her a sigh of relief.

Immediately caught up in this unexpected espionage, the pretty, young woman hastily stripped away her own skirt and blouse and thrust them at Judy. Hurrying to pull Judy's beige blouse and blue skirt onto her body, the girl spontaneously laughed. "Hey, this is fun. I've met some of those guys who won't settle for no!"

Ignoring the comment, Judy gently directed the secretary toward the restroom door with her hands on her back and instructed her, "Now then, go out there and call security. Oh, yeah, and have them positively escort the jerk all the way to the front door to question him. Understand?"

"Okay." The girl bubbled with excitement. She reached for the doorknob, then turned to Judy and exclaimed, "Say, I know something else that might help! I've got a sun-bonnet and sun-glasses in my car you can have!"

"No good." Judy stated. "If you walk out there to get them in those clothes, he might figure out what's going on."

"I'll get Shelley to go out and get them! She's the other girl out there. Even if he sees her, he can't suspect her of anything!"

Judy entertained her. "All right, but hurry. And, hey, you'd better call security first and get him away from that door. We don't want the pervert barging in here when she goes out to get the hat. And tell her to do it quick!"

"Gotcha!"

The girl opened the door, and then felt Judy's hand tugging at her arm. "And one more thing. If security should ask you, I was never in here. Okay? The guy saw you in those clothes and mistook you for somebody else." The young woman nodded with a grin, then vanished.

Five minutes later, Judy strolled out of the office, dressed in a red skirt and white blouse and wearing a pink sunbonnet over her blonde hair. Peeking over the top of the dark glasses, she cast a quick glance toward the front entrance of the building and saw two security guards talking with James Mortensen, who was pleading his case to them. Without breaking stride, Judy deftly filed outside in the opposite direction, climbed into her Corvette and screeched from the parking lot.

Thirty minutes later, she sashayed into the office of

Worthington Construction Company and saw Joe-Joe do a double take. By this time she was laughing about the whole thing. She quickly enlightened him. "Oh, and by the way, Hollywood, two more things. One, I guess you were right about wearing the disguise, and two, I didn't get those plans for the landscaper."

Chapter 35

While walking to the liquor cabinet, Antonio Tafino jabbered to his brother. "Lou, we haven't done anything with old Mortensen since that Cooke deal a while back. And you know, every time I talk to the skinny little jerk, he seems sorta down, kinda depressed or somethin'. Tell you what I think. I don't believe he ever got over that redheaded Mexican chick. Or what she tried to do to him."

Antonio settled into a high-backed leather chair, with a fresh scotch-on-the-rocks in his hand and laughed. "I'll bet after seein' the number Bigotti done on that apartment, her pretty little ass got scared real good. I mean, she completely disappeared from sight after that."

He quickly got very serious. "But I still got the word out to Alex to watch for her, 'cause I gotta know why that recorder was in Mortensen's place and what she's got on those tapes."

Twirling his cigar, Louis Tafino spread a faint smile across his thin lips and methodically blinked his eyes in accord. Seeing that, Antonio continued his spiel. "Tell you what else I think, Lou. I'm itchin' to get back to business and I believe if Mortensen could get some good lookin' young chippie to take care of his plumbing once in a while, he'd get back to bein' his old self again. Whaddya think?"

Raising his eyebrows, Lou uncertainly shrugged his shoulders. With a chuckle, Antonio ignored his brother's manner and lifted his glass toward him. "Tell you what, Lou, I just got an idea. I believe I'll call one of those high-class escort services tomorrow and fix Mortensen up with a strange, young piece of ass. That oughtta get him back on track. Think I'll get him a tall blonde. Hell, they're more fun than those Mexican broads, anyway! What do you think?"

Lou's thin smile spread a bit wider. He winked at Antonio.

Antonio grunted as he removed his shoes. "For tonight though, I'm gonna finish this drink then go to bed. I'll have Alberto take you home whenever you're ready."

Setting his empty glass on the end table, Louis rose to his feet and shook his head. Antonio's face reflected a touch of surprise, but then he stated, "I'll get Alberto."

****

The next morning, after wolfing down his breakfast on the veranda, Antonio ordered the butler to plug in a telephone. After dialing Mortensen's number, Tafino waited while Maryann put the call through.

"Hi, Antonio. Good to hear from you. How've you been?"

"Excellent. Say, Mortensen, I wanna ask you a question. Have you ever heard from that blackmailin' Mexican bitch?"

Mortensen froze. He didn't dare mention he'd just seen her last week and he certainly didn't want to tell Antonio about the grilling he got from those two stupid security guards! He still couldn't figure out how she got out of that building without him seeing her. Coincidentally, he was surprised that Tafino would bring up the subject of her right after that chance meeting. *You don't suppose this idiot knows about that, do you?* James took a gamble and lied. "No, Tony, not a word. I guess you were right about her."

Antonio bellowed, "See? What'd I tell you? Now then, Mortensen, I got a little surprise for you. Seein' as to how you've done everything like I told you to do, Lou and I want to celebrate a new beginning and we want you to have dinner with us on Friday night at the Scottsdale Resort. Not Margo, just you."

Except for an occasional lunch, Mortensen had never socialized with the Italians and even though not really wanting to now, he dared not refuse. He suddenly remembered the man's earlier death threat and turned ice cold. He nervously inquired, "Uh, okay, Tony, but is this something I'm going to like?"

Tafino roared with vulgar laughter. "Of course, Mortensen! You're gonna love this—I mean, literally!" He guffawed again. "Hey, like I told you before—you're good with the pigeons, so I'm overlookin' the one mistake you made, just like I promised. And since you seem to be pretty much back down to earth, all I want to do is show you I appreciate that and get the old ball rollin' again."

Sticky from perspiration, Mortensen felt glued to his chair. He hesitated, not entirely convinced of Antonio's integrity. *But, hell! I don't dare cross him!* "All right, Tony. Any particular time you want me there?"

"Make it seven o'clock." Click.

With one more call to make, Tafino's fat finger pressed the buttons for the number Alberto read from the directory. He told them what he wanted. Two days later, he received a follow up call from the escort service. Alberto handed him the phone. "Tafino here. What's the verdict?"

"Everything has been arranged, Mr. Tafino. The dinner date for your friend, Mr. Mortensen, will be escorted by limousine to the Scottsdale Resort on Friday, arriving at about seven-thirty. You'll be able to recognize her in a light blue evening gown. Her limousine driver will introduce you to her in the main lobby and as you've requested, we've assigned a gorgeous blue-eyed blonde. Her name is Sonya."

"Thank you." Click.

Chapter 36

The lace tablecloths, glittering chandeliers and gold enhanced wallpaper of the dining room were surroundings that James Mortensen was not accustomed to. He'd entertained at finer restaurants all around the valley, but this was above his usual social stature. The influence of money was visible all around him. This was society.

Feeling self-conscious, even though his rented tuxedo blended well with all the others in the room, he vainly attempted to show nonchalance. The second of his remedial scotch and waters didn't taste as harsh and bitter as his first and despite his initial discomfort, he found himself starting to relax somewhat. Antonio and Louis seemed right at home.

Ordering a third round of drinks for everybody, Antonio abruptly excused himself. "Lou, I'll be right back. I'm gonna go get Mortensen's surprise."

Aware that Lou wouldn't speak, Mortensen didn't attempt a conversation with him during Antonio's absence, however he held up his glass to him in recognition. He continued his surveillance of the place.

Soft piano music, accompanied by the light strumming of a guitar and the muted brush strokes of a snare drum suddenly filled the air with an old standard. As the music commenced, the overhead lighting dimmed, adding an embroidered illusion of enchantment to the room. The hushed conversations from the subdued crowd blended into an un-comprehensible buzz, just slightly lower than the strains coming from the musicians. Handsome waiters, well rehearsed in subtleness, and inconspicuous in their movements, glided perceptively at their appointed tasks.

Having been served with his latest drink, James Mortensen was imbibing the chilled blend when Antonio approached the table with a tall blonde on his arm. Holding her chair, the boastful Italian seated her next to Mortensen and declared, "James, this is Sonya."

"Hi, James." She said, melodiously.

Mortensen timidly looked up at her. Flabbergasted,

he recognized her immediately and without thinking, he blustered, "Tony, I don't believe this. Where did you find her?"

"What difference does it make, Mortensen? She's yours for tonight, so don't ask questions. Just enjoy her company." Snickering, Antonio reached across the table and slapped Lou on the arm. With his thin-lipped grin in place, Lou twirled his cigar, nodding agreement.

"But, Antonio, how did you know that she's—"

"Okay, James," Tafino interrupted. Leaning across the table, the Sicilian cupped his hand around his mouth and hoarsely whispered, "If it'll satisfy your curiosity, I'll tell you. I called an escort service and this young lady is the beauty they picked out for you. So, don't embarrass, uh, Sonya, right? Anyway, don't embarrass her by asking stupid questions. Okay?"

Suddenly, it hit Mortensen right between the eyes. *This is pure dumb luck! Of course—they couldn't know she's Jane's friend. How could they? For goodness sake, James, don't breathe another word!* With sweat popping out on his forehead, Mortensen reached for his handkerchief and began mopping his brow.

Suspecting that Mortensen's reaction to her was merely simple nervousness, Sonya professionally opened a dialogue with him. "Well, James, I understand my companionship is a reward to you for a job well done. Congratulations."

Leaning toward him, she patted his forearm. The scent of Estee Lauder wafted to his nostrils as his eyes rested on her breasts, bulging above the line of her gown. "Now then," she sang, "is there anything specific you'd like to talk about? Maybe some small talk, just to get acquainted?"

Her hand strategically remained on his arm. Turning to the Italians, Sonya acknowledged them, looking back and forth between the two as she spoke. "Gentlemen, I'd like to thank each of you for inviting me this evening. I'll do my best to help make this a very enjoyable get-together."

"It's our pleasure, Sonya. And say, we're drinking

scotch and water. If you prefer something else, just name your poison." Antonio bellowed.

"I think I'd like a whiskey sour. With ice, please."

"Waiter!" Antonio boomed.

Still staring at Sonya, Mortensen started to think a bit more rationally. *Mother of Mary, I can't let them know who she is! But how can I ask her about Jane without them knowing?* Still gawking at her, he drank in her statuesque beauty. *My God, look at her! She's gorgeous! That long blonde hair and those eyes. They're so blue! Maybe Antonio's right. Maybe I should just forget about Jane! Yeah, then I could let this girl, Sonya, take her place!* But with Jane entering his thoughts, a likeness of her pretty face and auburn hair flashed into his mind's eye. As the image of her slowly drifted to his earlier fantasy of envisioning them together, Mortensen began to experience a stirring in his loins and he squirmed in his chair. *My word, man, stop sweating! And, James, for goodness' sake, whatever you do — don't slip up!*

Futilely attempting to return his attention to the group around him, Mortensen was thankful Antonio had boastfully taken over the conversation. He was in the middle of telling a raunchy story to Sonya. Mortensen swiped his handkerchief across his forehead again. Although trying his best not to stare, James kept casting glances at the top of Sonya's dress, noticing that every time she moved, her breasts bounced above the small line of piping that trimmed the plunging bodice of her gown. Squirming in his chair, he felt the discomfort of a growing erection creeping downward inside the tight trousers of his tuxedo. *Go away!*

Quickly placing his right hand in his lap, James maneuvered himself in an attempt to re-position his uncomfortable member, all the while trying desperately to remain inconspicuous with his gyrations. *Damn, that hurts!*

Purposefully, he dropped his napkin onto the dark carpet in an effort to disguise his actions. He leaned down to retrieve it while his other hand feverishly pushed his uncooperative limb to a more comfortable position. But before he could get his hand on the napkin, the fingers of their capable waiter snatched it from the floor. As the servant deftly placed a new one on the table in front of him, he bowed to Mortensen, then whisked away to other duties. Embarrassed and sensing that all eyes were upon him, Mortensen thankfully felt himself soften and withdraw limp just as quickly as he'd stiffened. *Damn! That's a relief!*

Antonio's laughter was followed by his decree to the departing waiter for more drinks. "Bring us another round, young man." Pointing his fat finger at the mortgage broker, he added with a loud guffaw, "Maybe if we feed him enough of these, he'll stop tossing things on the floor." More repulsive laughter.

Mortensen strained a smile to the others. *Thank Heavens the obnoxious pig didn't know the real reason. Who knows what he might have said about that?* Feeling perspiration trickling down his sides, James excused himself for a trip to the men's room.

****

Somehow, James Mortensen managed to remain reasonably calm throughout the remainder of the evening. The booze helped. Small talk filled the balance of the conversation during their meal, with Sonya being overly attentive to him, constantly touching his arm, listening intently when he talked and in between, cooing comments to him. All the while, Antonio interjected his annoying laughter and leathery remarks. After eating, Louis twirled an unlit cigar and focused on light fixtures and paintings, then on to the tabletop candles enclosed in ersatz lanterns. He added nothing, save an occasional nod or stare.

Failing miserably to keep his eyes from her cleavage, James Mortensen answered all of Sonya's trifling questions.

"Yes, the Tafinos are business acquaintances. I'm a mortgage broker and I've arranged financing for many of their properties.

"Oh yes, I'm a graduate of Oregon State, in Business Administration. Ah, I see, that's what your degree is in as well.

230

"Aha, that explains it. So, the escort business is more lucrative than any job offers you've received. Interesting."

Checking her watch from time to time as the evening wore on, almost as if on cue, Sonya eventually announced, "Gentlemen, I've certainly enjoyed this evening, the fabulous dinner, the good company. Everything. However, since the bewitching hour seems to be upon us and my limousine will be arriving shortly, I'm afraid I'll have to be leaving. Maybe we can do this again sometime."

Looking at Mortensen, she smiled warmly. Rising from her chair, she leaned forward and placed a light kiss on his forehead. "Good night, James."

Briskly standing, Antonio extended his arm to her. "Please let me walk you to the lobby, honey."

"Why thank you, Mr. Tafino." Still smiling, Sonya placed her hand into the crook of his elbow. She exchanged glances between the other two men and caroled, "Good night, everybody."

In a panic, Mortensen drunkenly attempted to stand up. *Oh, hell no! I didn't get to ask her about Jane!* He reached out and tried to grab her hand. He had to let her know that he desperately wanted to talk with her!

Seeing him stumble, Sonya recognized the look of disappointment on his face. She'd seen that look a lot of other times before. He didn't want the evening to end. "Really, James, I must be going. Maybe there'll be another time. Okay?"

Turning her back, she strolled away with Antonio.

Although frantic, Mortensen somehow clung to a fragment of rationale and quickly reasoned with her last comment. "Maybe there'll be another time." *Yes, that's it! Antonio can tell me how to get in touch with her! I'll merely tell him what a good time I had with her and I'd like to do it again! Then, I can ask her about Jane!* His wide grin was to himself. *James, I am proud of you. As boozed up as you are, you came up with a solution. That's pretty good!*

Relieved, he yelled a thank you to her across the emptying room then sat back down. All at once exhausted and feeling his head spinning, James Mortensen was suddenly becoming sleepy and looked forward to going home.

Less than fifteen minutes later, with his eyes closed, while resting his head in his hands on his propped elbows, James heard Antonio's voice jar him awake. "Mortensen! Wake up! We rented a room for you. You'd better go on up there and sleep it off. Here's the key, it's number 216. C'mon, let's go!"

"Uh, no, no, Tony. That'sh okay. I'll get a cab. Margo will worry."

"Cab, my ass. You're way too smashed. Go on up to your room. I'll call Margo for you."

"Huh? Whut?"

"C'mon, Lou, we'll walk him up there."

Ignoring Mortensen's babbling defiance, the brothers guided the mortgage broker toward the lobby, boarded the elevator and ushered him to room number 216. Unlocking the door, they led him inside. Keeping the key, they closed the door behind them as they left the dimly lit room.

Spying the bed, James Mortensen sighed with relief. It looked very inviting. But as he staggered toward it, he heard a soft, feminine voice pleasantly say, "Hello again, James."

Straining his blood-shot eyes, Mortensen looked toward the corner and saw Sonya sitting on a chair. Her long, blonde hair nestled across her bare shoulders above the familiar light blue dress. Pushing her long locks behind her, she tilted her head back and huskily added, "You must have done a *very* good job for those guys, James."

Slowly standing, she ambled toward him with a sultry look on her face. Reaching behind her, she teased, "Do you want to undo this zipper for me? Or shall I do it?"

"Huh?"

Sonya's hand reached out and touched his cheek. "Don't be bashful, James."

With a look of surprise, he leaned backward and stared at her in disbelief. "Wh-what?"

"Okay, James, I'll do it for you." Skillfully moving both hands behind her, the beautiful blonde smoothed the zipper downward and dropped the front of her gown to her waist, exposing her perfect breasts. She showed them to him. While seductively wiggling, she shimmied the light blue dress over her hips, legs, and ankles, allowing it to fall limp to the floor. Side-stepping out of it, Sonya stood before him in bikini panties and high-heeled shoes. "There, James. Now you."

Mortensen rubbed his shocked eyes and stood there swaying back and forth, gawking at her. Sonya began tugging at his coat, clumsily urging it over his limp shoulders and arms. After finally getting his jacket removed, she started to fumble with the buttons on his shirt. But before she could finish, he stepped back and drunkenly mumbled, "I don't believe this! Jane's friend, un—hic—undreshing me."

"I'm sorry, James. What did you say?"

"You're Jane's friend, the lesbian. And you're taking off my, hic, my clothes. Just as I imagined."

"Whatever are you talking about?" Laughing, Sonya continued to tug at his shirt. "James, I believe you're very drunk and you've got me confused with someone else. My name is Sonya, and I'm here to give you a really good time, if you're capable."

Backpedaling, Mortensen plopped onto the edge of the bed and grabbed his forehead. With his eyes closed, he tried to reason. "Wait. I can explain this. Just give me a minute."

Slightly annoyed, Sonya stared at him and dropped her hands to her side. She heaved a huge sigh.

"Really," he said, "I'm just confuzzzed."

Breathing heavily, he looked up at Sonya in the dim light and lifted his hand, petitioning for patience. A lot of what he'd imagined was now right in front of him, but all at once, he felt depressed. Sitting there, James gripped the mattress, trying to gain some stability. Tears sprang from his eyes as his spinning head tried to comprehend. "I'm sorry, but I don't feel good about this. Jane should be here, too," he mumbled.

Seeing his sudden show of sadness and bewilderment, Sonya sat down beside him and tried to comfort him. "Whoa, James, what is this? Please tell me about it. Who is Jane? Your wife?"

Shuddering, he spouted, "No, no, no. I had a girl who worked for me. You know who she was—your friend, Jane. I saw you with her at Arizzzona State, uh, University. Last year. I thought she was interested in me, but she—I don't know. I can't think." Shaking his head, he held it in both hands, sobbing.

"James, I don't know anybody named Jane. You obviously have me mixed up with someone else."

"No, it was you, all right. Every night, you and her would walk from the law building into a dorm, uh, dorm-uh-tory. She worked for me, beautiful girl, auburn hair, tight blue jeans, gorgeous."

"But, I don't know anybody named Jane. James, what is this leading to? Hey, I'm here for you now and I'm paid for. Look at this." She placed his hand on one of her breasts, faking excitement.

He jerked his hand away and glared at her. "But don't you see? That was part of it. You, an' me, and Jane. We were gonna all do this together. Then Jane disappeared."

"Boy, you are drunk. James, I keep telling you, I don't know anybody named Jane."

All at once, Mortensen became angry. "Why are you lying about this?" he demanded. "I wish I had a picture of her. I know you would, hic, recognize her."

"James, I've got pictures of all my friends in my billfold. If you like, I'll show them to you and prove to you that I don't know anyone named Jane. Then, if you don't want to do what I've been paid to do, then I'm outta here and you can tell your friends their money was wasted."

Without waiting for an answer, Sonya stomped across the room, retrieved her purse and pulled out her billfold. Padding back across the carpet, she took a seat beside Mortensen and slowly started flipping through the photographs one by one until she came across a picture of Judy.

Mortensen shrieked. "That's her! That's Jane! I knew I was right! Just like I told you! I saw you walking with her! Every night. From the law building to that dormitory."

"James, I'm sorry, but that girl's name is Judy, not Jane. Now then, do you believe me?"

"Nope. That's her! That's Jane!" He banged his finger on the picture.

All at once remembering that she and Judy used to walk from the law building to the dormitory nearly every night, Sonya suddenly froze. *Maybe there's more to this than I realize!* "James, please tell me about Jane again."

"How many times do I have to tell you? Okay, I met Jane at a restaurant one day and she came on to me, hic, and when I hired her to work in my mortgage company office, I thought she was interested in me, but she never let me, hic, do anything. So I followed her to see if she had a boy friend, but all I ever saw was you and her together. I mean, I used to sit in my car every bless-ed night and watch you and Jane go from the law building to that dormitory. I figured that you and her were lesbians and that's, hic, why she didn't want anything to do with me."

"Well, James, I think you're very mistaken. This girl's name is Judy. And, believe me, she isn't a lesbian. And neither am I. Now then, I don't want to talk about this anymore. Either you get it on with me, or I'm goin' home. What'll it be?"

"Wait a minute. Did you say her name is Judy? She told me her name is Jane. Jane Romero."

"Yeah, that's right. Judy. Her name is Judy Carmelle. I never heard of a Jane Romero. But you can forget about her, whatever you think her name is. She had a problem of some kind with her employer and transferred to Vanderbilt University well over a year ago and I haven't heard from her since. I truly believe, James, that you have her confused with someone else who resembles her and you're so drunk, you can't remember. Now then, are you doing something with me, or not?"

Ignoring her question, Mortensen insisted. "No, damn it, I'm not confused. That's her! It was about a year ago that she quit workin' for me and disappeared. The stupid little whore was tryin' to blackmail me! And she's not at some Vanderbuilding. I just saw her last week. In an office building downtown. And when I tried to talk to her, she went into some office and got those ignorant security guards all over my ass. Then somehow, she disappeared on me again. I'm tellin' you, that's her!" He pounded his finger against her picture again for emphasis.

Sonya stared at him in disbelief. "Wait a minute. Did you say something about blackmail? Judy? Now I know you're mistaken. Judy certainly wouldn't be involved in anything like that! Besides, she couldn't have been working for you. She was working at the escort service where I work then she quit and took a job with some guy, doing legal work! James, why am I even talking with you about this?"

"Huh-uh. Nope. She was workin' for me and she was studying psy-uh-chiatry at A-S-U, Arizona State University."

Becoming more frustrated with him by the moment, Sonya decided to acquiesce. "Okay, James, if that's the way you want it, I'll agree with you. Now then, I'll tell you this one more time. I've been paid to give you a good lay, but if you're not going to quit talking nonsense to me and get down to it, then I'm outta here, and as I said, you can tell your friends they wasted their money!" Walking across the room, Sonya picked up her dress and started to slip it on.

Suddenly seeing his opportunity slipping away, James threatened, "Okay, okay. But if you do that, it'll make Antonio awful mad, and believe me, you don't want to make him mad!"

"Oh, really? And why is that, James?"

"Because Antonio's dangerous."

Recalling them in her mind's eye, Sonya suddenly

believed him. "All right, James. Then, let's do something. But without all the gibberish."

Removing the rest of her clothing, Sonya lay on the bed beside Mortensen and reached for his crotch, feeling him trying to stiffen. But, after failing with her efforts to arouse him, less than five minutes later, he was sound asleep and she left, two thousand dollars richer.

****

Staying out of sight, the two Italians watched Sonya enter the limousine. Antonio nudged Louis and laughed. "Let's go see how our friend liked that."

They walked through the lobby and took the elevator to room number 216. Once inside, Antonio shook Mortensen and hollered, "Mortensen, wake up! C'mon, wake up! How was that?"

James Mortensen groggily mumbled. "Go away. I gotta sleep."

"We'll let you sleep in a minute. Aren't you going to thank Lou and I?"

"No. She's a bigger bitch than her friend."

"Her friend? What's that about? Who's her friend? C'mon, Mortensen, wake up! Who's her friend?"

Mortensen groaned. "Oh, Antonio, you know, the, uh, the Mexican bitch. You know—Jane. Now, go away and let me sleep."

Not believing his ears, Antonio momentarily froze. "What the hell did you say? Mortensen! She's like who?" Shaking him awake again, the Sicilian bellowed, "C'mon, Mortensen, wake up! She's like who?"

"Oooohhh, leave me alone, Tony. She's like her friend, Jane. That's what I said."

"You mean the blackmailing bitch? The one who used to work for you? This blonde knows her?"

"Uh, yeah. Real well. But her name's not really Jane."

Antonio vigorously shook him again. "Mortensen, stay awake! If that broad's name isn't Jane, then what is it? C'mon, tell me!"

237

"It's Judy."

Antonio rolled him over onto his back and slapped him on the cheek. "Mortensen! Do you have a last name for this Judy?"

"Huh? Yeah, Tony, it's Carmelle. Her name is Judy Carmelle. And she's back in town. I saw her downtown last week. But, Tony, I didn't talk to her. Honest to God." Then James pleaded, "Now, please, leave me alone." Groaning, Mortensen drifted right back to sleep.

Suddenly wanting Mortensen to stay asleep, Antonio placed his finger to his fat lips for quiet and motioned for his brother to follow. Leading the way, Antonio stole across the floor toward the door. Together, the Tafino brothers silently left the room.

Chapter 37

Dressed in full disguise, Judy and I were both ready for anything when I placed the call to James Mortensen. Maryann routinely answered, "Mortensen Mortgage Brokers."

"May I speak with James Mortensen, please?"

"I'm sorry, he isn't in at the moment, however, I'll be happy to have him return your call. May I please have your name and number, and what it may be regarding?"

As I gave her the information, Maryann uh-huh-ed while she jotted everything down. "Thank you, sir." Click.

An hour later as Mortensen passed her desk, Maryann handed him the note and waited while he read her scribbled message. "Did he give you any of the details?" The broker asked.

"Nope. Just said he needs a mortgage."

"All right, Maryann. Thanks. I'll call him back right away."

Closing his office door behind him, Mortensen removed his jacket and placed it on a hook before taking his seat behind the mahogany desk. Reaching for the telephone, he anxiously dialed the number. Some new business would be welcome. Things were much too slow.

After the third ring, he heard Judy's voice at the other end of the line. It sang when she answered. "Worthington Construction."

Mortensen chilled. *No, it can't be!* He envisioned an image of Jane and the urge to merely hang up without speaking went fleeting through his mind.

He heard Judy say again, "Hello? This is Worthington Construction Company. Can I help you?"

Knowing that money was extremely tight, Mortensen eventually broke from his fixation. *Just pretend you don't recognize her, James.* He mumbled into the mouthpiece, "Uh, yes, sorry. This is James Mortensen with Mortensen Mortgage Brokers. I'm returning a call from a Mr. Worthington. Is he in, please?"

Straining his ear against the telephone, James listened intently to her reply. "Yes he is, sir. Please hold while I put you through."

I saw Judy nod and I picked up the receiver. "Hi, Mortensen. Worthington here."

"Yes, I'm returning your call. You telephoned my office earlier today about a mortgage. How can I help?"

"Well, sir, I'm in dire need of some financing on a piece of property I've just acquired. When can we get together to talk about it?"

Mortensen gave himself an elated grin. "I could see you tomorrow. What time could you come in?"

"That's a bit of a problem, Mortensen. I've got a whole lot going on right now and it's really hard for me to get away. Could you possibly come here to my office?" Propping my feet onto the desk, I winked at Judy, who was standing in the doorway.

"Why, uh, sure. Just let me look at my schedule." Not wanting to appear anxious and not sure how to handle seeing Jane again—*if it's her*—Mortensen stalled for several moments. "Mr. Worthington, it looks like I'm booked solid for the morning, but could I meet you somewhere for lunch?"

"No good, Mortensen. I've got everything we'll need to discuss it, right here in my office."

"I see. All right, then—I guess I could be there around two-thirty in the afternoon. Will that work for you?"

"Yes, sir. That'll work fine. I'm at 11330 North Scottsdale Road, Suite 1050."

"Wow, that's quite a distance from here, but don't worry, I'll find it. Incidentally, Mr. Worthington, may I ask how you might have heard about us?" Mortensen doodled on a scratch pad as he talked.

"Quite simple, really. I picked up the yellow pages and started calling real estate companies, looking for references. I decided that the first name to come up twice would be the guy. That's you."

"All right." The broker chuckled. For some unknown reason, he felt a sense of relief. "And if I might ask, Mr. Worthington, how much are you looking to borrow?"

"Just under two million." I winked at Judy again.

"On what type of property?"

"I have a garden type office building on Scottsdale Road, worth about three million dollars. But, hey, let's discuss all that when I see you. I don't mean to be rude, Mortensen, but I've got a dental appointment in about thirty minutes and I should be getting out of here. Got a tooth that's been killing me!" I fabricated.

"Oh dear, I see. All right, Mr. Worthington, I'll see you tomorrow. Oh, but before we hang up, could I please ask you one more quick question?"

"Sure. Shoot."

"Uh, by any chance—the girl who answered your phone—is her name Jane?" He kept quiet about the name Judy.

"No, it's Joyce. Why?"

"Oh, it's nothing really. She just sounds very much like a girl who used to work in my office and I couldn't believe the coincidence of that." A sense of alleviation softened Mortensen's feeling of disappointment.

"Nope. Couldn't be her anyway. This young lady came with me from back east. Been with me nearly ten years. Efficient as hell. Okay? Hey, I'll see you tomorrow, Mortensen. Thanks." Click. Click.

The second click was the tape recorder. Picking up the telephone again, I spoke into the mouthpiece. "This call was received from James Mortensen on Tuesday, March 10, 1981, at 2:18 p.m." Click. Click. The telephone company records would verify that.

Looking toward Judy, I said, "Holy Hannah, Girl, he recognized your voice! Can you believe that?"

"That's a little bit scary, but don't worry, Hollywood, he sure as hell won't recognize this face." She quickly pointed at me. "Or that face, either, for that matter." Her laughter seemed a bit hollow. *Let's hope, Joe-Joe...*

After having practiced our make-up for the past six

months for the benefit of our sub-contractors and everyone else coming into the office, it was becoming almost mechanical to apply it. And it was necessary to do it every day. After all, these were the Worthingtons and in no way could we permit a connection by allowing anyone we were dealing with as the Worthingtons to see the Pattersons.

Occasionally, we'd even wear it in the evening when we'd go out. The heads that didn't look away, stared in disbelief at *The Odd Couple*. With the habit of always parking our rented station wagon in the garage next to Judy's Corvette, we'd also try to make certain there were no neighbors about when we left in our get-ups. I'd sold the van several months earlier.

****

With microphone bugs, hidden cameras and tape recorders in place, we were ready for James Mortensen when he showed up at two-thirty. Timidly escorting him to my office, "Joyce" announced him. "Mr. Mortensen to see you, Reginald."

Standing up, I extended my hand and motioned for him to pull up a chair. "Great. Thanks, Joyce. Afternoon, Mortensen."

Accepting my handshake, the mortgage broker glanced back toward Joyce as she left the room. Shielding his mouth with his hand, he raised his eyebrows and whispered, "You're right, Mr. Worthington. That girl couldn't possibly be Jane." My only comment was a thin smile.

Without sitting down, Mortensen opened his brown briefcase and took out a pad and pen, which he placed on the desk. Reaching into it again, he pulled out a packet of official looking forms and handed them to me. "That's a package of applications, questionnaires, financial information requests, etcetera. I'd like you to fill these out for me and after you have them completed, I'll come by and pick them up. Those will get us started right away with the lenders."

Mortensen then cleared his throat and sat down.

Systematically pulling the aforementioned tablet squarely in front of him, he picked up the pen and was prepared to write. "Now then, Mr. Worthington, please tell me a little bit about the property you need the financing for."

Leaning back in my chair, I chewed on an un-lit cigar for a moment before holding it up for him to see. "I don't really smoke the damned things, but with the dental work yesterday, I can't chew my usual wad of gum, so..." Shrugging my shoulders, I laughed.

Showing patience, Mortensen nodded, gave me a forced smile, and re-crossed his legs.

"Okay, Mortensen, here's the deal. I got a-hold of this building by default, actually. You see, I'm a contractor and I built the damned thing for a guy named Patterson who had a mortgage commitment from some fly-by-night trust company. Anyway, the trust company couldn't make the last construction draw, so I filed a lien on the place. Since this fellow, Patterson, didn't have any more money, I arranged to buy him out and assume the property as well as the mortgage commitment. I removed the lien and everything seemed to be in order. Are you with me, so far?"

"Certainly. So, what you're telling me is, you need a mortgage to pay off the trust company. Right?"

"Yes sir, and pronto. But let me finish, there's more."

"Okay. Go ahead." He re-crossed his legs again.

"Now then. Along comes the City of Scottsdale, tearing up the entire street in front of the place, and Mr. Mortensen, have you ever tried to get tenants to move into a building that nobody can get to? Right now, the place is vacant. Hell, I can't even move in there! In my own building! Plus, old man Bowden, who owns the trust that gave the mortgage commitment, wants me to continue paying interest on the construction loan, when he can't pay the final construction draw of three hundred thousand dollars! Well, I refuse to do it. Do you blame me?"

Listening intently, Mortensen re-crossed his legs yet one more time.

"Say there, Mortensen, is that chair uncomfortable? I

can get you another one."

His face flushed. "Oh, no, the chair is fine. Just habit."

"Are you sure?"

Appearing a bit irritated, he uncrossed the legs and planted his feet on the carpet. "Yes, sir, I'm sure."

"Okay, good. Let's see, where was I? Oh, yeah. Anyway, since there's a vacancy factor in the mortgage commitment and since I've not paid the interest, this Bowden character has filed a foreclosure on the place! My personal opinion is—I think he may have gotten scared when Patterson filed a lien to protect the note I gave him as part of the buy-out. Or, it could be that the old man sees the potential value and wants the property for himself. But, for whatever reason, he filed it."

A quizzical expression came across Mortensen's face. "Who is this Bowden person you mentioned?"

"He's an old codger who just happened to have some money and wanted to invest it to make more. My guess is, the old guy wants to take as much of it with him as he can. The problem for him is that he gave this Patterson a mortgage commitment for more money than he had to lend."

"Isn't that illegal?" Mortensen questioned.

Mortensen, I almost have to laugh at the irony of you asking me that question! "Well, I'm certainly not a lawyer— I'm just a bricklayer turned builder, but you could be right. However, it's too late to think about that, now."

"Perhaps, but still, if he misled you or this Patterson fellow, then—"

I interrupted him. "Hey, Patterson didn't get hurt. He'll be getting his money back from me and then some. I gave him a pretty fair buy-out."

"Well, Mr. Worthington, I was just thinking that—"

I interrupted him again. "Look at it this way, Mortensen. Taking it one step further, in answer to your original question, let's assume that what he did is illegal. If I pursue that, it might take me forever to get this mess straightened out in the courts, especially if the old man dies and it gets into Probate Court. No, if I can get the mortgage, then that's the answer." I tossed the stogie into the wastebasket.

Mortensen crossed his legs again. "Mr. Worthington, I was just trying to say that perhaps by filing something against him, you could stop his foreclosure action."

There! He said the magic word—foreclosure! And directly into the hidden cameras and microphone!

"No good, Mortensen. If it's illegal, then it's a criminal matter and it wouldn't affect the foreclosure, which is civil. No, the only thing that could prevent it would be for me to file a bankruptcy." I didn't even know if that part was true. I hoped he did.

He obviously did. "Then why don't you just do that?"

"Hell, Mortensen, I ain't bankrupt! Just broke!" I hollowly laughed. "Actually, though, I'd already thought of that. My lawyer just laughed at me."

Staring blankly at me, he re-crossed his legs again. *Guess it is just habit.*

"Okay, but what if you were to start paying the interest on the place? Would this Bowden then remove the foreclosure?" *He said the magic word again!*

"What with? Hell's bells, Mortensen, I've got more money tied up in that place than I've received in construction draws! I mean, I do have a couple of other jobs in progress, but the profit from those doesn't come until the end and by that time, the foreclosure period will be long past."

"Yes, I see. A real dilemma. Huh?"

"Anyway, Mortensen, my opinion is, this old man Bowden is just being contrary and if I can come up with a mortgage, I'll get him out of the picture. If I can do that, I'll stand to make a lot more than I would've by merely building the place. So, can you do this for me, or should I call somebody else?"

Scribbling on the pad, he looked at me. "Oh no, Mr. Worthington, I'm sure I can handle it."

"Good. What do we need to do to get started?"

"First of all, do you have something to back up the worth of the property?"

"Sure. Right here." Reaching to the credenza behind me, I picked up a folder and handed it to him. "Now then, that's the original appraisal Patterson had done by Markham and Associates. Turn to page thirty-eight. You see, it was supposed to be worth two million, four hundred thousand dollars."

When he heard the amount, Mortensen gave me a suspicious look. "Do you mean it's not worth that now?"

Swiftly grabbing another blue covered folder from the table behind me, I placed it in front of him and said, "Sure it is. Now. But look at that one. That's an updated appraisal that Markham did for me after I bought out Patterson. It's projected to the time when the street improvements are completed. Page thirty-eight in that one, too."

Flipping the pages, Mortensen's eyes rested on the amount and he whistled. Smiling, he looked up at me and read it out loud. "Three million dollars. Just like you told me on the telephone yesterday. Hey."

"Exactly."

"Mr. Worthington, your situation should certainly be no problem whatsoever. Our lenders are willing to be a little more lenient than most. By that, I mean, they're willing to loan strictly on the value of the property, providing the value is there." He held up the appraisal in his right hand and patted the cover with his left. "And based on this, it certainly seems to be there."

"Well, that's good to hear. I called a couple of banks and savings & loans and those stupid frauds won't even consider it until that damn street is finished. Unfortunately, I don't have that much time. Hell, when it's completed, the rents on the place should be even more than they would have been without the improvements. But those idiots don't look at common sense."

Holding up the appraisals, Mortensen still had a wide grin spread across his face. "Can I get copies of these?"

"Take those. I've got more."

Bouncing from his chair, he put the notepad, pen, and appraisals into his briefcase, then snapped it closed. "Very good, Mr. Worthington. It looks like we can be of help. Incidentally, when is the foreclosure sale scheduled to take place? I need to know just how much time we have." *He said it again!*

Standing up, I recited, "Wednesday, May 20th. Ten o'clock."

"Ah, great, that gives us plenty of time. So, if you'll please contact me as soon as you have the information packet completed, we'll get started."

He held out his hand toward me, which I accepted. "I'll fill them out tonight."

"Mr. Worthington, it's been a pleasure talking with you."

"Yes it has."

Releasing my hand, James Mortensen ended his visit. Hurriedly exiting my office, he waved back to me as he passed through the reception area. He didn't look at Joyce.

But I did. Hearing the door slam closed, I walked to where she was sitting and placed my hands on her shoulders. "Guess that's it, Girl. Now all we can do is play it out."

She nervously squeezed my hands.

Chapter 38

Bubbling with excitement, Mortensen anxiously waited until Maryann left for the day before he made an anticipated telephone call. "Tony? Mortensen here. Have I ever got something for you this time."

After he'd explained everything, the moneyman cradled the receiver and leaned back in his chair. He rested the back of his head in the palms of his hands and proudly smiled to himself. *Maybe this will finally put me back in good graces with Antonio again. Not only that, another twenty thousand for this will put me at four hundred thousand in the safety deposit box.*

In his titillation, James Mortensen began to feel aroused, which led him to other thoughts. *I wonder why Antonio has never mentioned that girl Sonya again. Or the dinner party. I'd like to ask him about her, but I'm afraid to. But you know, I'll bet there are other girls as pretty as her in that line of work. Maybe I should just forget about her and Jane, or Judy, or whatever the hell her name is, and call one of those escort services on my own.* But he knew he never would.

However, still pumped, the mortgage broker made one more phone call. He got no answer. Hanging up, he left his hand resting on the cradled telephone and disappointedly looked at the picture of Margo. *Humph! She must be out shopping again. She never seems to be home anymore.*

Oh well, James—back to work!
****

Antonio Tafino lifted the two glasses from the serving tray that Alberto was holding in front of him. Handing one to Louis, he bellowed, "Drink up, Lou. We finally got somethin' to celebrate for a change."

Antonio groaned as he plopped himself into an easy chair and continued talking to his brother. "Yes sir, Lou, old Mortensen finally came up with something good. This one seems almost too good to be true. If it's anywhere close to the numbers Mortensen gave me, do you know what that means? A cool million in instant equity."

Toying with the unlit cigar, Lou traced a smile and leaned his head back against the high-backed Queen Anne chair. He continued to listen to his brother. "Hell, Lou, we shoulda fixed Mortensen's ass up with a tall blonde a long time ago!" Antonio roared with laughter.

Setting his drink on the petite round table next to his chair, Antonio rubbed his fat hands together to dry the drops of moisture left there from the sweating glass. "Speaking of that blonde, I thought about asking Mortensen exactly what she said about that Mexican bitch, but I changed my mind. I figure he was probably too drunk to remember." Louis frowned, showing concern.

"Yeah, Lou, it's still botherin' me about what that broad might've had up her sleeve with that tape recorder. I'd really like to get my hands on those tapes—I don't like loose ends." Listening intently, Louis reached for his drink.

"And while she was workin' there, she was usin' that phony name, too. That bugs me, to boot. What did Mortensen say her real name is? Judy something? Yeah, Judy Carmelle. That's it. Maybe knowin' that can help us track her down. I'll send Alex back out to that school."

Louis unwrapped a fresh cigar and began to twirl it. Alberto rescued the empty cellophane and left the room with it.

"Damn, Lou!" Antonio blared. "Why in hell didn't I think of this before? I know how we can locate that redheaded bitch! Alberto! Bring me the telephone!"

Chapter 39

Alex Bigotti sat waiting in his white Cadillac. *Thank goodness. The boss finally gave me something to do other than collecting rents from his deadbeats.*

Alex was watching the entrance to the Scottsdale Resort and when a black limousine pulled to a stop in front of it, he looked at his watch. *That should be them. Good. Right on time.*

He couldn't hear the conversation between the limousine driver and his passenger. Sonya Waverly was telling her chauffeur, "Remember, Mark, stay close. I may have to leave in a hurry. I don't like these guys at all."

"I'll be right here, sugar. Enjoy." Withdrawing his svelte frame from the driver's side, Mark circled the car and held the door open for the tall, stunning blonde. He vigilantly watched until she'd entered the glass double doors leading to the lobby before he glided back behind the wheel to park in the lot and wait.

****

Upon seeing her come through the door, Antonio Tafino bellowed a loud greeting across the brightly lit room, "Hey, there she is!" He conceitedly walked toward her. "Good evening, Sonya. Nice to see you again."

"Why thank you, Mr. Tafino." Giving him a cosmetic smile, Sonya held out her white-gloved hand for him to take.

"Hey, what's with this "mister" crap, anyway? Just call me Tony. C'mon, gorgeous, I'll show you to our table."

Gripping her elbow, he led the way into the plush dining room, talking loudly as they walked along. "Yessir, baby, old Mortensen raved about you so much, I decided to enjoy your company myself."

Sonya gave him a skilled look of modesty as they arrived at the rich, linen-covered table. As Antonio held her chair for her, he said, "You remember my brother, Lou?"

"Yes. Hi, Lou." She greeted him with a practiced smile. Not bothering to stand, Lou simply nodded, all the while methodically twirling the unlit cigar in his left hand.

After ordering drinks, Antonio continued his ploy of ranting about Mortensen's alleged comments regarding Sonya's beauty, her intelligence, her professionalism, eventually guiding his conversation into small talk about her, grilling her with questions about her college education and her likes and dislikes. Craftily leading from one subject to another, Tafino quizzed her about her affiliation with the escort service and about her relationships with the other girls working there, ultimately asking if they ever had discussions amongst themselves about their escorts or if there was any jealousy within the ranks.

Without wanting to directly ask Sonya about this Jane, or Judy, or whatever the hell her name is, Antonio skirted all around the topic with loaded questions. He had to be careful. He didn't want to mention the girl's name outright because it might raise a suspicion in this young lady's mind. And if Sonya walked out early, it would not only blow his alternate plan, but this blonde might contact the auburn-haired one and warn her. About what, he wasn't sure. Even worse, Sonya would then become one more unwanted connection to he and Lou and Mortensen and it was already coming too close to home as it was, which Antonio detested. *I have to keep those loose ends tied up.*

His hope was for a casual mention of the conversation she'd had with Mortensen. Perhaps that could lead to disclosure of the other one's whereabouts. Yet, with Bigotti waiting, Antonio knew he'd find out for certain later, but if he could discover it here in an arcane manner, then he could avoid both, the expense of Bigotti getting it for him, and more importantly, the attention that his handyman's methods would create if he somehow screwed it up. *But— hey—Alex is good. He wouldn't screw it up.*

However, as the evening wore on, an evasive Sonya parried her host's questions with home-worked casual replies all through dinner. "Oh, no, Tony, the first rule of this vocation is discretion. Not only amongst us girls, but more importantly, between us and the clients themselves. For the protection of everyone, really."

Even though experiencing some frustration by not learning anything with his approach, the mobster kept himself calm by ordering more drinks, ultimately concluding that he had no option but to choose his last-resort plan. However, time was running short and there was information he needed to know for Alex. Leaning toward Sonya, he lowered his voice and coarsely whispered, "Hey, tell me, baby—I'll bet in your line of work, you probably have a lot of guys wanting you to do all sorts of strange things—huh?"

By this time, Sonya was filled with divine steak and lobster, and after five or six strong whiskey sours, Antonio's obnoxiousness was suddenly striking her as funny. Feeling the effects of the liquor, she furtively looked from side to side, then leaned toward Antonio and teasingly pinched his jowl. "I'm not sure I know what you mean, Tony, my man. What exactly did you have in mind?"

When she saw the surprised look on Antonio's face, Sonya shrieked with laughter. *Damn! Why am I acting so giddy? Sonya, get a-hold of yourself!*

Pulling away from her with a loud pshaw, Antonio gave her a wave of his hand. "Nothing particular in mind, baby, I was just makin' conversation, that's all. I merely figured you must meet some real lulu's in your line of work—you know—guys who probably ask you to do all sorts of strange things. Truth is—I was hopin' you might have some interesting stories to tell ol' Lou and I."

"What kind of stories, Tony?" she giggled. "Give me an illush—illushtration—hic!" *My God, I don't understand this! Why am I so damn dizzy?*

Antonio rubbed his chin with his fat fingers then shrugged his shoulders. "Well, let's see, uh... Okay, like drugs for example."

Scowling with distaste, Sonya emphatically announced, "Oh, no. Nope. Sorry. I don't do drugs, Tony."

"You mean to say you've never tried drugs at all? You know what I mean, not even socially? Not even to please a client, or to make your job a little easier?"

Feeling the effects of the liquor more and more,

Sonya's tongue began to loosen. Giggling, she drew her mouth close to his ear and confessed, "Oh sure, I've tried a little cocaine a couple of times—you know—just a few lines with some of my college friends—experimenting—that type of thing. Why? Are you into that? Is that what this is all about? You want to do some?"

"Oh no, no, no, baby, not at all. I've never done that crap. I was just curious to know what it's like, that's all."

"It gives you a buzz—a high—you know."

"That's it?"

"Yup. That's it." Suddenly grabbing his hand into hers, Sonya asked, "Hey, Tony. Do you want to try some? I can line it up for you!"

Acting perturbed, Antonio frowned at her. "No! Hell, no! I just told you—I wouldn't want to get hooked on some kinda crap like that! I was just makin' talk! Now, shuddup about it!"

Man alive! Whew—this freak-a-zoid has a temper! Rubbing the back of his varicose-veined hand, Sonya sedately murmured, "Okay, Tony. That's all I was doing, too. Forgive me?"

"All right, baby." Turning away from her, Antonio bellowed to the waiter gliding past the table. "Hey, young man, can you bring us another round here, please?"

"Yes, sir."

Immediately turning his concentration back to Sonya, Antonio quickly allowed his mood to mellow and snickered. "Okay, darlin', no more playing around with examples of subjects—let's just stick to the subject of playing around!" Coarsely laughing at his own stab at comedy, Antonio nodded to Lou, seeking an audience. He then looked for attention from the waiter, who simply kept writing the order on his pad.

Still gripping his hand in hers, Sonya casually looked down at his short, fat fingers and suddenly started giggling. *Ha! I'll bet he's got a little, short, fat thingee, too! Amanda always says—just look at their fingers!* Thoroughly entertained by her own private humor, Sonya all at once burst into loud hysterics. Throwing her head back, she laughed out loud and popped right out of the front of her white gown. She immediately began tugging at her bodice and still cackling, she flashed her eyes wide open at Antonio. "Oops!"

Gazing at her exposed breasts, Antonio nudged her arm and laughed. "Hey, don't show 'em off in here, baby! I'll check 'em out later."

He then looked at Lou and displayed an okay signal before quickly turning his face back toward Sonya. Squeezing her hand, he said, "For now, though, honey, you'll hafta excuse me. I gotta take a short walk. Gotta unload some of this scotch."

"Bye, Tony," she sang. He rose to his feet and briskly walked away. Holding her face in her hands, Sonya leaned her elbows on the lace tablecloth and giggled uncontrollably. *Damn, I'm dizzy! What in hell is wrong with me!* Lifting her eyes to the front, the silent man at the opposite side of the table came into focus. Without forethought, Sonya teased, "Hey, Lou! Don't you ever say anything, man? Incidentally, am I supposed to do you, too?"

Shaking with laughter, Sonya looked into his glassy, watery eyes, which were perceivably fixed on her pretty face. She didn't detect the smirk spreading across his lips. He had it hidden behind his hand, which was rotating the cigar in his mouth. Eyeballing his fingers on the cheroot, Sonya all at once burst into roaring laughter again. Feeling her head spinning round and round, the young blonde just couldn't understand how only five or six mixed drinks could affect her this much.

She was totally unaware that she'd been treated to very strong triples, spiked with chloral hydrate.

****

Upon reaching the vestibule, Antonio Tafino plunked some coins into a pay phone and pressed the numbers from memory. Seated in the white Cadillac, Bigotti heard his mobile phone ring. He lifted the receiver. "Yeah, Boss?"

254

"Use cocaine. If the cops ask me later, I can tell 'em she just offered me some." Click.

Chapter 40

After getting the call from Antonio, Alex Bigotti methodically prepared two syringes and carefully checked the needles for an even flow. He set them on the seat next to him and grinned to himself. *There.*

Knowing he had plenty of time, Alex was in no hurry. He thought about the task ahead. *I don't even know why the boss is doing this. Hell, nobody's ever heard from that auburn-haired chick. She ain't gonna be no trouble, so why don't he just forget about her? But that's just the boss's way. That bitch recorded those phone calls for some reason and he ain't gonna forget about it until he gets his hands on those tapes. You know, it's no wonder those younger guys in New York told the boss to retire. I mean, he's still thinkin' like the days of Al Capone. Truth is, he's pretty lucky those guys in New York let him retire and didn't just eliminate him and Lou. Oh, well, I'm gettin' paid good money to do what he says, so what the hell! I just gotta be careful nobody gets caught. But, hey, Alex—you're good! Ain't nobody gonna get caught.*

Now then, let's review this thing. I'm supposed to take out the driver, pick up the blonde and drive her to the escort service parking lot. Then I make it look like they over-dosed together. But first, and most important, I gotta find out from the blonde where the auburn-haired bitch is. I mean, that's what this is all about. Right? He looked at his watch. *Time to go.*

Alex Bigotti exited the white Cadillac.

****

Mark Tyler was listening to the soft vibes streaming from the radio in the limousine. With his eyes closed, his head was resting against the back of the driver's seat. Suddenly hearing the passenger door open, he expected it to be Sonya, but when he glanced up, he found himself looking at a big man with a crew haircut and a heavily pockmarked face. Sliding onto the cushion beside him, Alex Bigotti waved a gun in front of Mark's face. "Hey, curly—we gotta talk!"

As soon as he saw the pistol in the other man's hand, Mark defensively blurted, "What the hell are you doing? I'm just a driver. I don't carry any money!"

"I ain't after your money, curly—so just shut-up and listen!" Bigotti growled. He waved the gun for emphasis. Holding a syringe in his other hand, the gangster showed it to Mark and squirted a drop of liquid from the needle. "Ever tried this stuff, handsome?"

"What the hell is going on? What do you want?" Mark leaned against the door, shying away from the intruder.

"Just want you to try a little bit of this "c" handsome. That's all. I mean, with you on a buzz, I get to take little Blondie home. Simple as that."

"Get the hell out of this car, you ugly slimeball!"

"Hey, handsome! I've got a gun here. See it?" Waving it again, Bigotti ordered, "Now, curly, do as I say, or I'm gonna scatter your brains all over the front seat of this fancy car!"

Petrified and not sure what to do, Mark stared into the barrel of the small caliber Smith & Wesson. "Just exactly what do you want, asshole?"

Still aiming the pistol at Mark's head, Bigotti snarled. "I want to take that tall blonde home with me, curly—the one you brought in here. To do that, I need to eliminate you from the competition, so give me your arm!"

Cringing away from him, Mark clambered for the door handle. *Hell, I've gotta get away from this crazy jerk!*

Instantly feeling a strong grip on his forearm, Mark released the handle and swung his fist at the big man's head. He missed. Feeling the cold steel barrel of the gun against his temple, Mark heard the man dictate slowly and coldly, "Handsome, you'd better hold still right now or I will blow your brains out! Now then, for the last time—give me your arm!"

Cowering away from him, Mark pleaded, "Hey, man, I'm a body-builder. I don't want that crap in my veins. If it's the blonde you want, you can have her! I'll just walk home!"

Mark again grappled for the door handle, but just like before, he felt the strong hand of Alex Bigotti pulling on his arm, jerking it away. "All right, curly, wait a minute. Let's make a deal here. Just give me your hat and that spiffy jacket then you can leave."

"What?"

"I said—give me your hat and jacket. Think about it, curly. The only way that whore is gonna climb into the back seat of this car is if she thinks I'm the limo driver—so I need your hat and jacket to pull that off."

"That's it? That's all you want?"

"Yup." Bigotti assured him. "Well, and I'll need to borrow this fancy car for a while. Hey, seriously, curly, I'm only interested in gettin' a piece of that good looking chick for myself, so I'm tellin' you—just give me the hat and coat, then you can go."

Stunned, Mark just sat there staring at him, trying to think. Bigotti raised the gun into Mark's vision again and viciously laughed. "Or, do you prefer to stay here and try to defend that whore's honor?"

I've gotta get away from this crazy goon and warn Sonya! Thinking quickly, Mark struggled to remove the coat, talking all the while. "Hey, man, I'm just the driver. That witch don't mean nothin' to me! You can have her! As for me—I'm outta here!"

Quickly flinging his jacket over the man's head, Mark scrambled to get the door open, but before he could exit, he felt the ugly man's hand grab his arm once again. With a painful twist, Alex pinned it against the back of the seat. Despite Mark's own strength, he was no match for Bigotti. Especially in the tight confines of the car. Moving instinctively, the killer threw aside the coat and kicked the passenger door open, allowing the overhead light to come on. Holding Mark's struggling arm in place against the back of the seat, Bigotti dropped the gun to the floor and grabbed the syringe from the dash where he'd momentarily left it. With Mark's lithe build, spotting a blood vessel was easy and Bigotti plunged the needle into Mark's bulging vein.

Keeping him pinned there, he squeezed the liquid into his victim's bloodstream while thwarting glancing blows from Mark's free hand.

When he felt the young chauffeur's body eventually go limp, Bigotti quickly exited the limousine and closed the door behind him so the light would go off. Cautiously walking around to the driver's side, he looked all around, assuring himself that all was quiet before he entered the vehicle again. With a grunt, he pushed Mark's flaccid body to the other side of the seat then forced him onto the floor in a heap. Donning Mark's jacket and cap, Bigotti checked his watch and settled himself behind the wheel. *Ten more minutes, then we go get the blonde.*

****

Flagging down their waiter, Antonio ordered one more round of drinks before telling Sonya, "Baby, after this, you and I are gonna retire."

In a giddy voice, Sonya slapped the Italian on the arm. "But, Tony, I'm too young to retire!" She squealed with laughter. *Damn-Sam! Why am I acting like this?*

All at once Sonya felt the front of her dress being pulled away, then a cold hand slipped inside and she heard Antonio say, "Then we get to see the rest of what you got under there. Huh, baby?"

Pulling back away from him, Sonya groggily looked around at the thinning crowd. She tugged at the top of her white gown. "Okay! But not here, Tony! Isn't that what you said?"

Even as drunk as she was, Sonya at once felt repulsed by his quick feel, despite the two thousand dollars in her purse. She wasn't looking forward to his grubby paws smothering her body. *But, at his age, at least it won't last very long. Besides, I'm so drunk, I won't even feel it! But why am I so drunk? I never get like this.*

At precisely eleven o'clock, a waiter approached Antonio and whispered into his ear. The Italian secretly slipped a large bill into the young man's hand, then turned to Sonya and declared, "Let's go out to the lobby, baby.

Something's come up. We'll have to take a rain-check on the sex."

"What?" She drunkenly mumbled.

"C'mon, Blondie! It's time to go!" Antonio roared.

Gripping Sonya's elbow, he roughly raised her from her chair, causing her to stumble before she gained her balance. Moving quickly, Tafino kept his firm grip on her arm and marched her stumbling toward the lobby. He came to a stop at the front door.

Immediately angered, Sonya blurted, "What in the hell is the matter with you?"

"It's nothing personal, baby, but they're forming a good card game in one of the rooms upstairs and the stakes are gonna be pretty big. I want to sit in on this one, so I gotta get rid of you in a hurry, that's all."

"Well, you don't have to be so damn nasty about it!" Sonya yelled. "Just tell me. I'll go!"

The Italian was pitching a game. He had to make her mad enough to stomp out of the resort and climb into the limo without hesitating. Bellowing loud enough for everyone to hear, he growled, "Blondie, I'll tell you this—I'd rather play poker anytime than spend the night with some whore who does drugs! Believe me, I can get a good looking trick anytime I want to, so get your ass out of here and I never want to see you again!"

Shoving her toward the door, Antonio turned and walked away in front of at least ten stunned witnesses. Shocked, and too embarrassed to argue in front of all those people, Sonya merely raised her head in proud defiance, flipped him off to his back, thrust open the door and staggered blindly toward the black Lincoln.

Not waiting for her chauffeur to come around and open the door for her, Sonya reached for the handle and missed connecting with it twice before her fingers finally wrapped around it. Holding her handbag under her arm, she used both hands to push on the button and struggled to pull the door open. It finally released and swung out toward the sidewalk. Still groping, she held onto the interior handle for support and started to climb inside. Stumbling, she grabbed onto the seat cushion, vainly trying to steady herself. She drunkenly mumbled out loud, "Okay, Sonya, just a coupla more inches."

Alex Bigotti intensely watched her movements through the rear-view mirror. *Come on, baby! Get in the car!*

Clambering to get a grip on the seat, Sonya was trying to lift her foot up onto the floorboard when she heard a feminine voice behind her. "Sonya? Is that you?"

Turning to look behind her, Sonya squinted in the direction of the voice. Not releasing her grip on the seat cushion, she chimed, "Hey, I'll be damned! Hi, Sandy. What are you doing here?"

Tottering, Sonya lost her grip on the cushion and laughed out loud at her own clumsiness. She heard Sandy giggle and return the greeting. "Hi there, Sonya. You're lookin' a little bit out of it—what's up?"

"I just had a really bad evening—hic—and I think I'm drunk. And believe me, I never, never, never get this way. What's up with you?"

"Well, Jolene, Christy, Cindy and I just had dinner here to celebrate Cindy's new promotion. We're on our way to Mr. Lucky's?"

"Mr. Lucky's?"

"Yeah—we're still celebrating. Hey, are you by yourself? Want to come with us?"

"Oh, I don't think so, Sandy. I'm not feeling so well. I should get back." Reaching aimlessly into the vehicle, Sonya fell against the seat, stumbling and giggling as she tried to maintain her balance.

"Oh, come on, Sonya." Sandy begged. "Come with us. None of us have seen you in a while. We probably have a lot to catch up on."

Alex Bigotti watched all this in the mirror. *Get in the car, Blondie!*

"Oooohhh, Sandy, I'm so drunk. I should get home. Really. Maybe some other time," she mumbled. Grabbing the car seat, Sonya tried one more time to climb inside.

Still concentrating on the rear-view mirror, Bigotti pulled the cap down further over his face and intently watched her. *Atta girl. Now then, let's go!*

With the motor running, Alex prepared to accelerate as he patiently waited, wanting to make sure she was inside and that the door was closed. But his patience was wearing thin. *Get in the damn car!*

As she made one more blundering attempt to climb onto the seat, Sonya cackled out loud. She glanced back over her shoulder at Sandy, who was extending her hand to help. With her head whirling, Sonya gave up the attempt and her head slumped onto the cushion and she moaned. She heard Sandy giggle and say, "I think you're right, Sonya. You are drunk! By all means, you better come with us. We'll get you sobered up then we'll take you home. C'mon, girl!"

Grabbing Sonya's hand and tugging at it, Sandy pulled the reluctant young woman out of the vehicle. But unable to control Sonya's limp body, Sandy's hand let go and they both went tumbling to the concrete curb, tangled together. Rolling into the gutter, they both squealed and, virtually incapable of standing up, they simply stayed there, laying on the ground and screeching shrill laughter. With Jolene and Cindy jumping in to help, they eventually gained their feet and brushed themselves off.

All at once, Sonya remembered how disgusted she was with the Italians. "Freaking Dagos!" *Maybe Sandy's right. Maybe I should go with them.*

Looking into the open door of the limousine without really paying attention, the young blonde yelled into the interior. "Hey, Mark, I'm going with Sandy and them. Tell Amanda I'll call her tomorrow. "Okay?"

Not waiting for his reply, Sonya slammed the door closed, and with all of them laughing and shrieking together, she tottered away with her friends to Jolene's car. Quickly climbing into the Plymouth Volare, the five of them sped away.

****

Stunned, Alex Bigotti continued staring into the

262

mirror at the empty rear seat. *Crapola! Now, what do I do? The boss is gonna think I screwed this up real bad.* He slammed his fist against the steering wheel and glared at Mark's body, slumped on the floor. *Sorry, curly. Guess you got wasted for nothing.*

All at once hearing a chorus of voices, Alex darted his eyes to the right and saw several patrons leaving the club. *I better get out of here!* Quickly shifting the car into drive, he alertly checked for traffic and pulled away from the curb, knowing it would be a long walk back to his car after he dumped the limo.

Grinding to a stop for a red light at the next intersection, Alex was considering his own fate. *Well, all I can do is tell the boss what happened and he'll just have to understand. I mean, I can't follow those crazy broads and take 'em all out. Hell—I ain't no butcher!*

When the light changed to green, he charged the smooth Lincoln into the intersection and saw something ahead. *Wait a minute, Alex, that's those broads right there in front of you. For Chrissakes, take down the license plate number! With the boss's connections, he can surely find out that gal's address, then you can find out from her where the blonde lives! Hell, she might even know the auburn bitch, as well. And hell's bells, if all else fails, maybe the boss can fix that blonde up with me. She don't know me! And I guarantee we'll get what we need from her then!*

All at once his dreaded long walk back to his car didn't seem quite as formidable. He grinned to himself. *Alex, not only should the boss understand the little misconnection that just took place, but he most likely is gonna praise your quick thinking for coming up with another solution so fast. Now then, you'd better get away from the back of that Plymouth before that stupid blonde whore recognizes this tuna boat and sees you ain't curly. That'll blow your other idea all to hell.* He took a right at the next corner and disappeared from sight.

Chapter 41

The insistent ringing of the telephone finally stirred Sonya from a deep, hard sleep. Despite the throbbing pain dulling her senses, she grappled for the receiver. Fumbling with it, she eventually got it to her ear and moaned into the mouthpiece. "Hello."

"Sonya, wake up! It's Amanda!"

"Whu-what? What time is it?"

"Sonya, c'mon. Wake up! I have to talk to you!"

"Ooooh! My head is splitting! Whaddya want?"

"Sonya. Listen to me. Mark Tyler was found dead this morning!"

"Huh? What did you say?"

"I said that Mark was found dead this morning!" Amanda repeated.

Sonya bolted upright. "What? Dead? Where?"

"In the parking lot!" Amanda exclaimed. "They found him in the limousine. He apparently overdosed!"

Clamping her hand to her forehead, Sonya held her eyes closed, trying in vain to stop the hammering in her head. She screamed into the telephone, "Wait a minute. What did you say? Mark's dead—and he overdosed? On what? Health pills? Vitamins?"

"Huh-uh, honey. It was drugs."

"That can't be, Amanda! Mark doesn't do drugs!"

"I don't know about that, honey, but when he was discovered this morning, according to the cops, he had enough of that stuff in him to kill an elephant! Did he take you home last night?"

"No. No, he didn't. I left the assignment early. I told Mark I'd talk to you this morning. I don't believe this."

"After he dropped you off at the resort, where did he go?"

"I told him to stick close because I didn't like the johns. He was waiting for me when I got dumped by that friggin' wop, but I ran into some old friends from school and went with them, instead of having Mark bring me back. I figured he'd return the limo and then go home."

"What time was that?"

"Mm, about eleven, I suppose. Maybe a little later. Whoa, hold on a minute, Amanda—I gotta go pee."

Dropping the phone onto her pillow, Sonya stumbled to the bathroom, banging into the door before coming upright again. Turning on the cold tap, she cupped her hands under it and splashed water onto her face. Once, twice, three times. Bracing herself against the vanity with both hands, she leaned against it with her eyes closed, muttering to herself. "Ooooh! My head is killing me! That's something else I don't understand. I never get hangovers!"

Grabbing a towel, she mopped her face and despite dreading the outcome, she forced herself to look in the mirror. Her unkempt hair straggled limp and her make-up was completely gone, save the dark blotches under her eyes from her mascara. Leaning closer, she touched her face beneath her swollen eyes. "Ugh."

Tossing the towel aside, Sonya reached into the medicine cabinet. After struggling with the lid, she managed to open a bottle of aspirin. Wolfing down four of them with a glass of water, she threw her head back when she swallowed, in an effort to let them slide down easier. Gasping and breathing heavily, with shaky hands, she soaked a washcloth in cold water. Taking that and the towel with her, she aimed herself back toward the direction of her bed. Halfway there, she turned back around, complaining out loud. "Damn! I forgot to pee!"

When she finally arrived back at her bunk, she stretched out and gently patted the washcloth onto her forehead before reaching for the telephone again. "Okay, Amanda, I'm back."

"My word, Sonya! What time did you get home, anyway?"

"Sometime after four. Oooohhh. Man alive, I feel horrible! And now you're telling me this about Mark? That's unbelievable!"

"Shook me up, too, honey, I'll tell you! Anyway,

Sonya, I thought I'd better call you before the police come. They're gonna want to talk to you. It seems you're the last person to see Mark alive. Are you—?"

Sonya interrupted her, "But Amanda, this whole thing is so bizarre! Mark never touched drugs in his life. Or alcohol, either, for that matter! What kind of drugs did they say it was?" Shifting her position on the bed, striving for some kind of comfort, Sonya replaced the wet rag, which had slipped off during her gyrations.

"A whole lot of cocaine, honey. Almost pure stuff. That's probably why he overdosed—he didn't know what he was doing."

"But, what the—? How? Amanda, he couldn't have done that. I know Mark well enough to know he wouldn't even think of touching that stuff! He was so damned health conscious with his bodybuilding and all. This is plain crazy!"

"Sonya, believe me, it's pretty cut and dried. They found the syringe in his hand and his prints were all over it, according to the cop I talked to. They're still investigating, but they're pretty sure that's what happened to him. They're impounding the car, but that detective told me with so many people in and out of that limo, tracing all the prints they're gonna find is damned near hopeless."

Thanks to his gloves, Alex Bigotti's would not be there.

"Did you say the cops want to talk to me?" Sonya nervously asked.

"Oh, yeah. Definitely. I gave them your address and phone number about half an hour ago."

"Then I'd better go, Amanda. If they see me in this condition, they'll think I'm a junkie. Or another corpse."

"Okay, babe. I'll talk to you later." Click.

****

While showering and dressing, Sonya couldn't push her memory of Mark away. With her thoughts bringing intermittent tears to her eyes, she refused to believe the asinine nature of the circumstances surrounding his untimely

266

death. And while thinking everything through, all of a sudden, she was afraid. Not knowing of what. Just afraid. Then she remembered something. Antonio Tafino. And all of his questions about drugs. Cocaine...

Her mind drifted over the events of the past couple of weeks and she attempted to piece it all together, searching for a reason for Mark's death, or someone to blame. She thought back to her first dinner date with the Tafino brothers. Having originally been indignant with James Mortensen's story about his so-called "Jane" and his tales of watching the two of them together, Sonya now began to wonder. Was it true? Was it really Judy? Is she somehow involved with all this? *Damn! It has to be. It's the only connection.*

Thinking further back, Sonya remembered when her friend left school and the escort service. All of a sudden, Judy had a new car, an expensive apartment, a lot of money, and somehow she seemed different. *I merely thought she'd met someone, a rich someone, and had fallen for him. But Mortensen? Naw! Can't picture that. Besides, he seemed to be looking for her. Who else? Antonio Tafino? Maybe for the money. But who could love that rotten dirt-bag? Anyway, whatever it was, ever since Judy left impulsively for Vanderbilt, I haven't seen her or talked with her. Jeez, I can't even remember the last time I did. But that Mortensen character was sure convinced she was his "Jane."* Then something else suddenly occurred to her. *Oh, hell, Sonya! And you told that Mortensen Judy's real name!*

Watching her image in the mirror as she applied her lipstick, new tears welled in Sonya's eyes and she stopped her mechanical movements. Standing there, she looked at her reflection in the glass and stared deeply into her own blue eyes. She moved closer to the reflection and hopelessly sighed, perhaps really looking at herself for the first time. Sickened by what had happened to Mark, the nausea stretched into her soul and she was becoming ill with all that her life had become.

Not only that, she was confused by the haunting fear

now nagging at her. She couldn't shake it, nor could she explain to herself the reason for its being there. Once more, for another unknown reason, Judy's face popped into her mind's eye again. *Just where have you gone, Judy Carmelle?*

With another longing gaze at her reflection, Tanya voiced aloud, "and even more importantly, Sonya Waverly, just where in the hell are you going?"

An impetuous, loud knocking at her apartment door crashed into her thoughts. Sonya jumped. Extremely nervous, she hoped it was the police, yet she dreaded that confrontation at the same time. Hesitating, she decided something at that very moment. *Okay. After I talk to them, I'm getting out of here. I don't know where to, but I'm getting out of here! Whatever Judy has gotten herself into, it doesn't involve me! And it has to be a connection with her, I just know it. She's the only common thread in all of this. Somehow, that Mortensen character has tied our friendship together and he thinks I'm in cahoots with whatever she's doing! And those two Italian guys? Now there's two scary lookin' dudes!*

Suddenly, Sonya heard the insistent knocking on the door again and shuddered. Tip-toeing to the entryway, she reached for the knob and started to turn it. But all at once, becoming even more apprehensive, she asked, "Who is it?"

A gruff voice on the other side of the door told her, "Detective Bearden with the Phoenix Police Department. Are you Sonya Waverly?"

Without removing the chain, Sonya opened the door a crack and studied the man on the other side. His receding hairline and off-the-rack blue suit told her he certainly resembled a policeman. "Y-yes."

While holding up his badge for her to see, the man offered, "Miss Waverly, we'd like to ask you some questions about a Mark Tyler." Then, motioning toward a younger, light-skinned black man beside him, Bearden added, "This is Detective Smith. May we come in?"

Momentarily closing the door to remove the chain, Sonya re-opened it, allowing them in. Turning her back, she walked to a cherry-wood end table near the sofa and nervously lifted a cigarette from the package setting there. With shaking hands, she touched her lighter to it and expelled a cloud of smoke above her head before speaking. "I, uh, just heard about Mark. Maybe an hour ago."

Staring into space, she uneasily puffed on the cigarette again and picked at the chipped fingernail polish on her left hand forefinger. Eventually realizing that the two men were awkwardly standing in the center of the room, Sonya apologetically motioned with a wave of her hand toward the sectional. "Oh, I'm sorry, officers. Please. Have a seat."

Tight-lipped, Bearden nodded a thank you and edged in the direction of the tawny colored furniture, followed by Smith. As they started to sit down, they heard Sonya offer, "I've, uh, just made some coffee. Would you care for some?"

"Sure. Thank you, miss." Bearden replied. In an effort to put the young woman at ease, he attempted to add a tone of pleasantness to his voice when he added, "black for me. Smitty?"

"Sounds good to me, too, but I'll have to doctor mine a little. I use cream and sugar, please." Without expression, Sonya briskly turned and walked into the kitchen, feeling their eyes following her.

As he studied her, Bearden raised his eyebrows while he stared at her rounded hips, moving gracefully within the confines of her too-tight denims. Having questioned Tafino a bit earlier, he had to ask himself—*and that old codger turned down that for a card game?*

While pouring the Chase & Sanborn, Sonya kept telling herself to try and remain calm. *Just remember, girl, all you have to do is answer their questions! Don't volunteer anything! Simply tell them what took place last night and stay aloof! STAY ALOOF!* Thrusting a hopeful look toward the ceiling for luck, she lifted the tray and walked back to the living room.

Carefully setting the refreshments on the coffee

table, Sonya picked up her own cup and seated herself into a dark blue casual chair across from the policemen. She pointed at the tray. "Please, gentlemen, help yourselves." As a quick afterthought, she hastily volunteered, "I'm sorry, I don't have any doughnuts."

When Sonya saw both officers simultaneously look at her with blank expressions, she immediately bucked forward in an involuntary spiel of convulsive laughter. Unable to stop, she spilled her coffee with her spasmodic shaking, causing her to laugh even harder.

Stunned, both detectives simply stared at her, frozen in their inexpressive poses. This caused her hysteria to surge even higher, as she uncontrollably quaked until her sides started aching, screeching shrill cackles until equally as instantaneously, she began to cry. Weeping unashamedly, the young blonde's shoulders trembled while the befuddled detectives incredulously watched in a complete state of helplessness.

Then, as abruptly as it all started, it seemed to just stop. Quit. While carefully setting the coffee cup on the table beside her, between sniffles, Sonya somberly peeked at them. Giving them a wave of her hand bordering on insouciance, she quickly darted her eyes longingly away toward the window—not really looking at anything. After a few moments, she heaved a sigh of surrender and swiped at the moisture on her cheeks while the patient investigators waited. She looked into Bearden's eyes. "Sorry."

However, before they could say anything, the tears began streaming again. Jumping from her chair, Sonya trotted to the bathroom. Returning with a box of tissues, the distraught young lady plopped back into her chair. After dabbing her eyes and blowing her nose, she slowly raised her eyes to meet their unsure gaze. She threw her long, blonde hair back away from her streaked face, brushing through it with her fingers. Shuddering, Sonya heaved another deep sigh and raised her palms out to them in a continued plea for patience. "Please. I'm sorry. Really. I-I guess I'm so upset about Mark, I'm not able to control myself really well right now."

Squirming on the sofa, both detectives mumbled a pooh-poohed acceptance of her apology and while Smith lifted his cup to his lips, Bearden spoke, "We understand, Miss Waverly, we see—"

"And, really, you guys—" Sonya blurted, "—I didn't mean anything by that remark about the doughnuts. Honestly. I could just as easily have said cookies, or cake, or whatever. But—" she innocently shrugged, "—I, uh, well, doughnuts and coffee sorta go hand in hand, so I said doughnuts." Her voice squeaked with the word doughnuts. Giggling again, she added, "Then when I saw the look on your faces, it struck me. Doughnuts and policemen. I didn't mean anything by it, honest-to-God. It was a slip. Sorry."

Very much relieved that her convulsions were apparently over with, Detective Bearden chuckled and brushed it away with a sweep of his arm. "That's perfectly all right, Miss Waverly. It's an old joke that we've all heard way too many times, but I've got to say, you pulled if off better by accident than most of those jokers do on purpose. Right, Smitty?" With a wide grin, Smith agreed.

After setting his cup back onto the tray, Bearden reached into his coat pocket and took out a notepad and pen. "Now then, Miss Waverly, do you, uh, feel that you're up to answering a few questions for us?"

"Yes, sir. What would you like to know?"

"First of all, we'd like to hear your version of what took place last night and when did you last see Mark Tyler?"

Starting from the time she and Mark left Parisian Escort Service for her assignment, Sonya relayed everything as she remembered it. "And that's the last I knew about Mark until Amanda called me this morning."

"I suppose your friends can verify that you were with them?"

"Oh, yeah. Sure. I'll give you their names."

"Tell me, Miss Waverly, did Mark do drugs often? At least, that you know of?"

"No! And that's what surprises me about this whole

thing! I've never seen him *ever* do any drugs. He said they were poison. I mean, Mark was a really health conscious guy."

"So, in your opinion, how is it that he could have died of an overdose? Any ideas?"

"I can't really explain that, Detective. Believe me, it's more of a mystery to me than it is to you."

"How about yourself, Miss Waverly? Are you into that scene?"

"No, sir. Not at all."

"We could get a search warrant."

Feeling numb, Sonya was not only not surprised by his questions, but for some unknown reason, she wasn't even angered or upset. "That's not necessary, Detective Bearden. You're welcome to look around here all you want. I've got nothing to hide."

Staring at her, Bearden believed her. He changed the subject. "Okay. Did Mark date any of the girls from the escort service? You, maybe?"

"No, we were just friends and co-workers. Mark is, er, was a real honest-to-goodness gentleman. I think he may have mentioned to me once that he was dating a dancer at Showgirls. I don't know her name. Sorry."

"That's okay. We can find that out." Slowly closing the notepad and shoving it back into his pocket, the policeman smiled at the pretty, young blonde. "Well, I think that about wraps it up for now, Miss Waverly. Smitty?"

"No more questions I can think of, Lieutenant."

When he saw Bearden stand up, the black man followed his lead then nodded to Sonya. "Thanks for the coffee, Miss Waverly."

As he ambled toward the entrance, Bearden smiled to himself, silently thankful that nothing had happened between this girl, Sonya, and Tafino. With no proof of any act of prostitution, except for the bragging words of the arrogant Italian, he saw no good in bringing it up. Opening the door, he kept his hand on the knob and smiled at her. "Thanks for your cooperation, Miss Waverly. If we think of anything else, we'll be in touch."

"Okay." She whispered. Silently closing the door behind them, Sonya trekked back to the end table and after lighting another cigarette, she slumped into the blue chair, thankful they were gone.

While she sat there, a wave of reminiscence came over her. She thought of the prior days at college, the fun of that, picturing Judy and the others. Fighting back more tears, she looked around the furnished apartment, listening to the absolute silence. Feeling hollow, she stared out the window and noticed the unusually dark overcast sky, then thought to herself. *How fitting.*

Resting her thoughts on the escort service, she all at once felt relief, knowing that nobody connected with the place knew anything about her background or her history before she began working there. As her life and all the people she knew fleetingly passed by in her mind, Sonya Waverly all at once smiled to herself, realizing she had the answer. She knew that Daddy would be ecstatic that his little girl was finally coming home. This time, for good.

Smashing the cigarette butt into an ashtray, she bounced up and started to work. Feverishly grabbing her suitcases from the bedroom closet, she haphazardly threw her clothes from the dresser into them. *The things in the closet can stay on hangers!* After hurriedly cramming everything from the bathroom and kitchen into grocery store bags, with several trips, she carried all of her belongings to her new Oldsmobile Cutlass, filling the trunk and back seat with no thought for organization. Traipsing back upstairs one last time, she ran from room to room, shutting off all the lights and taking one final look around. Satisfied, she went back outside and locked the apartment door before making a mad dash to her car.

Driving to the savings & loan, she closed her account, taking the balance in a cashier's check, payable to herself. She still had the two thousand dollars from last night in her purse. Wanting to know a reason, for their records, she lied to the teller that she'd decided to move to Miami.

Becoming more petrified by the minute, she shoved the check into her purse and anxiously ran out of the bank. With nothing else to be done, Sonya Waverly roared out of the parking lot and aimed the car toward Interstate 17 to Flagstaff, where she'd turn right and head east on Interstate 40, on her way to Omaha.

Leaving the city limits, her only regret was that she had no way to warn Judy. She didn't know where she was.

EPILOGUE
PART TWO

James Mortensen leisurely sat in his office with his feet propped up on his desk. *Only a couple more weeks to go and that Worthington property will be Antonio's. Man, am I ever glad that one came along. That put me back into good graces.*

Then, just as it did every day, his mind drifted back to the comely blonde named Sonya and while envisioning her nakedness, he filled with two emotions...regret that he hadn't taken advantage of her when he'd had the opportunity and, upon feeling himself becoming aroused, a wave of guilt for still wanting to. Casting a culpable glance at the picture of his wife, he had to clear away the latter emotion, so he picked up the phone and dialed his home number. Rinnng. Rinnng. Rinnng. Click. *Damn! Where can she be this time? Well, to hell with taking her to dinner. I'll just go back to work!* And for James, it was good enough. The guilt was gone and the vision of Sonya was back.

****

While Antonio Tafino swirled the ice around in his scotch, he stared at the glass in his hand. "Lou, I've been thinking. This thing with that woman and those tapes is all Mortensen's fault! As soon as this latest deal is over with, I believe we oughtta have Alex pay him a visit. I think it's time we find a new broker and get a fresh start. What do you think?"

A thin smile crossed Louis Tafino's oily face, but as he lifted the cigar toward his lips, a scowl replaced it and, with both hands, he drew the outline of a female figure in the air. Antonio caught his meaning. "Oh hell yes, Lou, I've still got Alex on her trail, but so far, everything we've tried has backfired and we've come up empty. But don't concern yourself—we'll find that Mexican bitch—hopefully before Mortensen's out of the picture." As Antonio laughed, Lou's cigar reached his mouth, and so did another smile.

****

275

Alex Bigotti sat in front of his television, sipping a beer, wondering what to do next. Even though it had been several weeks now, he was still angry at that stupid blonde whore. After forcefully getting her address from Jolene Wilson and going to the trouble of submersing Jolene's Plymouth Volare in the canal, with Jolene's already drowned body inside, it was only to find out that the blonde had already skipped out. Alex was at a loss. *There I was, waiting for her and all set to surprise her in that fancy apartment of hers, only to find all of her things gone. How in the hell did she get away so fast? Oh well, at least the one I drowned gave me a picture of the auburn haired chick and I finally know what she looks like.*

Finishing the last of his beer, Alex caressed the label with his huge thumb before setting the bottle on the table next to him with determination. *That's okay, Blondie, I'll find you. Nobody makes the boss get that mad at me and gets away with it.* He resolutely turned off the television and went to bed.

****

Detective Thomas Bearden was slowly perusing the records he was putting away. He had Jolene Wilson's file in his hand when one entry suddenly leaped out at him: Traces of soap. Could be bubble-bath.

Bubble-bath? He hurriedly reached for the telephone and dialed the coroner's office. "Bill, I have a question. A few weeks back, there was a young lady who drove off into a canal and drowned. Remember that?"

"Yeah, I seem to recall it. What about her?"

"Her death was ruled to be by drowning. But tell me, how in the hell could she have traces of bubble-bath in her lungs if she drowned in a canal? And why wasn't I told about that at the time?"

"It was in the report, Tom. Don't you guys read those things?"

"Never mind. Are you sure it was bubble-bath?"

"If it's written in the report that way, Tom, then it was bubble-bath."

"All right, Bill. Thanks." Click.

As Bearden cradled the receiver, he stared at his partner. "Smitty, I think we'd better try to locate that Sonya Waverly girl again. If I remember right, this young lady who drowned was one of the friends she was with the night that bodybuilder supposedly shot himself up with cocaine. That one never added up right, either."

"You think that Waverly woman had something to do with them two dyin'?"

"I know that when we went back to ask her a few more questions, she'd certainly disappeared in a hurry. And I also know this—if she's not responsible, then she could be in a lot of danger herself. Whatever it is, there's something fishy about all of this, so we need to find her and see if we can figure out just what in the hell it is."

"Where do we start?"

"Parisian Escort Service."

****

With every succeeding week that passed, following Mortensen's first visit to my office, I telephoned the broker once a week at first, then twice a week, until we had only sixteen more days before the foreclosure sale date. Using his memorized excuses, he gave me reason after reason why each application he'd presented had been refused. Of course, I made certain that I didn't mention the foreclosure to him again. The time was coming for that.

PART THREE

Chapter 42

The stage was set for me to begin my act of desperation with James Mortensen. Maryann put my Monday morning call through to him. "Mortensen? Worthington here! What's the latest on my mortgage?"

I heard him sigh. "There's nothing new since I talked with you on Friday, Mr. Worthington. It's only Monday. Let's give it a few more days."

I raised my voice. "A few more days? Mortensen, I've gotta have that mortgage! What about those two lenders you talked to last week? I thought you might have heard something from them by now!"

"No. Nothing yet."

"Well, rather than wait around for them to take their old, sweet time, why don't you give them a call?"

"Because, Mr. Worthington, I normally don't like to contact the lenders after I've submitted a package to them. If we act pushy, they're less inclined to approve us."

"That's bullshit! They either give it to us or they don't! I say go ahead and call 'em." I winked at Judy, who was standing in my doorway, taking it all in.

"All right, I'll get in touch with them both and get back to you this afternoon." Click. Click.

****

I took his return call shortly after two o'clock. "Okay, Mortensen, I hope you finally have some good news for me."

"Well, Mr. Worthington, I'm afraid not. The one trust won't have the funds available for another sixty to ninety days and the other one doesn't look at anything that's less than five million dollars. I'm sorry. This was the first time I'd submitted anything to either of them, so I didn't know that. However, I do have a couple of others in mind I can talk to."

"Well, when do you plan to talk to them? I need this mortgage, man!"

"Please. Calm down, Mr. Worthington. I'm doing the

best I can. Financing is very difficult right now. Nobody knows what's going to happen now that Reagan's in office. Everybody's sitting on things." Strangely enough, that part was true. "In any event, I have two labor trusts I haven't used before and I'd like to present it to them. Probably later this week."

"Later this week? What's wrong with giving it to them today?"

"Well—and this is awkward, Mr. Worthington—but you see, my secretary left the office earlier today feeling quite ill and the way she looked when she left here, I don't expect her back for a couple of days. Plus, it'll take her a day or two to catch up when she does get back. However, I'll tell you what—I'll have her take care of yours first—the minute she returns."

"Hell, Mortensen, if that's your only problem, I can let Joyce leave for the rest of the day. Why don't you let me send her down there to type those damned things for you? Believe me, she's good. I guarantee you, she'll have 'em whipped out in no time."

"Uh..." He hesitated.

"Seriously," I prodded him, "I want those things typed today. So, what do you say?"

"Uh, no, no. That's all right, Mr. Worthington. I'll tell you what. I'll stay late tonight and type them myself. That way, we can get them presented first thing tomorrow and we should have an answer back before the end of the week."

"I don't know, Mortensen. I really think you should consider letting Joyce do it. That way I'm sure they'll get done and get done right—not that I doubt your typing ability."

"Please rest assured, Mr. Worthington. When I first started in this business, I used to type all of them myself until I could afford to hire a secretary. And at times like this, when Maryann's away, I still type them myself. Besides, I'd have to review all the forms with your girl to familiarize her with them and that might take even longer than typing them myself."

"Hmm. Perhaps you're right. I didn't think about that. So, if you present them tomorrow, how soon can we expect an answer?"

"By Thursday, I'm sure."

"Good enough, Mortensen. I'll talk to you on Thursday." Click. Click.

Looking up, I saw Judy standing in the doorway with her head cocked to one side. She had her arms folded firmly in front of her and her eyes were glaring fire at me.

"Something wrong?" I asked.

"Was that really necessary?" She demanded. "I don't want anything to do with that stupid jcrk! What if he'd said yes?"

"Hey, hey, calm down. Believe me, I knew he wouldn't accept."

"Oh? And why is that? Because, all of a sudden in this get-up, I'm so freaking ugly?"

Is she serious? I shook my head in disbelief. Then as I got up and walked around the desk with my arms outstretched, she leaned against the wall, pouting coolly away from me. I enveloped her into a warm hug anyway and told her, "Hell, no, Girl! It's because he just bought two more days of stalling me and he wasn't about to give them back by allowing me to send you down there! Hey, listen, I knew what I was doing. I wasn't about to let you go over to that pervert's place. I love you too much to put you back into that kind of danger again." Grinning at her, I kissed her forehead.

"Oh." Pressing her face against my chest, she finally squeezed her arms tightly around me. "Okay, now I get it."

Pulling away, she looked up at me. "Joe-Joe, I'm tired. Can we go home?"

"Certainly. Let's go. Nothing more we can do here today, anyway."

****

At mid-morning on Thursday, James Mortensen burst unannounced into the office of Worthington

Construction Company. "Hi, miss. Is Mr. Worthington in?"

Rebounding quickly from the surprise of seeing him, Judy jumped to her feet. Walking somewhat slouched over, she moved toward my office without really looking at him. "Yes, of course. I'll show you in."

When she announced him, I sprang to my feet and leaned over the desk, extending my hand to accept his as he quickly brushed past Judy and approached my desk. "Good morning, Mr. Worthington. How are you today?"

"Fine, Mortensen. But plenty worried. I certainly hope you've finally got some good news for me." After motioning toward a chair for him, I sat down behind my desk.

He pulled the chair closer. "Not yet, I'm afraid."

"Hell, the way you were grinning when you came in here, I thought for sure you had something."

Without responding, he placed his brown briefcase on the desk and opened it. He extracted a thick packet of forms. Holding them in his hand, he said, "You know, Mr. Worthington, after I presented those last two applications on Tuesday, which incidentally weren't accepted, I've been thinking, the original information package you completed for me is getting a bit old and stale, and perhaps the reason I've been unsuccessful to this point is the fact we need to have it updated. So, I'm leaving this new set with you because I have a feeling that with more current information, there's probably a much better chance of getting this put together for you."

Plopping the papers on my desk before I could say a word, he pointed at them. "Would you mind taking the time to complete these for me? At your leisure, of course. No hurry."

Okay, Joseph, the time has come to bring up the magic word. "What?" I incredulously exclaimed. "Mortensen, you know damned well I only have six more days until the foreclosure sale takes place on my building, and now you bring your ass in here wanting me to fill out new forms? 'At my leisure'? What the hell is wrong with you, man?" Glaring at him, I pounded my fist on the desk for emphasis, causing him to jolt backwards.

He gave me a look of total surprise. "What did you say?"

"What did I say? You heard me!"

"No. What did you say about a foreclosure?" *Damn, he's good.*

I spewed the words at him. "Mortensen, you know exactly what I said about a foreclosure. I told you the first day you were in my office that my building had been placed in foreclosure by that old man, Bowden. And, at the time, you assured me you could get a mortgage for me and save the damn thing! So now, I want to know—where in the hell is my mortgage?" I was giving him my best panic-stricken act. *Hey—I'm pretty good, too.*

At this point, his show of surprise was approaching complete astonishment. "Oh my, no, Mr. Worthington, I had no idea your property was in foreclosure. My goodness— that completely changes everything."

I wanted him to admit it to the camera, so I repeated it to him through gritted teeth. "Mortensen, I know I told you about this foreclosure business on the very first day you visited my office. Are you now going to tell me you don't remember that?"

Innocently leaning back in his chair and shrugging his shoulders, the mortgage broker did even better than I'd hoped. "Honestly, Mr. Worthington, I'm certain you didn't tell me about any foreclosure. Let me assure you, I've been in this business a long time and I would have picked up on that right away. Especially since those types of things are special arrangements that I know how to deal with. Believe me, I thought we had all the time in the world! Had I known, I would have treated this entirely different."

My God, this man is truly believable. Now I know why it happened to me before. And to all those other people.

But by this time, with all of this now recorded on film, I didn't want to push my argument too far. Heaving a whooshing sigh of disgust, I relented, apparently giving up the fight. "Okay, Mortensen. So now what do we do?"

Believing he had gained the upper hand, Mortensen took charge, beginning with a sincere sounding apology. "My word, Mr. Worthington, I am really sorry. I only wish I'd known about this from the start. However, now that I understand the situation, I do have a few investors who specialize in distressed real estate. It's a little more expensive than our routine transactions, but I guarantee you I can more than likely save your property. Now then, if you will please go ahead and fill out these forms for me, I'll present them as soon as they're back in my possession. And I absolutely guarantee you, Mr. Worthington, I'll do my utmost to get them shoved through for you."

I gave him my best helpless pose. "All right. I'll fill them out this evening."

"Good. Can I pick them up in the morning?"

"Yeah, sure. But it looks like I'll be up rather late tonight, so don't make it before ten o'clock."

"I'll be here at ten, Mr. Worthington. After that, I'll immediately deliver the package to my investors personally. We should have their answer no later than Monday."

Standing up, he quickly grabbed his briefcase and shook my hand. James Mortensen whisked himself out of the office, not bothering to pay any attention to Joyce on his way out.

Watching through my window, I waited until I saw his blue Datsun leave the parking lot. Turning to Judy, I said, "Okay, Girl, phase four has now begun."

When I returned my eyes to the window, Judy walked deliberately up behind me and placed her arms around my waist. And as she nestled her head against my shoulder, I felt her shudder. "And this is the scary part. Right, Joe-Joe?'

Hell yes, it's scary! But, Girl, I can't let you know I believe that! "What did you say? Scary? Naw—not scary—just exciting!"

But I couldn't fool her like I did Mr. Mortensen. "Exciting my ass, Joe-Joe! It's scary!"

"All right, it's scary. Say, does it seem warm in here to you?"

"Well, it might be because I'm nervous, but, yeah, it does seem warm in here."

"Then let's go home. The mai tais are waiting."

****

It was Friday morning. Nearing mid-May, the weather was turning extremely hot, with the last two afternoons reaching well in excess of a hundred degrees. Early, even for Phoenix. Management had not yet serviced the air conditioning unit at our rented office. "We can't turn it on until it's serviced, Mr. Worthington." It was scheduled to be done on Monday.

That morning, I waited for James Mortensen to show up at ten o'clock. The telephone rang at nine forty-five. I listened to his explanation that something urgent had come up and even though he had to change our meeting to three in the afternoon, the mortgage broker assured me he was diligently working on my problem and he still intended to hand carry the paperwork to his investors, directly from my office.

Following a trip home for lunch, Judy and I returned at one o'clock. Although our meeting with Mortensen was not until three, we wanted to be there in case he arrived early. Sitting at my desk in the sweltering heat with nothing to do, I re-read the newspaper, even humorously checking the obituaries to be sure I wasn't listed. Itching profusely beneath the make-up, I scratched the lower part of my neck and swore. Cursing myself and Mortensen, I wished I'd insisted on sticking to the earlier time. While I was at it, I cursed management as well.

Trying to stay busy, I rifled through the papers I'd filled out the night before, all the while checking my watch every few minutes. Pretty soon, the big hand was inching past two-thirty and knowing that Judy was as uncomfortable as me, I walked to her desk. "Girl, this heat is becoming unbearable. Why don't you take the station wagon home and come back for me after I visit with our friend?"

Looking up at the clock, she squinted. "Naw, Joe-Joe. Only thirty minutes or so to go. I can stick that out." She then sent an airborne kiss to me.

"Sure?"

"Yes, I'm sure. Besides, it's not fair for you to suffer alone. And, hey, you never know—you might need me." With that, she smiled, turned the page of her book and resumed reading. I obediently trudged back to my office.

****

James Mortensen was prompt. After escorting him into my office at precisely three o'clock, Judy returned to her station in the reception area. As the mortgage broker approached my desk, I handed the completed forms to him. "So, Mortensen, what are our chances? I don't want that old man Bowden to beat me out of three hundred grand! And remember, it's too late for me to re-file my lien."

James Mortensen's face was flushed and perspiring. He appeared tired. "I'd say good, Mr. Worthington. Our chances are very good."

"So when can I expect to hear something?"

Without answering, Mortensen swiped his hand across his forehead. "Goodness, it's hot. Could I trouble you for a drink of water?"

I had to agree with him. "Certainly. I could use one myself."

Making my way to the reception area, I briskly approached the drinking fountain. Leaning down for a taste, I saw my dim reflection in the chrome and suddenly looked closer. *Oh crap! My goatee is peeling away!* Pressing it back into place against my skin, it stuck for a moment, than began curling away again. Trying one more time to make it stick, I found it was no use.

Inspecting Judy's face, I saw that her disguise was still in place, at least for the moment. *Good heavens! The woman actually looks comfortable! But what the hell, she's a female. They're used to wearing this shit!*

When I finally gained her attention, I showed her my whiskers and she gasped, giving me that shrugging, now-

287

what-the-hell-do-we-do look. Wig-wagging my hand, I lip-synced, "Don't worry. I've got it!"

Walking toward my office door, I held the goatee against my face and explained to Mortensen, loud enough for Judy to hear. "Say, Mortensen, you'll have to help yourself to the drinking fountain out here. That damn tooth of mine is acting up again and I've got to go to the restroom and apply some toothache medicine. I'll be back in a minute."

With a quick wink to Judy, I pointed at her telephone and promptly exited through the front door. I raced around the corner to the fast food restaurant next to our office building. Heading for the pay telephone, I reached into my pants pocket for some change. There wasn't any there. I checked the other pocket. Empty. *Damn!* Scurrying into the burger place, I got a bit luckier. With it being three o'clock in the afternoon, there was nobody in line and after receiving change for my dollar, I rushed back outside. Plopping a coin into the telephone, I dialed our number and impatiently began tapping my foot while I listened to it ringing.

When she heard it jingle, Judy cast a covert glance toward the waiting mortgage broker and nervously answered. "Good afternoon, Worthington Construction."

"Hey, it's me, Joe-Joe. It's more than the goatee. With this damned heat, my make-up's coming completely off and I don't think I can repair it. And, Girl, yours could go at any minute too, so keep your distance from our visitor. Now then, pretend that I'm the construction foreman, George. I'm going to ask you if Mr. Worthington is there. Say "No, he's not.""

She brilliantly carried it a bit further. "Uh, no, George, Reginald isn't here. But I expect him back shortly. Is there a message?"

"Just this—there's a fire at the construction site at the housing project, and even though the housing project doesn't exist, Reginald has to get down here right away. Now then, Girl, get rid of Mortensen with that story. I'll be in the men's room behind our office. Have you got it?"

"Yes sir, George. I've got it." Click. *I hope this*

works, Hollywood!

Springing from her chair, Judy ran panicky to my office doorway and, holding her hands to her face in shock, she screamed at Mortensen. "Oh, my goodness! There's a fire at our housing project construction site. I've got to go tell Reginald to get down there right away. Do you have everything you need, Mr. Mortensen?"

Standing up, he looked around my office before reaching for his briefcase. Snapping it closed, he shrugged. "Why yes, I believe so."

Without a bit of hesitation, Judy stomped to the front door and anxiously jerked it open. Nervously holding it for him, she impatiently bounced lightly up and down. Looking toward the floor with a show of self-consciousness, she mumbled, "Sorry to put you out like this so quickly, Mr. Mortensen. I'm sure Mr. Worthington will be in touch soon."

"Oh, don't worry, miss, I understand completely. I certainly hope the fire isn't a bad one. Oh, and tell Mr. Worthington I'll call him as soon as I hear something on this." He patted the briefcase, turned on his heel and marched out the door, not looking back as he strolled toward the parking lot.

Judy gave Mortensen one minute before stepping into the hallway and shutting the office door behind her. Walking off the few steps to the exit, she marched outside and jiggled into an awkward, slow pounding run around the rear of the building. Upon reaching the restroom, she double checked the parking lot and rapped on the door. "Okay, Hollywood, you can come out now. He's gone."

We went home to our air conditioning for the rest of the day.

****

Much later, following an early supper of cold cuts and salad, Judy and I were relaxing in the family room with our usual mai tais. Seated beside me in her skimpy, mint green pajamas, Judy stroked Socko's face. Hearing his loud purring, I offered, "Hey, gorgeous, if you'll pet me that way, I'll purr, too."

"Naw, Hollywood, you're too willing." Pointing at the cat, she pretended haughtiness and cooed, "This is spontaneous."

"That's okay. He's cool. I ain't jealous."

Having sipped the last of my drink, I stood up to fix us another one. When I returned to her side and handed her glass to her, I reached out to caress her bare shoulder and told her, "Judy, I guarantee those wops are gonna be in our office with Mortensen on Monday. You want the day off?"

"Hell, no! Why would I do that? Even as scary as they are, I'm not going to miss this. Besides, this is a together thing all the way. Remember?" With a sincere look in her eyes, she patted my thigh as I took my seat beside her again. "But thanks for considering, Galahad."

Scratching the cat's chin one more time, Judy abruptly said to him, "Okay, Socko, that's it. Now it's Master's turn. Shoo!"

Lifting him to her face, she snuggled a hug before letting him go. Escaping her clutches, Socko pounced down to the floor and shook himself. With one last glare back up at her, he pranced defiantly from the room.

Turning to face me, Judy moved closer and brought her hand up to the back of my neck, edging my face down toward hers. Slightly parting her full lips, she gently maneuvered their softness against me, nudging, tugging, nipping, caressing and ever so daintily creating a tentacle with her tongue. Pulling away for one brief moment, she whispered, "I love you, Joe-Joe."

Chapter 43

Speculating that Mortensen would play his game true to form and that I'd be unable to reach him all weekend, I preferred Judy and I be equally unavailable. So we left in her Corvette to spend some time at Oak Creek Canyon, leisurely sunning ourselves for two warm afternoons at Slide Rock in Sedona. Judy attracted a lot of attention. Dressed in her brand new, skimpy bright blue bikini, she was oblivious to the gawking stares from all the men and the looks of envy from the girls and women. Her imagination was too busy theorizing something else.

With her eyes shaded by the pink sunbonnet she'd gotten from the secretary with whom she'd exchanged clothes, and to which she'd become quite attached, she peeked from beneath it and quibbled, "Damn, Joe-Joe! Why don't those silly, gawking, teenybopper girls quit hangin' around us and go away? Can't they see that you're mine?"

Laughing at her, I laid my head back against the blanket and closed my eyes, bragging to myself. *If that's what the girl thinks, Joseph, then let her think it!*

Quite perfectly, as balmy as it was in the daytime, it chilled enough in the evening for us to sit before a cozy fire in our rented cabin, sharing our customary mai tais and each other's company. While stroking Socko's face, I rested my head against Judy's breast and asked, "There's just one thing I want to know. How in the hell did you get this ornery cat to accept wearing a collar and a leash?"

"Believe me, Galahad, it wasn't easy. He's even more stubborn than you are!"

"Good heavens, Girl. This is scary. You've tamed us both!"

"And both of you like it sooooo much!" She gave me a throaty laugh.

Sometime later, the three of us nestled together in front of the fireplace on a quiet Sunday evening. Without speaking about it, it was clear that Judy and I were sharing two different feelings at the same time. Both of us were torn between looking forward to—and dreading—the next morning.

****

On Monday morning, I silently thanked management for servicing the air conditioner, then I placed several phone calls to Mortensen's office and just as I expected, I didn't reach him. It was shortly after eleven o'clock when the three of them strolled conceitedly into my office in their usual guises—brown for the mortgage broker and black pinstriped suits for the two Italians. I was wearing dark blue.

James Mortensen greeted me. "Good morning, Mr. Worthington. I'd like to present to you, Antonio Tafino and his brother, Louis. They're the investors I told you about on Friday. They're interested in your mortgage application."

"Good to meet you, Worthington!" Antonio boomed as he extended his hand to me. Louis made no attempt to shake hands.

I offered chairs to them and after they were all seated, I took my own seat behind my desk and intently looked the three of them over. *Damn! These goons are even uglier than I remember!* With forethought, I was holding an unlit cigar in my left hand and I pointed it at Louis, who had already busied himself with studying the decorations. "Hey, Louis, I see you like cigars, too. Cheerio," I bellowed at him. Judging from his scowl, I'd patently disturbed him a bit. *Good.* I leaned back in my chair and waited.

Opening the conversation with his practiced oratory, Mortensen held out his hands, palms up, using them to accentuate his speech. "Mr. Worthington, here's what Antonio and Louis are willing to do..."

****

While answering their questions, I listened to the two of them, Mortensen and Antonio, bouncing back and forth as they made their presentation. Tafino wanted eighty thousand dollars in points and an increase of three percent in interest over the rate I would be paying the Bowden Trust. They were making it impossible for me to accept their proposal. *Joseph, they must want this one really bad, so why don't you give it to 'em.* "Gentlemen, I've got about twelve thousand dollars in the bank and a ten thousand dollar payroll to meet on Friday." Of course, none of that part was true.

It was Antonio who responded. "That don't leave you much to bargain with, Worthington. Can you borrow the eighty grand from somebody?"

"I doubt it, Antonio." He'd earlier insisted that I call him Antonio. "I'm extended to my limit, already."

"Well, Worthington, we'd like to see you keep your building, but we have to make something up front on our investment. You can understand that."

"Certainly I do, Antonio. But even if I was able to get my hands on the eighty thousand up front, when I consider that our friend, Mr. Mortensen here hasn't yet been able to secure a mortgage for me on a building with far more than one-third equity, how can you or I trust him to do it now? I mean—think about it—you gentlemen aren't interested in anything long-term, so you say, so if our buddy here fails, and if the city doesn't finish their damned street project pretty soon so that I can collect some rents, you could file a foreclosure against the place yourselves and I'd be hung out to dry."

"Believe me, Worthington, Lou and I are not the least bit interested in your building, so Mortensen will have to get the mortgage. Do you hear that, James?" According to script, Mortensen meekly nodded. All of it was being filmed.

Antonio turned his glare to me. "Now then, Worthington, I understand your cash-flow situation, but tell me—how much can you come up with between now and Wednesday?"

"Not a dime."

Antonio again glared at Mortensen. *James, I thought you said this guy was loaded! I'll deal with you later!* He retuned his cold gaze to me. "Then I'm afraid we can't help you, Worthington. Let's go, Lou."

Standing up, Antonio marched toward the exit and just prior to following suit, Louis took a moment to grin and show his cigar to me with a look of defiance. Looking pathetically helpless, Mortensen shrugged and left with them.

When I heard the front door slam, I ambled to the front office and winked at Judy. "Okay, Girl, only two more days and we can let it all start to hit the fan."

With a wide grin on her phony, ugly face, she gave me a big thumbs-up.

****

Waiting in the background on Wednesday morning, Judy and I watched the trustee conduct the sale. "I have a bid from the Joseph T. Bowden Trust, in the amount of one million, nine hundred thousand dollars. Do I have any other bids?"

Antonio Tafino stepped forward and conceitedly bellowed, "One million, nine hundred thousand dollars and one cent." Glaring throughout the sparse crowd, he dared anyone to top him. No one did.

"Are there any more bids to entertain?" the trustee asked. He only waited a few seconds before he pounded the gavel. "Sold!"

As we watched them all celebrate and congratulate each other, Judy and I, as Reginald and Joyce Worthington, drifted toward the exit. Looking back at all of them, Antonio, Louis, and Mortensen, I smiled and whispered one word. "Gotcha!"

I squeezed Judy's hand and we left the courthouse.

****

Five days later, sporting a curly blonde wig and exaggerated western attire, together with all my proper identification, thanks to Robert Tanner, I entered the courthouse to collect a cashier's check for Phillip Patterson in the amount of four hundred thousand dollars. After signing the forms to release the lien, I walked out with the money.

The next afternoon, dressed in my old man outfit, I went to the same office to receive Joseph T. Bowden's cashier's check in the amount of one million, five hundred thousand dollars, and one cent. The property now belonged to the Tafino brothers and the only loser of record was our fictitious Reginald J. Worthington. After three long years, payback time had arrived for Owen J. Hunter.

Chapter 44

As we entered the main downtown police station on Madison Street, Judy took one look at the cigarette-smoking collection of seedy people standing around outside and muttered under her breath, "Chee-rist, Joe-Joe—this place gives me the creeps!"

"It's a jail, Girl—it's supposed to give you the creeps."

When we arrived at the front desk, we were met by a uniformed young lady, whose official greeting was limited to a cold, what-in-the-hell-do-you-want stare and an equally cold, "Can I help you?"

"We'd like to speak with one of your detectives, please."

The policewoman cast a few glances of doubt back and forth between Judy and me. Acting disinterested, bordering on perturbed actually, she took her time in inquiring, "What's this regarding, sir?"

"I'd prefer to tell that to the detective."

"Sir, I'd prefer you tell it to me and if I can't give you an answer, then I'll tell the detective."

Seeing the expression on her face, coupled with her non-stop shuffling of papers, I could almost read her mind. *These people surely can't be taken seriously!* I glared deadpan into her eyes and my voice went cold. "Miss, I would like very much for you to please pay extremely close attention to what I'm going to tell you."

She stopped rearranging the files and looked at me. "All right, sir. You tell me."

"Thank you. Now then, miss, I could take the time to outline all of this to you, but then I'd have to explain it all over again when I *do* speak to one of your investigators. That will be after you will have spent a considerable amount of time telling him about our being here in the first place and why. Now then, young lady, I have every ounce of proof that several crimes have been committed and it's all right inside of here." Lifting my briefcase for her to see, I patted the side of it. "So, can we please cut to the chase and save your department and myself that considerable amount of time by permitting me to speak directly with a detective?"

Judy was standing by my side, nodding complete agreement with everything I was saying, all the while adjusting the glasses on her protruding nose. The curt, young officer glanced at her before bringing her eyes back to me. *Humph! I'll let the detective get rid of these idiots!* "Wait right here."

Indifferently walking away, she turned for one more dubious look at us before entering the squad room. I could hear Judy muttering under her breath. "That snippy, little bitch! Hell, Joe-Joe, if she could see the man you really are underneath all that garbage you're wearing, she'd probably have to go change her underwear!"

I had to force myself to not laugh. "Damn it, Girl— not now! I'm afraid my face will crack—literally!"

"I'm sorry, Joe-Joe. I guess I'm just nervous. I'm afraid we're going to screw this up royally."

"Baloney! Once we get into it, you'll lose that uneasiness and simply go with the flow. Don't worry, you'll do great. Oh-oh, eyes alert. Here he comes."

A stocky man with a receding hairline and a crisp, gray suit had come out of the office with the young cop and after whispering something to her, she nodded and he approached us. "Good afternoon. I'm Detective Bearden. What can I do for you?"

It was me who nervously told him, "We'd like to file criminal charges against some men who've defrauded us. What would that be? Conspiracy? Fraud?"

Scratching his head, the investigator sheepishly explained, "Well, sir, it doesn't work quite that easily. Can you give me some of the details of this alleged crime?"

I shifted my eyes toward the eavesdropping, young rookie, still with a smirk plastered on her face then repeated to Bearden what I had told her. "Absolutely, Detective. I can enlighten you from start to finish. We have a perfect case against these people right here in this briefcase."

Although somewhat amused himself, the policeman

tried his best to show us a great deal of restraint, simply because his experience had taught him patience. In over twenty years of being in this line of work, he'd heard stranger tales than this one. Tolerantly scratching his balding pate again, Detective Bearden opened the gate and invited us in. As we entered, he quickly looked away from us and coughed, in truth covering up a laugh. Fighting back a grin, he glanced all around the room before daring to make eye contact with me again. He cleared his throat.

At that moment, all of the fear and nervousness that had been welling up inside of me went away and a stream of confidence charged through my veins. "Detective Bearden, I understand your skepticism, but I guarantee you we have several legitimate charges to be filed and I'm telling you that I know of at least three people who may have died at the hands of the men guilty of defrauding us."

I hesitated a moment, allowing him to digest not only my words, but the somber tone in my voice as well before I continued, "In addition to us, these crooks have fleeced a minimum of thirty people with the same routine and if they're not stopped, they'll keep right on doing it! And who knows at what expense to some people's life savings. Or possibly, even their lives."

Not realizing that my voice was continually rising as I talked to him, I saw Bearden take a step back and shoot a rapid glance toward the uniformed young woman, who was standing aside with her mouth open, not quite sure how to take my high-volume spiel. I gave her a cold stare of my own. When Bearden returned his attention to me, my eyes were locked onto his and my jaw was clamped shut. After studying my face another moment or two, he said, "You know, sir, I believe you're serious about this."

"You bet your ass I am, Detective!"

"All right. Come with me to the detectives' room and let's see what you have, Mister…"

"Worthington. Reginald Worthington. And the young lady with me is Joyce Worthington."

****

Without naming names right away, I generally began telling him the story about the foreclosure, the tapes, and the films. After listening for less than fifteen minutes, the detective stopped me. "Mr. Worthington, I believe we should probably have someone from the DA's office in here to listen to this first hand, as well. Wait here a minute."

Leaving us alone, Bearden departed the room through a different door and returned a short time later, accompanied by a mustached Hispanic, about my age and dressed in a very current, three-piece camel colored suit. After sitting down and flipping to a clean sheet in his tablet, the Latino spoke point-blank to us. "Good morning, my name is Edward Granado. Lieutenant Bearden gave me a brief synopsis of your story, but perhaps you should start again from the beginning. Tell me, Mr. Worthington, how did you suspect that you were being conspired against in the first place? I mean, it took some planning on your part to set up and record all of this."

Notwithstanding that I was immediately not fond of Mr. Granado, I reminded myself that I needed him, however, when I gave him my answer, I knew I couldn't tell him the real truth. If I told him about Owen J. Hunter, the whole case might blow up, so I had to play it through as Reginald J. Worthington. That didn't prevent me from being as equally plainspoken. "Mr. Granado, when you've been in contracting as long as I have, you learn that your sub-contractors have a different memory of some conversations than you do. Believe me—these recording devices have rescued my butt a good many times over the past several years. It wasn't anything planned. I've always recorded my calls."

"I see."

And before he could speak again, Joyce Worthington tapped my arm with her elbow and chimed in. "Yes, Reginald but there's much more to it than that and you know it."

Surprised and puzzled, I cast a look of perplexity toward Judy. Not knowing where she was going with this, I

299

sent it back to her. "Of course, dear, you're right. Why don't you explain the rest of it to Mr. Granado?" *Come on, Girl— this better be good!*

Without hesitation, she stared directly into the lawyer's face and began rambling. "Well, Mr. Granado, I can tell you this much—I started getting suspicious about this mortgage broker when Reginald first told me that he'd called him. I thought his name sounded familiar. Then I remembered that my cousin was once employed by someone with the same name, so I telephoned her to talk about the guy she used to work for. Sure enough, he's the same man. And besides being a swindler, the man is an absolute pervert!"

Bearden chuckled. "A pervert?"

"Yes, sir. After he hired Jane—my cousin—he began to harass her all the time. I mean, Jane is a very beautiful young lady and it's certainly easy to see why all the men are interested in her, but—"

Upon hearing this, I had to turn my eyes away from everybody. I inwardly pleaded, *Girl, please don't look at me. I swear I will split a gut laughing! Please, whatever you do, just keep right on talking!* Thankfully, she did.

"—then she told me that when he really began to hound her, she put a tape recorder in the office and tapped his phone lines. Reason being, in case it became necessary, she wanted proof that he was sexually harassing her, but she decided it wasn't worth it, so eventually she just quit the job and dropped out of night school to get away from him. Anyway, after I informed her that this Mortensen had begun the process of securing a mortgage for Reginald, Jane told me about the suspicious dealings between him and those other men who ended up buying all the foreclosed properties. She also told me there were at least three people who came into the office after losing their properties, complaining and threatening to go to the authorities, but they all died very strange and very sudden deaths before they could do so. I'm sure Jane would give me her tapes of Mortensen's conversations, if we need them. I informed Reginald about what Jane had told me, but by that time, he was already involved with the man."

I saw where she was going. She was tying the murders to the fraud case! *Good girl! That's brilliant!* I squeezed her thigh beneath the table to let her know that I understood and before the Assistant District Attorney could intervene with more questions, I quickly picked up where she left off. "She's right, Mr. Granado. I decided to see if what her cousin was telling her was true, so I researched the public records at the Recorder's office and I located more than thirty people whose properties have been lost through foreclosure and have ended up in the hands of this man's crooked friends."

Knowing that this had not really been the source of those names (Judy found them—remember?), I sensed that if the police were interested, they wouldn't search the records downtown—hell, I don't even know if they could find those kinds of records downtown—they'd talk to the folks who'd lost the properties and I could give them those names.

"Anyway, Gentlemen, after discovering this and not wanting to get myself personally involved with these folks, especially since I was already entangled with the mortgage broker, I asked an acquaintance of mine to investigate for me. He went to see several of these people and discovered that in every case, this same mortgage broker had been hired to rescue their properties from foreclosure and they all told the exact same story about their losses that I'm telling you about mine. Now then, taking it a bit further, still following up on Jane's information, I also had my friend do a small investigation into the strange, unexpected deaths of the three men Joyce just mentioned. Do you want to know what I believe? I believe that at least two of the three were silenced by an agent of the men who bought these parcels. Maybe all three. So, in spite of my suspicions, I decided to allow the mortgage broker to continue with my mortgage procurement to see what would eventually happen. I further decided that if they are as crooked as it was beginning to appear, they shouldn't get away with it any longer. Therefore, I utilized my recording equipment, just as I normally do with my sub-contractors, and here we are."

"Mr. Worthington, Ms. Worthington, you've done your homework rather well. I compliment you," said Detective Bearden.

Granado nodded slightly and stated, "We'll have to look at your film and listen to your tapes, but if they substantiate what you're telling us here, a charge of fraud will get them five years each. Well, maybe less if it's their first offense."

"That's it?" I incredulously asked.

"Well, plus another five for conspiracy, which is going to be the hardest part to prove. Of course, we would also ask the court to order them to pay some form of restitution to all of the victims we can find."

Giving Judy and me a quick final glance, the Assistant D. A. closed his notebook and stood up while instructing Bearden, "Tom, after you get all the names and details from Mr. Worthington, I should be able to get a judge to sign all of the necessary search warrants, then your people can move on it." Bearden nodded agreement.

Then, Granado looked at me. "Mr. Worthington, may we hold these tapes and films for evidence?"

"Of course. But, Mr. Granado, I don't think we're finished here. What about murder charges against these guys? Can't we at least discuss the possibility of that?"

He looked at Bearden. "Detective?"

"I think we should hear what else they have to say, Ed."

The Assistant District Attorney sat back down. "Okay, tell me about these alleged victims, Mr. Worthington. What are their names?"

"There are three of them. Wayne Meeks, Ralph Blake, and a fellow named Edwin Cooke. But there's little to go on with him."

Bearden piped in. "Edwin Cooke? That name sounds familiar."

"His wife found him shot to death in his car several

months ago. I guess the police ruled it a suicide, but I—"

Interrupting, Bearden blurted, "Oh, yeah, wait a minute! I remember that one. Yeah, that was most definitely a suicide. I investigated that one myself."

Like I used to do in school, I raised my hand to speak. "Excuse me, Detective Bearden. I'm not questioning your ability or your methods, but just to satisfy my own ignorant curiosity—what convinced you about Mr. Cooke's death that it was a suicide and not a homicide?"

I saw his brow furrow. "Simply this, Mr. Worthington—there was a complete absence of foul play evidence. We found a pistol that we identified as both, belonging to and registered to Mr. Cooke. It was in his right hand and he had powder burns all over his right glove and temple. Does that explain it well enough for you?"

Ignoring the trace of sarcasm in Bearden's voice, Judy expressed a touch of her own when she volunteered, "I'm sorry, Detective, but that in itself raises a question in my mind. Edwin Cooke was left-handed."

Stupefied, the three of us stared at her. She stared back and said, "What? Why are you all looking at me so strangely?"

Suddenly realizing that she, as Joyce Worthington, couldn't possibly know this, the wheels in Judy's mind began to turn feverishly. She exchanged glances with the three of us before explaining, "I merely remember that Jane and I discussed this once during one of our phone conversations. In fact, she brought it up to me. I mean, Jane was pretty shook up about Mr. Cooke's death, since she'd seen him several times in the office just prior to it happening, and I remember her saying to me, 'You know, Joyce, after reading all about it in the papers, I remember seeing Mr. Cooke sign several papers in the office and I noticed he was left-handed. So, why do you suppose a left-handed person would shoot themselves with their right hand?'" Joyce shrugged her shoulders. "All I'm doing, gentlemen, is asking you the same question."

It was Bearden who responded. "That's interesting

Ms. Worthington. And I have to admit, it's a good question. But it doesn't prove he was murdered. Now then, do you folks want to tell me about the other two again?"

As I explained our theory, Bearden's memory faded back to the investigations of their deaths. With a studious look at Granado, he stated, "Bear with me a minute or two, Ed, and let me pull the files on those. This may be worth looking into."

Granado nodded, more impatiently than patiently.

Retrieving the folders from the closed cases files, Bearden rapidly poured over the paperwork and told the lawyer. "Okay, Ed, there's nothing concrete in here to support it, but Mr. Worthington's theories are making a little bit of sense to me, so I'd like to quietly re-open the investigations of each one. Who knows, maybe we'll come up with something."

Granado's choleric idea of the whole mess rapidly surged to the forefront as he heaved a sigh to the detective. "Tom, I'm beginning to wonder how much of my time is being wasted here."

The lawyer then glared at me. "Mr. Worthington, what are the names of this mortgage broker and his alleged co-conspirators?"

When I told him, Bearden thought aloud. "Tafino? Tafino? Oh yeah, now I remember. I just questioned him recently about the death of a limo driver. A young body-builder named, uh, Mark Tyler. Yeah—that's it—Mark Tyler. He was found dead from a drug overdose."

Instantly shocked, Judy screeched, "What? Mark Tyler? The one affiliated with Parisian Escort Service?"

Taken aback, the policeman nodded. "Yes, Ms. Worthington, as a matter of fact, he was. Don't tell me he's somehow connected to you people?"

"Oh, my God!" Judy wailed. "Not Mark! When did this happen? And what did Tafino have to do with it?"

Although puzzled, Bearden nevertheless jumped alert. "Early part of March, this year. It seems that Mark had driven a girl named Sonya Waverly to a dinner meeting with this Tafino character and the next morning, Mark Tyler was found dead in his limo from a drug overdose. Why are you asking? Did you folks know Mark Tyler?"

But Judy wasn't finished asking questions of her own. "Hold it. Wait a minute, Detective. Are you saying that Sonya went to a dinner meeting with Antonio Tafino? And that Mark was found dead the next day from an overdose? An overdose of what?"

"Cocaine," stated Bearden.

"That's impossible!" Judy screeched. "Mark wouldn't do any cocaine!"

"I'll ask you one more time, Ms. Worthington. How did you folks know Mark Tyler?"

Although still in a state of shock, Judy suddenly remembered where she was and who she was supposed to be. And me? I was becoming afraid that my outbreak of perspiration was going to unglue my make-up again.

But thankfully, Judy recovered very nicely, and as Joyce, she defended, "I'm sorry for the outburst, Detective, but hearing about Mark is quite a shock. We didn't actually know him that well, but you see, my other cousin, Judy—she's Jane's sister—is a very good friend of that girl you mentioned, Sonya Waverly. They used to work together at the escort service. It's just that I met Mark a couple of times through Judy and Sonya, and well, he seemed to be such a gentleman, not to mention a real hunk, and when you know someone, then learn all at once that they've died so unexpectedly, it's quite a shock."

"I understand, Ms. Worthington. I'm sorry I was the one who had to inform you about it and so out of the blue, at that," Bearden apologized.

Judy begged for more answers and crossed her fingers in her lap for luck. "Detective? I'm curious. Did you happen to question Sonya Waverly about all of this?"

"Of course. On the day Mark was found dead. We went back to question her a second time, but she wasn't there. We tried to discover her whereabouts, but it's like she's disappeared and nobody's seen her since. I've checked all of our missing persons reports, however there's none filed on her. But tell me, Ms. Worthington, do these Mark and Sonya people tie in with your conspiracy thing? Or is this merely coincidence?"

Touching her forefinger to her pursed lips, Judy thought for a moment, before suddenly bursting into another speech. "You know, Detective, there just might be a connection, now that I think about it. Yes—that's it! Just follow me here. Okay? I'll have to talk my way through this. Let's see, Mortensen was stalking my cousin Jane, who disappeared—well, not disappeared really, she merely got away from the horny toad. Now then, my other cousin, Judy, and Sonya and Mark all work for the escort service. Okay, let's take that a bit farther! Yes, it's making sense to me now. All right, somehow Mortensen makes a connection between Jane and Judy, and Sonya. Then he tells Tafino, who hires the escort service and they try to extract from Mark the whereabouts of Jane, for Mortensen, and when they can't, they have this crew-cut fellow we told you about earlier kill Mark. Then, shortly after that, Sonya disappears. Oh my God! Maybe that scary looking goon killed her, too!"

Deeply concerned for her friend, Judy darted frightened glances toward a tight-lipped Granado, a still somewhat skeptical Bearden, and a very disquieted me.

"Well, don't any of you think that's possible?" She charged.

It was Granado who grudgingly answered her. "Ma'am, Detective Bearden has already told you that Mark Tyler died from a self-induced drug overdose and he mentioned that he's talked with this girl, Sonya Waverly, since then. It was Mark's death that prompted us to talk with her in the first place. I like your theory, however I have one of my own. I think she got scared with the danger that can sometimes be faced in the business she was in and she's disappeared on her own. Where to? Who knows?"

With that, a miffed Edward Granado stood up and spoke to Bearden. "I'll get the paperwork started on the fraud and conspiracy thing, Tom. It does seem that we have a case there. In the meantime, you can finish up on the investigation of the murder angle and if you come up with something besides speculation, let me know. But, Tom, don't spend a lot of time on it."

Without another word, Granado left the room.

Upon hearing him slam the door, I breathed a sigh that was part relief and part disgust. "I understand he's a busy man, Detective, but I guarantee you that when these three people get arrested on the conspiracy and fraud charges, this big, ugly crew-cut mongrel will crawl out of his hole and Joyce and I are going to be his next targets. We'd rest a little more easily, knowing that there are people from your department watching our backs."

Slowly getting to his feet, Bearden walked over to the coffee pot and brought it back to our table. While he re-filled the cups he'd given us when we first got there—it seemed like a lifetime ago—he admitted, "You know, Mr. Worthington, with the absolutely solid proof you appear to have on this fraud case, something is nagging at me to strongly believe the rest of your suspicions. I'll notify you as soon as we make an arrest of these three, but I don't know if the captain will let me spring a couple of men loose to baby-sit. However, once we get them in here and start interrogating them, let's see what we can trap them into saying. Trust me, if they've killed some people, I want them as badly as you do."

"But, Detective—"

He didn't let me finish. "In the meantime, I have one more item to discuss with you, Ms. Worthington. I have an open file on my desk right now that I'm sure was a homicide made to look like an accident. The young lady who was killed was a friend of the other girl, Sonya Waverly, and she'd been out with Sonya and some other friends the night Mark was killed, after Mark and Sonya parted company for the evening. By any chance, did you know a girl named Jolene Wilson?"

"What? Jolene is dead, too? How did that happen?"

"So you did know her?"

"Not real well. She was also a friend of Judy's and I only met all of these people because Jane and Judy and I like to hang together quite a bit. We're all very close."

Even though I conjectured that Judy had no intention of being funny, this crack struck me as totally hilarious. So, to cover the laughter I couldn't hide this time, I pretended to choke on the coffee in my mouth and sprayed it all over the table. It did the trick. Everybody jumped clear. Adding to my cover-up, I continued to hack. "Sorry."

Eventually, after I wiped up the mess with some napkins, Bearden explained about Jolene. "By the time I discovered the bubble-bath notation on the autopsy report and went to her apartment to investigate, any trace of evidence that she'd been drowned in the bathtub was all gone. The only thing I got from her two roommates was that they'd been a little surprised and put out that Jolene had left the bathroom in such a wet mess. They came home that day and found it with water all over the place. Of course, by that late date, the room had been thoroughly cleaned many times over and all of Jolene's things had either been given to her family or thrown away. I suspect that her bubble-bath is buried at the bottom of a landfill someplace."

A discomforting quiet filled the room as the policeman finished his tale and slumped back into his chair. Tossing the pencil he'd been twirling onto the table, he shot a glance at each of us and admitted, "I pretty much messed that case up myself. I should have seen the notation on the coroner's report right from the start."

From out of the corner of my eye, I saw Judy shiver when she told him, "Well, Detective, I just hope you don't get the opportunity to botch up two more!"

When the detective's eyes bugged open, Judy darted a glance at me, then swiftly declared to Bearden, "Oh, Officer, I'm sorry, I didn't mean to put it that way. I should have said that I hope you don't get the opportunity to solve two more. I certainly didn't mean to insult you. Especially since you've shown such confidence in Reginald and me to admit to such a big mistake. Oh, crap! I did it again—I'm sorry. I better just shut my mouth!"

Bearden gave her a lukewarm smile. "I understand what you're trying to say, Ms. Worthington. And you're right about me having confidence in you two. By taking the bits of information I already had and putting it together with what you're telling me, I can't help but form the opinion that this is all connected somehow. With your continued help, perhaps we can figure it all out."

"Thank you, Detective. We'll certainly do whatever we can," Joyce Worthington confirmed.

"Good. By the way, do you think this Mortensen character and his two buddies are wise to your little program here?" He pointed at the tapes.

"Not a chance," I bragged.

"At least we hope not," Judy corrected with a stern look at me. "But I shudder to think about their mood when they do find out. Especially that Antonio creep. And even more-so if he gets released on bail."

"Let's cross that bridge later, folks. In the meantime, can I get you both to look through some mug books? Maybe we can put a name to this crew-cut guy you keep referring to."

Judy jumped up from her chair. "We'll be glad to, Detective Bearden. But can we do it tomorrow? We've, uh, been here a lot longer than I planned and I still have a few urgent things to take care of today."

"Tomorrow's fine."

He got up and moved to hold the door for us.

****

A few minutes later, after bursting through the double glass doors and leaving police headquarters, Judy began to run to where the station wagon was parked. "C'mon, Joe-Joe, let's get home! I've got to call Omaha and see if Sonya is there!" *Lord, please let her be okay.*

Chapter 45

Seated in his office with his feet propped on his desk, James Mortensen was feeling far better about himself than he had for a long time. Embracing Margo's picture with his eyes, he felt relieved that he was coming to a decision with his life. *It could be that Dr. Stone is right. It just takes time for all this confusion to pass. And perhaps I do work too much. Maybe I should take some time off. I know—I'll take Margo on a vacation someplace. If nothing else, maybe for once we can at least get away from this God-awful summer heat. Only bad side to that though is that I'll have to use some of my hoarded money to do it.*

Quickly picking up the telephone, he dialed his home number to tell her. There was no answer. *Don't tell me she's out shopping again! It seems that's all the woman ever does lately! And, hells bells, look at the time! It's after ten o'clock at night! She should be home by now! I wonder where in the world she can be?*

He tried in vain one more time to reach her and this time, her failure to answer agitated him and he slammed the phone down. *Of course, woman. That's just like you—never there when I really need to talk to you. And this time I even have good news! All right, you bitch, I'll teach you to treat me that way!*

Disgustingly turning Margo's picture face down, James leaned back in his chair and closed his eyes. A thin smile traced across his lips when his mind's eye conjured up the memory of the perfect large breasts of the girl named Sonya. That's really all he could remember about that night—her pretty face and those delicious mounds of flesh. *You know, I should get brave enough to ask Antonio where he found her. I mean, after his last purchase from that guy with the ugly secretary, his telling me that oughtta be the least he could do.* But James knew he would never ask Antonio.

He pictured the Italian in his head. *My God, he's going to make a cool million on that place, and in less than four months' time. And, huh! What do I get for my share? A*

310

meager twenty grand! That's another thing. Maybe I should approach him about giving me a percentage from now on instead of a flat rate. As soon as I find another one, I think I'll bring it up to him. But James knew he would never ask Antonio that, either.

He impatiently reached for the telephone and tried his home number again. Still no answer. Click. This time, James merely cradled the phone. Reaching for Margo's picture, he gingerly set it back upright and hatefully stared at her image. *Ha! There goes your vacation, you bitch! You can forget about that! That also means I won't have to use any of my money! Thank heavens I was smart enough not to tell you about it. The way you've been spending recently, I wouldn't have any of it left!*

He turned the picture face down once more and resumed his restful position in the high backed chair. He closed his eyes and brought back the vision of Sonya's bare torso, but this time, with a fresh idea. *Ha! I know what I'll do with some of that money! I'll buy some trinkets of my own. Trinkets with nice large breasts! After all, if stupid Margo can use all of our regular money for hers, then why can't I have mine? All I have to do is work up the nerve to find one.*

All at once, a loud, insistent pounding on his locked office door jarred James Mortensen from the vision. He jumped alert. *Who in the hell can that be?*

Scrambling to his feet, he turned off the light in his office and rushed to the outer door. He cracked it open. Standing outside was a slightly stocky man in a blue suit. However, James couldn't see the two uniformed police officers standing to each side of him. They were concealed against the wall, ready to pounce. James informed the man, "I'm sorry, but we're closed for the day."

"Are you Mr. James Mortensen?"

"Yes, that's me, but as I said—we're closed. It's after ten o'clock at night!"

"Mr. Mortensen, my name is Detective Lieutenant Thomas Bearden with the Phoenix Police Department. I have a warrant for your arrest."

311

Mortensen held the door open a bit wider. "What? What did you say?"

Bearden quickly stepped back as the two uniformed officers shoved the door all the way open, turned Mortensen around and slapped a pair of handcuffs on his wrists before he could even move.

"What in the hell is going on?" Mortensen shouted, trying much too late to wriggle away from them. "There's got to be some kind of mistake here. I'm a law-abiding citizen. What could you possibly be arresting me for? I haven't done anything wrong!"

"I'm afraid you'll have to come with us, Mr. Mortensen. You'll find out about the charges, once you're downtown and through booking."

"But, I'm telling you there has to be some kind of mistake here!"

Ignoring Mortensen's plea, Bearden turned to the patrolmen and said, "Okay, guys, let's get him out of here."

As he was being led away, James Mortensen was still pleading for an explanation when he unexpectedly saw his wife enter the hallway from the rear entrance to the building. Surprised, yet very elated, he yelled to her, "Margo! Margo, over here! God—am I ever glad to see you! Margo, you've got to help me here. I don't even know what this is all about and they won't tell me! Margo, please talk to them and tell them I haven't done anything wrong!"

Bewildered, the woman looked first at her husband, then at the two patrolmen, and finally at Bearden. Quickly approaching, she questioned the plain-clothes man, "Is this true? Are you arresting James? What on earth for?"

"Are you Mrs. Mortensen?"

"Yes, but what—?"

The policeman held up his hand, signaling her to silence. "Please, ma'am, I can't say anything to you until he's out of earshot."

As the officers proceeded to march him stumbling toward the double doors, they heard James yell over his shoulder, "Margo, listen to me! I want you to look in my desk and find the telephone number for a lawyer named Abe Sundstrom! Please call him and tell him to get down to police headquarters and get this mess straightened out. There's got to be something wrong, here!"

"All right, James!" She shouted.

"And, Margo, one more thing! Please be sure the office is locked before you leave!" Mortensen didn't hear her acknowledgement because, without slowing down, they whisked him through the double doors to a waiting patrol car, outside.

The investigator spoke to the bewildered woman. "Okay, Mrs. Mortensen, my name is Detective Thomas Bearden. I've just served your husband with a warrant for his arrest. The warrant is for fraud and conspiracy, but I'm afraid that's all I can tell you for now. His initial arraignment will more than likely be at nine o'clock in the morning, after which we'll arrange for you to speak to him."

"Detective, exactly what in Heaven's name is this all about? I can't believe that James is involved in any... conspiracy, did you say? And who on earth is he supposed to have defrauded?"

"I'm sorry, Mrs. Mortensen, I'm afraid that's all I can tell you for now. We'll be able to give you more details after he's been arraigned and talked with his lawyer. Plus, I'm sure the District Attorney will have some questions for *you* as well."

"Well, I can certainly tell you I know absolutely nothing about any of this! And why can't you just ask me your questions now?"

"Because, ma'am, without an attorney present on Mr. Mortensen's behalf, or yours for that matter, I'm not at liberty to say any more."

With her initial shock wearing off, Margo was becoming angry. "All right, detective, then perhaps I should *get* one present, and right away!"

Tom Bearden showed patience. "Mrs. Mortensen, even with an attorney, we'll be holding James overnight until he appears before the judge for his initial court appearance in the morning."

"And why is that?"

"Because, ma'am, he has to have an arraignment and enter a plea before he can be considered for bail. However, if you'll feel more comfortable having your lawyer contact us tonight for an explanation of the charges, I'll give you my card." He reached into his jacket pocket, pulled out a card and handed it to her.

"But, Detective, why can't you—?"

"We'll be in touch in the morning, Mrs. Mortensen."

Despite Margo's ongoing sputtering protests, Bearden left her standing in the hallway and briskly walked away. Helplessly watching the policeman's abrupt exit, Margo Mortensen whipped a middle finger to his back then huffed toward the door of her husband's office.

While slowly edging her way into the eerie silence, nervousness crept over her as she cast a long look around. *My God, it's hard to believe it's been two years since I've been in here! And isn't it strange? When I finally work up the courage to tell him what's been on my mind for such a long time, then deciding it was best to tell him here where he's most comfortable, I show up and the police are taking him away. It's almost amusing.*

To the contrary, her relief at not having to talk with him was nearly as strong as the astonishment she'd felt with his arrest. Moving farther inside, Margo stepped through the reception gate toward her husband's private office and flipped on the overhead light before going inside. She ambled toward his desk and when she surveyed the top of it, her eyes spotted a picture turned face down. Picking it up, she saw her own smiling face looking back at her. *Huh! This must have fallen over when James got surprised by those cops. No matter.*

She studied the snapshot for a moment before replacing it upright. *Speaking of photos, I'm having a hard time getting the picture of James in handcuffs out of my mind. And I just can't possibly believe what that policeman said. Conspiracy? And Fraud? James? Poor old automatic James?*

Margo Mortensen chuckled.

Even though somewhat diabolically amused, Margo was still rather sensitive to the hurt expression on his face when they took James out the door and she knew she had to call the attorney for him. She began searching through his desk drawers for Abe Sundstrom's phone number. While rummaging, she came across a small ledger book. Believing it to be an address book, she opened it. Written inside were several names with the amounts of five thousand, ten thousand, fifteen thousand, and twenty thousand scratched beside each one. Taped to the inside front cover was a key, which she instantly recognized as a safety deposit box key. Putting this into her purse, she left the book there and continued her search for the attorney's business card.

Eventually finding it, Margo Mortensen dialed the home number for Abe Sundstrom, waking him from a sound sleep. With an apology, she quickly explained to him what little she knew about her husband's predicament. The yawning lawyer agreed to contact Detective Bearden and vowed to get back to Margo as soon as he knew something concrete.

"Thank you, Mr. Sundstrom." Click.

Having finished her business there, Margo locked the office, hurried from the building and drove home.

Chapter 46

After spending the night with Rita, Alex Bigotti was sleeping late when the insistent ringing of the telephone rudely awakened him.   He fumbled with the receiver. "Hello! This better be important!"

"Bigotti! It's me, Antonio! Wake up! I got somethin' for you to do!"

Alex jumped alert. "Sure, Boss. What is it?"

"Lou and I just got sprung from the pokey! Some character named Worthington had us arrested for fraud. I got a lawyer workin' on it, but without this Worthington's testimony, they got no case, so here's what I want you to do — find that no good piece of crap and find that ugly witch of a secretary of his and eliminate 'em both!"

"Okay, boss. I'll take care of it. I'll meet up with you later to get any details you got on this guy."   Alex really wanted to go back to sleep.

"There's not enough time for waitin' till later, you dumb-ass! I want you out to my place right now!" Click.

****

The early June heat was already approaching one hundred degrees at ten o'clock in the morning when Margo Mortensen waltzed in, through the front door of her home. Dressed in a revealing halter-top and skimpy shorts, she still looked quite beautiful and very fit at age forty-two. All the looks she constantly received reminded her of that.

After turning on the air conditioner, Margo reached for the telephone and dialed a very familiar number. Fanning her face with her hand, she listened for the customary answer for Chez Charles. She heard the receiver lift and a young man sang it with a French accent. "Shay Sharl."

"Hi, Charles. It's me," Margo chorused.

"Well, hi there! This is a surprise. I mean, having you call me so early in the day. Is anything wrong?"

"Nothing at all, Charles, nothing at all. As a matter of fact, everything's right. And I mean perfectly right!" She gave him a throaty laugh.

With the clip-clipping of a pair of scissors at work in the background, the young hairdresser held the phone against his shoulder with his chin. He muffled a chuckle into it. "Okay. Want to tell me about it?"

Margo paused, trying to bait him and make him wonder. "Let me ask you something, Charles."

But instead of a response to her, Margo heard the hairdresser's conversation being directed to his customer, while he loosely smothered the mouthpiece. "What do you think, Christine? That length looks good, huh?" Eventually, Margo heard his reply to her. "What's that, beautiful?"

Margo ignored her irritation with him and simply asked, "On many of those nights when James worked late, do you remember how we'd imagine we were on an exotic cruise ship instead of in that motel room?" Margo always paid for the room. She paid for a lot of things for Charles.

"Certainly, gorgeous. And what was it you called it?"

"Our Little Fantasy, remember? Well, handsome, would we actually go on that cruise ship if it could be real?"

"Ab-so-lutely, dear." His words dragged while he continued to study Christine's coiffure. "Why do you ask?"

"Because. Good Old James was arrested last night and it looks like he'll be spending the next ten years or so locked up."

The snipping of the shears suddenly stopped. "Excuse me, Christine—I'll only be a minute." Charles gripped the phone in his hand and his voice became much clearer when he spoke to Margo. "You mean he's in jail? What in Heaven's name for?"

"Conspiracy and fraud. And his stupid lawyer says the D. A. has an air-tight case that'll probably stick."

Charles's voice lowered to a near whisper as he strolled away from Christine, out of earshot. "That's amazing! But, tell me, Margo, my love, how on earth does that get us on a cruise ship?"

"Charles, you won't believe this! It seems James had a secret safe deposit box. I've just been to the bank and, sweetheart, you'll never guess what I'm holding in my hands." Flipping through a massive pile of one hundred dollar bills, Margo Mortensen laughed deliriously into the telephone.

****

Judy was reminiscing to me about her earlier call to Sonya. "You know, Joe-Joe, when she left town, that silly Sonya was actually more worried about me than she was herself. Incidentally, without giving her too many details, I pretty much told her about us, but it's safe with her. And golly, she sounded so relaxed and happy to be home and working with her dad." Judy smiled warmly and took my hand in hers. "And she's glad we're in love."

Sitting across from me at my desk, Judy formed her lips into a smooch and sent an airborne kiss at me, then suddenly released her hold on my hand and reached for the telephone. "Okay. Back to business, Joe-Joe, I just got an idea."

Dialing the number from a long ago memory, she indicated for me to go pick up the extension. Holding her hand over the mouthpiece, she explained what she was doing while she listened to the ringing at the other end. "I'm sure glad Bearden gave us the names of all the girls who ran into Sonya that night. I'm going to see if I can get any information from Sandy. Hold on, Joe-Joe, she's answering."

"Hello."

"Sandy? Is that you? This is Judy. Judy Carmelle."

"Yeah, hi, Judy. How ya doin', babe? Jeez, I haven't talked to you in a long time. What's up?"

"Well, I've passed the bar for one thing, and I have a case I'm working on. Strange how these things come so close to home sometimes. I want to ask you a question about something. About three months ago, you and some of the other girls ran into Sonya Waverly at the Scottsdale Resort—remember that?"

"Yeah. Sure. And, wow, was she ever plastered!" Sandy laughed. "What about it?"

"Have you talked with her since?"

"No. Why? Is she all right?"

"She's fine." Thankfully, that part was true. "Anyway, do you remember anything unusual about that night? Anything that might have appeared strange to you? Other than Sonya being drunk, I mean?"

"I'm not sure I know what you mean, Judy. We bumped into her as she was about to leave in a limo. Man alive, she was sure mad as hell at somebody! Anyway, we talked her into going out with us and after getting her some coffee first—we were trying to sober her up—all of us went to Mr. Lucky's. We didn't get to stay there very long, though, because they closed at one, so we went over to the Casino House and danced until about three-thirty. Then we all went home."

"Doesn't the Casino House close at one, too?"

"Uh, off the record, no. At least not the back room. What's this all about, anyway?"

Sandy, if I told you the truth, it'd scare the crap right outta you! "Well, Sonya's limo driver was found dead of a drug overdose the next morning and the cops are looking into possibly charging Sonya with dealing the stuff to him, which is ridiculous! Anyway, I'm defending her." Judy fabricated.

"Wow! That ugly guy's dead, huh?"

Judy hollowly laughed. "I sure don't know why you call him ugly. I mean, I knew Mark myself and everybody thought he was a real hunk. Certainly takes a lot to please you. Hey?"

"Well, Judy, I'm sorry, but the guy I saw in that limo was no hunk. In fact, he was one mean-looking, pockmarked, ugly son-of-a-gun! Scary looking monster!"

"Are you sure this was the same limo that Sonya was taking?"

"Yeah. In fact, if we'd been able to remember where Jolene had parked her car in the first place, we probably wouldn't have even seen Sonya. Say, that's too bad about Jolene, too—did you hear about her?"

"Yeah, just recently, Sandy. That was a shock."

Leave it at that, Judy. "So, what else happened with Sonya that night?"

"Anyway, while we were searching for the Volare, we walked right past this limo parked out in front. Christy told us all, to secretly look at the driver. Boy was he giving us the once-over. The creep even took off his hat so he could get closer to the windshield for a better look. Man alive, he gave all of us the willies. We finally just ignored the jerk and kept on walking, and then, when we doubled back, that's when we saw Sonya stumbling all over herself, trying to get into the back seat. Like I said, she was really mad at somebody, and so drunk! Judy, you should have been there. It was hilarious!"

Not if you knew the truth, Sandy. Be-lieve me, not if you knew the truth. "Tell me something, Sandy—when this guy took off his cap, did you happen to notice his haircut?"

"His haircut? Yeah, it was sort of a crew cut. Military type, you know. Why?"

Judy instantly felt goose pimples rising on her arms as a chill went down her spine. "Do you think you'd recognize this guy again?"

Sandy laughed. "Good God no, Judy! Not if he's been dead for three months!"

"Cute, babe, real cute. However, the guy you're describing isn't the one who's dead. He's just a substitute driver," Judy alertly invented. "It was Sonya's regular driver who died and this is what we believe. This sub is the one who's providing the drugs to the people in the escort—I mean—the limousine service. Yeah, this maniac is very much alive and we're trying to find him. So I'll ask you one more time—do you think you'd know him if you saw him again?"

"Absolutely, Judy. You don't forget a face like that."

"I have to agree. I've seen him once myself. Okay, Sandy, that's about all I can think of for now, but if I come up with anything else, I'll be in touch. Oh, and if we locate this ugly creature, it could be that the police might want to ask you some questions, so don't be alarmed if they come knockin' on your door. Okay?"

"Sure, it'll give the neighbors something to talk about." Sandy chortled.

"Still full of the devil, eh, Sandy? Hey, buddy, thanks for your help."

"Glad to do it, Judy. And, hey! What do you say we get together sometime?"

"Will do, babe. Bye." Click. Click. Click.

After quickly hanging up the phone, Judy looked at me. "Holy salamander, Joe-Joe! Did you hear that? This means I was absolutely right about what I told Bearden! It substantiates that crew-cut must have murdered Mark and came damn close to killing Sonya, too! It's a good thing Sandy and the others came by!"

"Yeah, but I'm having a hard time tying Sonya and Mark to all of this. I don't see how it fits."

Judy stood up and pointed at the phone. "After talking with Sandy just now and adding that to what Sonya told me earlier, I'm beginning to piece a few things together, but before I give you my ideas about it, let's go grab a couple of stiff mai tais." She was already heading toward the doorway before she finished the sentence.

Once we were seated in the family room, Judy gulped a large swallow of her drink and leaned back against the sofa. She breathed a heavy sigh and brushed her long auburn hair away from her face. "Joe-Joe, I think I've got this figured out. That ugly clown was looking for me."

"How do you figure that?"

Judy proceeded to tell me that she'd learned from Sonya about the incredible, strictly by chance selection of Parisian Escort Service and an evening with Sonya as a job-well-done present for Mortensen from the Tafino brothers, and how Mortensen had recognized her as Jane's friend. "Do you know that rotten so-and-so followed me nearly every night and watched Sonya and I at school together? The crazy degenerate! He thought she and I were lesbian lovers! Ugh!"

While I sat there stroking Socko's head, I glanced at her and grinned. But before I could comment, Judy instructed, "And, Hollywood, don't you dare laugh or make any remarks or your days are numbered! You're much better off just re-filling this!" She thrust her empty glass toward me.

By the time I returned, Socko had left for the food bowl and Judy had mollified a bit. After taking the drink from my hand, she nestled against me on the sofa. I saw a lone tear streaming down her cheek and I lightly brushed it away. "Joe-Joe, I'm scared. Damn scared! Those people *had* to be looking for me. After his evening with Sonya, Mortensen probably shot off his mouth to Antonio about she and I being friends and that wop probably still wants to know what I recorded in Mortensen's office. I'm sure Mortensen reminded him about that, too. That has to be the connection to this whole mess."

I affectionately pulled her closer to me and she nuzzled her face against my neck while I gently rubbed her back. *And I told her there'd be no danger!* With her voice lowered to a near whisper, she said, "Joe-Joe, I think they're onto you and me and I also bet those wops know who put them in jail. They probably have that ugly crew-cut Frankenstein out there looking for us right now."

"Well, Girl, I don't want to scare you anymore than you already are, but I talked with Bearden today and he told me they're out on bail."

She bolted upright. "Oh, crap, Joe-Joe! Like I needed to hear that!"

"I certainly didn't like it either, but just listen to me—since learning that, I've taken a few steps to stay hidden from them. As you know, I've already turned in the station wagon and exchanged it for that Firebird sitting in the garage, plus, I've gotten in touch with Robert Tanner in St. Louis and he's shipping a complete new set of identification papers with different names, addresses, etcetera, including passports, for each of us. He's sending them overnight express, so I expect to have them the day after tomorrow."

"Okay, but what good will that do? We still look like us."

"That's true and that is a problem. So, I think we

only have one alternative—we have to separate."

"Separate?" She screamed at me. "Huh-uh, no way, Hollywood! I don't want to face these guys by myself!"

"Judy, listen to me—"

She suddenly moved away from me as if I were diseased with the plague. Interrupting, she said, "Oh, wait a minute. I get it! You're as scared as I am and you believe it's best we separate because you know these guys have all seen me in both, my natural face and that ugly get-up as Joyce Worthington, so they'll recognize me either way. But not you, no, sir! Unless you wear that stupid disguise, they won't recognize you at all. You're in the clear! So, I also suppose you're thinking the time has finally come to—*now*, let's get the girl out of it!"

I'd heard enough and I yelled at her. "Judy, shut the hell up! Stop being so damn dramatic and just listen to me!"

Her eyes opened wide in surprise before a thin smile spread across her face. "Damn, Joe-Joe, that's the first time you've ever raised your voice to me. Hell's fire, you are capable." *There she goes. Hop-scotching again!* "But I really don't see your logic in this."

"Judy!" I stared her down.

Leaning back, she raised her hands in surrender. "Okay, I'll be good and listen. Go ahead. Explain. But would you fix me another mai tai first? Please?"

When I returned and handed her glass to her, I didn't give her a chance to say anything more. I placed my hand on the back of her neck and drew her face close to mine. "First of all, Judy Carmelle, I love you, so why in the hell would I jeopardize, or abandon, the best thing that's ever come into my life? Don't answer that—just listen."

"I'm listening, Master, sir."

"Okay, here's my plan. First of all, I want you to stay out of sight in this house for the next couple of days until I get the new I. D's from Robert. Don't even open the door to let Socko in or out. Now then, tomorrow I'm going to take the tape of Sandy's conversation to Bearden. Maybe I can get him to bring her in to look through some mug shots. She might have better luck than us, and if crew-cut has a record, we can at least find out who he is."

"That's no good. How do you explain to Bearden that it was Judy Carmelle on that tape? He only knows me as Joyce."

"Simple. You've already told him about your cousin, Judy, who not only knows these other girls, but who happens to be a lawyer as well, so we asked her to make the phone call."

"Good thinking, Joe-Joe. Go on." She sipped her drink.

"Okay, here's the rest—I have to stay close and work with Bearden on trying to come up with something to prove that Antonio ordered those people killed. However, you don't. All you have to do is stay out of sight and eventually testify at their trial, as Joyce, or Jane, or both. Until that time, I want you to dress up as a sleek blonde and I'm putting you on an airplane to Hawaii or Acapulco, or someplace, until this thing cools down. You'll have plenty of money to stay as long as necessary and once they're locked up for good, we'll be together always, I promise."

"But I want to be with you, Joe-Joe," she whined.

"Judy, for God's sake, you're not even listening to me! Please pay attention! It simply makes sense for me to go alone from here. If Crew-cut is looking for us, he'll have to look a helluva lot harder if we're not together. And, like you said earlier, as me, they don't know who I am, so I'm free to roam wherever I need to. I mean, even if one of them remembers me from three years ago, they'll never make the connection that I'm Worthington."

I'd forgotten about Antonio seeing us together at the airport. He might know me as me. Thankfully, Judy didn't think of that either. "But, Joe-Joe—"

"Hey! Pleading Joe-Joe to me won't work this time! It's settled, so don't argue with me. Besides, it's only temporary."

"Promise?"

"I don't need to promise. I love you."

Another tear escaped down her cheek. Letting it fall, she wrapped her arms around my neck, and holding her body close to mine, she looked into my face and whispered, "Hollywood? Galahad? Owen? Or whoever you are at this moment, I'm really afraid right now, so would you please convince the man I know as Joe-Joe to make love to me?"

"I can do that."

Chapter 47

"Remember," I told Judy, "keep all the doors locked and don't open them for anybody—and don't answer the phone until you can identify who it is through the answering machine. If anything important happens, I'll either call you or come straight home. Now then, kiss me good-by and wish me luck."

"Can't I do the blonde thing and go with you, Joe-Joe? Please?"

"No. You'll be much safer here. Besides, since I'm on my way to see Bearden, how do I explain to him who you are as a blonde?"

"I could wait in the car."

I simply looked at her without making a comment.

"Oh, okay, *Reginald*. But where are you going after you see Bearden?"

"I've got to go to the office and make sure everything's okay there—and I don't want you in there in any color hair!"

"All right," she moaned. "But, Joe-Joe, do me one big favor. After you talk to Bearden, please take off the disguise before you go to the office 'cause all the bad guys know you in the Worthington get-up, but only Antonio has seen you as you and chances are, he won't show his ugly face there."

Damn—she did remember! "You're right! It might be better if I come back here first and dress up in the old man thing."

"No good, Joe-Joe. Crew-cut has seen you like that. Remember? And there's a good chance he *will* show his ugly face."

"You are right again. Looks like I'd better just take my chances as me. Okay Girl, I should get going."

Holding her close for a moment, I kissed her and whispered my love, then I walked to the garage, backed the Firebird into the street, and left.

****

With a tone of disgust in his gravelly voice, Alex

Bigotti barked into the pay phone. "Yeah, boss, it's me. Hey, I've been watching that friggin' office for half a day and nobody's gone in or out of the place. I think I better break in and search it. Maybe that'll give me something to go on."

"Bigotti? Do whatever you have to do! I want that weasel and his ugly woman out of the picture before this crap goes any farther. You got that?"

"Yeah, boss, I got it. And, say, boss—do you want me to keep an eye on Mortensen? Or maybe get Scottie to do it?"

"That ain't necessary. He's still locked up. It seems his frump of a wife hasn't posted bail, so he has no way of gettin' out."

"Why don't you spring him?"

"Hell, no! It's his fault we're in this pickle in the first place. The stupid, horny, skirt-chasin' asshole! Alex, you just concentrate on gettin' this Worthington creep and his ugly witch out of the way!" Click.

Hanging up the phone, Alex looked around before making his way from the hamburger joint back toward the office building. Acting nonchalant, he entered the double doors and approached the suite with the words *Worthington Construction Company* printed on the entrance. After looking up and down the hallway, he pulled out his pick and stethoscope. Putting them to use, he skillfully monitored each sound until he was sure all the tumblers had fallen into place. He gently twisted the doorknob, popped the door open, and slipped his big frame inside. As he slowly squeezed the door closed behind him, Alex listened. The dark office was completely silent. *Good.* He flipped on the light switch and after one last quick scan all around, he stealthily moved to the desk in the reception area and started his search.

Taking his time, he meticulously hunted through the drawers and, as he always did, Alex Bigotti systematically replaced everything exactly where he found it. His exploration came up empty. Next, his eyes settled on a file cabinet next to Joyce Worthington's typing table. Opening the lock was easy.

Alex began thumbing through the neatly categorized folders, not sure of what he was looking for. Just something. He pulled out the one marked Credit Reports and rifled through the papers. *Aha! What's this? Seems like this Worthington guy has an office in Indianapolis—that's where all these reports are from! Whoa, maybe that's where he is now! Oh crap, I sure hope the boss doesn't want me to go back there! I feel a whole lot safer right here on home territory.*

After putting the file back, he foraged deeper into the drawer. *What's this? Patterson Note.* He opened the folder. *Well, Alex, would you look at this! Our Mr. Worthington gave this guy Patterson and his wife a note for four hundred grand! Maybe Mister Patterson can tell me where he is. But where's Patterson?*

He remembered seeing that name on a previous folder, so the big man began fingering his way back toward the front of the files. *Uh-huh, there it is. Patterson Lease.* Looking inside, Alex Bigotti found our home address.

He reached for the telephone on the desk and made another call to Tafino. "I think I got what I need, boss. Maybe you and Lou ought to go someplace for lunch. Someplace real busy with a lot of people around. With all this other crap going on, you might need an alibi when I get rid of Worthington and his broad."

"We'll go to the resort."

"One more thing, boss. I been thinking about Mortensen again and I still think you should spring him. I mean, what if he sings while he's in there?"

"Good thinking, Alex. Lou and I will get him sprung and you can take care of him after you finish with Worthington and his ugly woman."

"All right, boss. Okay, I better go while their trail is hot. I'll check back with you later."

"Hey, Bigotti—remember—just like all the others— try to make this clean. We don't need no killings tied to us."

"Leave it to me, boss." Click. They didn't hear the second click of the tape recorder in my desk.

After swiftly replacing everything, Alex Bigotti left

the office of Worthington Construction Company.

****

I studied Thomas Bearden's expression as he listened to Sandy on the tape and, at length, I saw a thin smile spread across his face. "You bet, Mr. Worthington, I'll get her in here as fast as I can. And one other thing I intend to do this morning, is to question Mortensen again and see if I can get him to tell us anything. At the moment, we're letting him stew in a holding cell—at least for as long as I can legally keep him there before we have to transfer him to a regular block. You know, that must be some cow he's married to. We haven't been able to locate her to question her and she's made no attempt whatsoever to get him released. Hell's fire, his bail is only twenty-five thousand. Plus, I fully would have expected his lawyer to come up with something by now, but as long as he or Mrs. Mortensen doesn't, we'll continue to hold him, which gives us the upper hand."

"Well, not only that, Detective, he's probably better off in here anyway. I'm surprised that Tafino hasn't bailed him out just to keep him quiet. Let's hope he doesn't."

"A very good point, Mr. Worthington—and it gives me an idea. It's something of a stretch, but maybe I could press homicide charges against Mortensen on some of these strange deaths and have Granado explain to the judge the possible danger to him if he's released. If His Honor is willing to go along, maybe Ed can get him to revoke bail altogether. That'll give us two things. One, since nobody could get him out, we'd virtually have him in protective custody; and two, if he has all the blame thrown on him, it might frighten him enough to loosen his tongue. In the meantime, while we do still have him, I'll get his lawyer over here and we'll start grilling him, pronto."

"Excellent. Joyce and I will keep you posted about anything else that crops up at our end." With that, I shook hands with Thomas Bearden and left.

Climbing into the Firebird, I raced to the nearest gas station and removed the disguise in their restroom. Before going to the office, I detoured to the post office to check the box and inside was the express package from Robert Tanner, one day early. Elated, I trotted back to the car and postponed my trip to the headquarters of Worthington Construction. Instead, I aimed the car toward home, wanting to send Judy to safety as soon as possible. *Great! She can leave today!*

Chapter 48

Dressed in Levi's and T-shirt, Judy was seated on the sofa, mulling over the bottles of nail polish, trying to decide on a color. She didn't see the ugly face peering into the side window of the dining room.

With his hands cupped around his eyes, Alex Bigotti stared inside and spotted her immediately. Doing a double take, he leaned closer for a better look. *Holy crap! That's the auburn haired woman! I recognize her from the picture that other Fraulein had. Huh! So that's Mrs. Patterson?*

Alex took another close look. *Say—maybe this one knows where the ugly secretary is. Hot damn! The boss is gonna be happy about this! Maybe I can recover those tapes!*

The big man stepped back and made a long, slow, study of the neighborhood. Everything was quiet. He put out his cigarette with his fingers and stuck the butt into his pocket. *Okay, Alex, let's go do this.* He meandered to the front door and pushed the button.

When the doorbell rang, Judy froze. Quietly placing the bottle of polish on the coffee table, she slipped off the couch and crept barefoot across the carpet, cautiously making her way to the door. Once there, she looked through the peephole and inhaled a sharp gasp, holding her breath. *Oh my God! It's him!*

Backing slowly away, she frantically looked around the room then raced down the hall into the bedroom. Grabbing the telephone, she nervously pushed the numbers from memory and as she listened to the ringing at the other end, she anxiously implored. *Come on, Joe-Joe! Answer the phone damn it!*

When she heard the answering machine pick up the call, Judy muffled her voice with her hand and desperately pleaded, "Joe-Joe, if you're there, pick up the phone! He's here! Crew-cut is here!" She heard only silence at the other end. Then she anxiously whispered, "Joe-Joe, why in hell aren't you at that office, yet?"

Judy waited only a moment longer before she

frantically pushed the disconnect button. The moment she heard a fresh dial tone, she pressed the numbers for 9-1-1, but just as the operator answered, the phone suddenly went dead. She pounded the disconnect button again. Once. Twice. Three times. Still only dead silence.

Petrified, she dropped the receiver and raced back down the hall to the bathroom and quickly locked the door behind her. Immediately thinking better of that, she cautiously wrapped her fingers around the doorknob and slowly re-opened the door, straining her ears. It was very quiet. Slipping backward into the room, she kept her eyes on the doorway as she reached behind her and eased open a drawer of the vanity. Taking her eyes from the doorway just long enough for a quick look, she clumsily rummaged through the drawer and clamped her hand around a pair of long scissors. She removed them from the cabinet and stopped to listen again. Holding the shears like a weapon, she slipped out of the room into the hallway.

Deliberately tip-toeing across the carpet, Judy looked back over her shoulder then carefully peeked into the office and then the workout room as she inched her way back toward the bedroom. When she reached the end of the hallway, she looked back one more time before stepping into our bedroom. Once inside, she raced across the floor and scrambled into the closet. Petrified, she waited, all the while watching for movement through the slightly opened gap she'd left between the sliding doors. With her heart pounding, she felt like it was in her throat.

Panting and holding her hand to her chest, she vainly tried to slow her breathing while she stood there motionless, too frightened to move. *Please don't let him find me! Please, God. Oh, Joe-Joe—where are you?* She strained to think of what else she could do or where else she could hide. With no better choice, Judy just stayed right there, frozen in an attacking stance with her arm raised above her head, fearfully watching through the crack in the door and gripping her makeshift weapon until her knuckles turned white.

****

After slicing the phone line at the back of the house, Alex Bigotti forced his screwdriver between the aluminum frames of the sliding window and snapped the flimsy lock onto the carpet. Sliding the glass open, the killer hoisted his big frame to the sill and easily crawled inside. Hesitating for a moment, he watched from side to side and listened. Hearing only quiet, he weaseled across the family room and edged his way into the kitchen. Holding a pistol in one of his gloved hands and a piece of rope in his other, he peered around the corner into the dining room. Nobody there.

Gradually stealing his way through the dining room, he brought the living room into view when he looked around the corner. Slowly moving his ever-searching eyes all around, he spotted the small bottles of nail polish on the coffee table. *Aha! One has the lid off, so she must be alone.*

All at once, Alex heard a scratching sound behind him and he spooked. With his gun raised, he whirled around, took three big steps and looked into the kitchen. Socko was standing there watching him. *Stupid damn cat!*

Shooing at the animal failed to get Alex any results. Socko stayed put. Bigotti disgustedly edged back into the kitchen and tried to snag the cat to put him outside, but his hand just grabbed air as Socko moved away. In frustration, Bigotti kicked at him, barely grazing him as Socko jumped over his outstretched foot and bolted around the corner. Screeching wildly, the cat raced through the dining room, across the living room and down the hallway before disappearing into the workout room.

****

Hearing the sound, Judy tensed, at once realizing that Crew-cut must be in the house. Panic swept over her, but it temporarily mixed with anger at the thought of his harming Socko. Squeezing the handles of the shears tighter in her hand, first with revenge, then with fear, she prayed again. *Oh my God, Joe-Joe, please get my message and come home!*

****

After watching the cat disappear, Bigotti again

listened then slowly crept around the corner, slipping his way through the dining room and across the living room. Gradually progressing down the hall, he put the gun in his coat pocket and tightened his grip on the rope in his gloved hands. As he approached an open doorway, he stopped, again lending an ear for sound. Still quiet. He slipped his hand inside the room, flipped on the light switch and peeked around the corner. He was looking into a bathroom.

Treading softly onto the tile floor, he edged into the room to take a quick look around. Nearly tripping over something, he looked down to the floor where several dummy heads were lined against the wall. All but one was holding a wig. Alex reached down and picked up a brown one that was streaked with gray. He examined the shape and color of it. Checking the others, he noticed the strange variety. Blonde, gray, brown, male, female. He put the wig back.

Casting his eyes toward a large case on the counter, he walked over to it and carefully opened it. Inside, Alex discovered a wealth of make-up—whiskers, fake noses, scar tissue, moles, and a bevy of application tools. Staring at the inventory, Alex scratched his crew-cut head in bewilderment at the strange, elaborate collection. Glancing to his right, he saw various shapes and colors of eyeglasses neatly mounted on a rack next to the make-up kit. Returning his attention to the fascinating box, he reached inside and gingerly lifted a patch of wrinkled skin from it. He took off his glove and felt the rubbery texture. Then he put it back. In orderly fashion, he sifted through the other items and spotted several large pieces of realistic scar tissue and all at once, something struck him.

The boss told me that witch had a big scar on her neck! What in the—I don't believe this! But it's gotta be! All this make-up and crap? That auburn broad and the ugly secretary have got to be the same person! And that old skin? He lifted a piece of it from the box and fondled it, then reached down and picked up a gray wig. Holding it in his hands, he inspected it and began to put two and two together. *The old man in the van! Was that Patterson? Or Worthington?* He grabbed another wig. *And the tacky blonde who left with him! Damn Sam, I was right! That was her!* Astonished, Alex Bigotti just stood there, gawking at his discovery. *What is all this crap? Why would they go to the trouble of...?* He fingered the skin material again. *Ya know, if the auburn broad and the ugly woman are the same person, then I'll bet this Patterson and Worthington must be the same guy, too! Accordin' to the boss, he's real ugly, just like the woman!*

Like a bolt of lightning, it hit him. It could only be one thing. *Damn! I think these people are tryin' to set the boss up! But who in the hell are they? Why are they doing this? Could they be connected to New York somehow?* Alex quickly discarded that idea. *Naw. Those guys would simply have somebody kill him and Lou. This has to be something else. Mortensen?* Bigotti chuckled to himself. *Couldn't be him. He's too chicken-shit—plus, he ain't smart enough to pull off something like this.*

Alex couldn't come up with anything else, but he told himself one thing. *Whatever it is, Tafino, I get a big bonus for this!*

He carefully placed the phony flesh back into the box and crept back toward the doorway. With his mind working like a steel trap, he edged out into the hallway, all the while cautiously watching and listening. *This is gonna be easier than I thought. First, I'll choke her, then I'll wait for him to come back and with one bullet to his head, it looks like a lover's spat. A very convenient murder-suicide. Nice and clean. Just the way the boss likes it.*

Moving down the corridor to the next opening, he peered into the room with the exercise equipment. Ignoring the black and white cat sitting on the bench and staring at him, Alex looked into the office room across the hall. Total silence. He walked past the two rooms and snaked his way to the end of the hall, where two more doorways at opposite sides of the hallway had their doors wide open. A quick check of them both told him which of the two was the master bedroom—the unmade bed and the clear view of the second bathroom. Seeing the telephone receiver hanging limp over the nightstand, Alex smiled.

Once inside the room, Bigotti knelt down to look beneath the bed. When he saw nothing except several pairs of men's and ladies shoes, he reasoned. *Okay, she's not under there. That leaves the closet.* Climbing back to his feet, Alex snaked his way across the carpet one slow step at a time, mindfully watching and listening. When he reached the closet, Alex wrapped his fingers around the edge of the sliding door and swiftly jerked it open.

Terrified, Judy leaped backwards and shrilled a loud scream, momentarily stunning him. Seeing his gloved hand on the doorframe, she lashed out with the scissors as hard as she could, ripping the cloth and gashing the skin underneath. Bellowing in pain, Alex jumped back and grabbed his injured hand. The rope dropped to the beige carpet.

Vigilant, Judy sprang quickly from her hiding place, then frantically bolted past him and ran through the bedroom doorway into the hall. Hearing his guttural outcry, she raced toward the front door, screaming in terror, with tears pouring down her cheeks. Just as she rounded the corner into the living room, her feet slipped and she fell to the floor face first. Despite the carpet burns on both knees, she scrambled to her feet and ran to the front door.

In pain, Alex Bigotti ignored the blood streaming from the back of his hand and scooped up the rope. Angrily chasing her, he stumbled down the hallway into the living room, holding the cord in his hands.

Judy took a quick look back over her shoulder and, while she anxiously tried to get the door unlocked, she painfully broke a nail when her hand slipped away from the deadbolt knob. She grabbed at it again and heard the deadbolt unlock, but just as she placed her hand on the doorknob to open it, she felt herself being pulled back away from the door. Alex had caught her.

With a nasty laugh, Bigotti threw the rope over her head and wrapped it around her neck. Pulling her slowly backwards, he caused her shrieking voice to go silent.

Struggling to keep her balance, Judy tugged at the rope with both hands as her eyes began to water.

Without a word, Alex began to slowly twist the cord in his hands.

Chapter 49

Abe Sundstrom was certainly willing to defend his client, but if the allegations against Mortensen were true, Abe's conscience wouldn't allow him to permit the murders of several people to go unjustified. His unwavering ethics prompted him to inform Thomas Bearden of this, whereupon the lawman apprised him that even though Mortensen was aware, after the fact, that there were several homicides allegedly ordered by Antonio Tafino, Mortensen himself had no play in them and eventually those charges against Mortensen would probably be dropped. "However, Mr. Sundstrom, in addition to the fraud and conspiracy crimes, there is still the very likely probability he'll be charged with obstruction of justice regarding these alleged killings. However, that will depend upon how much James is willing to tell us. With Mortensen's cooperation, the D. A. is willing to deal."

"What sort of deal?"

The policeman outlined what Granado had told him earlier. "That's it in a nutshell, Mr. Sundstrom, and if you're in agreement, I'd like to present Granado's offer during my interrogation, but only when I think it fits. Please let me question James in my own way so we can hopefully get to the bottom of all this."

Abe Sundstrom stood up. "Assuming my client's defense is not jeopardized, you'll have my full cooperation, Detective Bearden. I'm as anxious as you are. Shall we go talk with James now?"

"Absolutely."

****

Sitting in his holding cell, James Mortensen slowly stood up and began pacing back and forth. *Why hasn't Margo or that skinny-ass lawyer gotten me out of here, yet?* Looking around, as he had a thousand times before, he saw only the hard bench, the metal toilet stool and four dirty gray walls. No windows and only that one steel door with the slim, wire imbedded glass, through which he really couldn't see much of anything. Shining overhead was a solitary light bulb, forty watts, and it stayed on twenty-four hours a day. When he tried to sleep on the blanket-less cold panel, it seemed much brighter than forty watts. Staring up at it, he thought of smashing the damned thing with his shoe, but then it would be total darkness and he wouldn't see anything. And, of course, he had no way of simply unscrewing it. There was nothing to stand on except the cold bench and it was bolted to the wall, too far away. Feeling as if he'd been there for years, it was hard to believe that it had only been a little less than two days.

Sitting his tired body back down, James combed through his limp hair with his fingers. He hadn't shaved in three days, his clothes were beginning to stick to him, and he felt totally abandoned. Nervously tapping his foot, he stared down at the floor while he held his stubbly face in his palms with his elbows resting on his knees. *How long can they hold me here this way? They don't even have a telephone in here so I can call Margo or that worthless lawyer. I tell you, I'm going crazy!*

He remembered his brief feeling of elation yesterday morning when the judge had set his bail at twenty-five thousand dollars, believing he'd soon be free. But now, the memory angered him. *That's a damn pittance, compared to what I have in the safety deposit box! If only Margo would come and see me, I could tell her about it and get released from this hellhole!* He slammed his fist down against the bench.

Painfully puzzled with it all, he pictured Antonio in his mind. *I wonder if he's in here someplace. And if he's not, then why in hell doesn't he get me out?*

Still holding his head in his hands, the heart-broken man began to cry. Just then, the metal door clanked open.

****

Several minutes later, seated beside his lawyer, a haggard James Mortensen looked across the table at Thomas Bearden. The detective spoke to him, "Good afternoon, James. First of all, I want to bring you up to date on a few things and then I'd like to ask you a few questions."

The mortgage broker nodded then studied his surroundings. *Even being in this room is a relief after being cooped up down there!*

"First of all, James, we've got news about your wife, Margo."

"Is she finally bailing me out?"

"No, it seems she left town in a bit of a hurry. That's why she hasn't bailed you out. However, we've managed to locate her."

"What? Locate her? Where is she?"

"We found her living it up on some island resort in the Caribbean with her hairdresser. Fellow by the name of Charles Cartier. Not only that, the feds down there have confiscated from the happy couple, over three hundred eighty thousand dollars in travelers' checks and cash. They're holding the money in custody and Margo will be back sometime tomorrow."

"What?" Surprised and shocked, Mortensen studied the policeman's face. "Why did she do that?"

"I'll have to let her explain that one to you, James. In the meantime, I have something else to discuss with you."

Mortensen didn't even hear Bearden. Instead, he convulsed a loud sniffle and rambled, "That's unbelievable! Margo ran away with Charles? You know, if it didn't hurt so bad, I'd think it was funny. I could've sworn Charles is gay."

Abe Sundstrom gripped his hand around Mortensen's forearm. There was a touch of anxiety in his voice. "James, I realize this news about Margo is a shock, but I'm afraid you'll have to deal with that later on. In the meantime, you're still in jail and I want you to concentrate on that right now. You're in serious trouble here and I believe you should listen to what Lieutenant Bearden is telling you."

Still stunned, Mortensen became at once embittered by his own attorney's seemingly uncaring candor and shot Sundstrom a look of infuriation. He started to object, but when he saw the grim expression on Abe Sundstrom's face and the man's words sank in, he slowly slumped back in his chair. James knew he was right. "All right, Abe, I'll listen."

Bearden spoke to him again. "Thank you, James. Now then, as you know, you and the Tafino brothers have been charged with conspiracy to defraud over thirty people with your little real estate scheme and we suspect that Antonio masterminded the whole thing. Am I right?"

"Yes." James whispered.

"Okay, then I want to explain something else to you. I've spoken with the district attorney's office and they're willing to talk with us about a plea arrangement. Would you be willing to listen to that?"

Mortensen just sat there with his eyes closed and his hands covering his face. His ears vaguely heard the words. He fleetingly pictured Margo in his mind's eye. Then Antonio. Even Louis. And with a lost feeling, the face of Jane flashed by, as well as the image of Sonya, standing in a motel room, dressed in only her skimpy underpants, beckoning to him with her hands holding her large breasts. All of a sudden, he imagined they were all pointing at him and laughing. Feeling completely betrayed he gladly let the images go. Lowering his hands, he glanced first at Sundstrom, then at Bearden. "I'm not sure. What's involved in all of that?"

Against the wishes of Bearden, Abe Sundstrom chimed in. "It's simple, James. If you're willing to enter a guilty plea and testify about the real estate scam, you'll receive a sentence of five to ten years. Otherwise, with more than thirty counts, you're more than likely looking at twenty-five years to life. As your attorney, I strongly advise you to seriously consider accepting it."

Bearden cast a scowl toward the lawyer and quickly interjected, "He's right, James, but you don't have to give us an answer right away because we're still sorting out the other charges."

"What other charges?" Mortensen's voice cracked as he asked the question.

When Sundstrom saw Bearden's cold stare, he went silent. Bearden said to Mortensen, "James, we're still looking into the possibility of charging you with conspiracy to commit first degree murder."

"What in the hell are you talking about? I haven't killed anybody!"

"We're not charging you with homicide, James. We'll be charging you with conspiracy."

"Conspiracy? Who am I supposed to have conspired to kill?"

"What about Mark Tyler?"

"Who? I've never even heard of him! Who is he?"

"He was a limousine driver for that escort service girl, Sonya Waverly. Remember her?"

"Yes, but—"

"James, it's our belief that Mark and Sonya were in the way of Antonio Tafino, who was trying to recover some conversation tapes made in your office by a girl who worked for you—Jane Romero. Do you remember her?"

Dumbfounded, Mortensen avoided Bearden's eyes and didn't answer. *How in the world does he know all that? And heaven help me, what do I say now? Should I tell him Jane's real name?* He decided against that—at least for now.

"Now then, James, let's start with this girl named Sonya Waverly. She was a friend of Jane Romero's. But you know that, don't you James? She's also the young lady whom Mark Tyler was escorting the night he died." Bearden then planted a seed. "Let me ask you something else, James. Do you recall how beautiful Sonya was?"

"Was?" Mortensen blurted. "Did you say *was*? Oh, my God, no! Don't tell me that ignorant Antonio had her killed, too? Just for those frigging tapes?" he shouted. Bearden's seed had taken root.

Jumping to his feet, Mortensen angrily shoved his chair to the floor and urgently began pacing back and forth. Bearden kept a close eye but let him pace. After several moments, Mortensen stopped and pounded the tabletop with his fist. "No! Damn it! No! Antonio, you rotten no-good slimeball! You've gone too far! You had no reason to kill her! My God in Heaven—that girl was beautiful!"

Disconsolate, Mortensen stood there, holding his

unshaven face in his hands then he began to cry. Moving quietly, Abe Sundstrom reached down and up-righted the chair then gently squeezed his client's shoulders and eased Mortensen back into it. When he was settled, Bearden compassionately offered, "James, would you like something to drink? Coffee perhaps? Maybe a cola?"

Still weeping helplessly, Mortensen whimpered, "Yes, sir. Could I have a cup of coffee, please? And could I possibly have some aspirin?"

"Sure, James." Going to the door, Bearden made the request to the officer standing outside, after which, the detective vigilantly waited right there until the officer handed a tray to him. He set it on the table in front of the other two men and after they'd served themselves, Bearden helped himself to a cup of his own.

Permitting Mortensen some time to recover, Bearden eventually spoke to him, "Okay, James, are you feeling well enough to continue?"

With his eyes still closed, Mortensen barely nodded.

"All right, you stated that Antonio Tafino shouldn't have killed Sonya, too. What did you mean by that? Are there other victims you can tell us about?"

Mortensen swallowed a gulp of his coffee and sat there, eyes open now, staring down at the table. He shook his head in disbelief. "He went too far. Way too far. And for what?"

Abe Sundstrom didn't like the avenue this conversation was taking and despite Bearden's prior statements to him, the lawyer knew his obligation was to advise his client not to incriminate himself. He grabbed Mortensen by the arm and leaned close to his face. "James, listen to me. If you are in any way involved in these murder allegations, don't say another word."

Heaving a sigh, Mortensen looked at Abe Sundstrom. "I have to, Abe. They have to be told the truth."

Without waiting for any further comment from Sundstrom, Mortensen glared at Bearden and stated with conviction, "Mister, I had nothing to do with killing anybody! It was Antonio. I'll do the plea arrangement for the other stuff, but in no way will I be accused of killing anybody. I mean, if all of those people weren't intelligent enough to manage their properties, they deserved to lose them, but none of them deserved to die for it."

"James, let's be sure we're talking about the same people. Every one of their names was listed in your little book of people for which you received a pay-off from Tafino. It's my understanding they were silenced for trying to expose your little operation. Do these names mean anything to you? Wayne Meeks? Ralph Blake? Edwin Cooke?"

Mortensen appeared astonished. "How do you know about all of that?"

"I'm a policeman, James, and policemen investigate. Are those the names of some of the people that Tafino ordered murdered?"

Solemnly bowing his head, the defeated man whispered, "Yes."

"Would you be willing to testify to that, James?"

"Hell, no! If I do that, Antonio will have me killed too!"

Bearden sent a masked hush signal to Sundstrom. "Okay, James, I understand your reluctance. But let me ask you in a different way. If you could be assured that Tafino would not be able to have any of his henchmen come after you, and that you and your wife would be absolutely safe and protected—would you then testify to it?"

Mortensen looked toward Sundstrom for a sign. The lawyer merely shrugged his shoulders, then directed Mortensen's attention back to Bearden, who asked, "What do you say, James?"

Although reluctant, the mortgage broker looked up at the detective and questioned, "Are you absolutely sure that Margo would be protected and no harm could come to her?"

"Absolutely, James."

"Then I suppose so."

"Good. I'll get Mr. Granado."

****

344

Upon returning with the Assistant District Attorney and a fresh tray of coffee, Thomas Bearden re-opened the conversation. "James, I believe Mr. Granado has an updated plea arrangement to offer you."

Edward Granado didn't mince his words. "Mr. Mortensen, I had a long talk with your wife just a short time ago and she appears to be quite remorseful for leaving you here to fend for yourself. And I also believe you're telling us the truth about these killings. It's our opinion that you didn't actually have anything to do with these alleged murders and—"

"I didn't!" Mortensen screeched.

Granado glared at him. "Please let me finish, Mr. Mortensen."

"Yes, sir. I'm sorry. But I tell you—I didn't."

"Now then, we understand your unwillingness to come to us about these killings at the time they occurred, because you had good reason to fear for your own life. We also believe that if you testify against Tafino about these killings, you'll be in a very unsafe environment within the prison system if your fraud and conspiracy trial ends up with a conviction."

"My God yes! They'll kill me! Go ahead and convict me if you want to, but I'm not going to testify against them."

"Well, Mr. Mortensen, before you make that decision, please listen to what else I have to say. Okay?"

A haggard James Mortensen looked at Abe Sundstrom, who urged Mortensen to listen. Mortensen looked back at Granado and mumbled, "All right. Go ahead."

"Good. Mr. Mortensen, the criminal roots of your partners are very deep and they go back a long way. I've talked with several authorities in New York City and learned they've tried for years to get Antonio and Louis Tafino convicted on many various charges, including murder, but were never able to get any of the indictments to stick. So, in order to get them put away, we've gotten approval from the feds to offer you another arrangement. Have you ever heard of the witness protection program?"

Mortensen shrugged. "I've heard of it, but I'm not sure how it works."

"In short, James, it works like this—in exchange for your undivided testimony against the Tafino brothers regarding all of these crimes, including the number of murders that have taken place, we'll give you and Margo your freedom and the chance to start life fresh in a new city with totally new identities and backgrounds. Does this sound like something you'd be interested in talking about?"

For the first time in three long days, James Mortensen had a reason to smile. It was a small one, but it was a smile. "Yes, sir. What exactly do I have to do?"

After hearing Granado explain the details to him, James Mortensen had one more question. "Does Margo know about this?"

"Not yet, James, but judging from my earlier conversation with her, I believe she'll agree. When we get her back here tomorrow, we'll all discuss it in my office in further detail. In the meantime, we'll be holding you here for your own protection, so why don't we take you someplace where you can get a shave and shower. And some fresh clothes."

With that, Granado stood to his feet, collected his notes and started for the door. Abe Sundstrom fell in step behind him. Tom Bearden motioned for Mortensen to come along, but stopped momentarily and looked at him. "Incidentally, James, just to relieve your mind, Sonya Waverly wasn't killed. She's alive and well for one simple reason. She just plain got damned lucky."

Chapter 50

"One-Adam-Emergency. Do I have a copy?"

Picking up his microphone from the dashboard of his car, the Scottsdale police officer responded. "One-Adam-four here. Go ahead."

"This is the Nine-One-One Operator. We have an emergency call from a number that's gone silent. Trace-back gives us an address of nine-one-three-eight North Seventy-Eighth Avenue. Are you in the vicinity? Over."

"I'm in the vicinity and will respond silent. Do I have back-up? Over."

"This is One-Adam-six. I'll back-up." The second officer replaced his microphone and shoved the accelerator to the floorboard.

****

As I turned the corner, I immediately saw the white Cadillac parked across the street from our house. *Oh, my God!* Wheeling sharply in front of it, I squealed to a stop, then scorched the Firebird backwards and placed it squarely in front of the Cadillac, blocking it to the curb. Leaping from the car, I raced across the street toward the front door just as I heard Judy's screams. When they suddenly stopped, I began praying as I reached for the door handle.

The damn door was locked. Fumbling with my keys, I finally found the right one and thrust it into the cylinder, then turned the knob. I shoved the door open with my shoulder and burst inside as Crew-cut was twisting the rope around Judy's neck.

When I rushed toward them, my foot kicked something and I looked down. A pair of scissors. Thinking quickly, I scooped them up and searched for a place to strike Crew-cut, but he kept Judy between him and me. As he further tightened the rope around her throat, he laughed.

Feigning left and right, I tried to circle behind him, but the big man moved around just as quickly, shielding himself with Judy's weakening body. Still struggling to get the rope away, her face was turning crimson and her inability to breathe was becoming critical. With no other choice, I slammed my body straight into Judy's, knocking them both backwards. Instantly losing his footing, Crew-cut back-pedaled and they both fell across the coffee table, crashing it broken to the floor beneath them. Losing his grip on the rope, Judy gulped for air as the pressure released from around her neck. Instantly tossing the scissors aside, I reached for her hands and yanked her to her feet. "Get up, Girl! Run! Go outside!"

Sucking in rapid breaths, she bolted away, choking and gasping as she stumbled through the open doorway. I was right behind her, but before I got outside, Bigotti had scrambled to his feet and grabbed me from behind. He spun me around and his huge fist crashed into my mid-section. I doubled over in pain, all at once unable to breathe. Clutching my stomach, I fell to my knees, trying to force my lungs to work. Without warning, I suddenly saw his foot coming toward my chin. Ducking away, I wasn't fast enough and I caught his boot against the side of my head. Bright flashes of light danced like spangles in front of my eyes and I felt my senses drifting away. Slumping to the floor with no air in my lungs, I couldn't get any there.

Forcing my eyes open, all at once I was looking straight into the barrel of a small caliber pistol, right in front of my face. Sheer instinct drove me to hit at it with my arm. Luckily, the surprise of that knocked the weapon from Crew-cut's hand and sent it sprawling across the floor to rest somewhere beneath the sofa, out of reach. Still standing over me, Bigotti growled and lashed out with another kick to my ribs, then slammed a large fist into the back of my neck, knocking me face down onto the carpet. As he watched me slump over and lie still, he assumed I'd lost consciousness, but I managed to open one eye just in time to see him go out the front door, rapidly in pursuit of Judy.

All of a sudden I felt a rush of air fill my lungs as my lost wind came back. As I gulped in deep breaths, the pain in my ribs made every inhale and exhale shoot sharp daggers through my whole insides. Filled with panic, I somehow wobbled to my knees then forced myself to stand up and move in the direction of the doorway. Stumbling outside, my burning eyes saw Bigotti in the yard across the street, dragging Judy toward his car. Trying her best to resist, she was fiercely kicking, scratching, biting, and screaming at him.

As he approached the back of the Cadillac with Judy in tow, Crew-cut reached for the handle of the rear door. I saw the door swing open. Petrified, I winced through my pain and broke into a run, heading straight toward them. I raced across the street and hurtled myself through the air, leaping onto the trunk of his car. Springing from there with my arms outstretched, I landed on top of them, knocking them both to the ground. Jumping up, I swung my leg and kicked Bigotti in the stomach, once, twice, again, as Judy rolled away from him.

All at once, his strong hands gripped my foot and he twisted my leg, shoving me backwards, slamming me against the car. Somehow, I quickly recoiled and as I saw him clambering to his knees, I swung my fist with all the strength I could put into it, squarely landing a stinging punch against his nose, spraying crimson all over his ugly face. Not letting up, I hammered at him with both fists, knocking him flat on his back.

Roaring loudly, Bigotti instinctively reacted and kicked out at me, dropping my legs out from under me. As I tumbled to the ground, he rose up like a cat and dove on top of me. With all his weight on me, I couldn't move. He wrapped both of his huge hands around my throat and started squeezing. I tried desperately to dislodge his vise-like grip from my neck, but kicking and thrashing as hard as I could, I couldn't get his bulk off of me.

Unable to breathe, I let go of his fingers and began swinging my arms wildly, but I was powerless to get them into position to land my fists on him. Frantically placing my hand under his bloody chin, I pushed upward as hard as I could, but he was too strong. Feeling my eyes stinging, I vainly grabbed his hands again and tugged at his tightening fingers, desperately fighting for wind. I could hear Judy's petrified screams in the background as I felt my strength slowly ebbing away.

Realizing this, Judy instinctively reached her hand down to Crew-cut's face and she raked her long nails across his eyes, gouging into his sockets. With a blood-curdling roar trumpeting from his throat, Bigotti blindly lashed out behind him to catch her, just as she jumped out of his way. On impulse, he grabbed at his eyes with a blood-curdling scream and when his hold on me loosened, an abrupt sensation of air came streaming into my lungs. As soon as I felt him topple off of me, I spun out of his reach, jumped to my feet and grabbed Judy's hand. "Let's get the hell out of here!"

Running to the Firebird, I grabbed the handle to open the door just as I heard a car screech to a stop in front of us, blocking the Pontiac. Another jerked to a stop in back of the white Cadillac. Two police officers scrambled out of their black and whites and came charging toward us with their guns drawn. The one in front yelled, "Hold it right there! Put your hands up against the car. Both of you!" Judy and I did just that.

The first cop demanded, "Okay—what's going on here?"

Judy burst into tears and pointed with her head toward the other side of the Cadillac. "That man on the ground over there just tried to kill us!"

Not even having seen him, both officers immediately rushed around the car to capture Alex Bigotti.

Slumping against me, Judy burst into tears and wept unashamedly. Holding her pretty face against my shoulder, I caressed her auburn hair with my sore, swollen hand. "It's all right, Girl. It's all over."

After placing Crew-cut in his patrol car, one of the policemen walked over to Judy and I. "Are you folks okay? Either of you need to go to the hospital?"

My insides were killing me, but I didn't want the exposure a trip to the hospital would bring. "I think we're all right, officer, but please promise me one thing."

"Sir?"

Cringing, I reached into my pocket to dig out my billfold and removed Thomas Bearden's card. I handed it to the patrolman. Pointing toward a scowling Alex Bigotti in the back seat, I told him, "Please keep that ugly mongrel locked up and under no circumstances do you let him loose. I'd like for you to please call the detective named on that card and tell him that this asshole is Antonio Tafino's hired gun. He'll know what you're talking about."

"All right, I can do that. However, we'll need for you to come down to the station and file a report."

I winced in pain. "Sure, sure. We'll take care of it."

"Are you sure you two don't want some medical attention? Ma'am?" He looked at Judy, who simply shook her head.

I glanced at his shirt. "No, Officer Billings, we're okay—you just take care of him." I indicated Bigotti.

Without another word, I took Judy by the hand and started walking toward our home. Officer Billings momentarily watched our backs, then entered his patrol car and drove away with Alex Bigotti.

Chapter 51

Later that evening, Judy and I moved from the house to an out-of-the-way motel, taking only the bare essentials with us. The following morning, I exchanged the red Firebird for a blue Buick Century. Having decided it was best to avoid our house and office for a while, we simply bided our time until we heard from Thomas Bearden, the sole person we had informed of our whereabouts.

The following week, we received his long-awaited call. Dressed in our full Worthington disguises, we walked into the courthouse for the arraignment of the Tafino brothers and James Mortensen. Detective Bearden greeted us in front of the courtroom entrance. He informed us of the still-secret plea arrangement for Mortensen and explained that they were arraigning him with the Tafino brothers as a front to maintain that secrecy. He concluded by congratulating us on our persistence and thanking us for the valuable information we'd collected. "Without your efforts, these guys could have gone on forever."

"Do you think you have enough evidence for a conviction, Detective?" asked Joyce Worthington.

"I'm sure of it. In addition to your documentation and Mortensen's testimony, we also have quite a bit of physical evidence from Alex Bigotti's apartment. The lab found traces of form oil on a pair of his shoes that's identical to the brand used on the construction of the bank building. Plus, they've discovered brake fluid on an old shirt of his, which matches the fluid from Ralph Blake's truck. They also found fibers from Bigotti's clothing and samples of his hair in all three vehicles involving Mark Tyler, Edwin Cooke, and Jolene Wilson. It seems that a good part of Mr. Bigotti's undoing is the fact that he's a real pack rat. The guy never threw anything away."

"Not only that," I chimed in, "but with that last tape I handed over to you—when Bigotti made the call to Antonio from my office—you practically have a full confession from both of them."

Bearden frowned. "Yeah, that would certainly carry a lot of weight, but according to what Granado says, we can't enter it as evidence because neither party agreed to the taping of the call."

I thought about that for a moment. "Detective Bearden, I believe there's an exception to it in this case. Since Bigotti made the phone call from my office without my permission and since I do agree to have all my calls taped, would that ruling still apply?"

Bearden looked stunned for a second, then he perked. "I don't know, Mr. Worthington, but I'll definitely bring that up to Granado."

Just then, the courtroom doors opened and as the three of us slowly moved toward the entryway, Bearden stopped and put his hand on my arm. He covertly looked around the hallway before he spoke softly to both of us. "Before we go in there, I'd like to make a strong suggestion to you two. Considering the history of Antonio Tafino, there may be more guys like Alex Bigotti out there and I think it would be very wise if you lie low during the next few months until their cases come to trial."

With a wide grin, I winked at him. "Thank you, Lieutenant. We appreciate your concern and wholeheartedly agree. But, to relieve your mind—I've already made plans for us to do just that."

"Somehow, Mr. Worthington, that doesn't surprise me at all." Shaking his head and smiling, the lawman turned away and walked toward the prosecution table.

As we moved arm in arm into the courtroom ourselves, Judy leaned against me and whispered, "I don't know anything about a plan, Joe-Joe. What is it?"

"I'll tell you later."

"Oh, you—" She pinched my arm and moved in front of me to a seat near the back.

****

As the three of them were being led into the courtroom in orange jail clothes and shackles, James Mortensen looked all around and instantly spotted Judy and

I. Gazing at us with hatred for several seconds, he moved his eyes away in disgust and continued searching the throng of people filling the crowded courtroom. At last, his eyes settled on Margo, who had taken a seat in the front row. After smiling bravely at her, he turned to face the front.

Shortly thereafter, the proceedings started and the State presented its findings to the Grand Jury. The three of them were bound over for trial and ordered held without bond. As the final gavel came down, I heard a squeaky, high-pitched feminine voice that resembled a cartoon character. Somebody was yelling at the top of their lungs. "Worthington, you no-good rotten scumbag! You're gonna pay for this with your life—I promise you! You better keep an eye on your back, you creepy looking, ugly moron, 'cause you're gonna die! I guarantee it! You will get yours, you asshole!"

Searching for the source, I knew it couldn't be Antonio. His voice was raspy. And it wasn't James Mortensen. *Could that be one of their lawyers? Huh-uh, I just heard both of them speaking up there and they didn't sound like that!*

Suddenly, I knew. My eyes settled on Louis Tafino, who was kicking and fighting, all the while continuing to scream high-pitched profanities at me as two deputies literally dragged him to a holding cell. I grinned and showed him my cigar.

Then I glanced at Antonio, who was staring daggers straight at me. Just before he was led away, he too pointed his finger at me in an unspoken promise, but for once, he didn't say a word.

****

Simultaneously, on the fortieth floor of a plush New York office building, four men in very up-to-date, dark suits were gathered around a conference table. The man at the head of the table spoke first. "So! Who called the meeting?"

A young man in his early thirties with a suave pompadour hairstyle carefully spread a newspaper on the table and pointed to a particular story. "I did, Mr. Calabrese.

354

Have any of you gentlemen seen this?"

"What's it about?" Mr. Calabrese asked.

"Antonio and Louis Tafino. It seems they decided to come out of retirement in Arizona and they've gotten themselves into a little jamb. Just like they almost did here before they left."

"Can their problems be traced back to us?"

"I don't think so, Mr. Calabrese, but I thought I'd better bring it up. Do you think we should do anything about it?"

Mr. Calabrese pored over the article then shoved it away. "No. If it can't be brought back here, then I say let 'em rot out there. Gentlemen?"

The others quickly scanned over the clipping, then nodded swift agreement. Mr. Calabrese pointed a finger for emphasis. "Okay. For now, we stand pat. However, if they contact any of us for help, either directly or through the grapevine, we'll have to eliminate them, which is what I wanted to do in the first place. We simply cannot have them connected to us anymore. Any comments or questions?"

There were none. "Good. Then I say this meeting is adjourned."

Chapter 52

With tears welling in her eyes, Judy asked, "But, Joe-Joe, they're all in jail, so why do we have to separate?"

"Judy, you heard what Bearden and Granado told us. These guys have mafia connections all over the place and they aren't going to stop looking for us, so please listen to reason! I have matters here that need taking care of and, Girl, as you very well know and have constantly reminded me, they all have descriptions of you in every disguise we've concocted, as well as knowing you in your natural appearance. But since they only know me in the Worthington get-up, I can do what I need to do as me and I believe it would be very unwise to have you with me when I do them. Not only that, I'm certainly not leaving you alone again anywhere in this town for any reason, therefore we have to get you completely out of the picture for the time being. So until we have to testify, I'm taking Bearden's advice and sticking to my plan. Like it or not, you're going to Hawaii."

The next afternoon, I put my still very reluctant Judy on a plane to Honolulu, using her new identity of Kathleen Pallenski. She wore a new blonde wig and dark sunglasses. Nervously standing with her at the airport, I kept a watchful eye all around as I gave her my instructions. "Okay. As soon as you get there, rent a post office box in your new name then telephone me with the number of it from a pay phone. Place your call to the pay phone number here that I gave to you earlier. I'll be waiting there at ten o'clock tomorrow evening, so call me promptly. I don't want to hang around there very long. Also, you might want to stay in a hotel, at least in the beginning. That way, you'll be surrounded by a lot of people most of the time. Finally, just one more thing. Remember, Girl, I love you and as soon as I'm finished here, I'll be with you. Okay? Now then, they're calling your flight, so you have to go."

Holding her close until the very last minute, I reluctantly released her when the final boarding call came.

After one last lingering kiss, Judy walked away to board the airplane. I turned my head away so she wouldn't see the tears in my eyes. I didn't know when I'd see her again.

****

Prior to going back to the house, I turned in the Buick and rented an Oldsmobile Cutlass on a day-to-day basis. The following morning, I practiced with my new disguise. It consisted of a hat like Robert Tanner's, a bushy black wig and mustache, and casual clothes. After leaving the house in my latest get-up, I went to a bank we hadn't used before and rented a large safety deposit box in the name of Reginald Worthington.

I then visited a car-hauling firm and hired them to ship Judy's Corvette to Nathan in Florida, and after arranging for our office equipment and household furniture to be purchased by an auction company, I sat down at my typewriter and authored three letters. With one last look around, I was satisfied that I'd taken care of everything and I left the office of Worthington Construction Company for the last time.

While driving away from the building, I gave notice to a black Mercedes pulling slowly into the parking lot as I was on my way out. During the past few days, I'd seen it several times, but so far, I'd managed to stay ahead of it. Traveling home at a high rate of speed to pick up my already packed luggage, I once again saw the black Mercedes in my rearview mirror just after I pulled away from the house. It parked in front of the place just as I drove out of sight around the corner. I didn't see the dark complexioned man stride to our front door.

After leaving the Oldsmobile at the airport rental agency, I telephoned Thomas Bearden. I requested that he place an ad in the personal column of the Miami Herald one week before Joyce Worthington and I were to return to testify. After saying good-by, I dropped the letters into a Postal Service drop box and caught a six o'clock flight of my own.

Chapter 53

Robert Tanner reached into his mailbox, retrieved his mail, and sorted through the usual junk before coming across a letter with a Phoenix postmark. He thought it was strange that his own residence was used as the return address. He walked into his house and seated himself at the kitchen table with a fresh cup of coffee before opening it. He had plenty of time. It was four hours before he had to go to work.

Systematically opening the envelope, he pulled out the typewritten page and unfolded it. A piece of paper unexpectedly fell from the inside and fluttered to the floor beside his feet. It landed face down. With a grunt, he stooped down to pick it up and when he turned it over, his eyes bugged huge. In his hand was a cashier's check in the amount of one hundred thousand dollars. "Lordy be. What in the world is this?"

Remembering the letter, he picked it up and began to read:

Dear Robert,

This is simply a little note to express my heart-felt thanks to you for all the help that you have so unquestioningly given to me. Having shown me your complete trust, I've been able to accomplish what I set out to do. The bad guys are behind bars and I've gotten back what is rightfully mine. I could not have done this alone and certainly not without the generous help you provided.

Since I've managed to profit from my little endeavor, I felt it only fair that I share that profit with those who lent a hand. Please take this tax-free gift as a token of my appreciation. It's time you bought that house, my friend. With warmest regards.

Your friend,
Opie

Closing his watery eyes, Robert Tanner picked up the letter and planted a big kiss on it. "Thank you, Opie. Oh, and Lord, thank you. Now I can do that. Yes, suh. Now, I can surely do that."

****

After the plane from Indianapolis touched down at Sky Harbor International Airport in Phoenix, Reginald Worthington departed the craft with his carry-on luggage and walked outside to the taxi stand. With his mind focusing on the letter in his briefcase, he climbed into the back of the cab and instructed the driver, "Take me to the Scottsdale Branch of the Valley National Bank, please."

Settling comfortably into the back seat as the Chevrolet pulled away, he took the letter from his briefcase and read it again:

Dear Mr. Worthington,

I am enclosing a cashier's check in the amount of fifty thousand dollars, which represents the income taxes that will be due on the building you and I constructed in Scottsdale, Arizona for a Mr. Phillip Patterson. Not having the credentials to do this on my own, I borrowed the use of your company's fine name to build it for him, but in doing so, I have unfairly made you responsible for the taxes. Although I fully expect the total taxation to not exceed thirty thousand dollars, please accept the remainder as your share of the profits for the use of your name. The enclosed safety deposit box key will allow you access to all the books and records of our joint project. The box is in your name and is located in the Scottsdale, Arizona Branch of Valley National Bank.

Should you decide to continue the operation of the Phoenix, Arizona branch of

Worthington Construction Company, you are very well established and highly regarded by our long list of sub-contractors. Of course, their identities and every other bit of information you'll need to continue will be in the box as well.

Good luck, Mr. Worthington.

Best regards,
Reginald Worthington

Reginald Worthington? That's very strange. And Phillip Patterson? That name sounds familiar. Wait a minute, I've got it! The writer! My goodness, yes. I've got a lot to thank him for, ever since he wrote that article. But what does he have to do with a building? And, what building?

Reginald Worthington looked again at the envelope in his hand then tapped it against his left palm and stared out the window. *I swear, I may never understand this letter and that check. Maybe the contents of that safety deposit box will give me a better clue.*

****

Judy Carmelle was sitting under an umbrella on the beach and studied the unopened envelope in her hand. *This has to be from Joe-Joe. But why in the world would he write me a letter? Especially so soon? Oh well, let's see what Bozo has to say.*

Ripping it open, she pulled out the letter and started to read:

My Darling Judy,
Loving you with all my heart prompts me to write this letter. In the very beginning, I told you there would be no danger. At that time, I truly believed that to be the case. Yet here we are, still not totally out of danger. I apologize for that and for having to send you away from me. I want you to know that watching you board that

plane was the most difficult thing I've ever had to do.

Now, the news. Ever since the bad guys' preliminary hearing, I've been followed nearly everywhere I've gone. I couldn't tell if it was one of Bearden's men or not, but I suspect it was not, since most detectives don't drive around in Mercedes-Benz automobiles.

Since writing this, I've also boarded a flight to disappear for a while. If they should happen to find me, I don't want them finding you too, so more than likely it will be three long months before we see each other again. That's how long it will be before we have to testify.

As you can see, I've enclosed a cashier's check for your part of our little venture. I'm doing this in the event something should happen to prevent me from doing it in the future. God forbid.

Please know and understand that I've taken these steps because I think it's best we continue to stay separated until everything back there is all over with. With your new identification and location, there is absolutely no trace of you, so they'll never be able to find you. I've done the same thing for myself, so please don't even try to contact me for those three months. You won't be able to do it.

In the meantime, you are in my heart and there you will stay until we are back where we belong—together again.

I love you,
Joe-Joe

Stomping from the beach, Judy Carmelle headed back to her hotel room. She wadded up the letter and tossed it in the trash.

Chapter 54

Unlocking the cell door, the prison guard gruffly informed the heavy set Italian man locked inside, "Tafino! You got a visitor!"

In leg irons and handcuffs, Antonio shuffled beside the sentry to the visitation room. He sat down and picked up the phone on his side of the window. A familiar, dark-complexioned man with cold eyes and slick, black hair waited on the other side. "Yeah, Scottie, what's up? Did you get it done?"

"Boss—that Worthington guy you wanted me to whack—is he black?"

"Hell no, he's not black! What the hell's wrong with you?"

"Then, boss, you're not gonna believe this. I went to Indianapolis just like you said. I went to Worthington Construction Company, just like you said. This Worthington character's been in the same place for fifteen years and he's black! So is his secretary. I made up some kinda story and talked to her to find out some things, and boss, they ain't neither one ever been to Arizona in their lives. Oh yeah, I checked on another thing, too. There's only one Worthington Construction Company in the whole damn state. So, whoever your guy is—it ain't him. I've checked out all his places in Phoenix, too and there's no trace of your Worthington anywhere. So, what do you want me to do now?"

"Bullshit! All right, let me think a minute. Okay, maybe we should get some help from New York. With some fresh troops in here, they might be able to scare this guy up. Besides, maybe Calabrese has a lawyer who can get Lou and I out of this mess. I want you to give him a call."

"I don't think that's such a good idea, boss. The word drifting down from there is—they're not real happy with you and Lou."

"Forget that! Get your ass outta here and go get a-hold of Calabrese!"

"If that's what you want, boss, then that's what I'll do. But I still don't think it's a good idea."

"Scottie, I don't care what you think! That's what I want, so just do it! Hear me?"

"Okay, boss." Scottie studied Antonio's face before he got up to leave. "Good-bye, boss." Click.

****

James Mortensen was extremely nervous about a lot of things. Having been swept out of town so quickly to start his new life, he still feared going back to Phoenix to testify. Having learned about Antonio's background, his anxiety increased day by day as the time grew nearer. Already, he'd slipped up twice and given his true identity away. He just could not get used to his new name of Donald Trout. Plus, he knew nothing about the floral business and he hadn't yet learned his way around Atlanta.

But I guess eventually it'll be okay. We do have some things in our favor. Margo—damn it—I mean Karen! That's her name now, James. You've got to remember that! Did I say James? I meant, Donald! Oh, crap, this is never going to work!

Disgusted, he kicked at an empty box on the floor then grabbed the sales slips for the three orders he had to deliver and began to study the one on top. *A box of dried Baby's Breath. Okay, what the hell is this stuff?*

Feeling helpless, he searched around the shop, looking for his wife. He located her near the front and formed a thin smile. *Ah, there she is. Doesn't she look lovely today? You know, I'm beginning to believe Doctor Stone knew what he was talking about. He said that thing for Jane would pass and I would see Margo in a different light.*

Then all at once, his smile turned into a frown when the customer she was talking to stepped out from behind a tall plant and into Mortensen's view. With the summer heat and humidity, 'Karen' was attired in a skimpy outfit and she was showing a lot of herself to the young man buying the flowers from her. She was laughing and playing a bit of touchy-feely with the man's arm while she carried on her conversation with him.

Swiftly experiencing a surge of jealousy, James watched the customer looking her over. *That's something Doctor Stone never told me about, though! Why is it that when I think of Margo being with that Charles character, or like now, watching her flirting with this stupid idiot, it makes me want her so badly? I just don't understand the excitement of that. Oh well, if it doesn't pass, at least it's greatly improved our sex life. But I sure as hell can't tell Margo about it—I mean, Karen, damn it!*

At that moment, his musing vanished as he looked toward the front again. *Ah, thank heavens! That young asshole finally left. I hope he doesn't come back here again!*

Breathing a heavy sigh, James Mortensen edged from behind the decorating table and began trudging toward the front of the shop. *Well, I'd better have her help me get started on these orders to be delivered.*

Chapter 55

Stepping from my rented bungalow, I trudged across the sand to the boardwalk and took a seat under one of the many gazebos. I was immediately approached by Marcelino, my eager, on-the-ball waiter, who was dressed in only white Bermudas and sandals. Shaking my head, I waved a not-now to him. Smiling, he bowed and walked away.

Gazing up at the azure sky, I could see small puffs of cirrus clouds drifting lazily toward the east, high above the deep blue of the water. That's a good sign. The other direction would normally indicate the possibility of storms.

All at once I felt the rapture of a warm, tropical breeze, which brought the smell of the saltwater with it. I closed my eyes and leaned back in the chair, breathing in deeply. I could almost taste the cleanliness of the ethereal atmosphere. When the short-lived wisp of wind subsided, I squinted across the horizon and watched the distant white sails bobbing lightly up and down with the gentle waves that were drifting toward the shore.

Absent-mindedly playing in the sand with my toes, my eyes followed the swells inland to the beach, where they were greeted by all the happy, energized youngsters frolicking there. Every so often, an occasional wave, bigger than the normal small lapping ones, would carry the smaller boys and girls backwards, drawing screams of delight from their small mouths. I listened to their faraway, squealing voices as they splashed in the edge of the ocean and disregarded their mothers' frantic warnings in several languages, mostly Portuguese, to be careful.

While sitting there watching all the people, even those passing closely by, at least to my mind, seemed to be far away. In the mix were families chatting in unison as they searched for their perfect spot on the sand, groups of adolescent children racing about, and young lovers lying side-by-side, oblivious to the goings-on around them.

There was a constant stream of topless young beauties parading across the beach and up and down the boardwalk, all looking for a variety of things. The right spot to catch the ultimate rays, the right look from the right guy, and an eye for the latest, up to date swim-wear, hoping they were either wearing it, or at the very least, carrying it with them. There were tall girls, short girls, heavy girls, thin girls. A real bevy of dark skinned and light skinned lovelies, all of whom were continually heckled by the ever-searching young men and ogled by the older, overweight ones, who wondered where their youth had disappeared to so quickly and longingly wishing it could come back, if only for one more brief time.

Mixing with the continual chatter of the beach-goers is the distant strains of guitar music somewhere off in the background, interspersed with the cawing of sea gulls, who are steadily searching for any bits and pieces dropped by careless eaters. From much farther down the boardwalk, I could hear the remote voices of the hawkers plying their wares and delicacies from their *barraças* and *carros*. The air was filled with the sweet, hot aromas of their specialties.

All of these things blended into the magic of Brazil. Taking it in, I inevitably beckoned to Marcelino and gave him my request.

While I lazily waited for his return, a bare breasted Brazilian girl with raven hair and dark skin, dressed in a patch of cloth that served as a bikini bottom, slowly sauntered by, flashing a wide, flirtatious smile. When I returned it, she momentarily lingered on the wooden sidewalk, coaxing me to drink in her exotic loveliness, which for me, was merely another landmark of the sculptural beauty of this place.

Jaguaribe. Within walking distance of Itamaraca Island just to the south and a scant thirty miles north of Reçife. Besides appreciating the picturesque panorama, it had taken me only a very short time to discover that despite the pervading poverty here, the Brazilian people enjoy life to the fullest. Every day is lived as if they are in a carefree, tropical paradise.

The dark haired girl with the ample, bare breasts was

playing on my earlier smile, inasmuch as she strolled by again, this time accompanied by a friend with dark blonde hair and equally as ample. They both flashed seductive smiles. During the limited time I've been here, I've witnessed this behavior many, many times and for the most part, it's simply innocent flirtation. That's what they'll do on the beach. Flash those smiles and mischievously blink their eyes, openly encouraging the men to gawk at them. And the men do look, winnowing the differences and making the inevitable comparisons that these young goddesses do and don't want them to make. But after a time, they all blend into a sort of sameness, similar to picture postcards, somewhat unreal.

For myself, there's only one comparison I can make. Despite their exotic beauty, none are as lovely as my Judy, and the only thing real for me right now is this emptiness that gnaws at my insides. It has only been two weeks since I put her on the plane to Honolulu and it seems a lifetime ago. Each day, I battle the same argument in my mind. *Go get her. What is life in paradise, if it has become paradise lost?* But then I tell myself, *No. Don't. She's safe. She's out of harm's way. Wait until the time is right.*

My trance was interrupted by the *moço*, who set a tall drink on my table. Sitting straight up, I told him, "No, *señor*, I didn't order a *cachaca*. I requested a *chopp*."

With a huge grin, Marcelino pointed toward the beach and said in broken English. "From the lady, *señor*, thees drink for you."

"What lady, Marcelino?"

He gave me another broad smile and pointed again. "Over there, *señor*."

Standing up, I stepped onto the sand and looked to where he'd pointed, halfway expecting to see the determined, bare breasted young lady from a few minutes ago. Instead, I saw the gorgeous, bronze body of a woman lying face up on a multi-colored striped *canga*, a short distance away. Wearing only a thong bikini bottom, her perfect breasts pointed skyward. The sun reflected off the lotion she'd generously spread across her smooth, evenly toned skin. At once, I was taken aback. *This can't be. But there certainly aren't two of them in this world that look like that. Is there?*

Squinting into the sunlight, I moved closer, trying to see her face, but it was hidden beneath a familiar pink sunbonnet, from under which a single lock of auburn hair was peeking out. In her hand was a tall drink, exactly like the one the boy had brought to me. As she began to giggle, her other hand lifted the brim of the hat and Judy peeked up at me. "Hi, Joe-Joe. Surprised?"

Surprised, hell. I was totally flabbergasted. I just stood there, incredulously staring at her laughing face. I finally managed to speak. "Where in the—how did—what in the world are you doing here?"

Placing the hat on top of her head, she sat up and commented, "Damn, it's hot here! Why in the world did you choose this place?"

"How in the hell did you figure out where I was?"

Standing up, she picked up the *canga* and shook it, then brushed the sand from her smooth hips and thighs. "C'mon, Joe-Joe, let's go sit under your umbrella."

Without another word and swaying her delectable bottom to and fro, Judy sashayed to my table and seated herself on one of the lounge chairs. Wrapping her delicious lips around the straw, she pulled some liquid into her mouth. "Aaahh. Damn, that's good!"

When she saw me standing like a statue on the sand, still watching her, she flashed a teasing grin. "Well, come on over here, boy. Don't you want to hear about this?"

Shaking my head in utter disbelief, I gingerly edged into the shade of the parasol and settled onto a chair, all the while continuously watching her as she nonchalantly stirred her drink with the straw. Peering into the top of her glass, Judy inspected the contents then whirled the plastic rod around and around again. Following one more sip, she held the mixture toward me and apologized. "Sorry, Joe-Joe, this was the nearest thing I could get to a mai tai."

Okay, Girl, I get it. This is a classic game of cat and

mouse and you're playing it to the hilt. All right. Two can play. Without a word, all I did was smile at her and reach across the table to place my hand over hers. I gently squeezed it, secretly thrilling to even the slightest touch of her.

She ignored my silence and patted the top of my hand. "So, Bozo. Are you glad to see me, or what? Incidentally, I brought your stupid, million-dollar check back to you. I don't want the damn thing! What was that all about, anyway? Didn't you think you'd ever see me again? And what kind of a name is Harold Smith? That is so average. Really, Joe-Joe, couldn't you have had more imagination than that?"

This time, all I could do was give her a sheepish grin. *Okay—she wins the game.* "All right, so when are you going to tell me how you did it?"

She ignored the question. "Goodness gracious, Hollywood, would you quit staring at me?" Thrusting her chest out, she laughed out loud and wiggled her breasts back and forth. "And stop grinning—after all, you've seen them before." Then she pointed toward the beach. "And many others as well, I might add."

I cleared my throat to speak, but before I could, Judy picked up her empty glass and started shaking it right in front of my face, exaggerating a sudden scanning search for Marcelino. "Joe-Joe, can we get another one of these? They're really good. Better than a mai tai, don't you think?"

When I breathed a huge sigh, Judy shot me a smile then laughed out loud. Filled with smug self-assuredness, she winked and, while continuing her search for the *moco*, she finally started talking. "First of all, Joe-Joe, you made two mistakes. Secondly, I pieced a few things together, and finally, I used a couple of things that I learned from you."

Finally attracting Marcelino's attention, Judy pointed her finger toward the empty glass. Indicating both of us, she held three fingers in the air to him. Grinning widely at her, the waiter nodded and scooted away.

"Now then. Where was I? Oh, yeah—of utmost

importance, Galahad is the fact that you should not have told me in your ignorant letter that I wouldn't be able to find you—"So don't even try"! That was mistake number one."

Looking directly at me, she winked again. Her lips spread into a smug smile. "Error number two—and this is good, Joe-Joe—I mean, really, really good!" She cackled before continuing. "Clever Owen went to all the trouble of getting those new identities for both of us, covering our tracks really well. I mean, nobody but nobody can track us down! Then you put your stupid, stuck-up cat on a plane with you and you don't even bother to change the little fur-bag's name!" Laughing out loud, Judy crowed, "Joe-Joe! That is rich! I mean, really rich! Incidentally, how is Socko?"

Blushing, I gushed, "Uh, well, he wasn't crazy about the quarantine period, but since then he's fine. Are you serious? That's how you found me?"

"Yep."

"But how did you trace down a cat? You couldn't have gotten that information from the airline. Flight information is confidential. Isn't it?"

"Normally, yes. But, Joe-Joe, you taught me a lot of things really well. Besides, you let me get close enough to you to know you and some of your habits. Let me explain."

Pausing momentarily, Judy waited for the young man in the Bermudas to serve us the new drinks and whisk himself away again, before she continued. "First thing I did, Hollywood, was narrow it down. I mean, this is the only time you got I. D.'s from Robert Tanner that included passports. And, Joe-Joe, you only need a passport if you're going out of the country and since I didn't, I figured you did. So, when I arrived in Phoenix from Honolulu, I went straight to an international airline desk and asked if there were any flights out of the country that had a cat on board. I wasn't sure of the date, but I assumed it was right after you mailed that really dumb letter to me."

Pausing from her story to sip from her glass, Judy took off the sunbonnet and set it on the table. With this break, I made an attempt to be serious for a moment. "Well,

Girl, spare me the details because it doesn't matter to me how you did it. I'm just glad you're here. I've debated every day about whether I should come and get you, but I wanted to be sure you were safe."

"Good. Now then, Joe-Joe, let me finish. You have to hear the rest of this. Okay? Now then—you know those little guys that sell you the tickets and give you boarding passes and so on? Well, I made sure I was talking to one of them when I asked for the information about a flight out of the country with a cat aboard on such and such a date, blah, blah, blah, and he tells me a bunch of bullshit! 'I'm sorry, Miss, but that's confidential information that I'm not allowed to give out'." Her nasal impersonation made me laugh.

"Well, Joe-Joe, I've seen you extract information from people many times by simply acting like you know what the hell you're talking about. Incidentally, you're quite good at that—especially with policemen." She giggled. "However, since I don't have quite that capability, I took the notion one little bitty step further."

Knowing she had me intrigued, she again sipped from her glass, making me wait for her to continue. So, playing the game her way and doing what she expected, I showed her my impatience. "Okay. And?"

"Well, sir, by design, I wasn't wearing a bra, so I just reached to the top of my blouse, ripped it wide open down the front, and exposed these." She wiggled again and sang with laughter.

"You really did that? Why?"

"Yes. Because I knew it would work! I simply told him—'Sonny, if you don't give me the information I want, I'm going to scream to the top of my lungs that you did this!' And, Joe-Joe, you've never seen anybody scramble like that boy did. Within three minutes, I knew about every flight that had any kind of animal aboard that had left Phoenix within a week." Then she gloated, "I would have had it in less than two, but he did take the time to stare."

She musically laughed again. "Of course, when I saw Socko's name, it was downhill from there. Well, I'll admit that tracing you from Rio was a little tough, but you did leave a good trail, Mr. Smith." Shrugging her shoulders, Judy giggled again. "And here I am, Hollywood."

"I really can't believe you did that." Although feeling a degree of embarrassment, I had to laugh at her story. Then, after ordering another *cachaca* for each of us, I tried to turn serious once more and told her, "Girl? I have learned one important thing in the past two weeks. Without you—"

Holding up one hand to stop me, Judy interrupted. "Hold it right there, Galahad. Let me tell you what I've learned—and I am very serious about this. No Bozo here! Okay? Now then, I know that you were simply trying to protect me from harm when you sent me to Hawaii, but Joe-Joe, my life is so empty if you're not in it every day, I'd rather die with you than live without you. So don't you ever do that to me again!"

"You took the words right out of my mouth, Girl, and I couldn't have said it better, myself." When I reached for my drink, all at once, there was a brief, awkward few seconds when we simply stared at each other in loving appreciation. I finally broke our mesmerized silence. "So, now what do we do?"

Just then, the fresh drinks arrived and we waited to be sure that Marcelino was out of earshot again before Judy suggested, "Three things, Hollywood. One, we finish these drinks. Two, we go to your little hut over there and make love. I mean, for a really, really, long, long time! And three, I've got something important to ask you about—our plans for the future."

"Okay. The first two are a given, but as far as the future is concerned, I rather imagined that after we testify in Phoenix, we could settle down someplace, start a little construction company, maybe make a few bucks and live a normal life."

"My God! How gloomy and dull!" Judy bolted straight up and banged her glass down on the table. "Joe-Joe, that's not you! And as you should already know by now, that's not me, either! Maybe at sometime in the past, okay!

But now? I don't think so. No, no, no. I have something else in mind. Please just listen to me. Okay?"

This oughtta be good! "Okay."

She picked the drink back up and leaned back in her chair. "Remember when I was at Vanderbilt? Well, there was this girl that I became friends with there. Her name is Rose-Marie Wanderkillen. She's from Atlanta. Anyway, her dad invented this weird, computer-programming thing and started a little business manufacturing it and somehow, when the company started to grow by leaps and bounds, he began bringing other people into it. He had some kind of a stock purchase program. To make a long story short, he was getting fabulously rich and all of a sudden, the people he brought into the company somehow made him a minority stockholder and pushed him out of his own company. Well, I heard from Rose-Marie a week or so before I left Phoenix so very damn fast and her father is nearly broke. She had to drop out of school with only about a year to go. I didn't tell you about this at the time—it seems we had a few things of our own going on—remember? Anyway, it didn't sound like it was on the up and up to me, so I called her from Hawaii last week and I told her we could look into it."

"You did what?" I exclaimed.

Judy shrugged her shoulders. "I told her we'd look into it for her father."

"My God, Girl. First of all, we're not even out of the woods with our own problems yet, and second of all—I don't know a damn thing about the stock market!"

"Neither do I, Joe-Joe. But we could learn. I mean, once Rose-Marie's father tells us exactly what happened, you'll figure out what to do."

Without another word, Judy quickly stood up and motioned for me to do the same. Donning her hat and picking up the drinks, she handed mine to me and hooked her arm into mine, pressing herself against me. We began a slow walk in the direction of the bungalow. Placing my arm around her waist, I snaked my hand under the thin strap of her bikini bottom and gently squeezed the soft flesh of her hip. I renewed my protest. "Seriously, Judy, I don't think we can do anything to help that young woman and her father. Come on, Girl, let's just stay here and enjoy each other for a while, then we'll settle down and do as I suggested. Besides, until we know for sure that the other thing is definitely over with, we have to stay incognito because it could very well be that Tafino has somebody else looking for us right now."

"Exactly! That's my point, Joe-Joe! Look, if I can find you this easily, then so can Tafino's hoods. Therefore, we've got to get out of here. And pretty soon!"

"But that other deal you mentioned—it sounds intriguing, but I just don't think we can handle it." *It does sound fascinating, but I can do cat and mouse, too, Girl!* I turned my head away to camouflage my smile.

Encouraged by my comment, Judy bounced in front of me so she could face me. Without breaking her slow stride, she began to walk backwards across the sand. "And why not, Hollywood?"

I showed her my best serious face and did what she thought I was good at. I acted like I knew what the hell I was talking about. "Because, Girl. I don't even know if Georgia is a community property state and it sounds to me like it's something that only a married couple could handle. I mean, with the stock market thing and all of that."

She stopped in her tracks just in front of the door. "Joe-Joe, do you mean that you'd be willing to—" Then, her mouth dropped wide open. "Wait a minute! Joe-Joe, are you asking me to marry you?"

I wrapped my arms around her waist and hugged her bare chest against mine. Kissing her lightly on the forehead, I looked into her dazzling, big, brown root beer eyes and told her, "Yeah. But only if you want to do that Atlanta gig."

A huge grin spread across her face. "Aha! Then I have it all figured out, Hollywood. Here's the plan! You and I will leave here as Mr. and Mrs. Berlinski, with their pet cat, Tuffie, heading for Detroit—for diversionary purposes, of course, known only to us. After two or three days there, you and I, as Mr. and Mrs. Addison, will leave Detroit for

Atlanta, along with our pet cat, Snowball."

"Snowball?" I stepped away from her. Showing mock concern, I looked into her beautiful face. "Did you say Snowball? What the hell kind of a name is that for him? He's more black than white! Snowball?"

"He's a *disguised* snowball."

Melodiously laughing at me as she pulled me through the doorway and back into her arms, I suddenly realized one more thing. We didn't have a cassette player. But no matter, because, although jazz and blues are okay, the sweetest music I ever heard was Judy's warm laughter as she kicked the door closed with her bare foot and drew me against her, placing those gorgeous full lips against mine.

Before closing my eyes, I glanced at our sleeping blue-collar cat, which was curled up in a ball and snuggled in his worn, easy chair. *Socko—I think we've both just been "Snowballed."*

EPILOGUE

PART THREE

And the three of them lived happily ever after—whoever they were.

D. A. Williams

Don, as he's know to family and friends, resides in beautiful Spokane, Washington with his wife, Sue, their cat, Linus, and a pet raccoon named Tulip. In addition to writing, he also designs and creates dioramas for model railroads, while Sue is a gifted artist. Together, they spend time camping and hiking in the great outdoors of the Pacific Northwest.

With three novels in print, D. A. Williams is presently working on a series of crime novels, followed by a sequel to It's Conspiracy By Any Name.